ARE

T'

66

2.

THE SWELL YOKEL

"When society grows ashamed of itself it seeks a victim." Was John Thurtell society's victim, or did he deserve the evil fate which befell him? In this new novel Philip Lindsay reconstructs a famous and sensational nineteenth-century crime, bringing before us as living human beings the various characters involved. John Thurtell, the "Swell Yokel", was the son of the Mayor of Norwich; in the early 1820's he came to London to seek his fortune—a fortune of which he was soon deprived by the rascally gamester Bill Weare. And thus Thurtell conceived a grudge—one of many—and thus, before much time was out, he had become a murderer. In telling the story of the crime, and of the many circumstances which surrounded it, the author writes with realism, a strong and accurate eye for detail, a sense of atmosphere, and considerable humanity. His central character emerges as a criminal and a man—a rogue, capable of a cold-blooded crime, but capable also of such emotions as love and equipped with marked courage, for he faced his final ordeal bravely. The other characters who were concerned in his story are conceived with equal vividness: the vain sensual Probert, his confederate; the one-eyed beauty, Anne Noyes, whom Thurtell came to love, and who showed so touching a devotion to him; and Pierce Egan, the sporting journalist who befriended the pair.

THE SWELL YOKEL

PHILIP LINDSAY

LONDON
HUTCHINSON

Hutchinson & Co. (Publishers) Ltd.
178–202 Great Portland Street, London, W.1

London   Melbourne   Sydney   Auckland
Bombay   Cape Town   New York   Toronto

First published 1955

Printed in Great Britain
by The Anchor Press, Ltd.,
Tiptree, Essex

DEDICATION

for

GILBERT *and* STELLA ODD

Dear "Bill" and Stella,

This is a tale I have long had in mind, and one reason why I delayed writing it was that my friend, the late Thomas Burke, had already used the theme in his Murder at Elstree *(Longmans, Green), 1936; but his treatment was so different from mine that I have dared risk the comparison, although deeply I envy him his splendid climax. The arrest of Thurtell, Hunt and Probert for the murder of Weare caused such a sensation at the time, 1823, that all classes were stirred to enthusiasm or horror. The aristocratic, the intellectual, the bourgeois and, naturally, the criminal classes all showed an agitation perplexing to understand today. No other murder in modern England made such éclat as this. The age was one of gambling, and in that lies something of the secret. We do not know how deeply involved Thurtell was in other crimes, but his arrest frightened the more important criminals into fleeing the country, and there must have been some terrible secrets which they feared he might reveal. Such fears, however, would have been confined to a comparatively small group, yet all Britain was roused by the murder and ensuing trial. Moralists, of course, seized it as a text with which to denounce the fashionable "vice," and the gamblers and legs seized it to make of Thurtell a kind of god of sport.*

My tale keeps close to facts. Only in chapter twenty-four have I cheated a little. The book growing bulky, I cut one night into two for the seemingly paradoxical reason of shortening the action: otherwise, I could not have easily explained the situations of Thurtell and Anne. One other point is not strictly historical, and this is the emotional situation between these two. For the sake of the story, an author must invent. Otherwise, he might as well write a direct historical narrative, and my rule for invention is not to outrage facts and to work only within their framework. Contemporary journalists at times confused the sisters, and this was the hint on which I seized. Although there is no proof of this love-affair, there is also no proof that it did not take place. And it is on this point that I make my stand when constructing a plot, violating

5

no known facts and inventing only what could have happened, and which perhaps did happen: who can tell?

Data for this tale are many. Apart from contemporary magazine and news-paper reports—I must particularly mention Herbert's fine, dispassionate reporting for the London Magazine, *February, 1824—there are many books, pamphlets and broadsheets about the murder, including the classic lines by William Webb, acrobat, linkboy and transported convict, which so en-chanted Sir Walter Scott:*

> His throat they cut from ear to ear,
> His brains they battered in;
> His name was Mr. William Weare,
> He lived in Lyon's Inn.

Of the books, probably the most important, I found, was The Fatal Effects of Gambling &c. *(Thos. Kelly), 1824. Like other of Kelly's publications, this is a thorough, well-written account and I suspect in it the hand of J. Curtis who in 1828 wrote the comprehensive work on Corder and the Red Barn. A* Complete History *of the murder, published by Jones & Co., 1824, is also very thorough, although largely a compilation of thefts from other publications, such as Pierce Egan's* Account of the Trial, &c. *(Knight & Lacey), 1824, from which practically everybody stole. Like most of Egan's journalistic publications this is a wretched production with pin-point type and crude woodcuts, the publishers doubtless relying on the author's reputation to sell the work regardless of its appearance. And if we are to choose by appearance, every honour must go to the publishers, Sherwood, Jones, & Co., who chose J. Nichols & Son to produce their* Account of the Murder, &c., *by George Henry Jones, clerk to the magistrates. Like all the books I have seen from these printers, this is a work of beauty, beautifully printed on hand-made deckle-edged paper and with charming lithograph illustrations by J. D. Harding. Put these drawings beside the coarse cuts illustrating Egan and one is ashamed of Knight & Lacey's meanness. There is another book which at first I neglected because it was a rushed publication brought out before the trial and contained wretched woodcuts. This,* A Full Account, &c., *1823, also published by Sherwood, Jones, I found surprisingly useful as it gave a detailed description of Gill's Hill Cottage and other facts and conjectures neglected by later publishers who had the trial itself to report. An extra interest attaches to this little work because it is the one which Thurtell's counsel, Mr. Andrews, quite rightly fulminated against as being, with reports in the* Times *and the* Morning Chronicle *and the play,* The Gamblers, *shameless in its abuse of the prisoners and in jumping to murderous* conclusions. Finally, there is Eric R. Watson's edition of the trial in Messrs. Hodge's Notable British Trials, *1920*, which is as scholarly as all the volumes in this invaluable series; and I can offer no higher praise than that.

As remarked, all Britain seemed struck lunatic on discovery of this murder. In Scotland, the mighty Scott, that connoisseur of criminous pamphlets, recorded the facts in his journal, remarking that "it led John Bull into one of his most uncommon fits of gambols"; and when in 1828 he was travelling north, he had to turn aside to look at what remained of the cottage and he reported in his diary its desolate condition. That a sporting journalist like William Hazlitt should become excited about the event was natural enough and—confusing Tom with his brother, Jack—he tells in the New Monthly Magazine, February, 1822, of riding in a coach with Thurtell to the great fight between Hickman, the "Gasman," and Bill Neat on December 11, 1821; and one is also not surprised when that boxing enthusiast, George Borrow, boasted of his friendship with Thurtell, giving an unforgettable portrait of him in Lavengro *and returning to him in both* The Romany Rye *and* The Zincali; but it is astonishing that Charles Lamb should have found time to jeer at Mr. Justice Park and that the echo of the murder should have inspired Carlyle to use the words "gigmania" and "gigmanity," and George Eliot to write of the "proud respectability of a gig." These uses of "gig" were the result of a misquotation. It was believed that one of the witnesses had defined Probert as a gentleman because he kept a gig, but in no report of the trial have I found this remark. Lytton added to Thurtell's gory glory by devoting a chapter of Pelham *to the crime; so you see, I am in the highest company! Sir Thomas Lawrence wished to make a cast of Thurtell's head for phrenological reasons; and William Mulready's excellent portraits of the prisoners have been fortunately preserved in the Victoria and Albert Museum.*[1]

[1] In *John o' London's* for June 2, 1905, the late Wilfred Whitten wrote an erudite and amusing essay on the murder, *Literature of a Crime*, reprinted in his *The Joy of London* (Newnes), 1943. I mention this essay because of a remarkable poem Mr. Whitten quoted, *The Owl*, by the Rev. John Milford, which is reminiscent of Beddoes—or should I say of Barham? We have space for only two verses:

> Owl, that lovest the cloudy sky,
>   A step beyond,
>   By the silent pond,
> I heard a low and moaning cry. . . .
>   "By the water's edge,
>   Through the trampled sedge,
> A bubble burst and gurgled by:
>   My eyes were dim,
>   But I look'd from the brim,
> And I saw in the weeds a dead man lie."

(Continued at foot of overleaf)

But I am racing too far into details, for there are other source-books that should not be ignored and I must mention at least some of the sporting volumes you generously lent me from your library. In particular, I am delighted to record the pleasure I found in Henry Downes Miles's Pugilistica, *vol. ii (John Grant), 1906, and in* Fights for the Championship *by Fred Henning (Licensed Victuallers' Gazette), N.D.; while J. Frank Bradley's comments on Thurtell in* The Mirror of Life and Boxing World *for September 2 and 9, 1916, were of great interest.*

For a novel one cannot write postscripts telling what happened to certain characters once the book has closed, but I think it only fair to the reader's curiosity to add that, after threatening to prosecute Egan for libel, Probert was hanged for horse-stealing in June, 1825. He died like a craven, gibbering with terror: "his limbs were completely palsied, and his agitation dreadful." Hunt was transported to New South Wales and was last heard of as servant to a Mr. Jonathan Slattery at Bathurst.

I think there is nothing further to hold you from turning the page, except to thank Mr. Gilbert H. Fabes of Rye for his help in collecting much of the material; and perhaps I should add a word about the slang used by my characters. This is always contemporary, however modern it may sound at times, even words which are considered American, such as "moll" and "frisk," for example, being good early nineteenth-century English. I hope the words used explain themselves in their context, but a comment might be made on "cross" which was similar to our "double-cross." To quote from Slang. A Dictionary *(T. Hughes), 1823, by that sporting journalist and envious hater of Egan, Jon Bee, editor of the* Fancy Gazette: *"The cross—cheatery and robbery; thus, when prize-fighters agree beforehand who shall win, 'tis a cross, in order to cheat third persons out of their wagers."*

For your sake, "Bill," as our modern Pierce Egan, I wish there had been more boxing in these pages, but by this date Thurtell had become too poor to continue promoting fights, although his love of the sport remained acute, as can be seen in his interest in Tom Spring, until almost the last moment. And

(*Continued from foot of previous page*)

> Owl, that lovest the midnight sky,
>> Where the casements blaze
>> With the faggots' rays.
> Look, oh! look! What seest thou there?
>> Owl, what's this
>> That snort and hiss . . .
> And why do thy feathers shiver and stare?
>> " 'Tis he, 'tis he . . .
>> He sits 'mid the three,
> And a breathless Woman is on the stair."

I hope that, with your great knowledge of this and of other sports, you will pass over any errors I might have made. At least, you and Stella know with what affection I write your names before this tale, hoping that it might interest you and be some return for the many happy times we three and Isobel have spent together.

PHILIP LINDSAY.

Sussex.

CONTENTS

CHAPTER ONE

A MARRIAGE IS PROPOSED

OVER the broken road the gig bounced and creaked, wheezing and whining as though asthmatic, while the horse stumbled amongst the furrows. Now that they had turned from the high road, they swept into darkness, although the sun, this July day of 1823, shone with the heat of early afternoon in a cloudless sky. Overhead, the untended hedges arched for their leaves to meet, hiding the blue from the earth. Crooked, suddenly twisting, and so narrow that the gig and its two occupants were whipped by branches as they passed, Gill's Hill Lane writhed through a miniature forest, although it was not a mile from broad Watling Street that was open to Elstree or St. Albans, and roughly a mere fifteen miles from London. Not only was it uncouth here, nature run riot, but it was strangely silent, even the birds drowsing in the trees and the bees resting in their hives. In that lane, dark and tortuous as a secret in a maze, between and under the shaggy hedges, all was shadowed and cool, drying the sweat icily on the men's faces, and they shivered as though they had been suddenly dipped into water. The smell of damp earth, of rotting leaves and bracken, was sickly sour, like the smell of a corpse; and it was perhaps this thought which made John Thurtell, the larger of these two large men, turn to his friend, William Probert, and say with a twisted upperlip:

"The very spot for a murder."

"Or," said Probert quickly, grinning yet looking sharply at his comrade, "for gallivanting, eh, Jack, boy?"

Thurtell never laughed, but now he smiled. The heavy lips did not part: only the corners crinkled up a little; and, as often when he was with his friend, Probert wondered uneasily what the man was thinking. He was so taciturn. That was the word he sought to describe the fellow! Taciturn. Unless he could talk sport or bawdy, John Thurtell rarely spoke. Silent, watching the company from under that jutting forehead, usually he sat, even his eyes shadowed by the outthrust brows, and only close acquaintanceship had taught Probert that the colour of those eyes was grey: blue to grey. And unless you could look into a man's eyes, you remained at a disadvantage; like a blinded bruiser milling with a two-eyed enemy, you never knew from where the next blow might swing. In that silence of Thurtell's, feeding on resentments, brooding on pride that could never be humbled but which could be easily, too easily, hurt, there seemed menace, a threat. . . . Not that he had anything to fear from the brute, grinned Probert to himself: he was Jack's pal; and he would have hated to have been his foe.

The black stock, over which showed the points of his collar, pressed up the too heavy chin and jowls, giving Thurtell's head a lopsided sullen look, the face being bottom-heavy. Indeed, all of the man was heavy—although he was not fat but lithe and powerful—save for the straight and almost delicate, gentlemanly nose that was marred only by the curl of the nostrils, showing hair. High and bony was the forehead, veins swelling on the temples, and the eyebrows were thick and queerly shaped—that over the right eye running more or less straight, and that over the left hooking up suddenly as though in a static twinge; while the upperlip was long and deeply furrowed, both lips outthrust, giving him a dogged look.

Ay, thought Probert: that was another word he sought to describe the man! Dogged! The fellow was a mastiff on two legs! Those were mastiff's jowls of his; and, like a mastiff, he could worry an enemy to death, could snap at him to kill, or at a flattering word could waggle into friendship. After all, it wasn't difficult to manage such a brute. At least, it was never difficult for a fellow as cunning as himself, thought Probert.

"Damn these twigs," growled Thurtell, dodging under a branch that almost toppled from his head the white hat sported by the followers of the fancy; "why don't you get your hedges clipped?"

Probert shrugged. "Not my hedges," he said complacently. "Not my ground. And," he added, laughing, "not my house, either. Expect to be thrown out any day now. My dog of a landlord's getting touchy about the rent; but I needn't worry over that. . . . Anyhow, they say they're going to clean up these lanes soon. Over forty years, I'm told, since they was touched. About time they did something about em."

"Ay," said Thurtell, ducking again. "Disgraceful. Beautiful country, too, for a hunt."

"Why should you worry?" Deep in his throat, lasciviously, Probert chuckled. "This is a lovers' landscape, lad. Plenty of hedges to hide behind. No one to spy on you. Even the most modest piece'd soon forget her modesty when she knew there was none to watch and tattle."

"I don't like it," said Thurtell, after a gloomy pause. "Damme, if I do!"

"What! Frightened of a woman! You, Jack Thurtell, frightened!"

Swiftly, Thurtell turned, face so close to Probert's that their noses almost rubbed and his small bright eyes glinted in their hollows, the muscles tightening on his jaw.

"Say that again," he growled. "Say that Jack Thurtell, Old Flash, is frightened of anyone, man, woman, God, devil or even Jack Ketch, and glory be, Bill Probert, you'll be the one to learn what fear is!"

"Hey, hey," cried Probert, forcing a laugh. "Easy, Jack! can't you take a joke?"

"Not that kind of a joke," said Thurtell, and elbowed the man aside.

Still smiling, his face white, Probert leaned on the rail of the gig and shrugged his neck in the black stock that had suddenly become tight.

"Never meant a thing, Jack," he said, darting at him a glance of hatred. "Just my foolish ways. Course you aren't frightened of Carrie. What man would be? As jolly a piece as any man could want, and willing, no doubt, to such as you. I didn't mean her, I meant marriage."

"If she's money, I'll marry her, though she's got two wooden legs and is hairy as an ape. But I don't want a wife."

"Who does? Women want husbands though, and there's the rub. But men want rhino and marriage's the easiest way to earn it, and Carrie's as handsome a lass as you'll find in a week in Soho; and she's got money coming to her out of Chancery. You're not still sweet on Mary Dobson, are you?"

"Mary's married now. You know that."

Probert roared his laughter. "Makes all the difference, don't it," he said, "when your mot becomes some other fellow's wife! Never troubled me much."

"I tell you—Mary and I are finished. She's a good girl and I like her. But we're finished. Now that she's married Walker and they're happy together, I respect her. And that's all. One thing about me—I never let down a pal: man or woman, I never let em down. Remember that, Bill Probert."

"I know it, what man doesn't?" muttered Probert, sinking back and letting the horse take its head. Impossible, unless one wanted a spill, to go fast along this twisting, narrow, broken lane; and he was in no hurry. He peered from under his brows at Thurtell and saw him with his great chin pushed out between the peaks of his collar, his upperlip sucked in, and his brow, under the white beaver, puckered with anger and thought.

"Well," he said at last with forced joviality, "if you don't want Carrie, just say so. I only suggested it to help you. You need blunt and she's going to get it. You've the insurance after you; you've lost your money and you'll soon lose the Cock; and here's a handsome filly that a lord'd be proud to name, and all yours for the taking; but now you don't want her."

"I didn't say that." Thurtell grunted rather than spoke, as though each word erupted from him. "Take her today, I would, but all this palaver, that's not to my liking. I like to say to a woman: Yes or No? And if she says No, to hell with her; but having to talk smooth, act the dandiprat, taking her hand and kissing it, whispering bloody lies into her hair. . . . That was all right when I was a boy. Did I tell you of that girl at Norwich?" He chuckled, deep in his belly. "Drowned herself for love of me," he said.

"Well, Carrie won't need to drown herself," said Probert dryly. "If you don't take her, Major Wood will; and I suppose even that'd be better than drowning."

"Major Wood? That bastard!" Thurtell's jowls began to swell and the underlip thrust further forward. "If he so much as touches her," he said, "I'll break his back."

"What's the good of that? You don't want her, so what the hell does it matter who has her?"

"I didn't say I didn't want the woman. I'm going to marry her. Be sure of that, Mr. William damned Probert, as sure as some day you'll be hanged."

"Not I," said Probert with a shiver.

"What of it? A quick death, a leap into the dark, and then you can doff your beaver to your old mate, Satan himself. But I'm having that girl. I need her rhino. If she's got what you say——"

"She has. I swear it. I should know as she's my wife's sister. It's hers when she marries."

"Then it's in my pocket," said Thurtell; "only I tell you, I don't want to marry. I like the fillies. Always have. Had more of em than most men. But marriage . . ." He leaned over to spit into the damp ground. "I suppose a fellow's got to come to it some time," he groaned.

"Ain't so bad after a time," said Probert. "D'ye think I wanted to marry Mrs. Probert? Who would, although she was handsome once?

Not bad now, so long as she keeps her gob shut. But her father was Bill Crook Noyes, who'd been a brewer until he retired to squat on his money-box. That's why I married her."

"And now you haven't even a brownie you've not stolen!" snorted Thurtell. "Yet you tell me to marry her sister for blunt!"

"Ah," sighed Probert, "'twas my ill fortune. I told you about it. With what she brought, I set up as a wine-merchant. And——" A sly smile creased his fat cheeks. "—failed for forty thousand quid, and my poor creditors never got one penny out of me. But money goes. 'Twas made round to roll round, as they say. But mine all rolled the wrong way, dammit. Like yours. Think, Jack! When you've got Carrie's dowry, you can take it out of Weare. You were a johnny raw when he plucked you. But now you're the sharp and, with capital, you could take him for a flat. I'd like to see that vulture turned into a pigeon for a change."

"I'll do him one of these days," said Thurtell; and Probert was startled by the fury with which he spoke. Thurtell and his lickspittle, Joe Hunt, were always talking about doing people, calling themselves Turpin lads, and Probert had never taken their talk seriously; but now, in the unnaturally low and vicious manner in which Thurtell spoke, he felt a shiver on his spine. This was no boast: there was hatred in that voice. In his pride, Thurtell had plainly never forgotten how Bill Weare had bubbled him when—the Swell Yokel, they had called him in those days—he had reached London from Norwich with a pocketful of guineas only to be diddled of every penny by snakish Bill Weare at blind hookey.

"I thought he put you right about that afterwards," said Probert, narrowly watching his friend, noting apprehensively the outthrust underlip, the lowering of the wrinkled brow. "Didn't he give you a slice of the blunt on the cross between Randall and Martin?"

Thurtell did not answer. As though crushed by the weight of his thoughts, he remained jogging to the slow motion of the gig, his head down over the chin swelling above the cravat. Then he turned slowly to Probert and looked fixedly at him.

"I don't forget an enemy any more than I forget a friend," he said at last. "Weare laughed about me. I heard of it. Called me the Swell Yokel; and him . . . what was he but a bloody waiter at the Globe in Fleet Street before he took to serving drinks in hells, and then to serving cards in hells? I'll send him to hell itself before I'm finished and he'll have my initials, J. T., carved on his carcase so that the devil'll need no introduction to the swine. Make a flat of me, would he! That blind hookey of his was rigged: I know it; and no man does that to Jack Thurtell and lives to brag of it. I'll do him yet; and Mr. Barber Beaumont, too. I'm going to do him."

"Beaumont? The fellow at the County Fire Office?"

"Ay, him. If it weren't for him, the fire'd be forgotten by now and I'd have had those nineteen hundred quid in my pocket which the judge said they ought to pay me. I'll wring his neck, by God. And anyone else that crosses me. And it wouldn't be the first time neither."

No. That was possible. The man was powerful, violent, his passions held in a tight rein. Proud and alert for insults, he was almost eager to find them in casual talk. He had been a soldier once—or was it a sailor? Probert was not certain, Thurtell's talk of bloody deeds at war being both at sea and on land—and such men can become hardened to bloodshed. In London he was feared, however blacklegs like Weare might snigger at him behind his back, and it was said that as an amateur he had once himself fought in the ring, and that when Martin had failed to appear at Jack Carter's benefit fight, Thurtell had taken his place and name and had stood up well to the Lancastrian Hero; and any man who could do that was one to be watched with fear and respect.

"As for the cross between Randall and Martin, I only got six hundred guineas out of it. I know Weare, the dog, made twenty times that. And he robbed me. I'll not forget it. He robbed me." Slowly, almost spitting the words, Thurtell spoke. "It's not the money," he said. "I've made more than that, and I've lost more than that; and I'll do the same again. But to have that bastard crow over me." The great fists clenched, then slowly opened. "To hell with Weare," he said: "let's talk of Carrie."

"With all my heart," said Probert. "When you marry her, Jack, we'll go into business together. We could open a hell in St. James's amongst the nobs and feather more than our nests."

"To be my own master again," sighed Thurtell. "Working with Lemming's all right, but I like to be on my own; and the returns aren't enough. Why should I waste my time breaking the heads of those who won't pay up like gentlemen just to fatten his reader? No. I'll marry the girl and we'll set up together."

"That's the brave lad I like to hear," chirruped Probert. "That's Old Flash to the life! She's waiting now; told her you were coming, and she blushed. Should have seen her! Red as though she'd been skinned she went."

"Yes," said Thurtell slowly, eyes half-shut, "Carrie should make a good wife. Pretty, fine shape, sweet pipe; can cook, I believe?"

"Like Ganymede herself!"

"Then I'll have her," said Thurtell, and crossed his arms on the resolution.

Seeing that his friend no longer wavered in his determination, Probert tickled the horse's rump with the whip, and the beast bounded forward, almost tossing them out as the wheels jerked on ruts. Then suddenly, as though a curtain parted above, the hedges fell apart and they saw before them Gill's Hill Cottage, a thin stream of smoke rising from one chimney to show that the kettle was on the fire.

Everything in the garden, if garden it could be called, was overgrown, weeds throttling flowers and running along the paths that curved around the dark cypresses. Behind the tangled greenery, the house could be barely glimpsed, even the doorway lurking half-hidden behind thistles and docks.

"I like it here," said Thurtell, looking with approval at the wilderness. "It's proper snug."

"Ay," said Probert grimly. "It's that, all right."

Through the open yard-gate he drove the gig and pulled up before the stable noisy with the buzz of flies about the dung and refuse-heaps, and the fierce barking of dogs chained nearby. Besides the stable, there were two outhouses, each opening into the other, the cow-byre being the furthest away. They looked as though about to tumble with rottenness and neglect, the doors swinging on loose hinges, damp-rot peeling the wood, and the rafters showing through the roofs.

"Where's that damned boy?" growled Probert. "Dick!" he bellowed. "Where in hell are you, Dick! Dick!"

A ragged boy of about twelve came running from the back of the house. Munching something that swelled his cheek as though he had toothache, he leaped the broken fence.

"Here I am, sir," he panted. "Shall I walk him for you, sir?"

"No need," said Probert. "He's not heated. Just give him a rub down and a feed. Come on, Jack. Don't let's go in the back way. Women never like it—same to them as being caught by a man before they've washed."

Thurtell did not answer. He followed his friend past the stables, through a narrow gate and into the parlour on the other side of the kitchen. This was a small dark room, its little windows obscured by the greenery outside, one small window being almost wholly blocked by a tall laurel in the yard. The carpet had been worn to thread in places, the chairs were common cane-bottomed chairs. A small chiffonier stood against one wall, close to an unlit stove, and there was a mahogany table in the centre of the floor, while under one unwashed window rested a sofa. The walls were bare, damp showing through the plaster, save for one thick looking-glass placed on the mantelpiece.

"Wait here," said Probert. "I'll tell em you've come."

Tiptoe, Thurtell peered into the little mirror, arching his throat to tighten the jowls; and he smirked a little, frowning only at the pock-marks pitting his skin. Apart from these, he was a handsome fellow in a manly way, the way that women liked, masterful yet gentle. Only, he groaned to think, he must now perform the tedious ritual which women's vanity demanded before they would consent to say Yes as, in their gratitude, they should be swift to say. This Caroline Noyes was a handsome lass. Often, idly, he had admired her, considering that he might woo her should he find the time; but never had he considered marrying her or any other woman. He liked his freedom, liked to come and go and be damned as he wished, and to love whom and when the spirit itched him; but to be tied down . . . No woman would tie him down, by thunder! . . . But when he was tired, late at night after drinking and gaming, it would be pleasant to find a fire at home, supper laid and a bed made warm for his entering. Despite the cynics, marriage had its good points, so long as the man from the first showed that he intended to be master.

The rustle of skirts warned him that the women were coming from the kitchen which opened directly into the parlour, and he swung away from the glass, assuming a bored and negligent air; but under the heavy brows, his pale eyes were alert.

Mrs. Probert entered first, to dip him a low curtsey. A small fat woman with a purpling face, sweat beaded her upperlip, for she had recently left the stove, and she glanced, archly, simpering, at Thurtell. He barely noticed her. His glance was on the girls that followed, her younger sisters, Caroline and Anne, both tall, dark girls with delicate complexions, the ebon curls dancing to their shoulders; only the unfortunate Anne kept one eyelid flatly lowered as though she winked, her right eye having been lost in some childhood accident. Nothing marred the perfection of Caroline's blue eyes. Boldly, wrinkling slightly at the corners, they gazed at Thurtell standing, legs apart, the muscles on thighs and calves showing hard through the tight trousers. Abruptly with a jerk of the neck, hand to his heart, he bowed, then stood again erect, still staring at her intently until she feared lest she blush.

"Well, Mr. Thurtell," clucked Mrs. Probert, "it does the heart good to see your bonny face again, does it not, girls? What I always says is, when Mr. Thurtell's here, a lady remembers she's a lady. There are too many men about who try to prove that she ain't, you know, but you're always a gentleman to the marrowbones, Mr. Thurtell; and that is what I always say, don't I, Bill?"

"Ay," said Probert with a grimace, "that you do, and often . . . but, Mrs. P., my love, I've something to tell you; and you, too, Anne. Come with me."

"One moment, love. I am sure Mr. Thurtell wishes to see his dear brother's children. Such loves, Mr. Thurtell, such lambs when they ain't naughty and kept away from firearms. They're in the fields. Shall I call them for you?"

"Not at the moment, please," said Thurtell. "Later."

"Come, wife," growled Probert, gripping her fat arm with such force that she squealed. "Come with me; you, too, Anne. Not you, Carrie. Jack Thurtell's something to say to you."

"To me!"

"Ay, to you. . . . Come, wife."

Almost he pushed his wife and her sister into the kitchen, then firmly closed the door behind them; and Thurtell was alone with Caroline Noyes in that dim shadowed chamber, sunlight through the leaves outside flickering in gold and silver on the dusty floor. In silence which every moment became more painful, they stared at one another, Thurtell with his chin up to stretch his jowls, and his eyes in their hollows glittering down at her; and Caroline poised, almost tiptoe, within her simple gown of strawberry-coloured sarsenet belted around the narrow waist, the stiffly starched petticoats spreading out the skirt to fall in a narrow bell to a little below the ankles. Yes, thought Thurtell approvingly, the girl was handsome, a little highly coloured at the moment—doubtless with agitation, finding herself alone with him—the eyes bright, the brows softly shaded, the nose a little uppish, almost supercilious, and the mouth full-underlipped, the chin small and neatly rounded as though with a sculptor's thumb. Her gown concealed her shape; but thought of that did not trouble Thurtell.

She was a woman: he wanted nothing more. Indeed, he really did not want so much.

Then she tittered, and he frowned, hating a woman's titter.

"La, sir," said she, "you stare as though I were a stranger or you would price my gown. 'Tis a new gown; do you approve of it, sir?" Lightly, she pirouetted before him, watching him archly, amused to see him like a blinded bull glowering at her and not knowing what to say. "The latest fashion, it is. Or my dressmaker's a liar. And these high shoulders. Are they not in the môde?"

Still, he did not speak; still with lowered head and furrowed brow he watched her as she sank back on the flat heels of her satin shoes and placed her hands together as though praying, the tips of her fingers under her chin.

"You know why I have come?" he asked suddenly, clearing his throat.

"To see your brother's girls? Shall I call them in?"

"No. They are Tom's concern and not mine. Come, lass, I'm no dabster at fancy talk. I'm Jack Blunt, a true Englishman, and have no knowledge of the faradiddles of drawing-rooms and ladies' parlours." He could not look at her. Before the amused smile dimpling her cheeks, he glanced aside, and now it was the turn for his cheeks to redden. "Then let me spit it out," he said, "and be honest with you. For that's my fashion. Take me or leave me. I'm no liar and I never break my word nor forget a friend or enemy. Such is my nature with all its defects. I tell you this first, do you understand?"

"No," she said, although she understood full well; and she could have laughed, only she feared to hurt him in his embarrassment.

"I've not said this to a woman before, nor asked this of her, not this exactly. But damme, why don't you help?"

"You bewilder me!" she sighed, eyes large and innocent. "How can I help you?"

"By marrying me, dammit, by marrying me. Surely that's plain enough? By marriage I mean church and all: the parson, the pew-opener, the beadle, the banns, bell, book and candle and all. There's an honest offer. Name the day, girl, and I'm yours."

Having brought out the dangerous words that could condemn him to a lifetime's sentimental imprisonment, Thurtell breathed more easily, as though after a swift bout he rested between rounds on his second's knee. Now he could look up and smile. But when he did look up, the smile slid from his lips, for Caroline, he saw, was smiling at him. Not with happiness did she smile, but with delight and malice and mockery in her eyes, although, when she saw him looking at her, quickly she drooped the corners of her lips.

"You honour me," she whispered, "and I am grateful, sir, for the compliment, but, I fear, my heart's another's."

"What? what's that? what?"

"I am already trothed," she said and raised her left hand that the diamonds in the ring might splutter when she moved them into a sunbeam crawling through the leaves over the window.

"You can't! Your brother-in-law said . . . I'll not have it. D'ye hear me! I'll not have it!"

He stuttered, unable yet to believe that he had heard truly. With a certain reluctance but with a grim determination to see it through for his pockets' sake had he come to this meeting, never conceiving a refusal possible. Even now he could not believe it. She was teasing him. That was the way of women. To tease a man, to coquette and torment him that they might find sweeter the moment of surrender. He knew so little of women, save the women of his world in which bargaining was swift and indirect proposals rarely needed, that he wondered whether this were not mere feminine play.

"Ma'am," he said harshly, "I'll not ask you again."

"That would be best," she said, "for both our sakes."

"Both our sakes . . ." He repeated her phrase like a half-deaf man uncertain whether he had heard correctly. "You really mean it, ma'am? This refusal—it is forever?"

"Forever," she whispered. "I am sorry, Mr. Thurtell."

"To hell with your sorrows!" he cried. "Don't talk like that to me, you sly slut. To dangle me as though I were a puppy at your skirts, to say Come Hither in a look, whore's looking, sidelong winking, and then to say No with your lips when the moment comes. . . . This is the way of an honest woman, is it! God be thanked I know so little of them. I've had better women than you, ma'am, ladies, well-bred, wealthy, young; they loved me . . . and yet you . . ."

There was no laughter now in her eyes or on her mouth as she stepped back when he stepped forward. For the first time in her life, Caroline realized that her mother had not been lying when she had warned her that men might prove dangerous to women. So easily until now had she twisted them to their knees, tormenting them with fluttering eyelashes or the barren kiss of a pout, that she had believed herself invisibly armoured in her chastity. Now as Thurtell stepped forward and she stepped back, panic robbed her of her wits, and she knew herself to be unarmoured, felt herself naked, blushing and naked and terrified, before that angry stare in the small grey-blue eyes.

"No," she whimpered, pulling up her skirt in readiness to run.

Then as though a hand had pushed against his chest, Thurtell tottered a little and stood erect.

"You have no need to fear me, ma'am," he said in a strangled voice. "I mean no harm to ladies. Someone has been before me with you. I see it by your hand."

"Why, yes," she said shrilly, laughing a little in her relief, "I am affianced to Major Wood."

"That bastard!"

"Sir! your language! Major Wood is a gentleman."

"Pah," growled Thurtell and stood back. "A fool and a coward," he said. "Tell him, he'd best beware of me."

"You would not dare! Because he has claimed my affections, you have no right to threaten him. He's done you no harm: at least, he meant you no harm."

Now, in her anger and defence of her lover, Thurtell saw that she was beautiful and he clenched his teeth to realize what he had lost. As though a genteel mask had fallen from her face, he saw the passionate woman, the true woman, that lived within the girl, her eyes gleaming, lips back to bare a flicker of teeth, and her chin up.

"By God," he said, as though awakening, "you are a woman, after all!"

"A woman? what did you think me? A silly puss to be flattered by your offer? If I had never met Major Wood, I'd not have married you, a beast, a tongue-tied bumpkin who can talk only of fighting men and dogs, of bears and badgers; and if you dare attack Major Wood, I'll . . . I'll . . . You'll be sorry for it, sir."

"He is safe from me," said Thurtell. Then suddenly—it was to him as though a devil sprang inside him, possessing him body and soul—he caught her by the shoulders, swung her into his arms and kissed her hard and long on the mouth. She punched him, tried to kick with her knees, wriggling and twisting to escape, but he had a giant's strength compared with hers, and she was helpless.

Suddenly he let her go and she staggered, almost falling.

"Beast," she stuttered, spitting and rubbing her mouth with the back of her hand, "beast, you beast! You've cut my lip!"

"Lucky it was only your lip," he said, and trembled with the longing not only to kiss her again but to thrash her into submission.

The chance was taken from him. Before he could move, she had run to the door, opened it and fled, leaving him trembling and feeling sick. He looked down at his hands and saw, to his surprise, that they were open, fingers crooked, as though of their own accord they had been prepared to close about her throat.

"What is it, Jack? what have you done? Carrie's weeping and laughing and swooning. What the hell have you done to her?"

He had not heard the handle turn, the door open and Probert hurry in. Now at the sound of his voice, he looked up with a bewildered, angry and almost frightened air.

"What have you done to her?" cried Probert again.

"Nothing, nothing at all," said Thurtell quietly. "Nothing, compared to what she's done to me."

CHAPTER TWO

A MURDER IS PROPOSED

ON THE west side of the Haymarket, that broad street flanked with ancient shops, stood the Cock Tavern. Like the shops around it, the Cock was old, but towards the south, the rebuilders were at work, pulling down and setting up again; and on the opposite side of the street, the newly built Haymarket Theatre behind its six Corinthian pillars, shining down their flanks with light from the gas-lamps behind them between the doors, pointed its pediment sharp against the starry sky. The street was quiet, save for the hubbub in the Cock, and, inside, lounging with his back against the wall, legs outthrust, John Thurtell sat with his hat tipped forward over his eyes, watching the customers. Riffraff. No money to be made from these sneak-thieves, these hangers-on of the sporting world, and their twopenny harlots quaffing beer and gin. Behind the bar, Mary Walker, who, as Mary Dobson, had accompanied him from his native Norwich in his assault on London, worked calmly, efficiently, pouring the drinks and keeping her hand out-forked for the money while watching the drinkers through stony blue eyes. Her husband worked beside her and carried the drinks on a tray to customers who were too lazy to stand up and get them for themselves.

He came to Thurtell and placed on the table before him and his brother, Tom, two tall glasses of rum and water. Thurtell nodded, not paying, and Walker skipped backwards, as though bowing from the presence of a king, or god, his head down and his lips curled spitefully. Thurtell did not notice. Moodily, hands in his breeches' pockets, he stared at Mary behind the bar, her dyed yellow hair shining like brass in the gas-light, her fat cheeks painted, her over-fleshed body's shape plainly shown in the simple blue gown she wore and which was, by deliberate choice, too tight for her.

Thurtell scorned sentiment, he blew his nose at the mention of love, but, as he sat there in the smoke of the tavern, with the shouting and the singing and the laughter about him, his gaze on Mary, his thoughts turned soft in memories. Norfolk. The fight at North Walsham with "Flatnose" and Tom Oliver pounding with bloody knuckles at each other while black clouds fanned overhead and split the sky with thunder, lightning, drenching them all, lords and black-legs, bruisers and backers, sharps and flats, tradesmen and beggars, sending them to run helterskelter, while, groaning, swaying, Oliver went down beneath the rattle of "Flatnose's" fists. "Flatnose" Ed. Painter. His man, "Flatnose." Good boy, "Flatnose."

He smiled. In their hollows, his eyes glinted like diamonds.

Mary had been with him that day in his barouche. A different Mary from this fattening woman behind the bar, although that had only been two years ago, in 1821. It seemed a hundred years ago with him cock of the provincial walk and Mary from Yarmouth his fancy lass in her finery, the envy of all country Cyprians. With high hopes had they driven south . . . to this. His lips closed, his hands clenched, his eyes narrowed, as he remembered William Weare and blind hookey and how, cheating, he had taken the golden guineas from him. He had bee. johnny raw then, perhaps; he was so no longer. He was a man now, merciless, hard, unafraid. London had strengthened him; but Mary . . . not Mary. . . . The brave laughing girl of Norwich, costliest lass in the town, had found herself a sad figure amongst the multitude of women drawn every year to London and its wealth.

They had been happy then, comrades rather than lovers. He liked her still. Now, watching her, seeing when she lifted an arm to take a bottle from a high shelf how the chestnut hair showed at her armpit where the damp gown was split, he felt a sudden gentleness, a wish to stroke her, to kiss her; and he wondered why he had been sufficiently generous to let her marry that mooncalf, Walker.

He could not see Caroline here. He saw her always in the disorder of Gill's Hill Cottage, playing with Tom's young daughters, or strolling pensively over the grass, or watching the beauty of her own reflection ripple in the pond beside Probert's cottage. But here? here amidst cursing, blaspheming, bawdy thieves and whores: no, he could not see her here . . . Yet, given the chance, given the opportunity of catching her alone, he'd smash that smug cat's smile from her gob; he'd humble her.

"I'd soon flog the sauciness out of her," he growled.

"Eh? eh?" Startled from his own gloomy thoughts, Tom turned to stare at his brother. He was a few years younger and was not so powerfully built, yet there could have been no mistaking their brother-hood. Tom was a minikin to John's manakin, a reflection in miniature, although almost as well-built physically. But where John's features—

save for the delicately modelled nose—were strong, Tom's were weak, the kind of face that seemed all profile, shifty-eyed, shadowy, without firm outlines. "What—er, er, what, er—did you say, J-j-jack?" he asked.

"Did I speak?" Thurtell turned to stare at him. "That's dangerous. To talk aloud."

"It—it—it was only about some wench, ab-b-bout flogging her, or—or—or something."

"Caroline Noyes," said Thurtell, taking a long drink of rum. "I don't like hurting women, Tom. You know that. I can be as gentle as a lamb when treated right. Look at Mary there. I made that girl. What was she but a cheap good-for-little in Norwich! I brought her South. Set her up. Showed her the town. And now I let her marry that little dandiprat, Walker, and I let em both work for me. I'm fair to who's fair to me."

Not only his stutter kept Tom from speaking. That stutter often closed his lips when witty thoughts, while drunk, rose to his palate, but love of his brother now kept him tongue-tied. He had always worshipped Jack; he worshipped him still; but there were times when he wondered, and was ashamed of himself for wondering, whether he were not occasionally mistaken. In Norwich, Mary had been a jolly lass, the toast of the taverns and the envy of every shop- and bar-girl, with tradesmen's and squires' sons jostling to toss coins into her lap. Now, already fattening, her skin an unhealthy white, her hair losing its gloss, she toiled behind Jack's bar, the wife of his tapster. When bringing her to London, he had scarcely raised her out of her station.

"I'm not going to forget that woman," said Thurtell. "It's not the refusal. A man has to expect such things at times. There're sure to be some women who can say No. It was the way she said it. I almost thought she was laughing at me! And I won't have that."

"I—I—I think you l-l-love her, Jack," smiled Tom.

For a long moment Thurtell was silent, staring blindly at the noisy crowd; then he turned to his brother and said slowly:

"By God, Tom, I believe you're right! I hadn't thought of it before. I must be in love with the cow! Else why should I be always thinking of her, she a young and foolish, giggling creature a man'd tire of in a week? That's what it is! Love! Glory be! who'd have thought it! Old Flare in love in his old age! for I'm old, Tom, for all my twenty-nine years, I'm old in sin and wickedness. . . . So old at times I think of slinging all this, of settling down, following in dad's

steps, becoming a merchant, an alderman with a wife and kids at home.
When it came to it, I suppose I'd jib; but it's good to think of. And
when I do have silly dreams like that, the bloody wife of mine has a
mug like Carrie Noyes's—curds and whey with eyes like broken ice."

"B-b-brighter than ice," laughed Tom.

"Ay, I'm no poet. Blue as, what can you say? well, blue, anyhow.
I never thought a woman could get under your skin like a prickly heat.
There's only one cure for that."

"B-b-but you c-c-can't. She said No."

"If I can't have her," said Thurtell slowly, "I'll have him;" and
that crooked left eyebrow of his arched high to a point while the right
flattened down as the lid drooped in a vicious wink.

"What's this?" cried Probert, pushing his great bulk through the
drinkers, "what's this I hear? who are you going to have, Jack?"

"Shut up," said Thurtell, eyeing him coldly. "You always talk too
much."

Behind Probert wriggled a tall handsome fattish man, dark-skinned,
dark-eyed, with great black whiskers like brooms on his cheeks, and
moustachios worthy of a Spaniard. He seemed to bounce rather
than to walk, as if his boots were soled with air; and although his dark
coat and trousers were worn and shiny and his hands not clean, he had
about him an appearance of ultra-amiability, almost of gentility,
impossible to repulse. He swooped, a plump and amiable crow,
towards the table, brown eyes rolling, long tongue lolling from his
lips as though he were dying of thirst; and even in his anger, Thurtell
could not resist smiling when he saw him. There was something about
the sprightly sycophancy of this man, Joseph Hunt, a professional
singer—whenever he could find employment—that appealed to him
and he preferred his company above most others.

"Be a pal, pal," said Hunt quickly, rolling his eyes, "pour the
bingo down a poor fellow's throat before he croaks. O, O, I die before
your eyes and not a drink amongst all your hard hearts."

"Rums!" shouted Thurtell to the bar. "Four rums here!"

At the prospect of liquor, Hunt stood up and gave a jig, elbows
out, while in a surprisingly sweet tenor he piped:

> "There's a difference between a beggar and a king,
>   And the reason I'll tell you why.
>   A king cannot swagger, nor get drunk like a beggar
>   Nor be half so happy as I—as I."

"Sit down," said Thurtell, "I'm in no mood for fun tonight."

"Sorry, my lord," said Hunt, quickly drawing a chair up beside Probert at the table. "I will be as glum as you are merry; I'll be Bob Logic to your Corinthian. What shall we patter of? Kings and sepulchres, beagles and bruisers——"

"No," said Thurtell harshly. She had said that he could talk of nothing but fighting men and dogs and bears and badgers; and, after all, what else was there worth talking about? "We've got to get some money," he said.

Hunt yelped rather than laughed, as though the idea were too absurd to mention.

"What's it look like?" he cried. "What's it smell like? taste like? It looks like drops of sunlight and it smells like brandy and tastes like pigeon-pie. What did you want to bring that up for, Jack?"

"Because it's time somebody did," said Thurtell. "Here's us four, as clever a pair of pairs as you'd find in all London; and what are we? Nothing. Nothing, dammit, only a few shillings between us. I started right, but bloody Weare rooked me. I know. I know! You've heard all that before, but I ain't forgot yet. Then there's Tom and me have a nice fire in an empty warehouse with an insurance company that wants to nab us for it and won't cough up a penny-piece. There's Bill Probert, bankrupt yet penniless, who was doing well with his jigger at Elstree before the excise heard of it and now he's got to stop brewing better booze than any you'll buy in London. And there's you, Joe, with the Army and Navy Tavern which you had to give up purely because you couldn't meet your bills. It ain't right."

"It ain't, indeed," groaned Hunt. "Give me another drink, Jack."

"What are you going to do about it?" asked Probert quietly, slouching in his chair, chin on his breast. "Take to the road and be hanged?"

"We're Turpin lads!" laughed Hunt and cocked an invisible pistol at Probert. "Bang!" he shouted. "You're dead, Bill, dead as a flounder; and having got your life, I want your purse. Why should lads stay honest when a pistol can be bought and a horse be hired and every lady loves a highwayman!"

"Shut up," said Thurtell quietly. "You've got it, Joe; but not quite right. The days are over for highwaymen. You know that. The money's made today by rats like Lemming who hire stout fellows like me to guard em and do their robbing with a crooked E.O. table or a rolly-polly board. We could take a hell in St. James's. I've considered that, but there are too many at the game, and you need capital, rich furnishings, quarts of fizz and good food. We can't do it, dammit."

"We could go around the fairs," suggested Hunt.

"Shut up. So that's out. We've not the capital for a hell nor to work at race-meetings like Lemming or to put on a cross at a fight. Tom and I've tried the insurance and we got away with it; the judge gave judgment for us: only the insurance company won't pay, the bloody cheats. And I think, under another name, we might do it again."

"Not under my name," said Probert hurriedly. "After my bankruptcy, I can't get no more credit."

"After having been in Newgate," sighed Hunt, "my good fame is gone forever."

"Cowards," said Thurtell quietly. "I thought it'd be like this. A fine pair of jackanapes. I know. You want me to do all the work; and then, like fleas, to live on me. Is that it?"

"Well," said Probert uneasily, clearing his throat, "I'd do it if I could, Jack; you know that; but who the hell'd trust me, 'cept a woman? and I don't know any women now with any canaries left worth pocketing. I need rhino as much as any of you. I've got to leave Gill's Hill. Since I got rid of the jigger, I can't pay my rent and I can't see where a farthing's coming from. . . . If only you could have married Carrie and got her cash."

From the black hollows under Thurtell's brows a milky gleam showed for a moment as he turned towards Probert, and his great fists clenched.

"You know why that failed?" he growled. "You'd let the wench take up with the bloody landlord of yours. Why didn't you stop it from the first?"

"I didn't think there was anything in it——"

"You didn't think! You've signed Wood's death-warrant, that's all you've done, and you've lost us a mint of money. You should have kicked his backside when he first came sniffing near her. What's the use of a fellow like that for a brother-in-law when he makes you pay rent? he'd not give you the smell of a goblin unless you put down your I.O.U. on a Bible for it first. You've let the money get out of your family, you fool."

Probert said nothing. He remained sunk in his chair and slowly sipped his rum, knowing that it was dangerous to provoke Thurtell while in this angry mood.

"There's only one thing to be done," said Thurtell. He lowered his voice so that all had to lean forward to catch what it was that he said.

"I've got to marry the girl," he hissed.

"B-b-but what ab-b-bout Major Wood?" gasped Tom.

Thurtell slowly winked and tightly smiled.

"We're the Turpin lads!" cried Hunt with a whoop.

"Have you seen my stick, my pretty walking-stick?" continued Thurtell, with a quiet smile at Hunt to remain quiet. "Looks like wood, don't it? Hawthorn, mayhap?"

From behind his chair he pulled out a knobbly walking-stick.

"Feel it," he said.

Gingerly, Probert took it in his hands and weighed it. "Mighty cold for wood," he said, and twirled it in his fingers. "Don't look like wood to me," he said, and smelt it; then he sucked the round top, watching Thurtell all the while. "Don't taste like wood either," he said at last.

"I can't show you here," whispered Thurtell, tenderly taking back the stick and dangling it in his hands, "but you're right, Bill. It's not wood, though you'd think it was. It's a gun, an air-gun. Made of tin painted to look like wood. You screw off this top here, and the air-pump, which is separate from the rest, but small enough to slip into your pocket, can be fixed in a moment and the gun filled with air. Then, it's just—present arms, fire! and blaze away, my jolly boys! get em between the eyes!"

With held breath, the three men stared down at that innocent-seeming weapon. A knobbly stick, like a piece of Irish bogwood, perhaps, swayed across Thurtell's palm. Yet in its hidden muzzle lay death, quick death, silent death, coming with no warning on a dark night to a man strolling without thought of danger in the street. It might have been any of them, that victim. The enemy unseen, the blow like an invisible wasp stinging you; heard and felt as you toppled down, not knowing how you had died. . . .

"The calibre's small, very small," whispered Thurtell, exulting to see their intent, anxious, almost frightened eyes watching the secret gun as though he had evoked a devil to paralyse them into silence. "The bullet's no larger than swan-shot. I've tried it. There's nothing like it in the world. It'll send a bullet through an inch deal board at a moderate distance."

"Where'd you get it, Jack?" gasped Hunt.

"No matter that. I've got it; and I got it for Mr. bloody Barber

Beaumont of the County Fire Office. I've been trying to get him for some time till I got sore feet hanging at the back of his house in Regent Street, the way he usually sneaks in and out. And I've stood evening after evening in the door of that house of Ward's on the corner of Sherrard Street, waiting for him to come out of the fire office; and all the time I've had this gun over my arm, aching to use it. Well! I think I'll let Beaumont pass for a time. I'll use it first on Wood. Then I'll marry the girl——"

"N-n-no," gasped Tom Thurtell, his hand on his brother's shoulder. "N-n-not bloody murder, J-j-jack. I—I—I'm in any-anything; but not, not m-m-murder, Jack. D-do-don't do it."

"You go home, Tom," said Thurtell with sudden tenderness, smiling at his brother. "You're right. I don't want you in this. Go home and wash your ears and forget everything you've heard."

"B-b-but you don't mean it, Jack?"

"Go home," said Thurtell, catching him under the elbow and lifting him to his feet. "This is nothing to do with you. You've heard nothing."

"B-b-but you don't mean it?"

"I said—go home!"

Tom Thurtell stood uncertainly, staring down at the three, but he was used to submitting to his brother's dominance. Giving John a last imploring look, he turned quickly and pushed through the drinkers to the door.

"I'm glad of that," said Thurtell, sitting back. "Tom's a stout lad, but he's not the stomach for these things; besides, he's got those pretty kids of his. We'll leave him out of this. Now, look here, Bill: when Wood comes to London he lodges in Castle Street with you, don't he?"

"Ay," said Probert sulkily, the blood beginning to leave his cheeks. "But he's not there now."

"When's he coming?"

"I . . . I don't know."

"Then find out. And don't think you can back out of this like Tom. Tom's my brother, he's got two fine girls, he's done nothing wrong 'cept against the insurance. You're different. It'd be hard to find anything you've done right, and a little murder won't make much difference to your soul."

"It's not my soul I'm worried about," growled Probert. "It's my neck."

"I'm not asking you to do anything: just to tell me when he's

C

there. All you'll have to do is to find him dead in his bed, an empty pistol at his side, and raise the house with your bawling. They'll not blame you. How can they? You'll be out most of the night, roistering wherever you can find most folk who'll remember the hour. It'll be felo-de-se, and Caroline'll find herself a widow before she was a wife. How's that?"

"Don't like it," said Probert, blowing out his cheeks. "Why can't you do it somewhere else? why pick on my lodgings?"

"Because Wood's there, too, you fool."

"You've got this air-gun. You could get him in the dark, walking home at night . . ."

"How am I to know what time he's coming home? Expect me to hang around with every bloody police-officer in Westminster to quiz me, and for the watch to start asking questions? I don't want to get hanged any more than you do. And I'm not going to be hanged, I tell you that!"

"I still don't like it," muttered Probert. "I don't."

"'Hark,'" trilled Hunt, "'I hear the sound of coaches, the hour of attack approaches. To your arms, brave boys, and load!' We're the Turpin lads, and may the devil go hang!"

"Hush; now, listen to what I've got to say . . ."

"I still don't like it," muttered Probert, sinking down inside his coat. "Why have you got to kill the bastard in my place?"

"I'm telling you. Now, listen, and speak low. . . ."

Three heads drew closer together, the cropped head of Thurtell, the bushy head of Hunt as he leaned forward, giggling, and the scantier hair of Probert moving forward over his skull as he frowned and knuckled his fists. And in the uproar of that tavern, under the babble, the singing, the quarrelling, the cursing, the love-play, none could hear a word they said; although from behind the bar, Mary Walker leaned forward, straining, straining; but she heard never a word that she could understand.

CHAPTER THREE

DEVIL TAKE THE CLOCK

CASTLE STREET formed the west side of the block of which the south side was Duke's Court; the north, Henning's Row; and the east, St. Martin's Lane. At its lower end was the Upper Mews Gate opening on to the royal mews from which the horses were already being taken to be stabled at Buckingham Palace; and with the going of the royal horses, it seemed, the district was beginning to decay, like neighbouring Leicester Square with its tangle of weeds dusty around the broken metal statue of King George I dressed like a Roman soldier and riding a horse copied from King Charles's horse at Charing Cross. These were not so much streets as footways; too narrow for carts they were usually damp and sunless, stagnant with the reek of old cooking and slops tossed out of windows, playgrounds for children whose parents believed them safe away from traffic. Like their homes, most of the inhabitants lived in a state of disrepair, unwashed, untidy, and their clothing tattered. The women looked half-asleep, for only at night did they really awake, their eyes alone seeming living and sullen with angers when turned towards a stranger venturing near; the men were furtive, quick walkers, sidlers, stealers into doorways, and either obsequious or belligerent in manner. Only the children, of which there were many, showed any interest in life, but even they were peaked and wary like their parents, their faces older than their years and their knees in a chronic state of rash.

Castle Street was broader than its neighbours and therefore cleaner, although itself far from clean. Here were warehouses, taverns, brothels and lodging-houses; and No. 35 was a lodging-house in which the lodgers could eat with the landlady and that wench-of-all-work, her fat, energetic, spot-faced daughter, and the landlord when he was not in hiding. Thurtell knew it well, many of his friends staying there when they considered it time for them to disappear discreetly for a while, and he would be able to creep in unseen while Probert amused the women downstairs; then he could kill his enemy in silence, and creep out again.

Having arranged the murder and rehearsed it again and again, until he almost believed that it was already done, he found that the most important detail was lacking. Major Wood rarely warned the landlady when he might be expected, and as he disliked Probert and Tom Noyes, the only other lodgers, he never discussed his affairs with them. His visits to London from his home in Hertfordshire were occasional, unexpected and, usually, brief.

"Tonight I hear," said Probert one day, drawing Thurtell into a corner of the bar of the Cock; "he sent to say he'd come."

"Tonight!" Thurtell's face grew pale and his lips set tight. "Anyone else in the house?"

"No one. Noyes has gone to his sister's. Are you backing out?"

"Backing out? what do you mean? You were the one who wanted to back out, not me."

"I didn't like it at first," said Probert with a shrug. "That's true enough, but thinking it over, I see you're right, Jack. We need the rent; at least, I do. Damned Wood's getting pressing and not a stinking soul will trust me with a farthing. Something's got to be done. And now's the moment, lad. You'll find no better time to serve him."

"Tonight? He'll be there tonight?"

"Ay. I'll keep the old woman and her wench merry in the kitchen. They'll not hear you, and Wood goes early to bed. Let's say midnight. He's on the first floor, the room opposite mine."

"Midnight," said Thurtell. "I will do it."

Until now it had been merely a pleasing thought, a threat against a rival with which he could console his vanity, but at Probert's words, he realized with a clarity he had not felt before that this was no longer an idea, a day-dream. It was a bloody deed which he had sworn to commit.

"Mary!" he shouted. "Two brandies. Large uns. Leave em naked, will you! You don't want water with yours, do you, Bill?"

"No," said Probert, watching him narrowly as he seized the glass and drank the neat spirit at a gulp. "I've been finding out about Carrie's fortune. Mrs. P.'s a bit vague about it, but it runs into thousands. She was always papa's pet, she and Mrs. P., and he left most of his fortune to the three girls, Anne coming in for her whack. The others get a little, but not so much. Tom raised what he could on his, but the Jews drove their usual bargain and after he'd inherited he found that he owed more than he got. Once Carrie's married and the money's out of Chancery, you'll be able to buy a coach and four if you want one and live like a duke in St. James's."

"Tonight? midnight?" Thurtell drew himself erect. He even managed to smile. "I never did like the cove," he said, "and I suppose the next best thing to kissing a girl you like is beating a man you hate. I'd rather I had him in the ring with his mawlers up than letting him have it without his knowing what's hit him. That takes half the sport away, don't it?"

"I don't know," smiled Probert. "I've not croaked anybody, yet. But it's got to be done quiet. Don't give him the chance to yell, if you love your neck."

"I'd rather flog the bastard first. Too easy for him to be banged out of life and not know it. He might be dreaming of her at the time and be able to carry the dream to heaven."

"Ay," chuckled Probert, "or he might be having a nightmare to carry with him to hell."

Although the day was cold. Thurtell's hands were clammy and there was sweat between the fingers, and Probert noted the raising of his voice and the flash of the small eyes. No other sign did he give that he was preparing his spirit to kill. But now and then, while they talked of sport, of boxers and gamecocks and slow horses, he would say suddenly, casually, something about Wood which showed that, under the chatter, his mind was teasing with the problem of the night.

"I've got an old pistol," he said. "I'll slip it into his hand to let em think he done it himself."

Then, again, while Probert was telling him, for the hundredth time, of the dirty way Tom Cribb had kept the championship against the black Molyneux, he said:

"I'd better clean the gun. I've not used it for weeks and we don't want any mistake, do we?"

Probert glared at him, infuriated. Here he had been at his wittiest and Thurtell hadn't heard a word. But he swallowed his rage and said with an assumption of amiability:

"Ay, you don't want anything to go wrong."

"It won't. This air-gun can't miss at close range. I think I might slash him with it first; wake him up, you know; then let him have it straight between the eyes."

"No," cried Probert. "Don't give him a chance to squeak, for God's sake and your own neck."

What satisfaction in killing a sleeping man? No more than in making love to a dead woman. In murder, as in love, the other party must be awake for the full pleasure to be relished. But like a cowardly assassin, to tiptoe to his bed, to place the stick to his temple, and let fly . . . the idea depressed Thurtell, although he had no intention of backing out.

That was impossible. If he acted the coward, Probert would have contempt for him and the tale would soon be tattled throughout London, as such tales always mysteriously were revealed. Old Flash, the Bully, had funked it. Thought of such ignominy made Thurtell twist on his chair. The terror that walked with him had brought him a living as one of Lemming's men hired to protect their leader and to thrash or mutilate anyone who failed to pay his gambling debts. It had not been work he liked, for he fretted at being employed by others and he felt degraded in being merely one of a gang of blacklegs and sharpers. Nevertheless it filled his pockets on occasions when they were empty and he did enjoy the prestige of being feared, of seeing the flats watching him warily at the race-course and ducking obsequiously at a word.

"I'll see that Carrie marries you right enough," said Probert, detecting indecision in Thurtell's eyes. "She'd have had you at a bounce if that dog hadn't bitten her first. Of course, being a woman, she'll weep for a while and put on black, but it won't last, and you'll be there and I'll be there to act the pander when she softens. She's a fine woman, Jack."

"Fine enough," said Thurtell with a shrug.

"With a pot of gold, too."

"Ay, that's what I'm thinking," he said; but it was not the truth. For the first time since early youth when he had wooed a neighbour's wife in Norwich, he felt excited at the thought of a woman. He had grown to look on the sex with a kindly tolerance as little more than children to be coaxed and petted, but Caroline's refusal of his hand had changed her from a pretty girl into a cold goddess who must be ravished for his pride's sake. He could not shake her image from his mind. At night it kept him sleepless; it sat beside him at his meals, and in company he only half-listened to what was said, speaking silently to the dream that was more real in his imagination than the living people about him. This haunting exasperated him and he strove to exorcize it by drink and exercise, but always it remained, a taunt, a jeer, an insult that needed blood in recompense. That blood, blood of her lover, would be his that night, the Lord be thanked. . . .

When he had managed to shake off Probert, he walked up to his bedroom and took out an old pistol which he loaded, then fired up the chimney, bringing a shower of soot upon him. He had been prepared for that, however, and had donned an old coat that was past soiling, and which he had intended to wear as a disguise lest an acquaintance see him near Castle Street. But now, he felt, it had become too filthy even for such use and he would shake behind him at every step a sooty trail for the thief-takers to follow.

Better to use the boat-cloak he had bought for dark uses; and he took it out of its box and hung it from his shoulders. Greasy, sticky, it defied the weather and made him look like a tar on the spree. Yes, he would wear this, he decided.

And having decided that, he found that there was nothing further for him to do save sit and brood and drink. He did not want to get too drunk. He might lose control of his hatred if he did and might start mawling with the bastard, causing an uproar that could expose him for hangman's meat. Not that he believed they would ever hang him. The idea made him smile. Only the fools, blunderers got hanged. The clever fellows like himself, the rum sharps, knew what to do to escape suspicion; and, should it be required, Mary would swear on a stack of Bibles that he had never left the tavern.

He had not believed that he could feel like this again, elated yet anxious, unable to remain still while not wanting company, just as he had felt when he had been a boy mooning at the fat old adultress's window in the moonlight. Yes, the feeling was the same. It was not a new experience, after all, he decided ruefully, and he felt that he had been cheated. How could one measure love-play with an elderly woman against the greatness of the act of murder? Yet they felt very much the same in anticipation. It had been the same, too, when on the *Bellona* he had seen the doomed French schooner drift towards them. His hand had closed about the hilt of his cutlass, and he had held his breath, finding his heart beat painfully. Love and death. Were they allies, after all? in killing Wood would he know pleasure such as he might have felt in Caroline's arms? A rum thought. . . . There could be no link between the two.

Yet like the ambitious boy he once had been watching the sun go down to curtain love-play, now he walked up and down his little room, glaring through the unwashed window at the feeble light of a rainy afternoon, waiting, waiting for sunset, for the silence of the night and a tiptoe assignation.

"God curse it," he muttered, "I've never known time drag so damnably."

He did not want to go downstairs to the bar because he did not wish to talk, nor did he want to wander to other taverns where friends might recognize him; and he did not want to wear his boat-cloak in the light lest it be remembered. Was the first murder always like this? he wondered with a grin: like one's first love-affair? did one, as with women, lose one's doubts in time and eventually take the matter as casually as a grown man takes the kiss a woman offers? There were professional murderers at work in London, men employed by Lemming and other rulers of the sporting world, and they showed no remorse, no fears. But they were few, most backsliders being punished with a slit nose or a dozen broken bones rather than with killing which might bring the police too busily to work. Soldiers killed and were applauded for it. And what harm could the slaying of a mercenary landlord like Wood possibly do to the world? He had no mother and brothers to mourn him, and he lived a pursey, smug life on his half-pay, playing the Hertfordshire squire over a few acres. He could easily go and the world would scarcely notice.

Devil take the clock! Thurtell listened to the striking, counting carefully. One. Two. Three. Four. Five. . . . Only five o'clock; and he had to wait until midnight! He would go mad before then, exhausted after killing a hundred phantoms in his mind, stabbing, strangling, shooting them who were always in the shape of Wood—slim, dark and soldierly with cold blue eyes and an abrupt manner of speaking. Once Wood was in the grave, he grinned to think of Caroline's tears. She had rejected him, the only woman who had ever rejected him, and she would pay for it. But he would have to be clever. He'd have to hide his thoughts and simulate woe with a graveyard-face, sighing at Wood's goodness, his damned nobility and blasted honesty, until Caroline agreed to marry him . . . Heigh ho! it would be different then! At night, on the bridal night, perhaps, when he held her helpless in his arms, he would whisper the truth, telling her how he had murdered the rogue. A wife cannot bear witness against her husband, that being treason; and she would have to live with him, her heart heavy with the secret that the hands which fondled her were red with the blood of her lover. He chuckled, lying on the bed, and seeing that moment clearly in the dark. O, she would hate him, and that would give salt to his love.

On the stairs, quick footsteps. A woman's footsteps. For a wild moment, he half-believed that this was Caroline Noyes running to visit him; then the door opened and he sank back on the pillows when Mary opened the door and peeped in.

"Thought you'd gone out," she said.

"I'm not going out," he said. "Not all night. Remember that."

"Are you sick or something? what are you doing up here all by yourself?"

Impatiently, he twisted on the bed, not wanting to talk, and women were always inquisitive. They couldn't be trusted, not even Mary who had secrets of her own which, if revealed, would have had her transported, at the least; nevertheless he wanted to tell her everything. He wanted to say, quite casually: "I'm going to murder a cove tonight." The words trembled on his tongue, and he thought how astonished she would become, how awed and excited, how proud of him, if only she knew the truth. After all, he had loved her for a time and he did not doubt that she loved him still. They had been happy; yet he had given her to Walker in a moment of quixotic generosity. Now he regretted the gesture. That was what he needed—love— in this moment of tensed emotions that would not let him remain still.

"Come here," he commanded.

"What you mean, come here? I'm Mrs. Walker now, I'd have you know, and the old times are passed for good."

"Come here," he said more fiercely. "I want you."

She laughed. To his astonishment and anger, she laughed. There was a ring of malice in that surprisingly girlish laugh; of pleasure, too, and of triumph.

"Catch me if you can," she laughed. "Goodnight, Mr. Thurtell, and sweet dreams to you."

Before he could spring from the bed, she was gone, slamming the door, and he heard her racing down the stairs. A feminine and low revenge to mock at him, to taunt him, when until she'd met him she'd been a common strumpet. Damme, he had put her in this tavern, had let her become respectable by marriage, and here was his reward! She tittered at him when he asked a small service. Blast the woman! Blast all women! If he had had Caroline there, he'd have cut her throat . . .

Impossible to remain longer in this room. The walls seemed closing on him as the shadows deepened, drawing around his bed, and he leaped up and, rearranging his disordered stock, brushing down his coat and breeches, he walked slowly down the stairs. Best to be seen about as usual. There were hours to wait. . . .

No drinkers in the bar yet at this early hour. Only Mary behind the bar, her fingers in her hair gazing at nothing. When he entered she turned and smiled at him maliciously but she did not speak.

"Bingo," he said. "A large un."

While she poured his brandy, he watched her with desire and hatred. It would serve her right, he thought, to give her warning; but he dared not do it. She knew too much as it was, and with Beaumont's case against him soon to come up in the courts he could not have her appearing for the prosecution.

"Feeling better?" she said with a smirk as he swallowed the brandy in quick gulps.

"Never felt better," he growled. "I'm going to get married. D'ye know that?"

"Poor girl," sighed Mary with an exaggerated shudder. "Who is the unhappy wretch?"

"Someone better than you," he snarled. "A lady. And she's what you've forgotten you ever were—an honest woman, modest and beautiful."

"Where the hell, Jack Thurtell, did you meet a modest woman?" She laughed, patting her curls. "Ah, you can't gammon me," she said. "You're angry with me and think to make me jealous. Let me tell you this, damn you, I'd not care if you turned Turk and had a hundred wives to cuckold you. You're nothing to me now. Understand that. Nothing. Of course, you'll not believe it, but I love Mr. Walker and I'm faithful to him."

Thurtell laughed, shaking with rage. "That nincompoop!" he cried. "And a woman of spirit like you, Moll! I've often wondered why you married him, that crab without a shell."

"I tell you, I love him," she said, beginning in her turn to grow angry. "Which is more than I ever felt for you. You were useful, that's all. I was sick of Norwich and the silly boys there and the drunken squires stinking of cowdung, and I wanted to see London. So I worked you up to taking me."

"You, you worked me! Don't try and gammon me. I took you because I got lonely at night, and I often wonder why I wasted my time."

"And what have I wasted? Nothing, I suppose? I was a brave girl in Norwich, I could do what I liked, charge what I liked; but here . . . here I'm only a bar-girl, chalking up drinks for you that you'll never pay. I've wasted my life. Wasted it! And think what that means to a girl who's not getting younger every day! In Norwich, I might have married some swell when I had him lushed. But here . . . I wouldn't marry any of the trash that comes here, no! not if they was to have a real parson and a church and everything for it, I wouldn't."

Tears glittered on the soot of her lashes, smearing the lids, and her thin lips trembled, the fair hair, touched with dye, seemed to turn sulky in the oil-light, becoming lifeless.

"And let me tell you this, too," she cried, "now when I'm worked up to telling you the truth. I've had it too long corked inside me and I've got to let it out or burst. You're a fool, Jack Thurtell. You're a flat, that's what you are, and these London coves have laughed at you, plucked you and laughed at you. Look how easy Bill Weare plucked you at blind hookey!"

"I'm going to kill Weare one of these days for that!"

"You're always talking of killing people, you and that bushy-faced pal of yours, Joe Hunt. You're Turpin lads, you say! you're always talking about ripping people up and shooting em, but you'd swoon if you saw a corpse. All talk and no doing, that's your trouble. And I'll be pleased if you'd take away the damned bayonet you left at our place in Whitcomb Street."

"Frightened your Will might stick you with it some night?"

"I'm not frightened of Will. He's a good man. But I don't want anything of yours in my place. That's all. Anyhow, what do you want a bayonet like that for when you'd be scared to use it?"

"Don't be too certain." His mouth was dry and he found it difficult to speak. "I might use it on an ungrateful female before I'm finished," he said thickly, "just to see if you're cleaner inside than out."

He dared not thrash her and she knew it; damn it, she knew it; and that was why she could smirk and spit in his eye, and he could not retort. What had she been when he first met her? A fishwife from Yarmouth stinking of rotten herrings for all the powder and perfume she sprayed on her carcase. He had bought her finery, carried her to London . . . and here was all the thanks he got for it! Insults, gibes, when she realized she was safe from vengeance. If she hadn't known so much about the fire—what a fool he had been to have her living with him in that building, seeing him spread the wood-shavings, the old rags, and strike the tinder-box!—he'd soon have shown her who was master with a razor cupped in his hand—only the edge showing beyond his fingers—when he drew it down her nose or cheek.

"Hullo, Turpin, my lad," cried Hunt; and, relieved to escape Mary's mocking smile, Thurtell turned to greet his friend as he pranced into the bar, his splendid whiskers brushed and oiled, his tall hat on the side of his dark head. "I'm having a rum. Or is that bingo? I'll have a brandy, too, light of my life, my love."

"Who's paying for it?" demanded Mary.

"I wish you wouldn't be so damned inquisitive," grinned Hunt. "Like all women, you talk in questions. You should listen to Mrs. Hunt! Where were you last night? who was that fancy piece I saw you with? why don't you get some work? The sphinx never asked so many damn questions that a man can't answer. Give me that drink, now, sugarlips, please."

"Where's the money first?" asked Mary, cold-eyed, unsmiling.

"O, give him a drink, for the love of God," snarled Thurtell. "We can afford at least that for a friend. Come over here, Joe. She puts acid in the liquor with her evil eye. . . ."

As though submitting regretfully to male unreason, silently protesting at this waste of good brandy, Mary poured Hunt a large glassful, then turned her back.

"Some day," muttered Thurtell, leading his friend to a table against the wall, "I'm going to kick her so hard she'll pop out of the roof. The airs these females give emselves! Took her out of the gutter I did, a common trollop, made a lady of her, squandered fortunes on her dirty back . . . and now look at her! Thinks she's the queen of the Haymarket and that her breath don't stink."

"When you going to do it?" whispered Hunt, shaking, his eyes glittering. "Is it going to be soon? Has Bill found out when he'll be there?"

"Tonight," whispered Thurtell. "But keep your trap shut."

"Tonight!" Hunt leaned back in his chair, smiling and taking a deep breath. "Wish I could be with you," he said. "I'd like to see it. Give a hundred quid to see it, I would."

"Pah," said Thurtell, with a modest shrug. "It's nothing. Only thing I don't like, I can't stick the pig for fear he squeals. It's got to be my gun and there's no satisfaction in just pinging a fellow when he's asleep and don't know what's hit him."

"You're really going to do it!" Hunt gazed at Thurtell as though he were a beautiful woman; with awe, joy and delight, he stared at him, and he laughed, hitting his fist on the table. "Our friends had better be civil in future, eh, Jack," he squealed, "else we'll know what to do with them, won't we?"

At ease again, Mary's taunts forgotten, Thurtell lay back, almost purring before the homage in Hunt's eyes.

"Ay," he said. "I'll look after you, Joey. Nobody's going to treat you bad while I'm about. Get these glasses filled again. Tell that bitch to chalk em up to me. . . ."

Quickly, Hunt seized the empty glasses and darted back to the bar.

"Same again," he said, "only larger this time. Jack's in a brave mood tonight, Moll, ain't he? Never seen him look so brave before. I'd feel sorry for the man that got on the wrong side of him. He'd slit him up like a cheese."

"Pah," sniffed Mary. "And that's about all he ever will slit— cheese," she said. "Him and his talk. Never trust a man who talks too much. That's one of the first things a woman's got to learn. They talk because they're frightened to do anything. Pah to him!"

Hunt gaped at her, his face turning grey with rage.

"You'll know different some time," he said. "There's things I could tell you that'd uncurl your hair, my pretty, ay, and not let you sleep o' nights. But I'm a friend. My lips are sealed. Only take heed, my girl. Turpin rides again!"

"If he does," she said, "you'd best watch out. From what I've heard, Dick Turpin was a man. He didn't go clacking about doing this or that. He just done it and said nothing. You all talk too much."

Before the contempt in her eyes, Hunt lowered his lids and when he took up the refilled glasses his hands shook so that he spilt some of the liquor.

"She's a bad woman, that," he said to Thurtell when he had returned to the table. "You don't want to trust her, Jack."

"Trust her!" jeered Thurtell with an angry laugh. "Some morning she's not going to wake up again; and we'll fix it so that that damned husband of hers get strung up for doing it to her. There's sport for us to come, Joey boy. First Wood; then bloody Beaumont; and her; and—and another female; and others. Understand this, Joe, I'm a man of my word; and no man's going to stand between me and my happiness. There're three or four names on my list, but Wood stands first. After that, we'll see . . ."

"Can I come with you tonight, Jack? Let me go as far as the door, eh, and carry the stick?"

"Perhaps, perhaps . . ."

Suddenly Thurtell shivered as though a drop of ice ran down his spine, when he heard the clock strike seven. Seven. Eight. Nine. Ten.

Eleven. Midnight. Then Castle Street. How could he live through the hours? Seven. Eight. Nine. Ten. Eleven . . .

"This brandy's like water," he cried. "Get us another. A large one, Joe."

Midnight. The door opening on silent hinges—Probert had promised to oil them well—and the shape that was a man on the bed; and his stick raised quietly, carefully aimed. By God, he wished, he wished that it were over!

CHAPTER FOUR

THE STROKE OF MIDNIGHT

NOT quite midnight and very dark. The moon blotted by racing clouds, only the broader streets lighted by gas or oil, one was blind after stepping out of the door. In narrow streets, in lanes and alleys and rookeries, one could not see an inch ahead but, arms out, stumbled forward, cursing gutters and heaps of muck and the cats that screamed when trodden on. Nobody was abroad, it seemed, once the brightly lighted taverns were passed: except shapes, darker than darkness, like creatures in an inky ocean flitting, floating, noiselessly past. Thieves. And now and then a drunken harlot whining, laying a bony hand on one's arm, stinking of gin and stale sweat. Tap tap in the blackness went Thurtell's metal stick shaped like bogwood; tap tap on cobbles and paving-stones, rattling against the walls, along railings struck like a metal harp, that stick led the way.

"The very night for a murder," whispered Hunt, giggling.

Thurtell frowned and tapped him with the stick. He did not like such talk. One never knew who might be listening, tiptoeing at one's elbow, unseen in blackness, and he regretted having agreed to let the fool accompany him.

"Hey!" squealed Hunt, leaping from the touch of the stick. "Put that down. It might go off."

"It will," said Thurtell, "when I want it to."

Although Castle Street was not far from the Haymarket, that walk through darkness took longer than Thurtell had expected. There was a smell of fog in the air, mixed with exhalations from unclean homes, and it pressed clammily around his fingers and down beneath his boat-cloak on to his throat. He spat but he could not spit out the odour of decay. It pressed upon him as though amorous, seeped through his clothes and made his hair feel greasy. He could feel it tickle his throat as though sprouting there like a fungus, and his eyes smarted.

"Damn it," he whispered, "I hope I've counted right. This should be 35."

"Ay, ay," said Hunt, feeling along the hidden wall. "It's 35 all right. I remember this loose brick under the window. Pulled it out once, thinking there might be treasure there. Uh! just dirt; dirty dirt at that. You got the key?"

"Bill's left the door unlocked. Wait here. No; for your own sake, mizzle! Go back to the Cock and, if anyone asks for me, say I've got a cold. I'm lying down, say!"

"I'd like to go with you. I'd not interrupt, I promise. I'd just like to watch. Just to know I've seen it . . ."

"Go back to the Cock," said Thurtell. "There'll be other uns you can watch. This is mine alone. He's got to learn that what's mine's mine. I'll have no poaching for the woman I love."

"I—I don't want to go away . . . You know, I'm not afraid, Jack. I may be only a singer but I'm no coward, for all that. You laugh at me, I make jests, and you all laugh at me. But the real Joe Hunt's a very different person underneath. He acts the fool and often he could kill those who laugh at him. Yes, I've often felt like that. I could kill em when they laugh." His hand was on Thurtell's sleeve and his voice dropped almost to a whine as he pleaded. Like a woman, thought Thurtell, pleading to a man who was tired of her.

"I'm a rum one for all that they laugh," said Hunt hoarsely. "I sit at home and writhe when I think of what I'd like to do to em. Nothing to eat, nothing to drink, my wife half-starved, and me having to be a clown for a copper or two. It gets a man down, it does; it gets him here, in the bread basket, and I've felt like running through the streets shooting at people, any of em, just shooting at em. And Wood's the worst of em. Thinks he's a gent, he does. I'd like to croak him, but I've not your strength. I'm tall but I'm only a weak fellow. But I could help you; I could, Jack. I am as leery as any fellow you know. Let me help, please."

"No," said Thurtell, and he placed his hand tenderly on the hidden shoulder of his friend. "I understand," he said. "I've felt like that myself at times, when everything's against you. Mr. blasted Beaumont stirring up the insurance, Wood who boned my girl, Moll thinking she's queen of hell because I let her manage the Cock, and dainty-nosed pieces like Carrie Noyes who don't know a man when they see one. . . . We're going to alter all that, my lad. We'll be in the rhino soon, a couple of swells together. And I'm starting tonight. I'm starting alone. This is a private matter I'd share with no one, even with you. So scarper . . . I'll find you in the Cock."

He could not see Hunt leave him. He heard only the reluctant pad of his steps fading away, and more firmly he gripped his stick and stood on the front step of No. 35. Probert was already at work. From behind the curtained window in the basement he heard a woman squealing, then laughter, and the clink of glass. Grimly, contemptuously, Thurtell smiled. There was no doubt that Bill Probert had a way with the ladies, and he was not wholly lying when he boasted, as he often did, that no woman whom he wanted could escape him, for if he could not get her by fair means, he would say, he'd assail her by foul; and certainly he was notorious for his amours, although— Thurtell spat—he had little discrimination and cared not for age or looks so long as the chase were feminine. Tonight, while he worked in silence for the good of them all upstairs, the short-legged black-whiskered dog downstairs would be having the sort of sport he liked best, even though the landlady was nearer fifty than forty and her daughter was fat as a slug, although as active as a spider.

At his touch, the door swung open. No sound. Well-oiled, the hinges did not squeak. As though of its own accord, the dark house invited him to enter, and on tiptoe he stepped into the passage, carefully, slowly closing the door behind him. He needed no light, yet he had brought with him a dark lantern, which he now took from under his cloak and unshuttered. Its pale circle of candlelight showed the greasy boards of the floor and the worn steps going up with their rickety railing.

Still tiptoe, holding his breath, taking minutes over each step, Thurtell ascended, pausing whenever a board creaked, and listening. Only his own heart could be heard like thunder in his ears and his hands left damp marks on the rail. Up, slowly, up; and hold your breath; unscrew the gun; slowly, now; keep it at the ready, finger on the trigger. Death in his hand. It was good to feel, companionable, his pal with him on this adventure, one who could never blab, who acted faithfully, without argument. Slowly, surely, pump in the air . . .

With every step lifting him higher towards the man he hated, Thurtell felt a lightness in his limbs, a buoyancy also of the heart; and without knowing it, he smiled, tight-lipped. What love of woman could equal this? what fever in an embrace could equal the fierce pounding of his heart that made him catch his breath as though on ecstasy? His body seemed merely a casing for his spirit and he could already feel himself in that bedchamber as though the deed were done. Another step. Another, and he would be there.

Suddenly, a jangling in the air made him pause and almost lose his footing. The sound of bells from the sky; then the slow, sonorous

D

striking of a clock. It was the first stroke of midnight. Two. Three. Slowly, he breathed easily again and wiped his forehead with his sleeve. Four. Five. Now was the moment. With that clanging overhead, he'd not be heard. Quickly, with a few paces, he reached the door, turned the handle and flung it open, the gun raised in his right hand, the lantern swinging in his left.

The circle of light raced along the bed-length, showing uncreased quilt and untouched pillows.

Wood was not there.

Furiously, Thurtell swung the lantern around the plaster walls mapped with damp. There was nobody here. Nor under the bed. That chest was too small to hold a man. Wood was not here: and when he realized that, he felt the angry tears spring to his eyes. He had been cheated! All that day of waiting, the anxiety, the watching of the clock, the walk with Hunt through the dark, all for no purpose. Wood was not here. His rage was such that for a moment he could not see, his eyeballs seeming to strain under the lids, and only with a fierce effort did he check the impulse to smash everything in sight. That would have been foolish, the uproar bringing others to catch him. Yet he had to destroy something, he felt, something; and wildly he looked about him for anything he could break.

Then he heard steps on the stairs. Quick steps. The panting of a man; and shivering with relief, he covered the lantern with his cloak, ready to swing it out when his enemy entered, and he poised the stick for firing. His finger was on the trigger when the door was flung open and almost he pressed it before he heard Probert cry:

"Jack! are you there, Jack? Where are you?"

"I am here," said Thurtell in a shaking voice and sank back on to the bed, shaking as though he awoke from a debauch. The stick clattered to the floor and he did not bother to pick it up but he took the lantern from under his cloak because the metal was hot and was burning him.

"Here's a pretty to-do," he said in a flat voice. "Where's Wood?"

"He's not coming, dammit. Just sent word that he's staying elsewhere. He didn't say where."

"With Carrie. I bet a thousand it's with Carrie! If she plays me false, by God . . . Where else would he stay? He's with Carrie."

"No. Carrie's at Elstree. Miles away. Some wench he's picked up on the corner, no doubt. He sent a boy to tell he'd not be back. That's all I know. The boy was gone before I could question him."

"The whore!" said Thurtell furiously. "So smooth-cheeked with me, so daintily virtuous, the liar, while with him . . . Now I will have to kill them both. Tell me, where she's staying?"

The light of the lantern lit up a round piece of worn carpet: nothing else. Behind it, the great bulk of Thurtell on the bed was scarcely a shape to Probert, and he wished that he could see the fellow's face. This conversing with a solid shadow was faintly frightening, like talking to a spirit that had Thurtell's voice.

"I give you my word," he said, "he's not with Carrie. She's staying with Mrs. P. tonight at Elstree."

"You can't trust any of em. Money. That's all they want. And once they've got it from a man, what do they care? Like Mary. I can go into the gutter now she's married and steals my money out of the till. And this Carrie Noyes. Wood's a gentleman, to her; he's a major, ain't he? Well, I'm a lieutenant of the marines. I never use the rank. I scorn to use it. But him——"

"He won't be here, I'm telling you . . ."

"There'll be other nights. Other times. I'll get him yet."

Slowly he stood up and wondered at the heaviness of his legs and the dullness of his mind. As though after the excitement of that walk up the stairs, his heart seemed exhausted, and his body felt tired. Slowly, he moved and slowly bent to pick up the stick. Like an old man, he was: weary, no longer interested in anything, and not even angry at Caroline's suspected night with Wood. He wanted to go home to bed. That was all.

"Come and have a drink downstairs," urged Probert. "We've got some bingo and the women are merry. There's two of them and only one of me. . . ."

"No," said Thurtell, "I don't like drabs."

Squaring his shoulders, he walked as though he were a marine again, and found satisfaction in making a great amount of noise on the stairs in recompense for his laboured ascent, stabbing at the wall with his metal stick as he walked.

"See you tomorrow," he said at the front-door.

"Have one drink; come on." Uneasily, Probert peered at him but could see only blackness, an ebony statue on the step. "The women are ripe for sport and the night's young."

"I'll see you tomorrow," said Thurtell firmly and strode into the dark, deliberately making all the noise he could, kicking at stones and hitting his stick against the walls. But he felt sick. Strangely. As though he had been drunk and wanted to vomit. His stomach shivered, and he leaned a moment against a wall to steady himself. This was absurd. If he'd killed the fellow, it might have been understandable to feel queasy. But he hadn't killed him. He had killed nobody. The shot remained in the gun; and he looked about him, seeking a cat or dog or rat at which to aim. In that darkness he could see nothing, and the bullets would stay wasted, unused, in the barrel.

Slowly, half to himself, he began to swear. As he walked back to the Cock, kicking aside anyone who approached, he cursed. He cursed Wood. He cursed Probert. He cursed Caroline. He cursed Mary. He cursed the world and all the people in it, for his hatred was all-embracing; and the dark city about him, murmurous with people in the shadows, was to him so hateful that he wished he had a bomb to throw idly, anywhere, so long as it slew the fools.

"Tomorrow," he said, "tomorrow I will kill him. He might escape me once. Even twice. But not for ever. I'll get him yet."

In that thought there was some consolation; and as he considered it, the more pleasant it became, gradually soothing his anger. Had he not been thinking that murder was like love? and in love, there was often deeper joy in expectation than in consummation. Now he had longer time in which to savour the deed and to feel the power cold under his hand, death like a snake in his stick, caressing the metal while enjoying thoughts of what it would do, of Wood dead, of Carrie kneeling at his feet.

Almost he laughed, jauntily swinging the stick and jeering at any woman who dared pluck his sleeve. This stick was power. That Wood was still alive did not matter. Let him have his run before he was struck bloodily down. Ay, let the poor fool laugh and make merry and plot a future with Caroline as his wife. All the more appalling to him then would it be when he saw, in his last moment, the pout of this secret gun aimed at his heart. Ay, ay, that would be good; and Thurtell was almost glad that he had failed.

White-faced, Hunt leaped from his chair when he saw him stride into the crowded bar. The black whiskers of which he was so proud seemed even blacker against the pallor of his skin, and his eyes were large and ghostlike.

"How did it go?" he whispered hoarsely.

With an amused smile, Thurtell called for two brandies and water from Mary, and he grinned at her when she gave him a disdainful toss of the head. He did not answer Hunt until he had carried the glasses to his favourite table in the corner.

"For the love of God, Jack," moaned Hunt. "Tell me, tell me everything. Did he see you? Did he put up a fight? Was it quick? Did he squeak?"

"He wasn't there," said Thurtell quietly.

Hunt sank back, shaking, against the wall, and he ran his fingers through his thick black hair. "Not there?" he whispered. "And I've been sitting here, imagining all sorts of things, wondering when you'd done it while I watched the clock, worried when you was late. . . . And all the time he wasn't there!"

"No," said Thurtell. "He wasn't there, I'll have to try again."

"Again? Glory be," groaned Hunt, "I don't think I could bear another like this. I've been sitting on nettles. And all for nothing! I wouldn't go through it again. Not for a hundred quid."

"That's all right, Joey," said Thurtell, patting his thigh and taking a long drink which his dry throat craved. "I'll take you with me next time. I promise."

"I . . . I don't really know if I want that either," muttered Hunt miserably. "I don't think I'm much good at this, Jack. Too much imagination. That's my trouble. It was worse than when Mrs. H. had her first infant. Waiting. Waiting. My heart won't stand it." Suddenly he laughed, rolled his eyes and clutched his chest as though about to swoon. "A tender plant, my heart," he grinned, "but it's tough enough. Did you see Bill?"

"Ay," said Thurtell, and chuckled. "Thought he was Wood. Almost got him between the eyes. Just about to shoot when he called out. That'd been a rum go, wouldn't it?" he said, raising the arch of his left brow and grinning at Hunt. "They might have thought Wood'd done it. Then we could have gone to his hanging, eh?"

"Why didn't you do it? That'd have been deep. Who'd have believed him, no matter how he cackled? Everybody knows Bill's a bad un as it is, and a bad un he is, too, although a good fellow, but they'd sure to have hanged Wood for it. Think of that, Jack!"

"No," said Thurtell solemnly, "I stand by my pals. I couldn't do a thing like that to Bill."

"I was only joking. . . ."

"Were you?" asked Thurtell slowly, watching him with that raised inquiring eyebrow, the other eye bright, cruel. "I hope you were, Joe.

There's one thing I hate. A nose, Joe. A nose. I hate it above anything. D'ye understand me?"

"I'm no nose! You can trust me, Jack. Gord love me, Jack, you don't think I'd blab, d'ye? I'd rather die than talk!"

"You would die," said Thurtell, "if you tried it. Now get us another brandy, quick."

He leaned back in his chair, unable yet to believe that he was sitting in his own tavern with noisy friends and strangers drinking about him. That midnight hour in Castle Street seemed as though it had happened years before to somebody else; already it was almost a dream. Yet at his side rested the metal stick with its metal knobs to make it look like bogwood; and in its vitals there lay, ready for a finger's pressure, death in a little shot that should have killed already; and which, he swore, would kill, straight to the heart of Wood, before many days and nights were over.

CHAPTER FIVE

A SECOND CHANCE

STROLLING back from the Tennis Court in Windmill Street late in the afternoon, Thurtell walked jauntily, swinging the mufflers, those gloves stuffed with wool over the knuckles, and proud to show the bruise over his right cheekbone. To be one of the fancy was the aim of all young men, were they dukes or city-clerks, and he felt it far from impossible that some awed youngster, seeing him pass, might think he was the great Tom Spring, Jem Ward or Bill Neat. Certainly, he felt their equal, shouldering his way amongst the passersby, haughtily with right uplifted brow cowering any man who stepped before him, and looking with condescending admiration at any pretty woman. Few were the coins in his pocket, but he felt himself a king amongst dwarfs. He was the intimate of Tom Spring, most cunning of battlers, who with a feint, a duck and a blow could floor men twice his size; and being Tom's friend somehow gave him a share in the champion's glory.

They did not know, he felt scornfully looking at the little men scuttling about him: they did not know that this huge fist of his, harmless to them for the moment while it swung the blood-stained mittens, had tapped the claret many a time from an amateur's lordly nose, nor did they know that it had only a few minutes since clasped the strong hand of Tom Spring in friendship. Unrecognized, a giant, he strode amongst mere mortals, and he smiled because he was the intimate, not only of Spring, but of mighty "Flatnose," Ned Painter, who now kept a tavern in Norwich, and of Tom Oliver, Abe Belasco, Josh Hudson and the terrible black Molyneux who should have been champion had he not been cheated of his rights in his bout with old Tom Cribb. . . .

A fine upstanding girl like Caroline Noyes, with passion sparkling in her eyes, could not really prefer a dullard like Major Wood to a handsome, charming, powerful fellow like himself. He had mistaken what she said. Perhaps she had meant merely to tease him, woman-fashion, making her person appear more valuable by refusing it for a time until she had pampered her vanity sufficiently for her to be able to say Yes. He had been hasty, that being his nature.

No woman liked to be thought easily captured. Her sex demanded sweet tyranny over a lover because she feared lest, once she submitted, her power might be gone. Yes, he would give the pretty filly a second start. And he was glad now that he had spared Wood. Such a murder would have been unnecessary and it would be a subtler revenge to leave him in the toils of jealousy after he had persuaded Carrie to change her woman's weathercock-mind. The next week-end at Probert's he would prove it; and first he must make certain that Probert would have her there for him to woo again.

"It's no go, I tell you," growled Probert that night in the Cock. "Course you can come Saturday, Jack. Always pleased to have you. So's Mrs. P. If I were of a jealous nature, I'd be staring mad, the way that woman rattles on about you. You've an advocate there that should melt Carrie. But she don't. I tell you, it's no go."

"You can't take heed of what a woman says," smiled Thurtell, malevolently eyeing Mary behind the bar. "They're weathercocks and don't know themselves what they're saying or doing half the time. Remember a girl at Norwich. As fancy a piece as ever you'd want, a real dandyzette with her flounced short petticoats and her painted cheeks and lips; but prim! Ay, she liked to pretend she was what she ain't, liked to have fellows on a hook and, just when you thought you had her, to wriggle away from you. There she was, giving you the Go Ahead with every roll of her eyes; and she had a sister, such a one she was! head down in the poke bonnet, prayer-book always in her hand, eyes never raised. . . . But just you get her in the dark! She was all what her sister wasn't but pretended to be. Couldn't understand it. Can't understand it now. Why should one look like a she-saint and the other like a game woman, when each was the opposite of what she pretended? Women are deep uns, Bill, as downy as they make em, and you can't believe a word they say. They're worse than men when it comes to fiddlefaddling and telling lies."

Frowning, Probert glanced at him from under the brim of his white hat tilted forward. "That's true enough," he said with one of his quick, too charming smiles that flashed his teeth like new dice, "but I ain't sure about Carrie. She seems really nutty over Wood. I tell you, there's only one way for you to win her."

"I tried it. You know that. And it didn't come off."

"You heard about King Bruce and the spider, didn't you? When he was hiding in a cave and giving up all hope of getting away, he sees a spider spinning. Down comes Mr. Spider, tumbling again and again out of his web, but back up he always crawls. 'Ho,' says Bruce, 'what a spider can do I can do better.' So he ups and he floors his enemy."

"That's what I mean," agreed Thurtell. "I'm going to try Carrie Noyes again."

"I wasn't thinking of her," muttered Probert, "but of bloody Wood. You didn't get him the first time. You will the next."

"I'll get him when I want to. But I'm thinking of Miss Noyes now."

"It's no good thinking of her till you get rid of Wood. With him out of the way, you'll have both the girl and her money." He leaned closer, peering hopefully into Thurtell's eyes while he whispered. "You won't get a better chance than now to serve him," he said. "Noyes's away and there are no other lodgers in the house, and the old man's still in quod."

"I tell you I'm going to do it. When I want to." Thurtell wriggled and drank his brandy and water. For the moment, he had lost interest in Wood. That night when he had stolen to the man's room on a futile errand remained to nag him, but he half-felt that, having invaded the room with murderous intention, the act was more or less already committed and Wood was dead. All his interest now was concentrated on Caroline. To win her would be more satisfying than killing her lover, for the man's sufferings would become then the greater.

"If you mean to do it," hissed Probert, "why don't you do it at once? You know I can keep the women engaged downstairs."

With sudden fury, Thurtell turned on him. "Damn your great eyes," he cried, "if you want it done, why don't you do it yourself! You're big enough and ugly enough; and there's the air-gun at your service."

Probert forced a laugh; the eyelids fluttered over his deep blue eyes, and he turned away with a shrug.

"Now, now, Jack," he said soothingly, "you know I only want you to have the woman and don't want Wood to get her first."

He could feel Thurtell glaring at him, although he pretended not to notice; then to conceal his confusion, he made a great deal of noise pushing back the table while he took up the glasses and carried them to the bar. As he walked, assuming a careless gait, he could still feel Thurtell watching him; and although, by habit, he gave his usual seductive smile to Mary when he ordered the drinks, his thoughts were not on her. He could feel, as though it were a living thing, the intensity of Thurtell's glare on his back, and he sighed. On occasions, men could be as difficult to coax as any female, but he did not doubt that in the end he'd have the big fool doing what he wanted him to do, killing Wood and marrying Caroline that they might share together the spoils of her dowry.

"I'll see she's there Saturday," he said, putting the refilled glasses on the table. "Truth is, Jack, things are hard with me at the moment and I can't entertain my friends as I'd like to. There's the wife and her sister, Anne, and Tom's two girls, and that nuisance, Tom Noyes, has been hanging about, feared to show his nose in London for the moment. There's talk of his wine business being seized and him along with it. Then there's the lad to look after the stables and things. A lot of mouths to feed." He groaned. "I don't know how I keep em fed, I don't, for I've only my wits to work with since they took my jigger."

"I'll bring something with me, a leg of pork or something. But you're certain Caroline'll be there?"

"I'll see to it," said Probert.

When, on Saturday afternoon, Probert pulled up his black gig before the Cock he was annoyed to find Thurtell, dressed in his best toggery, the white castor of the fancy on the back of his head, and because there was a nip in the August air, his brown three-caped box-coat over his arm, waiting for him at the door. He was feeling thirsty, as usual, and had expected at least one drink before setting out on the dusty road to Elstree, but Thurtell was impatient to be off. Nor did he heed Probert's casual references to a glass of bingo and his nostalgic comments on the taverns they passed until along the Edgware Road he insisted on stopping at the Bell at Kilburn.

"Haven't been here for weeks," he explained. "Was sweet on the barmaid once but I'm told they caught her fingers in the till and she ain't there any longer, so it's safe now."

Contemptuous of Probert's mastery over women, Thurtell followed him into the old low-ceilinged tavern, and reluctantly ordered brandies and water. Having had his fill of drink before setting out, he did not suffer Probert's furry tongue and was therefore annoyed at having to stop when his impatient nature urged an immediate encounter with Caroline. He swallowed the drink at a gulp, then paused, glass in hand, to stare at a small, lean man seated in a corner, who was looking carefully through the pages of a pocket betting-book.

Startled by the sudden stiffening of his friend, and the fixity of his glare, Probert swung round, and grinned.

"Bill Weare!" he cried. "What the hell are you doing in the country?"

The little man swiftly pushed the book away inside his waistcoat, and, recognizing the two, smiled with tight lips. He was neatly dressed in a blue coat with gilt buttons and had a dazzling collar and wristbands, all closely fitting to his boyish body. But he was not a boy. Seemingly ageless, with a touch of the East in its features, was the dark face, the brown eyes lightless as pebbles, the cheekbones high and shining, as though polished; and his chin was so small and his brow so broad that the shape of his face formed almost a perfect triangle.

"Mr. Probert," he said dryly, "and Mr. Thurtell. Well met, gentlemen."

He made no offer to buy them a drink. Coldly, yet with a certain sardonic amusement in the curl of his fleshy mouth, he looked at them and sipped his brandy and hot water.

"An out-of-the-way place for fellows about town like you," he said. "I never thought the rural amenities would appeal to such town-birds, although, I suppose, Kilburn's no more the country now that it has its own chapel and its own coaches and the houses are sprouting everywhere."

"It's country to me," said Thurtell, glowering at him. "And what brings you here, Bill?"

"The same as yourself, no doubt," smiled Weare, daintily lifting his glass again. "Country air, excellent brandy, boundless opportunities for sport in the landlord's garden, the waters to be drunk if you like such stuff, and . . . and tradition, ghosts, you know: all that. . . ."

"Ghosts? whose ghosts?"

"Ay, master, that's truth," said the landlord, leaning his elbows on the bar and speaking in a thick hushed voice. "We have our own ghosts at Kilburn; many a maid has seen em and swooned so that she couldn't be blamed afterwards for what happened to her. There was a lord, hundreds of years ago it was, what loved his brother's wife in Saint John's Wood yonder——" He jerked his right thumb at a barrel in a corner. "—and being greedy and wanting er all to imself, he ups one night and does for is brother in a dark lane; and he carries the wife ere, to Kilburn. As she wouldn't listen to what the dirty dog asked her to do, he locked er in a dungeon and forgot about er till she died. That's why he built the priory that was, in remorse of conscience, and the stone where his brother lay, that stayed dark red, blood-red, forever."

"Hey, hey! where's this blood-red stone?" grinned Probert.

"Can't say," said the landlord. "Never seen it, but Kilburn has its istory, gentlemen—bloody murder and ghouls and remorse and ell and everything what you might see at the Surrey Theatre any day tonight."

"A highly moral tale," said Weare in his thin, sneering voice. "Take heed, Mr. Thurtell, never covet your brother's wife and you'll commit no murder."

"I covet no man's wife, and as for killing because of a woman . . . Pah! I've not found em so difficult to get that you've got to kill to steal em. When it comes to killing, there's only one thing worth risking your neck for."

"And that, Mr. Thurtell?"

"Yellow boys," said Thurtell, lunging forward, hatred in his face, "rhino, rent, bustle, blunt, pounds, shillings and pence, call it what you like. That's the stuff a fellow needs to jingle in his pocket. That's worth risking your neck to get, not women. You know it, too, Mr. Weare. I've never seen you chasing the fillies."

"I am affianced," said Weare coldly, "to a respectable young lady in Bayswater. I do not follow trulls."

"I wasn't talking of trulls either, nor of respectable young ladies. I was talking of Women. Of women, Mr. Weare. And trulls or respectable young ladies, they're not much different under their skirts, for all that I've found." With difficulty he controlled his hatred. Whenever he looked at Weare's leathery face, the carefully combed whiskers, the agate eyes, his palms itched to close about his throat. In his early days in London this man had made a flat out of him; at blind hookey, he had robbed him of almost every penny he had possessed. That was something Thurtell could never forget or forgive. "Come, Bill," he said, "we must be going."

"Good sport, lads," chuckled Weare with a friendly flourish.

"Good plucking to you, sir," grinned Probert, and bowed.

Thurtell did not speak. His hatred of Weare was too strong to be controlled, and he hurried from the inn beside its leafy oak and quickly sprang into the gig. More slowly, Probert dragged himself up beside him and cracked the whip. Sideways, he looked at his companion, and noted the outthrust lip, the brows drawn over the little eyes, the arms crossed tightly across the great chest; and although he did not want to distract the man from the pursuit of his sister-in-law, he was relieved to think that his mercurial energies had switched from love to enmity. Carrie was forgotten while he brooded on Weare.

"Wonder what his woman's like," said Thurtell after a long silence as they rattled towards Edgware. "Bet she's got a fat purse, or he'd not be after her. Can't imagine that fellow marrying for love!"

Probert did not answer, and when he pulled up at the Bald-Faced Stag about two miles the London side of Edgware, Thurtell made no protest but leaped from the gig after him. Quickly, he drank, saying little, his mouth twitching and the eyes shining when the light struck them in their hollows.

"Wonder what he was doing in Kilburn," he muttered. "Ain't nothing in Kilburn, not for a man like him to bother about. Only apprentices and such with their wenches going there sometimes since the spa's neglected. None of the swells."

"Probably been to hire a carriage," said Probert. "Good stables near there, I'm told; and cheap."

"*He'd* think of cheapness. A skinflint old Elwes'd have been ashamed to own. Never met a man like him. What's he do with all his money?"

"Carries it with him, they say . . ." Probert paused and his eyes lit up; and over his glass he looked at Thurtell standing, watching, smiling at him. "Ay," he said breathlessly, "he don't trust banks. I've heard him say it myself. Once he put five hundred quid in Morland's and couldn't sleep all night with thinking of it and he had it out first thing in the morning. Heard tell he's worth at least two thousand. May be more. Probably is, because he don't spend much, and he always carries it with him."

"And now he's going to marry some poor creature for her gold! Eh? Do her a good turn to put a stop to that. . . ."

"Ay," said Probert slowly, "it's worth our thinking of."

So deeply did they think of it that neither spoke during the ride to Elstree, although they stopped at inns and taverns on the way. There was no need for them to speak, each well knowing what the other was thinking. Little Weare, cheating Weare, a man of darkness who shunned the light except to go to a race-meeting or to a battle which he knew to be on the cross; miserable Weare, never known to spend a penny unless it could hook a flat; Weare waiting day and night with a cue in Rexworthy's newly fitted up billiard-rooms, waiting to snare some flat to a wager on a game. A notorious sharper, a dead nail, ready at all times to pick up a flat, either to nibble for a sprat or to tackle a heavy jack; no one, except the mysterious Bayswater lady perhaps, would miss his going and many would rejoice not to see his long nose dipping towards the cue or hiding behind a hand of cards. Besides, he had made a flat of Thurtell; and that could not be forgotten.

Only once during that ride did Thurtell again unchink his thoughts. As, to the howling of dogs, the gig drove into the yard of Gill's Hill Cottage and the boy, Richard Addis, ran forward to catch the reins, he said suddenly to Probert in a casual manner, as though continuing an interrupted conversation:

"It'll be Wood first though. That is unless she decides to have me."

Probert did not answer. He wanted no discussion of secrets within sound of the boy's long ears. He grunted, hoping that his wife had been able to keep Carrie from running away before their arrival, and tenderly he lifted from the gig the leg of lamb that Thurtell had bought.

The day which had opened coldly had now become hot, and Thurtell regretted having brought his box-coat. There was a heaviness in the atmosphere and no wind stirred the trees or ruffled the bushes and weeds, while from the neighbouring pond came a reek of decay and the croak of frogs. But Thurtell scarcely noticed the weather, save to mop his brow with his handkerchief, as he followed Probert through the flowerless garden and into the parlour. Entering that small room, cool after the tense heat outside, he felt a little angry and he clenched his teeth, remembering the last time he had been here. From the kitchen next-door sounded the shrill voices of women: protests, almost a shriek of "No No No!" that might have been Caroline's voice. Could she be refusing to see him?

Thurtell began to tremble, the skin tightening on his skull, as he tried to listen; then he heard a door open and he ran quickly into the garden, just in time to glimpse a white skirt flutter near the wash-house. In half a dozen strides he had caught up to Caroline and gripped her shoulders.

With a moan as of fear, she stumbled, almost fell, then stood still, trembling. In her haste she had forgotten her bonnet, and the black curls, shadowed blue, shone in the dull, fierce light, tossing behind her as she swung round. Huge were her blue eyes and the mouth was pale, drooping a little open.

Having her so close, sensing her panic as a beast senses another's fear of it, he felt rise high within him rage mingled with exultation.

"Why are you frightened of me?" he asked.

Trembling, leaning back in his arms to escape his kiss, she half-lay and for a moment she could not speak.

"Pray, Mr. Thurtell," she gasped at last, "pray, as you are a gentleman, release me."

"Not until you tell me why you ran." His linked his fingers, dragging her against him by his grip on the small of her back. "Tell me," he said again.

"Why must you have this scene? Had I known you were coming today, I'd not have been here; but this is a trap. I am ashamed of my own sister to subject me to such humiliation." Slowly, Caroline was regaining control of herself and was able to speak more steadily, while with loathing and scorn she glared up at him. "I thought at our last meeting," she said, "I'd made it plain what my regards were towards you."

"A woman's privilege, to change her mind," he whispered.

"Not when that mind is resolute. Do not deceive yourself, sir. Under no circumstances, if I had never met Major Wood, I would not have considered a proposal from such a person as you. Have I made myself plain?"

Even yet he could not believe it; he dared not believe it. The urge to embrace her violently, to make her suffer under his kissing, was so powerful that he feared to continue holding her in his arms. With a sudden twist, he spun her from him, and she would have fallen had she not been close to the rotting wall of the wash-house.

"I came," he said, "to give you your last chance. After this, I'll not ask again."

"I pray you keep your word," she sobbed, smoothing down her muslin skirt.

"You will be sorry for this. Ay," he said grimly. "You will be sorry for it."

"Whatever you might do, whatever you might say," said she, little fists clenched, "I will not be sorry for this."

He tried to laugh, but could not. "Your fist," he said, "is clenched, and 'fist', my girl, is a masculine word. When a female makes up a fist, 'tis said, she's no longer a woman and must be floored like a man." He raised his own clenched fists, mutton-fists, into a boxing-attitude and sparred at her. "Put em up," he said, "and I'll mash your beauty so that Major bloody Wood'll not know your mouth from your ear, nor your nose from your chin."

"No," she whimpered, hands stretched out while she backed away, stumbling, afraid to turn lest he leap on her back.

He laughed. It was the first time she had heard him laugh, and it sounded to her more like a bark than a laugh.

"Did I frighten the pretty lady?" he jeered. "Do you think a man like me'd lay a finger on a woman? It was all fudge, I tell you, all gammon. Lady, I'd kill a man that hurt you, even though it was myself. That's what I think of you. I'm a tame old stallion you can spur without fear of a toss. I honour you, ma'am: indeed, I love you, and admire you for your spirit. You've more bottom to you than many a man, by gad, and I'm proud to call myself your servant."

Warily, she stood away from him, half prepared to run when he held out his hands. From side to side, her bright eyes darted, seeking escape; but there was no escape. Amongst the bushes, the tree-roots, the tall grass, she would be easily tripped in her skirt if she attempted flight; and the safest thing, it seemed, was to accept this offered friendship, while remaining on the alert.

"I—I forgive you, sir," she whispered shyly. "But you frightened me. You are so headstrong, and I am only a maid."

"A maid of beauty," he said, and taking her offered hand, he raised it to his lips and kissed the pucker of knuckles. "We are friends now?" he asked.

"Friends, ay," she said, still watching him cautiously; but as he offered no affront, stooping low beside her like a humble courtier, her blood cooled a little and she grew ashamed of her recent terror. As he said, it had probably been only his crude sport; if so, it was sport she did not wish to encounter a second time.

"Your cavalier," said he, "begs to escort you to roast lamb when Madam Probert has done the cooking to your liking."

"Thank you, kind sir." She curtsied, dimpling into a smile. He was like most men, a big boy, and easily handled by a clever woman, after all; and she, little fool, had thought him a monster with no respect for her sex. She smiled at him, pouting as though to tempt a kiss. Hugely, he leaned down above her, seeming to enfold her small body in his massive strength, and quickly she stepped aside. Girlishly, she laughed, angry because fear like a drip of icy water still rippled down her spine, making her shudder. They were in the daylight, in dull yet hot daylight, the sun concealed behind grey clouds, and there were her sisters, her brother, her brother-in-law, the children and the boy, Dick Addis, all within squeaking-distance. She had only to scream and they would race to her rescue; yet something of her fear still clung to her, damply inside her hair and on her scalp and pressing against her spine, so that, to prove how insouciant she felt, she arched her shoulders, pouting her bosom, and almost danced tiptoe by his side.

"We will be like brother and sister," she said, ogling him from the corners of her eyes. "Always friends, won't we, Mr. Thurtell?"

"I—I don't know," he said, "brothers and sisters aren't always friends."

"But we will be, for always, won't we?"

"Till death," he said, and smiled.

"Yes," she murmured, and she shivered. "Till death, my friend," she said, and wondered at the sudden chill about her heart.

CHAPTER SIX

A CHALLENGE TAKEN

SO PLEASANT was Thurtell's manner, so gracious was he towards Caroline when they returned to the cottage, that Probert whistled when he saw them. Having been confident that Caroline would reject the man, recalling her squeaks of revulsion at the mention of his name, he had expected an angry or, at least, a dour Thurtell; instead, the fellow smiled, a lady's man, so far as so crude a cove could ever be a lady's man.

Delighted, he grinned and raised his eyebrows and was astonished when, in reply to his silent inquiry, Thurtell glumly shook his head.

"Jack," he said, taking Thurtell's arm and drawing him into the vegetable-garden, away from the women and children indoors, "what's happened?"

"What you said'd happen," said Thurtell quietly. "No: it was No; and no doubt about it. The girl don't like me."

"Can't understand it," muttered Probert. "If she turned you down, what are you grinning for?"

"I hope," said Thurtell, drawing his wood snuff-box from his waistcoat-pocket and taking a dainty sniff, "I hope that I have something of the gentleman left in me. I am not going to force my attentions on a female when they can give her no pleasure. The bitch is a coquette, Bill, a scheming minx who needs a thrashing to knock that cat's smile off her gob. I leave her husband to do that—if she ever gets a husband—poor little virgin widow."

Seeing the slow smile curl the fleshy mouth, the underlip pushed forward and pressed up against the upper, Probert caught his breath in a spasm of fear. Thurtell was a brute, but a brute easily guided should a cunning man hold the reins, he had believed; and now he doubted that: it was as though a master suddenly saw a quiver of hatred in his dog's eye and a baring of its teeth. This was unexpected and therefore frightening, this coldly controlled hatred and the unspoken viciousness shown in the curl of Thurtell's lip.

"So you're going to do him, after all?" he whispered.

66

"The moment you tell me he's back in Castle Street," said Thurtell, "that'll be the last time he'll ever open his peepers. I only wish it was tonight."

"I don't know," muttered Probert, "I can understand the girl giving you the go-by if she were nutty on some other fellow; but I don't think she is about Wood. It's only talk, Mrs. P. tells me. She says the silly chit don't know her own mind and don't really care much for the fellow. But I don't know."

"It's Wood, all right. She told me so herself."

"Then, I suppose, it must be him. . . ."

"I'd like to send her his head in a hamper, labelled 'Boil well for female eating,' and his giblets along with it; but I suppose it'll have to be the air-gun, and silence, after all." Thurtell shrugged, and the branch of the hawthorn tree he held in his hand snapped suddenly, sagging from the bough; and he looked at it, surprised. "Look here, Bill, I'm not staying tonight. I'll have dinner; I've got to have that; but I'm going back to London straight afterwards."

Probert shrugged. "Whatever you want," he said.

"So I'll need your gig," said Thurtell. "The boy can come in with me and drive it home again. But if I had to sit here all day and night, looking at that smug grin of hers as though she'd swallowed a mouse, I'd hit her on her smeller before I knew what I was doing. And I don't want her to think I bear any malice. . . . That scran smells good. Will we go in and eat?"

Frowning, Probert followed Thurtell indoors, running his fingers round inside his sticky cravat. He had not expected Caroline to say Yes. All the same, he was disappointed. Murder could never be a safe affair; someone always blabbed, talked too much; and he didn't trust Joe Hunt . . . but when the moment came, he'd be careful, if possible, to slip aside and let this brute of a Thurtell take all the risk and the blame.

Ill-humouredly, he strolled into the parlour and looked at the out-wardly merry scene before him: Tom's two little girls stood, hands behind their backs like coy little ladies, while they piped a duet about two little snowdrops caught in the snow. Before them, straddling a chair, arms crossed on its back, Thurtell sat, nodding his head in time to the music. In a corner on a stool, Tom Noyes crouched, strangling a yawn and gazing at the cracks in the ceiling. Alone on the sofa, half-reclining, lounged Caroline in a loose posture which showed under the clinging muslin the shape of her long plump thigh, and her black curls like ink-squiggles against the pallid cheeks and throat; while dreamily she smiled approval and, from under her eyelids, watched with mingled fear and amusement every move that Thurtell made.

Quiet she remained, coy and slow in gestures, eyelids half-lowered at the dinner-table in the kitchen while the others laughed and jested, their faces reddening, sweating, with the heat from the stove and the heat in their bellies. Mrs. Probert had placed Caroline on Thurtell's right, and the girl leaned a little away from him as though afraid of being jabbed from her stool by a cock of his elbow. Small were the signs she gave of any inward perturbation, but Probert noticed them and read the truth. Also, he noticed that, although almost over-polite, Thurtell at times, beneath his breath, let slip an oath and, when he thought Caroline was not watching him, darted at her pale beauty a glance of murder. And Caroline, sharp wits sharpened under the titillation of the man's lust and anger, missed nothing that Thurtell said or did. She rolled her shoulders and puffed out her bosom and when she laughed she laughed too shrilly.

Undeceived by Thurtell's elaborate courtesy, she could almost smell the sweat of his anger and that excited her, making her tremble deliciously, laughter always a-gurgle on her lips. The others took no heed of her wriggling as she sat with shoulders back, a queen in de-lightful danger on her throne of beauty with an amorous rebel at her side. Her brother, in his usual manner when at the table, wasted no time on talk but ate as though he were to be hanged in the morning and would find no opportunity to eat again. Mrs. P. ate voraciously, like her brother, stuffing the food on knife and fork into her loose mouth and chattering doughily through the mess on her tongue, laughing, squealing, giggling, behaving like a lewd young girl—for all that she was fat and well over forty and had a moustache—coquetting with Thurtell. Glumly, on Thurtell's other side, Anne Noyes sat, eating with pecks as though she feared poison in every dainty mouth-ful, her one brown eye scorning Thurtell and her sister while the lid over the other hung like a grey curtain concealing, Thurtell felt, an ill-willing witch with thoughts too wicked to be revealed by two open eyes. At a small table, Tom Thurtell's two young daughters gravely ate with the thirteen-year-old boy-of-all-work, Dick Addis, and the fat cook, young Susannah Woodruff.

After everyone had risen from the table, bellies pleasantly taut with food and wine, and strolled into the parlour, Thurtell announced his immediate departure for London. He had forgotten, he said, an important engagement that must be kept that night. While he spoke, he looked at Caroline seated between her sisters, the three women's white muslin skirts joining to give the impression that they were some triple-headed Venus; and he set his teeth to see the relief, mingled with the vexation of a child losing a doll it wishes to tear to pieces, that gleamed in her pupils before the long lashes fluttered down.

"The regrets are all mine," he sighed, kissing Mrs. Probert's fat hand. "But I'll soon be back, ma'am, if you'll permit me to intrude again into your Eden here. I do declare! the three of you ladies look like the Three Graces and I only wish I were a painter that I could immortalize such triple beauty."

"O, la, sir!" tittered Mrs. P., giving him a playful slap. "The things you do say! you'll have us all blushing again!"

"A blush becomes the rose," said Thurtell, and was more surprised even than Probert at his own impromptu poetry.

"Till we meet again, sweet lady," he said, taking, in its turn, Anne's fat little hand to kiss. The knuckles suddenly rose, stabbing at his teeth and almost bruising his lip, and he stared down at her, astonished. Anne Noyes's expression had not altered. With the same inflexible stare from that dark gimlet-eye, she looked up at him, her pale lips curved scornfully, and he was relieved to turn from her to lean over Caroline's dimpled knuckles.

"Your servant, ma'am," he whispered, pressing the knuckles hard against his lips: "always your servant, ma'am."

Faintly blushing, taking a deep breath to press out her bosom's pointed shape, coyly Caroline looked at him, no longer afraid. Almost could he read a challenge in those blue twinkling eyes and in the insolent curve of her mouth and the droop of her fleshy underlip. Still with the air of a queen accepting homage, she looked at him invitingly but with a threat in the invitation, as though she would have tempted him for the delight of having him afterwards thrashed for his temerity, had that been possible.

"Do Carrie's fingers taste better than mine?" asked Anne suddenly and, it seemed, seriously.

That was why Thurtell disliked the woman: he could never tell her serious from her mocking moods; and now, flushing, he dropped Caroline's hand which drooped languidly into the shadows of her lap.

"Do they?" cried Anne. "Tell me, please, sir. Are ladies' hands of different savour, according to the soap they use? some sweet, some sour, some sticky, some cool, some hot, some dirty, and some lewd? I ask only from curiosity, being a woman with a very open mind."

"They are hands," muttered Thurtell. "All ladies' hands are sweet."

"What! when they are filthy, when they sweat, when they've been scratching pigs or peeling onions? All savoury like Queen Lady Macbeth's, is that it?"

"Ay," said Thurtell, "all savoury to him who loves em."

"What! do you love us all! Hey, here's a Turk, sisters, a regular Bluebeard who likes to eat us poor females for supper and pick his teeth afterwards with our polished bones in splinters." She squeaked with a pretence of horror, pouting at him; and his hands itched to smack her, for all things which Thurtell hated, he hated ridicule the most, and he was never certain whether this woman mocked at him or not. "Would you marry such a cannibal, sweet Carrie?" she lisped.

"There is no talk of marriage," snapped Caroline, tossing her ringlets. "You do talk nonsense."

Annoyed, she itched away from her, but Anne was sitting on the side of her gown and she feared to tear the delicate cloth with a sudden jerk.

"Of course I do," said Anne, "being a woman, what else can I talk? That is why men like females, because they are fools and swallow whatever they're told. Is that not so, Mr. Thurtell?"

The obvious retort to that would have been too cruel, too easy, to make, yet it lay balanced on Thurtell's tongue and, seeing malice twinkle in that one dark evil eye, almost he spoke it, telling her that she need never fear any man's love, whether she be a fool or wise one.

"I must be off," he said, taking up his hat. "Farewell, ladies."

"Farewell," said Anne; "and promise me, sir, you'll eat no females on the way with those big teeth of yours, however tempting they might look."

Flushing, angrily he turned to the door leading into the garden, not even looking to see whether Caroline regretted his departure; and it was not until with Probert he walked in the clean air, swishing at the heads of thistles with his whip, that his blood began to cool under the glare of the hidden sun. The dogs had started again to howl. He heard the rattle of their chains, then choking sounds, throttling the barks, as they bounded to the end of the chains and were thrown back.

"Take no heed of Anne," said Probert. "Poor bitch, she feels the loss of that lamp. It makes her bitter against men and jealous of her sister. Pity, she'd not be bad if it weren't for that; you can see by the way she gets heated that she's as bob-tailed as any of em if given half a chance. But what man would when she's only got one ogle. . . . A pity. . . . Waste of a good woman."

"I don't like her," said Thurtell; "and I wouldn't like her better if she had forty ogles. Come on. . . ."

Whistling, young Addis was at work in the stables, harnessing the horse to the gig, excited at the thought of riding to London in the company of a magnificent swell like Mr. Thurtell who was a friend of all the champion boxers in the country.

"See you tomorrow," said Thurtell, "in the Cock. Then we'll map out what's to be done. Until then, goodbye, Bill . . . and kiss the bloody ladies again for me, will you, and don't forget Miss Anne?"

Probert grunted, annoyed at Thurtell leaving when he had been looking forward to a boozy night with him and Tom Noyes over a bottle or two of rum; but he waved his arm in farewell as Thurtell took the reins out of the boy's hands.

From there, in the stable-yard, the parlour-window could be barely glimpsed at an angle beyond the falling fence and around the thick tree; but Thurtell believed he saw, for one fleeting moment, a paper-white mask pressed to the dirty glass—the pale face, he believed, of Caroline watching him go.

Damn the girl! damn both the girls in their virginal gowns! Carrie with her graceful body and lewd smile masking a heart of ice that would sting if you touched it; and her bob-tailed fidgety sister, flea-bitten with desires no man would stoop to heal, and her hawk's eye . . . how did the song have it?

> Gimlet eye, sausage nose,
> Hips awry, bandy toes!

although that was a bit of a libel, he had to confess. If you could only close your own eyes to that one damned lamp, Anne'd have been a prime piece of property for a fellow who wasn't too particular; and her dainty nose was most decidedly no sausage, nor by any manner of means—he had often walked behind her—were her hips awry or her small feet in the kid shoes and her ankles in silk stockings in the least bandy; but the unfortunate would-be blossom with that fizgig dial and the one lamp . . . Stupid of him to be angry with a poor lass starving for a man; while her sister . . .

She was very like her sister. Egad, they'd have been a pair of peas if it hadn't been for that empty ogle! of course, worry and being despised by men had wrinkled poor Anne between the brows and hardened the lines beside her mouth, and her skin had a faintly greenish tinge like cheese about to go rotten . . . but that was not her fault, she couldn't help pining like an old lily with its petals open for a bee. . . . He should pity her. And pity her he did, his good humour and self-complacency restored.

Until he thought of Caroline again; then he spat over the side of the gig.

Love was a bug that bit only poets, sucking out their thin blood. Ay, only poets, women, fools, old uxurious codgers and dream-fed youths could feel that flame; it was not a disease from which grown men suffered. His natural manly pride was hurt; that was all. He didn't love Caroline or any other woman; no, not Caroline. It was her rhino now in chancery that he lusted for, not the silly female herself.

There was one thing to be said about that disappointing day, he consoled himself, jogging slowly back to London with young Addis. He had acted with cunning, calming Caroline's silly fears, so that now, after he'd got rid of this Wood fellow, she'd scarcely dare accuse him of having caused his death, whatever in her wizened heart she might suspect. And the next time he attempted the man there would be no mistake: she'd find herself a widow before she was a wife. He would stay in Probert's room from early in the afternoon, the air-gun ready. waiting for the Major's step on the stair. Ay, every night from now on he'd sleep at Castle Street, the gun at his side, so that there'd be no risk of his not hearing the bastard outside.

Reaching the Cock, he sprang into the street and tossed a half-crown into the lad's lap and told him to drive slowly home; then he strode indoors, yearning to fondle his air-gun again.

There were not many customers in the bar, and Mary, half-asleep and lounging against a barrel, raised her eyebrows at his entrance but said nothing. Past her and up the stairs he hurried until, in his room again, he closed and bolted the door and drew the air-gun from amongst the fluff under his bed. It was not his gun, although he coveted it. No common pistol betraying its presence by the swelling of the pocket had given him such satisfaction as he found in gripping this weapon of concealed death. Since first it had been shown him in Norwich, the property of an old friend named Harper, he had ached to own it; and only with great reluctance, and with many anxious instructions about the care of its delicate mechanism, had Harper allowed him to borrow it for a time; but Thurtell had no intention of ever giving it back.

Raising it now at arm's length as though carelessly pointing, he pulled on the nob. Little more than a pop, like the opening of a bottle, a common sound that would attract nobody's attentions, and a crack showed around a hole in the wall, exposing a broken lath. Had Wood been standing before that wall, he'd have been a dead man now. Straight into his heart it would have gone.

"Straight into your black heart, you bastard," he said, and fired, pop, again and saw the plaster flake and spit out.

That he should have to wait until Wood decided to revisit London was an intolerable thought, and to escape it he wandered down to the bar. Nobody there he knew. Only Mary watching him with a cocked, contemptuous eyebrow, and a few ragged topers murmuring together over their pots. And such must be his company, perhaps for days! O, he moaned, gulping brandy and water, he would go mad long before then. Never had the craving for a woman's kiss been so tormenting as was to him this craving to destroy the man he hated.

Yet he knew little of Major Wood. Twice only at Probert's had he met the fellow and had disliked him because of his air of gentility, his attitude of condescension, as though he were of superior clay. Yet he was only a half-pay major with a small estate in Herts, and his parents were probably socially far inferior to Thurtell's. A smallish man with the shoulders-back carriage of the military, with his tightly buttoned coat too tight, his boots polished to black mirrors, and his abrupt speech and gestures. That a gay girl like Caroline could love a stick such as that seemed absurd; yet it was apparently true.

For him to remain still was impossible. Restlessly, Thurtell walked from tavern to tavern, calling in at Rexworthy's to see if Weare were about that he might pick a quarrel with him, but he found only strangers with cues over the green cloth under the gas-lamps flaring inside the reflectors opening above them like huge petals. Even Hunt could not be found; no one he wished to see could he find; and he avoided acquaintances with whom he could not openly discuss the revenge that dominated all his thoughts.

Wearily, he dropped to bed, but he could not sleep; and the next day was no different. Hunt he could not find at home; Probert had not come back to the City as he had promised. Alone amongst thousands, brooding, Thurtell walked the streets, scarcely seeing those whom he elbowed aside; and when he returned to the Cock for dinner, his legs ached although his thoughts remained undulled and his spirit as fidgety as ever. In this tired yet fuming state, the dishes cleared away, he sat over his brandy, re-enacting for the thousandth time the death of Wood. On the bed lay Wood; himself, love's avenger, smiling, stick raised and aimed, stood at the door. Then, ping! perhaps a faint moan and the dark blood oozing through the nightgown. Ping! ping! again: ping!

A shadow fell across his table, darkening his clenched fists, and Thurtell looked up; then he remained gaping, not believing what he saw, thinking he lived still in his imagination.

Before the table stood the lean figure of Wood, yellowish whiskers brushed out like a lion's mane; his dark hat straight on his head, his clothing neat, clean, undistinguished, but gentlemanly, and in his hand a stick—an ordinary stick, of plain wood, not of metal.

"Mr. Thurtell," said this solid apparition, "I would speak with you in private."

Leaning slowly back to give his wits time to work after the shock of seeing the man whom he had been carefully and efficiently murdering in his imagination for the last few days, Thurtell forced a smile.

"I have no secrets with you, sir," he said. "Say what you will, and say it here. Sit down."

"There's a lady concerned," said the major in his quick, harsh voice. "I do not wish her name mentioned."

"Then don't mention it," said Thurtell.

The major took a slow breath and tightly gripped his stick, but his eyes never shifted from Thurtell's eyes.

"This lady——" he began at last; but Thurtell interrupted him.

"This anonymous lady," he said mockingly; "this Madam Unknown who doubtless has private reasons for concealing her identity; but I can assure you, sir, she need not worry. No police officers are in this tavern to hear anything you say about her."

"Do not try me too far, Mr. Thurtell," said the major, stuttering a little. "I am a soldier, sir, and I have a soldier's temper; but I have sworn to remain calm." Trembling, standing erect, he half-closed his eyes while he struggled to control his anger. Then, in a low voice, he continued:

"This lady, sir, I have known only for a year or two, but the little I have known of her has taught me to respect her for her virtues as well as for her womanhood. Admiring her long from a distance, imagine my surprise when yesterday she came to me and told me that you, sir, that you had designs upon my life!"

"Indeed, sir, you flatter yourself! Your life, indeed!"

"Upon my life," continued the major, plainly determined to remain master of his rage. "I was astounded, scarcely knowing you as I do, but the lady, in her fears for my safety and in her own fears of your passionate nature, said sufficient to make me understand that she was not entirely disinterested in my humble self."

"What!" cried Thurtell, and his jaw drooped. "Do you mean to tell me, sir, that you are not affianced to Miss Noyes!"

"I suggested that no names be mentioned; as you, sir, have mentioned that pure and noble lady's name, I will say that I am proud to tell you that she yesterday accepted my heart and hand. This was a consummation I had dared not dream of. Long have I admired the lady, but never did I consider myself worthy of ever becoming her consort. At least, sir, I must thank you indirectly for that. Had you not frightened her about my safety, I would never have discovered the truth of her heart."

The major gave him a quick bow from the hips, then stood again to attention; and Thurtell could only gape at him, having no words on his tongue. What the man had said was too astounding to be credited. Caroline had not been this fellow's betrothed! She had said that she was only that she might be able decently to reject his unwanted proposal! And if that excuse had been a lie, a base lie, being a woman's, why had it come to her lips unless in secret she had hankered to marry this dull, ramrod of a fellow? What could she have seen in him? what could any woman have seen in him?

"She—she told you—she said—she said that she loved you?" he muttered, and he ran his hand across his eyes.

"She me honoured with that confession, sir. Not in such plain words, but in a look, a sigh . . . I say no more. That lady is to become my wife. For that, I repeat, I must indirectly thank you. But I want it understood, sir, that you molest her no further. As for your threats against me, I scorn them. Were you a gentleman, you would have sent a challenge in the manner of a gentleman instead of frightening weak women. Nevertheless, I am prepared to meet you, swords or pistols, whenever you should wish it."

Thurtell began to laugh. As was his way, he did not laugh aloud but bubbled within. There was to him something absurdly comical in the victim coming to his killer like this and offering to be killed, and his laughter could not be controlled.

"Don't be a fool," he gasped. "Do you think I'm going to get out of bed in the early morning just to shoot you in Hyde Park or somewhere, then find myself lumbered for it and, perhaps, hanged? If you want to fight, let's use our hands like men, with mittens or without, and not shelter behind a gun or a sword."

"I fight like an officer and a gentleman," said Wood, "not like a ruffian. If you refuse my challenge, I will know how to think of you in future; and you shall know what to expect should you dare pester Miss Noyes again. . . . Good day to you, sir."

Abruptly, he turned on his heel and, head in air, marched off, while Thurtell with both hands gripped the table-edge to keep himself from leaping up and running out and thrashing him. Almost he choked with the hot anger in his throat, and he could not see clearly; but he dared not move. To reveal his hatred of the man in public would bring talk after this bloody major had been croaked, and then he might be suspected of the murder. Therefore, trembling, he remained in his chair, glaring after the slim figure striding stiffly off; and he was glad that few had been present to watch that quarrel.

"Who's your military friend?" cackled Mary, leaning over the bar. "Thought for a moment he was going to hit you."

"Go to hell!"

"Thanking you, Mr. Thurtell," said she, "I'm already there, having to work for you. But you might tell me who he was so that I'll be able to say I can't serve him next time he comes. And who's this Caroline Noyes you was quarrelling about? No relation, I hope for her sake, of that caggy chap, Tommy Noyes, you bring here sometimes?"

"You know too bloody much," growled Thurtell. "If you don't want your throat cut, my girl, you'll wear ear-muffs when you're in here. If I find your nose poking into any of my business, I'll snip it off with a razor. And I mean it."

"Pah," she said, tossing her yellow curls, "you're always talking. How many times have I heard you say you were going to stick somebody and then done nothing about him? Why! I've lost count of the times you was going to slash my giblets, and they're still there, safe and warm as they ever was."

"Don't be so damned optimistic about that," he growled, and shrugged away. "I might do you yet some time."

She laughed, showing her pale gums and bright teeth, while briskly she polished a glass that squeaked against the cloth; and back into his chair Thurtell sank, angry and bewildered.

So much had happened so rapidly that as yet he was unable to sort them into their correct patterns. Only was he glad that he had held tight the ribbons on his rage and there had been no public brawl, although he felt rueful at having mentioned Caroline's name; and Caroline . . . this was the astounding revelation from which his wits had not yet recovered . . . Caroline had never been betrothed to this cock-sparrow! That was something which Thurtell felt it difficult to credit. . . . Nevertheless, he feared sickishly that it must be true, there having been no reason for Wood to have lied about such a question. And if it were true, how could Caroline have been so unwomanly as to have declared herself loved by a man who had not spoken of his love to her? In their fear of being snubbed and made to appear foolish, girls were usually cautious in claiming husbands without reason. . . .

Thurtell's head ached with the effort to unpuzzle this mystery. That Caroline had lied, pretending a lover she did not possess at the time, was something he found it difficult to believe. It was not as though she were some sallow old witch who had to satisfy her pride with a phantom. A woman as attractive as she did not have to bed with a dream. Yet she had said . . . and Wood had said . . .

Why should she have lied?

Why should Wood have lied?

Could it have been that she had exposed a secret hankering for a man that it might protect her from his proposal, quickly saying anything to escape his pressing her?

Why? why? why?

All that evening, all that night through which he dozed and did not sleep, waking suddenly, tingling alert, with hot eyeballs and fevered skin, Thurtell puzzled and groaned and tried to find the truth, the woman behind the pretty mask. And it maddened him to fear that he might never uncover the truth, for only a fool would accept a woman's unproven word. If only to hurt a man for some inexplicable feminine reason Caroline might have said anything, no matter how wild and cruel the accusation or confession; and he had never intended to hurt her. Why then should she suddenly hate him, flinging at him a lie in the shape of this damned Major Wood?

When at last, after eternities, the dawn glowed mistily through his dusty window, the enigma of Caroline remained still sphinx-like, unsolved by him. But while he shaved, glaring at his own reflection in the cracked glass, he swore that, if he had to slap-bang the smile from her pussy-face with his fists, he would make the girl spit the truth at their next meeting. But one thing this revelation had done. It had hardened his resolution, and with even deeper satisfaction could he contemplate the shooting of Major Wood. . . .

When at last that evening he saw Probert struggle through the other drinkers towards him, he gazed dully at him, although his heart was pounding until he feared it must pound itself to a stop.

"Couldn't get back any earlier, damn it," muttered Probert. "Get me a drink."

Thurtell nodded to Mary to pour another brandy, but he did not speak. Tight-lipped, he sat and with cold eyes stared like a statue at his friend.

"Thanks, love," said Probert, taking the glass from Mary and gulping down the liquor. "That's better," he panted, slapping his chest. "That's what I needed . . . I've got something to tell you, Jack, something important. It was lucky I hung on at Elstree, else I'd not have heard. . . . Are you listening, Jack?"

"I'm listening," said Thurtell, sitting like a statue, but watching him.

"It's about Carrie, the bitch . . ."

"I know. She told Wood that I might kill him. Did you tell her that?"

Slowly, Probert's joints seemed to loosen until he sagged in his chair, and his cheeks turned greenish.

"Before God, Jack," he whispered, "of course I didn't! You don't think I'd blab on you, do you? I'm in this as deep as you and I want him out of the way just as much . . . Carrie's a sharp girl. She must have guessed it from your talk. . . . What the hell are you looking at me like that for!"

"If I thought you'd blabbed, Bill Probert, I'd break your neck," said Thurtell, his small eyes like silver under the brows. "I've said nothing to her, nothing about Wood, anyhow, that should have made her know what I meant to do. How then did she guess?"

"Women guess strange things," croaked Probert, beginning to sweat. "They're like animals, they can sniff things, you know, don't need words. Spit my death, Jack, I told her nothing. If I had, do you think I'd have heard her talk later about how she'd been to Wood? . . ."

"Is it true," asked Thurtell, "that she wasn't Wood's fancy piece? That's what he told me. He said that he couldn't believe it at first when she ran and blubbered to him. Which of em's lying?"

Weakly, Probert shook his head. "I—I don't know, Jack," he sighed. "I wish I did. That Carrie's deep, and all women are liars. And this means, damn it, that our game's up."

"What do you mean—it's up?"

"Why, if Carrie knows, or suspects, that you're after Wood's blood, and Wood knows it, too, they'll rattle to everybody about it. Then if he was found in his bed, what'd they think? Knowing that you and I are pals and me living in the same house as him . . . We'd never get away with it, Jack. Never!"

"I have now," said Thurtell, "every reason to wipe the bastard out. Do you think fear of any consequences is going to stop me?"

"But you can't, Jack. They'd be on us at once!"

"I always knew that you were a coward."

"I'm not a coward, but this'd be madness. Can't you see it?" Desperately, sweating, Probert leaned across the table, fists raised imploringly. "It was different before. There was no link between you two—well, no link they could prove—and I had no reason to kill the cove—but, now . . . You know women! Carrie'd be yelling her head off and we'd be in quod before you could say Damn it! You can't do it like that, you can't, Jack."

Contemptuously, Thurtell looked down at him; then he spat, widely missing the spittoon on the floor.

"Don't be so scared," he sneered. "You need have nothing to do with it. I'd rather you weren't in it, anyhow. I want to have fellows with me I can be sure won't blab."

"I never blabbed!"

"I'm taking no risks, whatever you did. I'm looking after this game from now. It's nothing more to do with you."

Vainly, Probert strove to conceal the look of relief that shone in his eyes, but Thurtell noticed it.

"Coward," he jeered again. "Look at the size of you, as big as me almost; you'd be a giant if your legs weren't so short; and you haven't got the spirit of a tomtit like little Joey Hunt! I'll be glad to go to work without you."

"No, Jack, don't talk that way. I'm with you up to my neck; I tell you I'm not scared, but it'd be madness to start again in Castle Street, particularly when he knows that you're after him. . . ."

"Be quiet," said Thurtell. "Shut your mouth and your ears and get me another drink."

Still shaking, stooping obsequiously, Probert took up the glasses and carried them to the bar, while, picking his teeth, Thurtell watched him under puckered brows. Then again he spat and, to his delight, he spat into the centre of the spittoon. The success of this shot so delighted him that he spat again, and again the gob plopped into the centre of the sawdust bowl. Such sudden success so excited him that when Probert had returned to the table with the drinks he was astonished to find Thurtell wagging his head and grinning to himself.

"Just watch me, Bill," chuckled Thurtell. "That must be four paces away at least, yet I can lob one clean in the centre with one spit; and I've got all my molars, too! It's cheating to spit between a gap in your teeth. Look, now!"

"BravO!" cried Probert, clapping his hands. "Almost did it! Again, Jack! Bet you a brown you can't do it first shot. . . ."

The other drinkers turned to watch, their chatter fading to a murmur, as, straddling his chair, Jack Thurtell, grinning like a schoolboy, cleared his throat, took careful aim, pouted, and spat once more.

"BravO!" cried Probert again. "Dead centre, my lad! You're the boy for me. Now have another shot. . . ."

A minute ago he had been trembling, sweating, his clothes seeming too large for him, expecting any moment to be beaten if not murdered; and now, as though there had been no dangerous suspicion between them woven by a woman's tale, he laughed with Thurtell and clapped him on the back. Others joined them, chalking out distances from which the competitors were to stand; and Mary from behind the bar muttered and cursed at the mess they were making of her floor with their filthy globules in the sawdust.

Like a boy, Thurtell laughed, swelling out his chest. No one in that bar—he proved it—could spit so far nor so accurately as he.

CHAPTER SEVEN

THE CHALLENGE CONFIRMED

ONCE set in his determination that the impertinent Wood must be killed, Thurtell became impatient with every minute that separated him from his desire. The quicker the man was dead, the more contented he would be, even though Caroline might have said the truth that under no circumstances would she become his bride. The question of marriage was no longer of real importance. All that mattered was that Wood must die. No longer was it a question of getting his hands on the woman's money or of desiring her dark loveliness, it had become a question of pride. And Thurtell prided himself that he had a proper pride. No one had ever insulted him and escaped his wrath uninjured. No one, he often declared, would make a flat out of John Thurtell . . . yet Bill Weare had done exactly that. . . .

Whenever he thought of Bill Weare, Thurtell's fists clenched and his neck swelled with hatred. It was not merely that Weare had rooked him—he had been a johnny raw then, fresh from Norwich and had had to learn the hard way—it was the manner in which he had managed it that rankled like an open ulcer in his memory. After fleecing him of about three hundred quid, when he had shown his empty pockets, Weare had refused to lend him five of his own pounds back. "I'm neither a Jew nor a banker," he had said, with that scornful smile on his heavy mouth, "but I'll lend you a pistol if you want to earn some more to give me." For him, Old Flash, the Bully, the sporting king of Norwich, to be treated like a silly boy was something that Thurtell could not forget. Even when Weare, repenting his foolishness and perhaps growing afraid, had told him of the cross arranged in the fight between Randall and Martin, he had not been appeased. He had taken his share, six hundred guineas, but even that heavy sum in his pocket could not recompense him for such an insult. From that moment he had determined on revenge, although pretending friendship that he might await the chance to strike.

But he must, for a while, put aside that sweet thought and concentrate on killing Wood. This time he would not tell Probert of his plans. As that big coward had refused to help in a second attempt in

81   F

Castle Street, he would make his own plans. The fellow's arrogance seemed to bring ill-luck on his coat-tails. Whatever he might make from the killing—it would not be much, Thurtell feared; a half-pay captain, even though he had a small country seat, was unlikely to carry large sums on his person—it would be whacked between himself and Hunt, and Probert could go sniffing for his unearned share.

Yes, he would have Joe Hunt for ally, and perhaps young Ennison, his brother's servant, a pale-faced pimply youth with adenoids who was his slave. Neither of them would dare to blab. Even should the affair miscarry again, they'd not scoff and prick at him as Probert continually pricked him about the failure at Castle Street which had not been his fault. This time, the planning would be his own and it could not fail.

First, he must arrange the setting. Castle Street being ruled out, he must find another place. That was not far to seek. He knew the perfect place, close to the Thames in Westminster, where once he had been taken for a game of rolly-polly. Manchester Buildings. Most of these houses, all built alike, were practically empty, being rented mainly by bachelor members of the parliament, and there were always some to let, for they were ill-kept and the street was dank with river-mists. Behind Cannon Row, the houses stood, dingily respectable on the exterior, although once the doors were shut, the inhabitants were known to hold riot on occasions. A squeal or two in such surroundings would awaken little interest in the neighbours. Ay, that was the place! Besides, they needed somewhere to store whatever goods he and Tom could obtain from tradesmen with fraudulent bills. As a bankrupt, Thurtell himself was unable to trade, but he had nevertheless managed, under false names and with false references, to amass a certain amount of negotiable goods which were hidden in a cottage which his brother had hired in Kensington. This cottage was small and too over-looked by neighbours to be really suitable. From it, they would carry every-thing to Manchester Buildings, near the tempting Thames which, wellnigh every night, carried some unknown's corpse to its watery burial, and they would trade from there. That was all that Tom need be told, Thurtell being determined that his brother should not be implicated in anything more dangerous than common swindling.

Having decided on the stage for the drama, he wasted no time. Merrily he set to work. There was Cousins, the linen-draper in Kensington, who held some of their stock and could be relied on to give a reference. He was interviewed and, with insolent reluctance, finally agreed to say that, so far as his knowledge went, Thomas Thurtell was a respectable gentleman who might be trusted. With this cautious document, the brothers hurried to the solicitor in Berner's Street, a slow-speaking gentleman called Assretis who, after much hemming and hawing, demanded five pounds to pay for the agreement. They had been prepared for this, Tom having pawned a looking-glass on the way; and with the solicitor's clerk and Joseph Hunt —who had trotted at their heels all morning—they hurried to the house.

A man of affairs, a man with little time to waste on talk as though his thoughts were far away on vast commercial deals, Thurtell strutted through the house, poking his gun-stick at the walls to see whether they were sound, stamping on the boards and complaining about the stink of dampness and neglect.

"Don't want none of these old fixtures," he growled, crumpling the faded curtains in his fists. "When my family come down from Norwich to join us, I must have all new fixtures and furniture. Otherwise, the place might do. . . ."

Once Tom's signature was on the lease, his brother took command like the general of an army, sending Hunt and Ennison off to hire a wagon from Daffern in Compton Street that the goods might be transported from Kensington and the other secret places in which they were concealed.

"This gives us a clean start," he said, and already he felt that in these new surroundings he was cleansed of the past. "Here we can begin again, and if we should have to do a moonlight," he laughed, "we can take everything down to the river and hire a wherry. I'll leave Ennison in charge so that our mugs mightn't be seen about here too often. He can sleep here, live here like a lord, and see that the bloody bailiffs don't come sniffing about."

Wearily, Tom Thurtell leaned against the wall and watched his brother, seeing his self-confidence return in his swagger, in the hard depths of his voice and in the brilliance of his eyes. Always Jack was the same in the way that he could bounce up again after he had been floored; and Tom envied that resiliency. Nothing daunted Jack. Already he had forgotten that they would soon be charged with conspiracy and perhaps arson because of the fire in Watling Street, and he seemed unable to see the dangers in the future. To Tom, however, those dangers were very plain, and he was weary of this hole-and-corner life, always just one step ahead of the law. It could not continue indefinitely; but what could he do save cling to his brother's coat-tails and pray that their luck might change sometime? His own luck had always been invariably bad.

Forced into marriage with a woman he had thought should prove only a night's diversion, he had sulked in matrimony, then had fled with the children from Norwich, having failed in business to the tune of £4,466. Luckily, his chief creditor had been his father and, with his help, he had managed to make a composition with the creditors. Everything now had therefore to be arranged in his name, although the true negotiations were being made by Jack. This Tom did not complain at, being grateful to submit the future into his brother's capable hands; but lately he had begun to fear. Whatever they touched collapsed, perhaps because they were unable to resist using capital as ready money and trusted too greatly to luck at cards, dice or the races. Their winnings, owing to their being on the inside of many cross deals, had on occasions been large, but they had never remained content to pocket the money. Whatever might be in their pockets, Jack would argue, could easily be doubled; and, trusting to his own acumen, he would always begin to gamble again; and that would be the end of another dream. Again and again, the same: poverty, a few days of wealth; then, poverty once more. Up and down, mostly down, living always on the knife-edge of fear, supping one night in the luxury of a St. James's hell and on the next night gnawing bread and cheese around St. Giles's or in Covent Garden, the brothers lived, always hoping, always expecting, and almost always losing. There could be no end except jail to such an existence, Tom was aware, yet he knew of no other method of making money.

There had been the bombazine factory in Norwich of which Jack had been so cock-a-hoop when first their father had set him up in it; and there had been his own farm for which their father had paid a yearly rent of £800. Both now were gone; and Tom was honest enough to confess that he could blame no one but himself for his stupid failure. The farm had been left in the hands of a bailiff who had robbed him while he had roistered in Norwich or, with his brother, had travelled the country from race-meeting to race-meeting, cock-fight to cock-fight, bull-baiting to bull-baiting, boxing-bout to boxing-bout, both drunk and joyous, while keeping the prettiest, and therefore the most expensive, high-fliers they could find. A boozy, gallivanting life had it been with few moments of sobriety; and, of course, the inevitable crash fell suddenly. His farm sold up, Jack's business in the bankruptcy courts, the brothers had ridden to London to a wealthier and, they believed, easier fortune.

Failure again: always, failure . . . Jack's capital rooked from him by Weare; then a miserable existence as petty cheats, touts, the bullies of Lemming going about his, and not their own, dirty business. They had thought then to settle in a tavern where they could attract the flats to a game of cards or to the E and O board in the upstairs-rooms of the Black Boy in Long Acre. With Mary Dobson who had travelled from Norwich with Jack to stand behind the bar, and a rogue they had thought a friend, Cowdrey, as manager, it had seemed that a fortune must soon be theirs. Their young brother, Henry, before going off for a soldier, had cheerfully signed the lease, and the authorities therefore could not charge them should the bills remain unpaid. Even unpaid bills, however, could not keep the Black Boy profitable when their friends had unquenchable thirsts and so few coins with which to pay for cooling-mixtures.

They had established an ordinary and, of course, had neglected to pay the butcher's bills; they had given evening parties and had found in the morning that their returns did not cover their outlay. Mary Dobson was the jewel they had relied on to draw the swells and tulips; and there she had not failed them. Every man with a twinkling eye for a prime puss had strolled to Long Acre, but whatever Mary may have earned went into her pocket instead of the till. At the time, the brothers had not grudged her that, Jack having long since let her gad her own slippery way, and they had congratulated themselves on a packed tavern night after night. Alas, their popularity had proved their downfall. The rioting, the singing and brawling, the horde of thieves, rooks and harlots who had made the house their home, led to a suspension of their licence, other taverns and brothels growing jealous of the riotous success.

Again, down and up; up and down; and mostly, down. Following the fancy to race-meetings and boxing-bouts, watching the pugilists training at Wade's Mill in Hertfordshire and gambling there night after night, living day by day, often hour by hour, feverishly, working as few men worked to grub up a few pounds. Then the return to commerce; with £500 lent them by their father, they had bought hugely on credit to sell for ready money below market-price. A brisk but only temporary business had resulted until, pressed by creditors, they had resorted to fire and would have been in jail had not the judge, Mr. Justice Park, taken such objection to the defendants' counsel that he had given judgment in their favour. Brief victory. Barber Beaumont of the County Fire Office, raging at such a verdict, had caused an indictment to be made against them for conspiracy to defraud. The next term, proceedings would begin, and Tom was not looking forward to them. Not only his stutter made him helpless in the box, his courage ran out of his heels amongst all those wigs, and then he scarcely knew most of the time what it was that he answered.

Now, again, Jack, with that threat hanging over them, had started a similar fraud, most of the goods this time being bought in Hunt's name. This could not continue forever; they would hang at last.

"C-c-can't we start something l-l-legal, for a change?" he asked suddenly. "I-I-I've got my kids, and I-I-I don't want em to suffer if-if-if I've got to go to jail again."

"You won't go to jail, my boy," said Thurtell, giving him one of his rare affectionate smiles that changed his sombre countenance almost into beauty, as though candles had been lighted behind the grey eyes, the hard lines of the skin smoothing out and the brows lifting amusedly. "You'll not be involved more than's needful. I give you my hand on that. But, Tom, we can't go on like this. Soon I'll have to leave the Cock——"

"L-l-leave the Cock!" cried Tom, aghast.

"Ay, I've not told you, didn't want to trouble you, but things aren't going too well. The butcher's cut off our credit, blast and rot him. Only owe him about eleven quid but he'll send us no more, he says, unless we pay it. And how in hell can we pay him? There're bills for about nine hundred quid soon to fall due and I've realized all we can on what's in the cellar."

"B-b-but where's it all gone!"

Thurtell shrugged. "A gentleman don't ask things like that, and no man that's a gentleman pays his bills. It's low to pay such scum as tradesmen. The only debts we can acknowledge are debts of honour, and I've had to settle those first, of course. And I think Mary and that damned husband of hers keep birdlime on their fingers; but what they take is almost nix beside what we owe. I'll have to leave the Cock soon, mizzle off somewhere, lie low for a time, I suppose."

"Go-g-good God," moaned Tom. "W-why didn't you tell me?"

"Didn't want to tell you, didn't want to trouble you," said Thurtell, kicking up dust as he walked up and down the uncleaned floor. "It'll all come right in the end, Tom," he cried with a forced smile. "We only need one good cleaning up and then we'll get out and live as country squires. We might be down on our luck for the moment; but at the same time, don't forget we're downy coves and we'll come out best in the end. I feel it in my bones. I've an idea, an easy way of getting my hands on a fortune; but I don't want you mixed in it. If it comes off, you'll have your whack; if it don't . . . well, you won't have to suffer."

"I-I-I don't l-like it, J-j-ack. It's no-no-not what you was saying to Bill and Joe about that m-m-major somebody I hea-hea-heard you magging about?"

"Forget you ever heard about any major," cried Thurtell in a suddenly fierce voice. "You don't know the fellow—never heard his name. That's all you've got to know. . . . For the love of God, Tom, be a man! leave everything to me. It can't go wrong!"

He had always said that: It can't go wrong, he had said; and it always had gone wrong. Always! Thomas groaned. The complete faith he had in his brother was beginning to crack after such continual disappointments. With his courage, his self-confidence, his energy, Jack should by now have become a great man, an alderman, or even Lord Mayor of London, instead of living this hunted life, relying on each day to bring coins to carry him through to another day, borrowing, pawning, promising, and rarely paying. Something was wrong with the universe when one born to greatness should have been frustrated at every turn. Jack's generosity had much to do with these failures. Scorning to take a tradesman's attitude towards money, he had given it away when he could not spend it, relying continually on that devil Luck which visited him but rarely. Had he remained a bombazine manufacturer at Norwich, content on small but growing returns for hard work, by now he might, like their father, have become an alderman and even mayor.

Had he exerted himself as strongly towards the right as he had towards the left, long ago he would have been wealthier and even more respected than dad. Instead, after the will-o'-the-wisp of easy money, a quick kill, he remained penniless.

Sadly, Tom recalled their youth in Norwich and the splendour they had known, the swells they had been considered in their finery, and the dreams of wealth, wine and opulent ladies that had spurred them to spending as though they would never have to wake up again.

"I—I wish w-w-we could start again," he sighed.

"We *are* going to start again!" cried Thurtell, slapping him on the back. "If my plot comes off, and it *will* come off, we'll be in the money. Forget the past. Look ahead, my lad, look ahead."

But that was something Tom dared not do. Better to look back to a ruined past than towards a future which might spell disaster; and he wished, with all his heart he wished, he could have the proud confidence of Jack whom nothing, it seemed, could daunt.

True to his word. Thurtell kept his brother as much as possible in the dark, as he did Probert. To Hunt alone he confided his plot, knowing that from the whiskered chaunter he could always expect praise and admiration. And enthusiastically, proud to become a Turpin lad, Hunt joined in the game.

"Let me try the gun," he begged Thurtell. "Just once."

"Haven't tried it myself lately," said Thurtell, looking complacently down at his metal stick. "Better do it, perhaps, before I fire at Wood. Can't have it sticking at the wrong moment. See that bird out there, out of the window there! Just watch him, my lad. . . ."

From his pocket he took the air-pump and, unscrewing the top of the stick, slipped it inside.

"Got sixteen charges in it," he said, and, raising the gun, he pulled on one of the imitation-knots.

Nothing happened.

Again, he pulled on the knot. Again, there was silence while the bird still sang on the tree.

"God damn it," snarled Thurtell, "it's never stuck before."

Impatiently, losing his temper, he pulled with all his strength; then he hit the gun against the wall, and afterwards, threw it on the floor and kicked it.

"Glory be," he cried, "thank the Lord we tested it in time! Think if that'd happened when I had Wood in front of me! or Barber Beaumont!"

"What are you going to do now?" Gently, timorously, Hunt picked up the gun and examined it closely. "You can't use pistols here. The noise'd give you away."

"I'll not use pistols," cried Thurtell, the veins swelling on throat and forehead as he raised his clenched fists. "I have these which God gave me, haven't I? They'll not give me away or let me down like that bloody toy!"

"What! what! you'd strangle him? beat out his brains?" whispered Hunt, sweat on his forehead. "That'd make a fine to do if he shouted! Fate seems against you, always, Jack."

"Who am I," shouted Thurtell, "to care what the bloody hell fate might do! I'm master of my fate, and I'll prove it. Let guns go rusty and knives blunt, there's always a brick to be tied in a handkerchief, a razor to slip up your sleeve; or, if all else fails, there's one's hands to use! This time, Wood's going to get it if I'm left with only my boots to kick him with!"

He seemed to grow, his shoulders to broaden, his length to expand, and Hunt watched him with apprehensive worship as though this were not a human being but Satan himself who stood before him. Nothing seemed beyond the power of such a man, one so strong, so iron-willed, so resolute and so callous—the kind of man that Hunt would have given half his life to have been. But he was weak-willed and weak-bodied, the butt of fools who, to earn a meagre existence, had to play the jester before those whom he despised.

"Jack," he breathed, "by God, I don't think there's anything you couldn't do if you set your mind to it!"

"Those aren't idle words," grinned Thurtell, his good humour returned by the praise. "There's nothing I can't and won't do when I'm set on it. I've been idle, Joe: let the other fellows, like Bill Weare, get away with it too often. It's my easy nature; I hate a quarrel, and I despise those mean souls who think too much of money. But I'm changing, and soon I'll surprise some folk. They'll find it's not the old, easy-going fellow I used to be that they'll have to deal with in the future. I'm starting a new career and I'll have no pity for man, woman or maid that gets in my path. And you're my pal in this, Joe; we'll share alike, profits and dangers together, and to hell with bloody Probert!"

"Partners!" cried Hunt; and there were tears of happiness and gratitude in his eyes; "we'll live and swing together! Give me your hand, my partner, my pal, my good old Flash!"

Smiling, feeling himself a king before a pauper, Thurtell offered his huge fist, and Hunt seized it in both his hands; and for a moment, Thurtell almost believed he was about to kiss it.

"Ay," he said, squaring his shoulders. "From now, Joey, we're partners; sink or swim or, as you have it, we'll swing together!"

Proud he felt, all-conquering, and generous, too, in accepting this amusing yet too weak chaunter as his partner in murder. To the devil with Probert! Here was the only friend he could trust, Joe Hunt with ever a smile at misfortune, a fellow without envies or rancours, humble and eager to please, it seemed.

"Who touches you, Joey," he cried, "touches me. We're more than partners, we are friends . . . And we must get quickly to work."

So he instructed Hunt to find out slyly what he could, particularly to learn not only when Wood was expected in London, but whether there were any friend whose name might be used to decoy the fellow to Manchester Buildings.

Delighted to show his cunning, Hunt set gleefully to work, dancing at Probert's heels, listening with patience to Noyes's grumbling at his lack of rhino and his curses on chancery that held up his father's money which should, he swore, have come to him. Sympathetically, Hunt cursed with him, drank with him, condoled with him, slipping in now and then apparently careless questions about Wood and when he might be expected again to sleep in Castle Street. Then, while he drowsed over his gin one evening with Noyes in the Brown Bear in Bow Street, Noyes casually remarked that he wondered what Wood, after he married, was going to do with the female he kept in Kensington.

Almost running, Hunt sped to the Haymarket, grinning with delight to think how his cleverness would serve Thurtell. Here was the bait for which they had been seeking and had feared they would never find! Now would they be able to decoy the bloody major to his doom, and none could possibly suspect that they had a hand in it!

Thurtell grinned, his eyes gleamed, when, in the Cock, Hunt whispered his discovery to him.

"Name of Brew. Lodges at Cousins's, in Kensington. What they are together, you can guess if your mind's as dirty as mine. All I know's what I got out of Noyes. They have a great friendship, says Noyes, and that's all he knew. Said he believed she was an old trot with half a leg in the grave, but that's probably what the bloody major told your girl just to gammon her."

"I don't care if she's a hundred so long as her name'll lead him to the slaughter. When's he coming down?"

Woefully, Hunt shook his head. That was something he had not yet been able to learn, but he was certain that he'd discover it the moment Noyes heard.

"We'll just have to wait on luck," he sighed.

Thurtell felt that he could wait no longer. It was Saturday, a bright sunny day, and the country called him. He'd hire a gig and drive into the country, idling along the road towards Edgware; and if he continued on to Elstree—who knows?—he might glimpse Caroline. Or he might see Wood alone and have the opportunity of killing him. The weather was too good to waste indoors and his legs needed stretching. Even if he saw neither Caroline nor Wood, the clean air would refresh him after these days and nights indoors.

At Cross's stables in Whitcomb Street he hired a gig and set off towards Tyburn, driving slowly through the traffic until, in the Edgware Road, he flicked the horse with his whip and lolled back, taking deep breaths of countrified air, his tall hat well back on his head for the breeze to fan his forehead. No one watching would have suspected that there was murder in his heart! A proud thought! it made him look contemptuously down at passers-by, those weaklings timid of bloodshed; what would they have done had they been able to read his heart? Ah! then there would have been shouts of horror and disbelief, squeaking and swooning of females, and the traps would have come running from their bolt-holes; and all because one man was amongst them, a man who had no common fears.

The idea enchanted Thurtell, and he smiled. But these creatures had no need to be afraid, he thought disdainfully: he'd not cut their useless throats—the swag-bellied merchants with their fat dames, the whistling lads and the skittish, crummy girls, the shopkeepers peering like bats from the darkness of their dens; they could all sleep without fear at night. Already he had marked those who were to be visited like the Egyptians in the night. First, Wood; then Barber Beaumont; then Weare; then others who had insulted or had cheated him.

Thurtell whistled at the prospect, then he cursed because the air-gun had proved a failure. After all the trouble he had taken to borrow the damned thing, too! But perhaps it would be better to use his hands, more satisfying to strike with a brick or a knife or . . . He had it! . . . Those dumb-bells with which he exercised at Hancock's would be exactly the thing he needed! Good weight, six pounds each, and easily gripped! Ay, he'd borrow those dumb-bells tomorrow and begin to practise on his own shadow against the wall.

Then, when she heard of her fancy man's disappearance, or the fishing of his body out of the Thames, Caroline might remember him and her knees would knock and she would swoon, realizing what it meant to have Jack Thurtell an enemy. After that, perhaps he could threaten her into submission. Ay, ay. He would let her know, in a glance, that he was the killer avenging dishonour, and, with a word slipped in here and there, make her understand that she would be next if she would not consent. Quickly, the red would fade then from those cheeks and the eyes would lose their impish sparkle.

He could see her now, near-swooning, shivering from him . . .

He saw her then and, in his surprise, he almost ran his horse into a hitching-post. For a moment, he thought that he dreamed, and he blinked, then looked again. Caroline! not pale, not blanched with horror or fear; Caroline with her head tossed back in her bonnet, showing her pretty teeth and gums when she laughed! Caroline in a gig pressed tight against the driver, damn her! hand on the man's thigh while he whispered into her ear! Caroline plainly giggling, red-cheeked with happiness, holding on her bonnet with one hand; and Major bloody Wood grinning into her phiz, one arm about her jimper waist, the dog! A pair of lovers—damn it, the man was old enough to be her father—they passed, too intent on one another to notice the gig pulled to one side and the huge man in the white castor turning to glare after them.

Chase them, ay, he would catch them and kill them! To grin so shamelessly into each other's faces! Called herself a good girl, did she? liar, jilt, a good girl! no better than any dirty trull or flaunting Cyprian with skirts too high who rubbed against you in the Garden! To think to make a flat of him, talk high and bloody mighty about her getting married, a dainty piece, too good for anyone below the rank of a stinking major! A marine, God dammit, was better than any army-major! He'd soon show who was the better man; a lieutenant in his majesty's marines, real fighting men, or some damned major in the army who'd curled his whiskers in St. James's and had never tasted a sniff of power in all his baby-days! . . .

Thurtell's rage was so great that it almost stifled him, and he flogged his horse to make it turn, but by the time he had swung the frightened beast back on the way to London, the gig had disappeared. Not even a spit from a puddle to show him where it had gone: up some side-street to some filthy bagnio, no doubt, and she pretending to be an innocent woman! . . .

He had been her flat too long, too bloody inocent! From now, Thurtell swore, he would be relentless in pursuit, and if he had to shoot the accursed major in an open street, shoot him he would, or strangle him—that would be better!—with his bare hands! Towards London they had been bowling. Good. He, too, would go back to London; and this time, he swore, and he spat and cursed in swearing, the dandi-prat major would not escape the fate which he deserved.

CHAPTER EIGHT

NOW OR NEVER

THAT night Major Wood did not sleep in Castle Street. Thurtell sent Hunt to the house to make inquiries. No, he was not expected that night, the landlady told him, but he had sent to say that he would be there in the morning. No, no, no, not with any lady. There had been no mention of a lady. The major was not the kind of gentleman who consorted with females. A proper gentleman, he kept to himself, and always polite, paid the rent regularly, never had to ask him for it once. . . .

Where did he sleep? The thought tormented Thurtell, driving away all hope of his own sleeping. While he lay on a lonely bed, blankets twisted about him in his tossing, feeling the heat like a damp hand on his skin and in his hair, blasted Wood lay with a long-legged lass at his side. Caroline. Of that, Thurtell was convinced. Now, indeed, was there every reason for Wood's death! For such stolen happiness he must be made to pay.

All was ready for the amorous sacrifice. The house in Manchester Buildings was packed with the goods which Tom and Hunt had obtained on credit. From a friend, Hancock, Thurtell had borrowed the pair of heavy dumb-bells, each weighing six pounds. A clout with these, slap-bang, a blow from each hand, as in boxing, and there would not be more than a few splinters left of the major's jaw-bone. Then, in the night, a boat untied on the Westminster mud-bank, a box, loaded with iron, containing a gentlemen *en route* to the Styx, heaved to the bottom-boards to be heaved out again in the middle of the river. Goodbye, Major busybody Wood! gone with a bubble. . . . Thurtell felt that then, and only then, would he be able to sleep soundly again, his angry spirit appeased.

Yet there was still another day and night to be dragged through somehow. It would have been absurd to have allowed his impatience to speed the deed until all possibilities of a slip had been examined and the plot found to be perfect. So long as Hunt played his part—and damn it, the fellow should not fail: after all, he was an actor—nothing could possibly go wrong. On Hunt depended almost everything. The rogue was faithful and energetic and enthusiastic, and he should be able with his mobile phiz and wheedling pipe to convince Wood that there was no danger in accompanying him to Westminster.

"Of course, of course, I know what to do," insisted Hunt that evening in the Cock. "Ay, I know the name! I'll not forget it. Didn't I tell you about her first? 'Mrs. Brew at Cousins's in Kensington wants to see you urgently. Don't know what the trouble is. Young woman ran up and asked me to hurry to your honour to tell you to come at once. At once, if you please, sir. Seemed real urgent about it, sir, as though someone were dying or being murdered——'"

"Don't say anything about murder."

"Of course not. I was just running through it to show you I ain't forgotten. Wish it were over, don't you?"

Curtly, Thurtell nodded, and drank deep of the brandy.

"Like waiting at the theatre for the curtain to go up, afeared you might forget your lines or say the wrong damned thing. But nothing can go wrong. I'll pull a sad phiz and have the gemman worried sick lest his wench be dying. He'll not stop to think. And if he wants to know why she's at Westminster and not Kensington, I'll say she's had some words with Mr. Cousins, which is another thing she wants to consult with him about."

"For heaven's sake, don't overdo it! Here's two tales twisted already and enough to make a saint suspicious. First, you say you don't know a thing, that a strange woman sent you to Castle Street; then you say that you know she's quarrelled with Cousins; now, if you're a stranger, how the hell are you to know anything about Cousins?"

"I got carried away by my part," muttered Hunt sulkily. "That happens to the best of actors."

"Then don't let it happen on the morning."

"I won't. I'll say she's had a rumpus with Cousins and wants to consult the major before she goes back."

"And if he should say he'd prefer to go there alone and asks you the number of her house and the street?"

"I've thought of that! I'll say I can't recollect it but could lead him to the very door."

"BravO!" cried Thurtell, clapping him on the back. "That calls for another glass of clap of thunder. Get em filled up again, will you, Joe?"

That was the only danger, that in his gusto in the part of second

murderer, the fool might babble too much and cause Wood to become suspicious. Thurtell realized that the fellow knew of his hatred,
knew that he waited the chance of killing him, and therefore he would
be on the alert. Fortunately, he had heard nothing of Hunt who had
never been to Elstree; and the tale sounded plausible, worrying enough
to make him hurry to help a friend in her mysterious embarrassment.
Then, once he had opened the door in Manchester Buildings and had
stepped inside—ah! then the dumb-bells would fall, one to the right,
one to the left, and perhaps a third quickly to break his smeller, and a
fourth hard on the adam's apple to stop him squeaking. Blood and
muscle seemed to sing in Thurtell's arms as he conjured the scene
behind his eyes and saw the bloodied face jerk back before his
blows.

When Hunt returned with the brandies, Thurtell looked dazedly
at him, faintly smiling, as though only half-awake from his dream of
successful murder.

"I don't know how I'm going to get through this night," he
muttered.

Yet, strangely, that night he slept. He had expected another of
those tortured nights; but, perhaps his body being too tired to suffer
further, he sank swiftly into slumber and then gaped to find it early
morning, the serving-wench, Lucy Slater, shaking him by the shoulder.

"It's gone past five, sir," she said; "I thought you wanted to be
wakened early."

"That's right, yes, of course. Thank you, m'dear."

He shook himself and blinked. Today was the great day, yet his
accursed head remained stuffy, blast it, and he felt tired. But he had to
be up, he must waste no time, or Hunt would be at Manchester
Buildings before him, and that might prove disastrous.

At first, he thought that he would not shave. Why shave when he
was going only to an assignation with one who soon would have no
eyes with which to see? Then he decided that it would be an ill omen to
start the day with carelessness. He must wash and dress as though
preparing to meet a woman.

Cold water on his face and around his eyes revived him, and by the
time he had finished shaving and dressing, he felt himself again. In the
bar, he drank half a tumblerful of brandy—to keep out the cold, he told
the sceptical Mary—and strutted away, swinging his stick and walking
briskly to keep his blood flowing healthily. Safer not to take a hackney.
The driver might remember him should questions later be asked and

might lead the traps on his trail to Westminster. And he had time enough, if he walked quickly through the rushing crowd hastening to work, it having been agreed that Hunt should call on Wood promptly at seven to make certain of finding him in. There were no preparations to be made. The dumb-bells were ready with the red shawl he would toss over his head and use as a disguise. There was only Ennison to be sent off that he might not become an evidence against him should there be a trial, which Thurtell certainly did not expect.

Telling him to go to Tom's room in the Cock to see whether he were wanted there for some duties, Thurtell sent the lean youth racing off; then he had the empty house wholly to himself. House of echoes and of little furniture. With boxes and bales of goods stacked to the ceiling in two rooms, it resounded with every step he made and turned his coughing into thunder. And it was cold. River-mists coiled across the windows and seeped through the walls, showing in damp patches here and there, and blotting out the sun rising in the sky. From the river sounded the calling of boatmen, the whistle of a boatswain, sounds that drifted faintly through the heavy atmosphere and seemed to come from no particular point but from a confused, diffused direction that might have been south, east or west, or even north. An empty house, an empty street, an empty city, it seemed; and he alive alone amongst the ghosts.

Pish to ghosts! There were no such things as ghosts. Bugaboos invented by nursemaids to silence children. But if there had been ghosts, which he did not believe, this was the kind of house that they might haunt. Empty, silent, echoing, with mists wetting the windows, and the nearby boats ringing and calling like dead men sailing they knew not whither. There were no ghosts here now. There were no such things as ghosts anyhow, anywhere. But if by some chance they should exist, they should show themselves thankful to him, for today he intended to add another to their company.

Rubbing the dirt from the glass with his sleeve, he peered through a window into the street. No sign yet of Hunt. Nor of Wood. Nothing but a cat moved below, a cat crawling on its belly in a crouch as it slid towards a sparrow pecking at horse-dung. All the houses appeared empty; and that he knew was not so, most of them being inhabited; yet they showed never a blink of life. What could the damned time be? could he have come too early; or was he too late?

As though to answer his question, with a whirring overture, Great Tom of Westminster in its tower beside the bridge began to strike slowly. One. Two. Three. Four. Five. Six. Seven . . . Anxiously Thurtell waited, holding his breath, his head to one side. There were no more hours to sound. It was seven o'clock in the morning and he had less than half-an-hour to wait. Unless they hired a hackney and were driven here; then they would be earlier, of course. He must remember, too, that Wood might not be dressed by this time; he might be a late-riser and not get up before eight, although that was unlikely in a soldier and a countryman. No, he'd have already breakfasted. Sitting at the table at this moment perhaps, living over again the heaven he had enjoyed in false Caroline's embrace. To him would enter Hunt dressed in some of Ennison's clothes which Thurtell had lent him, in an apron and fustian jacket, as though he were a servant. Bowing, calling the dog Your Honour, tipping his dark forelock to him, Hunt would tell his message, exciting the rascal more with what he did not tell than by the little that he said. Quick questions, and few answers. Then, down the stairs and into Castle Street, Wood hurrying, Hunt at his heels, they would scamper. Already, no doubt, they were on the way here.

Shaking with anticipation, Thurtell kicked off his shoes that he might not be heard when he attacked, and then slipped out of his coat. He should have thought to bring a mirror so that he could have seen himself in his disguise and made certain that he should not be recognized if, by some accursed ill-luck, Wood should escape. But under this red scarf, his face was well concealed. A bloody veil, it fell around him, turning the world to red, apt colour for the deed he contemplated. In each hand he gripped a dumb-bell, and he pressed his nose against the smudgy glass, peering for the first sight of his victim.

A dozen fears raced through his thoughts to shake him with doubt. Wood may have been warned about Hunt; he might have already left Castle Street before Hunt arrived; he might have quarrelled with Mrs. Brew and wanted nothing further to do with her; he might know, perhaps, that Mrs. Brew was abroad or in the country; he might, having been warned by Caroline of danger, be too suspicious to accept Hunt's tale; he mightn't have stayed the night with Caroline, after all; or with some other woman; he might have returned to Elstree to see Caroline again; he might be still too drunk after a heavy night to be able to leave his bed; he might have a woman with him and be furious at being discovered with her; Tom Noyes might have seen Hunt and, in terror at the recognition, Hunt might have abandoned the

G

enterprise; Wood might insist on bringing friends to protect him, and again then would Hunt have scampered off. . . . Anything might have happened. Anything.

It seemed to be his fate, Thurtell groaned, always to be in a state of suspense, continually waiting on somebody else. If only he could have managed everything alone, he'd never have failed. That was the one person, the only person, on whom he could rely never to fail him or to lose courage at the sticking-point.

He caught his breath and swung back from the window, for the moment unable to breathe as the blood ran to his head, inflaming his cheeks, then quickly ebbed and left him cold and shivering. Hunt in Ennison's fustian jacket and white apron had turned the corner. No mistaking those greasy shining whiskers and the jerky gait. And at his heels, striding as though on parade, Major Wood with his beaver erect on his head, not tilted a thousandth of an inch to either side, his coat tightly buttoned, a stick in his hand.

Now. Not a moment to be wasted. Now. The dumb-bells, where were they? Where had he put them? Ah, yes, on the mantelpiece. Heavy in his hands, he weighed them, widening his chest and swinging his arms. Now the cloth. Over his head like a satanic beekeeper's net when he goes to the hive. There was nothing else. No. Nothing.

Tiptoe, swiftly he ran to the open door, paused a moment, listening, then began to scamper down the stairs. He had reached the bottom step and was turning towards the passage when he heard the key in the lock and the squeal of the unoiled bolt dragged back; and, under his breath, he cursed himself for having been so laggard.

Just as he reached the turning into the back parlour, the front-door swung open and Hunt and Major Wood entered. Major Wood entered only a step while, chatting gaily, Hunt strode forward; then Wood stood stock-still, face bloodless, as he gaped at the tall figure of a man with his coat and shoes off, holding a dumb-bell in each hand, and with a red shawl shimmering over his head to his shoulders. He had no need to see the face to recognize Thurtell. Backwards he swayed, stumbling, then suddenly he turned and bolted.

"God damn the dog!" cried Thurtell. "After him."

Had he had his boots on, he'd not have paused. Reckless of who watched out of windows, he'd have chased the rogue and have killed him in the daylight, such was his fury. But he could not run like this, without a coat, without shoes, devil damn it!

He let the dumb-bells fall, clang, to the floor, and he groaned and shook himself as though he were feverish. Again, ay, a second time, Wood had escaped him. But the third time . . . Could there be a third time? would it be possible after this to catch the rogue off-guard, alone?

O, God, he sobbed, why should my luck always be out!

Panting, Hunt tottered back and banged shut the front-door. For a moment he could not speak while he fought to breathe.

"He—he got away," he gasped. "I—I did my best, Jack, but he got away. Saw him running round the corner of the Buildings and thought it best not to follow, too many spies about."

"Lucky for him he ran," said Thurtell in a flat, weary voice "Else, he'd never have run again."

"He'll have the traps on us," groaned Hunt. "He'll go straight to them, and they might be here any moment. Let's go."

"He'd not be such a sneaking knave as that," cried Thurtell indignantly, "damn it, the man's a soldier and must have some honour. This is a private quarrel, and not for traps. And he'd not drag Miss Noyes's name through the courts."

"He'll do it," wailed Hunt, "I know he'll do it; he was stark crazy with fear. You didn't see how he ran. He'll do it, I tell you!"

"Well, what if he does? We'll deny it."

"We must do something, something," sobbed Hunt. "Mother of God, we're trapped. There must be something! I know, I know! Let's get away from here, let's go to Tom's. We can write a note there and send it to him; not sign it, of course. . . ."

"Of course," said Thurtell mockingly. "And what are you going to write in this note?"

"O, O, we'll say—we'll say that it was a sheriff's officer that wanted to nab him. We'll say it was a bum's stratagem to decoy him here."

"He'd never believe it."

"No matter, it's something for us to do. And we must do something, we must; and it might work."

His jaws moved as though he were chewing and his eyes glanced hither, thither, terrified of shadows. He put his hand to his neck, then swiftly drew it down again.

"What are we going to do?" he squeaked.

"Coward," said Thurtell quietly. "Must I always work with cowards who fail me? First, Probert; now you, Joe, although I did not expect much courage out of you, my lad."

"I'd have killed him! Honour bright, I would. I'd have cut his throat or carved him with a butcher's knife; ay, ay, I'm not afeared of blood." Hunt tried to stand erect, but his legs were shaking, and he drooped. "Don't think too hard on me, Jack," he whined. "I ain't like you. I'm not strong and I haven't got your stomach. But I'd have killed him. It wasn't my fault it went wrong."

"No," said Thurtell, "it wasn't your fault."

"So let's get away before the traps come. If we hurry to Tom's and write that letter, Ennison can carry it for us—Wood don't know Ennison—and even if he don't believe it, the traps might. We'll get Tom to swear a debt against him, or you can swear it, and that'll make it seem as though it were true, won't it? Come on, Jack! If we hurry, we can cut across the Park to the Haymarket and we'll have that letter at Castle Street even before Wood gets back."

"All right," sighed Thurtell, his strength returning in his scorn for Hunt's agitation. "It can do no harm, I suppose."

"Harm? It can do much good. No one can think we had a hand in it then. Come, come, come, Jack! Where's your shoes and coat?"

Thurtell nodded his head towards the ceiling and Hunt ran up the stairs, barking his shin in his haste. Howling and hugging his shin, he hopped on, and Thurtell slowly smiled. He was exhausted and no longer interested in killing or even in living. Whatever he attempted, failed; even a simple matter like a murder, performed expertly almost every night by ignorant rascals somewhere in England, failed once he had taken it in hand.

Sometime his luck must turn. Sometime . . . Sometime.

CHAPTER NINE

TALK TALK TALK

HAD the traps suddenly arrived and accused him of attempted murder, Jack Thurtell would have smiled and shrugged his shoulders, not even bothering to deny the accusation. Almost with relief would he have accepted arrest, the struggle within him being resolved by circumstances he could not control, and his countless worries, those hornets of fear, barred from him with his liberty. Soon, he and Tom would have to defend themselves in court against Barber Beaumont's accusations of conspiracy and arson; soon, he would have to flee the Cock with creditors snapping at his heels; soon, he would have to devise some new tricks for making money. A failure in murder as well as in love, he could read no happy future ahead: only, until the grave, a succession of kicks whenever he tried to rise; only again and again, the rekindled hope, the effort, and then the ultimate betrayal to hammer him back into the mire of misery.

Indifferent as he was beginning to feel about his own fate, amusedly could he watch Hunt's panic when, back at the Cock, in Tom's room they argued means whereby they might keep Major Wood from calling in the police.

"Leave it to me," he said, and took pen and paper from a cupboard, setting them on the table.

"W-w-what are you g-g-going to write, Jack?" asked Tom.

"There's only one thing to write," said Thurtell with a grin at Hunt twisting in a chair and pressing his shaking hands between his knees: "what Joe suggested. Write as though we were a friend advising him to keep out of the way, saying that there are several writs out against him."

"It won't work," moaned Hunt. "I know it won't. He'll have gone to the traps already and have sworn out warrants against us. They're probably at Manchester Buildings by now, asking the neighbours what they heard. Once they get on your trail they never let up, the bastards; and they know me. I've been through their hands before, and now I'm a marked man to em."

"What was it they nabbed you for?" asked Thurtell.

"Never mind that now," growled Hunt, with a shiver. "I've had my time in Newgate and I don't intend to have it over again. They've got no respect even for gentlemen when they have em in there with the fetters on your legs. I've got a sister married to a captain in the Austrian service and my brother's sung at the theatre in Covent Garden, but that don't matter once you're in quod. You're just dirt, I tell you, dirt. I don't want to go there ever again, by God."

"You won't, my boy, you won't, if only you keep your head. The traps can smell out a frightened man, that's how they bone most fellows." While he wrote in a backward hand, different from his own rounded one, Thurtell chuckled and talked as though there were nothing to trouble him. "Today, Joe, you and I are going to show our dials in every street we know," he said, "from Bow Street to St. James's. We'll swagger along with our sticks like a couple of swells on the spree. And you'll laugh, if I have to break your neck first; and you'll flash those molars and sing and cut your capers, as usual. Come on."

"I—I can't do it, Jack."

"Come on." Thurtell towered over him; and, making little whimpering noises, Hunt pulled himself to his feet. "Give us a song," said Thurtell, "and grin, damn you, grin."

But the grin when it came at last was too horrible even for Thurtell. He smacked it from Hunt's lips, then drew him out of the room and down the stairs, Tom following miserably with the letter to be carried by Ennison to Major Wood in Castle Street.

"Where you been?" asked Probert, turning from the bar as they stamped towards him.

"Talking," said Thurtell. "That's why we're thirsty. Buy us a drink, Bill. We need it."

Probert grimaced as slowly he pulled a few shillings from his trouser-pocket and counted out sufficient with which to pay for four brandies.

"Funds getting low," he muttered.

"*Getting* low!" cried Thurtell with a snorting laugh. "We're all on the rocks, Bill, all stony broke."

"What's wrong with Joey?" asked Probert, suddenly noticing Hunt. "Are you sick, man? Spew it up; that's the best thing; get rid of the poison, then you can drink again on a clean stomach."

"I'm all right," growled Hunt, with a furious glance at Probert. "I need a drink, that's all, so shut your gob."

"Lookee, Bill," said Thurtell suddenly. "There's something you can do for us."

"Anything, Jack, anything within reason." Probert tried to speak lightly, but a wary look had come into his large brown eyes that wrinkled at the corners apprehensively as though expecting a blow.

Away from the other drinkers, Thurtell led him and Hunt and Tom to his favourite table in a darkish corner. There, when they were seated, Thurtell, faintly smiling, never shifting his steady glance from Probert's eyes, said quietly:

"I want you to swear a debt against a fellow for—let's say, twenty-nine quid. Sounds more real if you don't make it a round sum. Twenty-nine pounds seems like a real debt."

"Of course I will," said Probert with obvious relief that the demand for his help should have been in such a trivial matter. "And who's the poor cove what owes me twenty-nine pounds?"

"Major Wood," said Thurtell.

"Eh? eh? Major Wood? What's your game this time, Jack?" Probert sank back in the chair, still smiling, but his eyes were grave.

"I want him out of the way for a time, that's all."

"He'll get bail . . ."

"Anyhow, I want a debt sworn against him," said Thurtell. "That ain't much to ask a pal."

"But I can't do it, you know I can't. What'd the women say? how could I explain it to them? Besides, I'm a bankrupt. I can't have debts."

"So you won't do it?"

"I can't. Have a heart, Jack, I'd go to quod myself if I tried that, contracting debts when I haven't my discharge. Let Joey do it."

"Joe can't do it. I don't want him mixed any further in this."

"If you'd only explain," groaned Probert. "I don't like being in the dark. Besides, it wouldn't work. If Wood saw my name on it, he'd know it was gammon, and he'd want to know what I meant by doing it. I'd have all the females after me, badgering me."

"All right," said Thurtell. "I'll get somebody else. Come on, Joe. We've got to hurry . . ."

"Don't go like this!" cried Probert. "Have another drink, boys; I've got a few more shillings in my other pocket."

"Haven't time," said Thurtell. "I've got to get that warrant sworn."

"But where are you going?"

"Anywhere, everywhere." He gripped Hunt under the armpit and hauled him upright. "See you later, Tom. Goodbye, Bill."

Probert half-rose to hurry after them, then he sank back into his chair. Whatever game Thurtell was playing, it was doubtless a dangerous one and he was better out of it; but he had not liked the cold glitter in Thurtell's eyes and the scorn ringing in his voice. Confident though he usually was of being master of any situation, Probert for once began to doubt his fascination that Thurtell could so easily turn from him; and it was not until he noticed a half-drunken trot cocking a lewd if glazed eye at him that his self-satisfaction was restored. Nevertheless, he remained uneasy. . . .

"What have they been up to?" he asked, leaning towards Tom who sat, arms crossed, head down as though oppressed by a weight of fear or misery. "What's this game about having Woody up for debt? I don't understand it."

Tom shrugged and did not answer. He knew a little more about the plot than Probert, although there was much he did not understand, and what he did know depressed him with forebodings of disaster.

"They're mistaken," said Probert after a long silence in which, heavy brows raised, he had kept his large and beautiful dark eyes intent on Tom, a whimsical smile on his heavy pouting lips, "ay, very much mistaken if they think they can do anything to Woody. He ain't a man to be frightened by threats or bailiffs. There's only one way to deal with him, quick and final, as Jack should know."

"Th-th-they don't tell me m-m-much," said Tom, "and I d-d-don't want to know anything."

"Very wise of you," said Probert, "very wise, indeed, my lad. Can't say I want to know much either, but I wouldn't like to see em run into any trouble. Jack's so headstrong, so—so belligerent at times —understandable why some fellows call him the Bully—he might do something rash. . . . And Joey's all right in his way, but it's a weak way; he'd be no use in a tight corner. . . ."

Tom showing no sign of interest nor making any attempt to speak, Probert heaved his great bulk out of the chair, said a friendly goodbye, winked at Mary behind the bar, and wandered into the street, frowning while he sucked his teeth and wondered what Thurtell and Hunt could be up to with their talk of sending a bum to the major. From tavern to tavern he strolled, rarely drinking, his coins being few, while he sought Thurtell; and he was beginning to despair of ever finding the fellow when he entered a tavern in Orange Court and saw him with Hunt leaning against the bar and talking to a burly ruffian whom Probert recognized as being one of the dangerous Lemming's gang.

When he swaggered in, their voices fell instantly to silence and they turned warily to eye him.

"It's only Bill Probert," said Thurtell. "You can talk in front of Bill."

"Ay, gentlemen, you can say anything to my face," grinned Probert, swaggering to the bar. "I've only got one good ear: what goes into it don't go out of the other. What are you all having to drink?"

"The usual," piped Hunt. "Claps of thunder, my boy!"

"Four brandies," ordered Probert of the landlord.

The Hunt of some hours ago had become a very different Hunt. The craven, green-cheeked coward who had trembled in the Cock was now skittish, merry and truculent, his courage sailing bravely again on a brandy-ocean.

"If your talk's private, gentleman," said Probert with a bow, "say the word and I'll mizzle and leave you to it."

"It's private," said Thurtell, "but that don't exclude you, Bill. This gentleman here has just offered me five hundred quid."

"Five hundred! . . ." Probert pursed his lips into a soundless whistle and widened his large eyes while he stared admiringly at the big ruffian. "What've you got to do to earn that much?" he cried. "Blow up the House of Parliament or whisper to a jockey at New-market?"

"Easier than either," said Thurtell, with an indifferent shrug. "Nothing much really. There's a young gentleman of the name of Graham who's been foolish enough to lose a heap of blunt at rouge-et-noir in a certain place in St. James's, and he's squealing. They want to stop that squeal. And another cove, you know him, Captain Kelly. . . . The silly ass is making himself obnoxious to certain friends, and that can't be allowed, can it?"

"Five hundred pounds," said the burly ruffian, glaring earnestly into their faces, "and every one of em a good un, paid on the nail. They might come to more than that if you care to wait a little. You see, the fellows that are ready to pay have to live in France and they're getting sick of eating frogs. They've got home-sickness bad, but they're being persecuted and don't dare show their noses over here.

Now, if Graham and Kelly were out of the way, there couldn't be no prosecutions against em, could there?"

"Who's putting up the blunt?" asked Probert. "Have you got Lemming's word for it?"

"That's the question!" cried Thurtell eagerly, as though the suggestion had been his and not Probert's. "If you can get Lemming to pass his word for the money, it shall be done."

The stranger shifted uneasily, and took a long sip of brandy. "I'll speak to him," he muttered. "I've no doubt he'll undertake to pay. When I get his answer, I'll see you again."

He finished his drink, waved a brief farewell, and strode off, plainly worried despite his air of confidence.

"If Lemming passes his word for five hundred quid, it's sure to be paid," said Thurtell, and by the shining of his eyes, Probert realized with a sigh that the fool already believed the money to be practically in his pocket. "The men they want put out of the way'll be disposed of in a week, and I'll do it in such a manner that the public'll believe they killed themselves."

Probert sighed. Off again on fantasy, encouraged by Hunt's noisy approval, the Swell Yokel was racing. Just as the fool almost believed that he had the five hundred quid in his pocket, so did he begin to believe that he was killing or had already killed Graham and Kelly, neither of whom was a simpleton.

"You won't find it easy to get Graham," he said suddenly. "He's fly to most tricks; and as for Kelly . . . there's not a sharper fellow in London."

"That's what's going to make it interesting," said Thurtell, his cheek twisting with annoyance. "Anybody can do for a shopkeeper or the plebs, but when it comes to a cove like Kelly . . . well, that needs cunning. . . ."

"Ay, Jack," giggled Hunt, "you're the boy for the game!" and skipping into a hornpipe, he sang the song of the Buffaloes:

> "Bloody head and raw bones!
> Bloody head and raw bones!
> Be not perplexed,
> This is the text:
> Bloody head and raw bones!"

"And what about Wood?" asked Probert quietly.

"Damn and blast Wood," cried Hunt, "what's the use of killing him? Barber Beaumont's the man we want out of the way. Why don't you do for him now, Jack?"

"Never fear," said Thurtell with a quiet smile. "We'll have him safe enough soon, you may depend upon it."

Talk talk talk. Talk of doing Barber Beaumont, of doing Wood, of doing Graham and Kelly and many others. Depressed, yet forcing a smile to his fat lips whenever a smile was required, Probert drank with them and felt as though he were a man having to tolerate the boasting of two small boys. While they talked like this, they would never do anything. By now, Wood had probably raced back to Elstree; Beaumont slept comfortably in his bed at night; and Graham and Kelly need suffer no fears if their only dangerous enemy was to be Thurtell.

"I'll tell you what we'll do!" Smiling, Thurtell leaned forward to whisper, and excitedly Hunt leaned to catch his words, while with a sigh, Probert pretended interest. "I'll invite Kelly to meet some young gentlemen to play," said Thurtell. "I'll tell him that they're wealthy flats. I'll tell him to come to the Park to meet em: he'd suspect nothing in the Park; and when he comes, I'll be waiting with my air-gun—when I can get it to work again—and I'll immediately go up to him after he's had it and I'll drop a discharged pistol into his hand."

"Just as you were going to do to Wood," Probert could not resist saying, "yet Woody's still alive and kicking."

Hunt glared at him ferociously, Thurtell gave him an angry glance, but the fantasy was too exciting to be interrupted by any sceptic.

"The moment anyone comes up," continued Thurtell, "I'll say I saw him in a duel. I'll say that he fired without effect at the other cove; that the shot was returned and he'd fallen, whereupon the other cove run off. They'd never suspect me then; how could they?"

"Brave!" whispered Hunt; "that's the kind of fellow I like! ready for anything, frightened of nothing, you're the boy for me, Jack! That'll be five hundred goblins in our pockets; and Kelly'll be only the first of dozens."

"Ay," said Thurtell, nodding briskly. "I've been remembering a rogue of an attorney named Springfield in Norwich. When I went bankrupt, the dog used me ill and I might have had my discharge, like Tom, if it hadn't been for his interference. When I take the gun back, I'll use it on him before I hand it over."

"But I thought the gun was no good," said Probert.

"I'm having it seen to, it'll soon work again." Impatiently, Thurtell shrugged from any doubts.

"What about Wood?" asked Probert in a casual voice.

"I told you, I'm dealing with Wood my own way." Almost with hatred did Thurtell glare at his friend. "He's booked, and he'll get it if I've got to go to Elstree to give it to him."

"I don't want the traps snouting round Elstree," protested Probert quickly. "You can do him somewhere else, can't you?"

"Why are you always scared of the traps? You got rid of your jigger, didn't you? What else are you afraid they might dig up at Gill's Hill? Don't tell me you've been burying corpses with the weeds in your garden!"

"Not me," said Probert, managing to laugh. "Only corpses you'll find there are empty bottles and some rabbit-bones."

"And you've got a pretty little lake next door," murmured Thurtell, "just right for shoving corpses into."

"They float," said Probert. "And I don't want em floating near my place. No thank you!"

"Tie a rope round the neck," said Hunt, banging the table with his fist, "and a lump of lead on the other end of it. He'd not float till Trumpet Day then. Queer thing, talking to a boatman once down at Wapping, fellow made a living fishing dead uns out of the Thames, and he told me, swore blind it was truth, that drowned men float on their backs and the females on their faces. Shows how contrary the sex can be; even after you've pushed em into the river, they don't forget their modesty; or so that fellow says."

"Believe anything of females," growled Thurtell with sudden gloom; and Probert knew that he was thinking of Caroline.

"Got to go back to Gill's Hill for the week-end," he said in a careless manner. "Like to come down with me, Jack?"

Almost, Thurtell said Yes. Probert saw his mouth open and his eyes light with eagerness; then suddenly the eyes dulled, the mouth grew thinner, and he sat back in his chair.

"No. Thanks," he said, "there's nothing to take me there now. Not for a time, at least; not until she's wearing her bill of sale, her widow's weeds, and that won't be long, whether she marries the bastard or not."

Probert did not answer. He smiled in an amused fashion which he knew would madden Thurtell.

"I tell you," shouted Thurtell, "I'm going to do it!"

"I never said you weren't. . . ."

"Then take that bloody grin off your face." Trembling, Thurtell tossed the remainder of his brandy down his throat. "Or, by glory, it'll be your turn next, not his."

Probert knew better than to speak when Thurtell was in this furious mood. Besides, there was nothing more to be said. He had stung as he had intended to sting the man, and he had now only to wait to see whether the poison would work under that thin skin.

CHAPTER TEN

TRAILING THE BAIT

LYING awake that night in the Cock, Thurtell shivered, remembering the insulting smirk on Probert's thick lips. Now that he was alone with none to watch and criticize him, he could relax, could loosen the muscles of his face and neck, and sink into misery. In company, he had to maintain a façade of callousness, the air of a man bloody, bold and resolute whose proud spirit suffered no doubts, no fears; a man who had no interests in the world outside gambling and boxing. But at night, naked to his own thoughts, he shivered in the dark, while he recalled the past that should have been so glorious. Had the traps cornered him at such a time, in the dead-spirited early morning before the dawn crowed hope, he'd not have struggled against them or denied anything of which they should accuse him. Almost with relief, as an escape from self-accusations and self-pity, would he have given his wrists for the handcuffs, his legs for the darbies, the struggle then being lifted from his heart, freeing him of innumerable stinging worries, the gadflies of debt and deeds misdone, while bringing peace with loss of liberty.

Slowly the sun climbed over the skyline, glossing wet roofs, lighting up the puddles in the streets and turning mud to gold; and with its light glimmering on his windows, Thurtell felt courage steal back as though his blood, after being near frozen, had begun to thaw, returning manhood with his strength and dissolving the night's bogles around his bed.

Now in the light he could smile again. He even managed to whistle while he washed and dressed. At nighttime, alone in bed, one peopled the dark with terrors of one's own making. That suggested an argument for marriage, the only convincing one that made domesticity appear tolerable to Thurtell: at night, he would not then be alone, he would have a woman to clasp as buckler against his conscience and the threats of jail; but he did not want to think of marriage, dammit. That meant thinking of Caroline and her rejection of his offer; and since she had rejected him, from having been to him merely a pretty, kissable wench, she had grown into a goddess made sacred by his desire. If he could not have her, he swore, no other man would have her. Her lover must die; and, should she flout him after that, he might take satisfaction in snipping off her nose or scarring her as the rebellious harlots were mutilated by Lemming and his myrmidons should they attempt to work for themselves or try to conceal any of their earnings from their masters, their bullies.

Thurtell smiled at his own reflection in the glass while he shaved. That letter warning Wood that writs had been issued against him had doubtless gagged the coward; and last night, to clinch the fellow's fears, Thurtell had written him another letter, signing it by the name of Clarke—the first name to enter his head—saying a man called Curtis had instigated his arrest. The name, Curtis, had been suggested by Probert, who had heard from his wife that the major had once had some unhappy business dealings with someone of that name in the city. This second letter Hunt had carried to Castle Street and sent up to Wood; then to convince him finally that someone, not Thurtell, was plotting against his liberty, a drunken friend they had chanced on in their drinking had been cajoled and bribed into swearing a debt against Wood for £29. By now, on that false accusation, the major would probably be in a sponging-house trying to convince the sceptical bums that they'd pounced on the wrong fellow.

Following that exhausting night with the phantoms in his bed, Thurtell was surprised to find how energetic he felt when, after a breakfast of toast and chops, he descended into the bar for his morning-glass of brandy mixed with rum and diluted with hot water and sugar. The sharp yet sweetish drink refreshed him, opening his mind and clearing his eyes, and had an army of traps invaded the tavern, he would have scorned whatever they might think to do to him.

Impatiently, he waited, seated at his favourite table, for the arrival of Probert who should be able to tell him the latest news about Major Wood. Hunt arrived before him, walking in his usual brisk manner as though always late for an important engagement, his hair freshly oiled, which made his forehead and temples greasy where the oil had run, and his huge black whiskers brushed and oiled until they shone like polished coal. Whatever might have been his fears yesterday, they had apparently vanished during the night. The Hunt that had moaned in terror, not knowing what to do with his hands, squeezing them one moment between his knees, and the next under his armpits, had become as chirrupy as a bird, and graciously he accepted Thurtell's offer of a hot rum and sugar.

"I trust you slept well?" he asked.

"Very well," lied Thurtell.

"Shows the effect of a good conscience," trilled Hunt. "Although, I must confess, my slumbers was a little disturbed by my chagrin at our failure yesterday to get to grips with a certain bloody major. A pleasure postponed, of course; and a pleasure missed can be a pleasure found, as the husband said when he threw his boot at his wife and hit her fancy man by mistake. On whom do we settle next?"

"I'll get Wood, if I can and when I can," growled Thurtell. "I'm waiting for Bill, want to know if the coward's bolted to Elstree or intends to meet us like a man, face to face and fist to fist."

"And while we're waiting to get Wood, who then?" asked Hunt, his eyes greedy as he watched his friend who yawned as though uninterested.

"I haven't decided yet," groaned Thurtell; "want to hear from Lemming before I start on Graham and Kelly; and I'd have to go to Norwich to do that bloody attorney, Springfield. Perhaps I'll see if I can catch Barber Beaumont before the trial comes off. I want to hear what Probert's got to say about Wood before I make up my mind."

It seemed that Probert would never come. Seconds became minutes and minutes hours while Thurtell and Hunt sipped their drinks and waited uneasily. Tom Thurtell joined them and, as usual, sank silently into his chair with a brief nod of greeting. Whether he were naturally taciturn or timid of speaking because of his stutter, Hunt could not decide; but the man's contemptuous, sullen attitude jarred on his usually high spirits. Even at his most extravagant jests or bawdy songs or most outrageous puns, Tom rarely smiled. He seemed a man aware of impending catastrophe who found himself helpless to save either himself or his friends but waited with fretful patience for the drop to open under his feet.

At last, when he was beginning to believe that the traps must have nippered him, Thurtell saw Probert stroll into the bar. His brown castor on the back of his head to show the thick dark hair brushed carelessly across the low slanting forehead, his chin high in the loose cravat, a sluggish smile on his heavy mouth that was always pouting as though faintly scornful of whatever company he might be in, he pushed his way to the corner in which Thurtell sat between Tom and Hunt.

"Where the hell have you been?" growled Thurtell, not stirring to answer his greeting or to call for a fourth glass.

"Where?" Probert raised his thick brows as though astonished by the question. "About your business, my dear fellow," he said. "Where else do you think?"

"My business? what do you mean?"

"I have been consoling the unhappy Major Wood," said Probert, putting on a rueful countenance. "The poor fellow languishes in the grip of bailiffs, the victim of some unprincipled, stony-hearted creditor called Curtis who swears that he owes him money. Wood, of course, denies it like a man. They always do, as the sheriff's officer explained to me over a pint; but when I learned that this Mr. Curtis was hurrying from the city to explain his ungentlemanly act, I thought it discreet to retire. So here I am."

This was one of the few occasions on which Probert had heard Thurtell laugh. At the thought of Wood in a sponging-house, Thurtell tossed back his head and cackled until he wept. Quickly, Hunt joined the merriment with a trilling, self-conscious sound as though he were the villain in a drama exulting over the hero's discomfiture. Probert grinned, pleased to find himself rewarded with Thurtell's approval; and only Tom remained unexcited. Unable to understand what the jest could possibly be in the wretched Wood having been nabbed on a false oath for a debt he didn't owe, he stared gloomily at his companions.

"That'll teach him," gasped Thurtell when able to speak again. "That's his first taste of what he's going to get. By God, today, if I can raise the wind, I'll buy a pair of pistols and shoot the bastard some night when he's going home to Castle Street."

"He's leaving Castle Street," said Probert. "Or so he told me."

"What! is he so lily-livered that he's sneaking off to hide in the country where Carrie's skirt might protect him? They'll not save him; though she cover him with her body, I'll shoot through two sets of guts, that's all, and pierce em both together."

"I'm afraid that'll have to wait," sighed Probert.

"For a time, perhaps; let things die down a little. I'll leave him for a month or two. Then, when he thinks he's safe, I'll get him when he least expects it."

"Even then it won't be easy, Jack," muttered Probert. "He recognized you yesterday and he'll be doubly on guard against you now."

"I don't believe it! If he'd recognized me, he'd have told the flats and had me boned."

"He talked about that." Uncomfortably, Probert shuffled in his

H

chair, his eyes looking at the table. "He knew it was you, all right; but he said he was keeping his muns shut because of Carrie. Seems to think she wouldn't like to have her name mauled in court."

"I don't believe it." Thurtell's face grew red, and his jowls swelled. "That's just gammon. Trying to pretend to her that he's a noble fellow, the bastard! If he's going to marry the mort, why should he care if her name stinks when he's the cause of the stink? He was fishing, that's what he was doing, trying to get you to say too much." Suddenly, he lunged across the table, his face so close to Probert's that their noses almost touched while he stared fiercely into his eyes. "You didn't say too much to him, did you, Bill?" he asked.

Sweating while he tried to assume an offended attitude, Probert returned the glare from Thurtell's little eyes.

"Of course I didn't," he growled. "Don't be a fool, Jack. I wasn't born yesterday. He got nothing out of me."

"I hope, for your sake, that's true," said Thurtell, slowly sitting back into his chair, but still intently, suspiciously watching Probert's large and friendly dog-like eyes.

"Well, if we can't get the major," groaned Hunt, "who can we do instead? Until we hear from Lemming, Kelly and Graham are out, and that lawyer-cove's too far away in Norwich. So I suppose it'll have to be Barber Beaumont again."

"Yes," growled Thurtell, still watching Probert, "I suppose so, blast it."

"D-d-don't, J-j-ack," exploded Tom suddenly. "Th-th-they'd k-k-know you did it. Th-th-the trial coming soon an-an-and him d-d-dying like that, they'd k-k-know you did it an-an-and they'd nab you quick."

"They won't nab me," smiled Thurtell, speaking in that gentle, faintly condescending way in which he always spoke to his brother, as though they were boys again when the few years between them had seemed unbridgeable. "But if we can get Beaumont out of the way," he said, "there's no evidence against us, except——" Darkly he looked up from under his jutting brows towards the bar on which Mary leaned her elbows and bosom, gazing into some feminine dream in the tobacco-smoke; and slowly, still watching her, he took a pinch of snuff and pushed it up his nostrils. "She'd not dare blab," he said slowly, but there was little assurance in his voice.

They all turned to look at Mary. Her hair appeared to be duller than usual, as though it were long since it was washed, and the rouge was carelessly rubbed into her cheeks, emphasizing the chalky colour and texture of the skin; her brown dress had been carelessly donned, one shoulder slipping down her arm, and the paint was smeared over her mouth. Rarely in the mornings did she trouble to undergo a careful toilet, waiting until late afternoon or evening when the more gentlemanly customers were likely to call.

"She knows I'd kill her if she blabbed," muttered Thurtell; and at that moment, Mary caught him looking at her, and she raised her brows contemptuously, then turned to give Probert a honeyed smile.

"You can trust her, all right," said Probert, with a chuckle. "Just leave her to me, my lad. I can handle her."

"Can't you think of anything but women, damn you?" Thurtell turned on him in a fury which surprised himself. "I'm sick of your damned mutton-mongering!" he cried. "Take her if you want to, but don't talk about it."

What was he angry about now? Probert lowered his eyelids but watched him through the lashes. Was he thinking of Carrie and Wood that he was becoming so hot about women and their pretty ways? or was he jealous of Mary? He had let the girl marry Walker, but that did not mean that he had necessarily surrendered all seignorial rights. Anyhow, some men—Probert knew the feeling well, suffering from it himself as he did—felt that once a woman had been theirs she had no right to look at other fellows, but for the rest of her lonely life she had to remain virtuous, doting on his memory. But never before had Thurtell shown a gleam of jealousy. No, this anger resulted from something else, from lack of sleep perhaps, or from fear?

"Let's get out of this place," said Thurtell suddenly, springing to his feet and tapping his castor on his head.

"Where do you want to go?" asked Hunt.

"Anywhere. I don't care. Anywhere, so long as it's away from here."

Yes, thought Probert with secret satisfaction, groaning as he hoisted himself to his feet: yes, the fellow was worried and that explained his irritability. In such a tense condition as this, he might do any reckless deed to explode his tormented feelings; and this was the moment, he felt, when the murder of which he and Hunt were forever talking might be brought near to consummation. He had only to wait, smiled Probert, to be friendly and keep silent, watching for the opportunity; for unless Thurtell robbed or killed someone of wealth, Probert's own future looked dark indeed. Wood was furious about the rent and any day now he might send the bums along, particularly as he suspected him as Thurtell's friend. Money had to be found, and quickly found; and the only man he knew savage enough and sufficiently reckless to kill for blunt was Thurtell, once he had been wrought to the sticking-point. Once on that point, his vanity could be relied on to keep him spinning there until the deed was consummated.

With Tom, Probert drifted along the streets behind the quickly striding Thurtell who had Hunt dancing beside him, walking apparently aimlessly, walking only because Thurtell could not keep his legs still. Down the Haymarket they went, and Probert for a moment wondered whether they were making for Castle Street. If that was the fool's intention, to assault Wood in his room, he decided that he had best quietly slip away; but Thurtell turned instead to the other side of the street, making for what in a gayer age had been the Spring Gardens where city-folk had come to drink and listen to the fiddlers; now, like the present age, it had turned degenerate, although there were still some fine houses there, such as the large, if decaying, Berkeley House to the north, and many of these houses opened on to St. James's Park.

They were going to Rexworthy's, decided Probert, and he wished he had some coins to risk, being fond of a game of billiards when he could find a novice to challenge. Anyhow, he thought, it would be better there in the warm than walking about doing nothing.

"Who're you going to play, Jack?" he shouted.

Thurtell paused, being far ahead with Hunt, and waited for the lazier pair to reach him.

"What do you mean, play?" he asked.

"Ain't you going to Rexworthy's?"

Thurtell looked about him as though for the first time realizing where he stood. Apparently, he had been striding on blindly, purely to walk the energy out of his legs.

"Yes," he said, his face brightening. "Let's see if Lemming's there."

Lemming was not there; but on one of the high seats that ran the length of one wall so that watchers could overlook the game on the green tables under the funnelled lights, Probert saw the small lean figure of William Weare. No one else, save Rexworthy himself, was present at this hour. The master of ceremonies and the spider were patiently waiting for the flies to enter, and they looked up hopefully at the noise of Thurtell and the others stamping in.

At sight of Weare, Thurtell stood stock still and his cheeks grew sallow. Behind him, Probert sidled close to his back and whispered, his sour breath hot on Thurtell's cheek:

"Looks like fate, don't it, Jack? the very cove what cleaned you of three hundred quid that night at blind hookey and told you to go thieving for some more when you asked him for a fiver back?"

Yes, Probert was right. As though fate, in this moment of wrath and despair, had relented towards him and led him to the sacrifice waiting to have its throat cut, there sat William Weare smiling amiably at him, the bastard! With the same tight kind of smile on that night of their first meeting had he told him to go thieving when the rogue's pockets had been heavy with his money. The sinews tightened on Thurtell's throat when he recalled that moment and the feeling of helplessness that had almost choked him while the little cheat had grinned up at him, at Old Flare, as though he were a flat who would not dare answer when insulted.

"Why," he cried with a merry smile, hand outthrust, "if it's not my old friend, Mr. Weare! How are you, Bill?"

"I'm all right," said Weare, limply taking his hand, shaking it and then dropping it as though it were a damp rag. "Things are pretty quiet at the moment, though. Feel like a game, Jack? We won't play for high stakes. Say, just for a few browns, eh? You should be able to manage that."

Thurtell stiffened at the insult which hurt the more because it was near the truth. Weare had heard—such news soon was whispered through St. James's—that he was cleaned out, and the rogue who had plucked him, who had left him open to ruin, now deliberately rubbed salt into that memory. Thurtell had been seeking a victim, keeping an open mind to take the first flat he might encounter, and this insult concentred all his hatred of society, his rage against fate and those wealthier or more fortunate than himself, upon this one small lean dark man with the contemptuous look in his cold dark eyes. Here was the victim he had sought, the true author of his downfall, the man who had taken from him the spoils with which he might have built a prosperous future. Often, idly, had he considered revenge as, in moments of rage, he swore to murder anyone who had ever thwarted him, but it had remained purely a thought, until now. This was the one man in England whom he would really delight in killing.

"Well," said Weare in his dry, supercilious manner. "Will you play me for a few browns, Mr. Thurtell?"

Trembling with excitement though he was at the thought that he was soon to kill this man, Thurtell yet managed to smile, and he found, when he spoke, that his voice sounded more than friendly, that it was almost caressing, in fact.

"I don't play for browns, Bill, any more than you do," he said, smiling. "I don't mind being honest with a friend. I'm cleaned out at the moment and need a flat, not a sharp like you. And that reminds me . . . you might be just the fellow for it . . ."

"For what?" asked Weare, with faint curiosity.

"We'll not talk of it here. Let's take a stroll. It's a fine day and I like the park, the flowers, the bees, the women, the guards in their red coats, the canal and its waterfowl. . . ."

"What the devil are you talking about!"

"I was trying to tempt you to take a stroll in the Park with me. I prefer it where there're only birds to listen to what you say, for I've a proposition might interest you: there's money in it. . . ."

"Money?" said Weare. "All right, if there's money in it. . . ."

"There's money enough," chuckled Thurtell. "Indeed, I hope to redeem my fortunes with this plot; and if you're interested . . . Don't go!" he called to Probert, Hunt and Tom. "We'll not be long. Wait here for me."

He needed a moment away from the room to give him time to plot, and he did not want Rexworthy to listen to what he was going to say. A large and amiable, but very cunning, dog, and an old friend of Weare's, Rexworthy could not always be trusted and he was liable to remember for future use any secrets he might chance to overhear.

Into the Park, Thurtell led Weare who followed reluctantly, and after they had walked a few yards, he turned with a tight smile, and said:

"I think we're safe here, Bill. Don't always like Rexworthy knowing too much, and if I talked in front of Probert and Joe Hunt, they'd want to be in it, too; and we want to keep it to ourselves. It's no good having others in when they've got no rhino in their pockets and only want some of the winnings without taking any of the risks."

"And you expect me to take these risks?" murmured Weare with his tight smile. "You are a queer cove, Thurtell."

"I'm like other men," said Thurtell. "I want to live. I'd not have you in on this, Bill, if I could help it; and that's the truth; but you're the only cove I know at the moment who's got any of the ready, and I need backing."

"I never lend," said Weare primly. "I told you that before."

Recollection of that insult sent the blood to Thurtell's cheeks, and Weare smiled the wider when he noticed it. To taunt such stupid oafs as this with their ridiculous belief in their superior cunning was always a pleasure he could not resist.

"I wasn't going to ask you to lend me anything," growled Thurtell, when anger permitted him to speak again. "I was going to suggest that we became partners for a day: that's all. It's like this. I've become acquainted with a young gentleman who's just come into possession of a large property, and he has an inclination to gambling. But the trouble is he can't be tempted to play unless it's for large stakes."

"Who is this young gentleman?" asked Weare, turning to stare into Thurtell's hidden eyes.

Thurtell grunted, grinning. "I may have been a flat once," he said, "but I ain't one any longer. D'ye really think I'd tell you his name so that you could scamper off on your lonesome and leave me high and dry? I'm not that kind of a fool."

"Well, when can I meet this . . . this young gentleman of yours?"

For all his suspicious nature, Weare was hooked. Thought himself cunning, did he, the cleverest sharp in London? Well, this time he was dealing with somebody sharper than himself. Thurtell chuckled deep in his throat and glanced sideways at his companion, noting with delight how bright his eyes had become, and how alert his manner.

"That's the trouble," he said. "This young gentleman don't like going to hells, doesn't trust em, and I told him he was right in that."

"Of course, of course," said Weare impatiently. "It's better to keep such a fellow to ourselves; don't want him plucked by every leg in town."

"That's what I thought," said Thurtell. "Now this gentleman, he lives in Hertfordshire—I'll tell you that much—has given me an invitation to go down to his country-house and to bring a friend with me for two or three days' shooting. You like shooting, don't you?"

Weare gave a brief nod. Everybody knew that he would ride any distance for a day's shooting. That was why he kept so many dogs in Lyon's Inn, in the hope of sport.

"So now you understand," said Thurtell. "Here I've got the kind of wealthy young flat a fellow dreams of plucking, and scarcely a brown in my pocket. But I can't let him go. I've been thinking hard for days who I might let in on it, but all my pals are as hard pressed as myself. If I could find somebody else, do you think I'd have asked you to join me?"

"No," said Weare, "I certainly wouldn't have expected it. That was why I was wondering. . . ."

"I've got to have some bank behind me. If you can provide the rhino, we could go down together and you could introduce cards, hazard, backgammon, what you like, after dinner, and we could make a famous thing of it."

In silence, frowning, Weare paced the grass beside the tall Thurtell who looked down on him with contempt and hope. The tale he had told rang true; and Weare notoriously could never resist the possibility of making money, even by honest means, so that when an offer like this was given, a wealthy young noodle and a week-end's shooting, he would have to succumb to the bait.

"All right," he growled at last. "I'll think about it."

They had reached the Chinese bridge which the king had built across the canal during his regency; and, with blind eyes, Weare stared at it as though he were counting the broken sticks. Knowing that he was turning over the proposition in his cautious mind, examining it from every point in search of flaws, Thurtell said nothing.

"Yes," said Weare again, "I'll think about it."

"Better not think too long," jeered Thurtell. "I might meet somebody else with a pocketful of the ready; so you'd better make up your mind here and now. I'm not going to hang about for weeks waiting for you."

"All right," said Weare abruptly, "I'll do it. When do we go?"

His relief and joy was such that Thurtell could have sung aloud. The cautious, the miserly Weare had been gammoned! he had agreed to ride to his death!

"You'll have to bring all the money," he said. "I've got nothing."

"Yes, I can do that. . . ." A doubt had crept again into Weare's voice at the mention of his bringing money with him. "But wouldn't it be safer to play for I.O.U.s?" he asked.

"That's the end of it!" cried Thurtell. "We'll talk no more about it. I'll send to Lemming, he's never one to haggle at a bargain. I.O.U.s, indeed! so that the fool can wake up with a sick head in the morning and stop the cheque at his banker's! If that's your way of doing business, Bill Weare, it ain't mine; so I'll give you good-bye and a thank-you and have a look for Lemming——"

"Don't be too hasty, damn it!" Weare glared at him, biting his lip. "I'm taking all the risk, aren't I? and what are you doing?"

"Taking a greater risk, introducing you to my flat. I was a fool to think of it!"

"Don't be so bloody hasty, and leave Lemming out of this. I know for a fact that he's down at Margate at the moment, operating from there, so you couldn't bring him in if you wanted to. When do we start?"

"I've told you, I wash my hands of it. . . ."

"Don't be a fool. I'll put up the rhino." He placed his lean, strong fingers on Thurtell's forearm and he tried to smile winningly. "Come on, Jack, when do we set off?" he asked wheedlingly.

"Well," muttered Thurtell, "if you're really set on it, and no damned talk of I.O.U.s, I should say in about a week. . . ."

"No earlier!"

"You don't want to rush it. I've got to see him again first, remind him of the invitation, tell him how much you like shooting, and let him suggest a date. We don't want to make him think we're too eager."

"No," said Weare, "you're right;" and he smiled, his suspicions vanishing. This fool was as clear as glass, even though he might be dirty glass, and it had been absurd of him to think that such a simpleton as Thurtell could act a part so convincingly.

But what Weare did not know was that all his life Thurtell had been attracted to the stage and that he prided himself on his imitations of the tragedian, Charles Kean, which, at the smallest prompting, he would perform in any company, even in professional company. And the part he favoured most, the skin which he believed most closely fitted him, was that of Shakespeare's King Richard the Third who boasted that he could seem a saint when most he played the villain.

CHAPTER ELEVEN

STRATEGIC RETREAT

COCK-A-HOOP, merry, smiling often, John Thurtell had lost his sullen, withdrawn manner. The man who, save when with intimates, remained usually silent, wary, distrustful, seemed delighted to meet others and was able even to talk on everyday topics that did not touch him personally. Hunt danced at his side, shrill with merriment, like a little dog, thought Probert derisively, gambolling and yapping for his master's occasional condescending pat. All his talk was of "Turpin lads" and of cutting throats and slitting people up; and, listening to him as an indulgent father might listen to the prattle of a favourite son, Thurtell would smile and cock his head, seeming to purr with inward satisfaction.

Like a schoolboy waiting impatiently for holidays to start, Thurtell could not remain still; an inward excitement, an expectation of wonderful adventures kept him strained like an over-keyed instrument whose strings might snap at any moment. Ay, thought Probert, at any moment, at somebody's careless word, at a suspected slight, he would be liable to spring up with those huge fists clenched for hitting or open for throttling.

His distrust of Probert remained, although it was not so strong as formerly. No longer did Probert seem to hang back, entering only now and then with an air of condescension into his and Hunt's plotting. Of the three, however, Hunt had become the most enthusiastic, for there were occasions when poverty, the continual threat of bailiffs to his home in Golden Square and the blank future ahead, robbed him of his professional entertainer's mask of clown and left him bogged in self-pity and in terror; and the necessity to wait until all details should have been perfected irritated both him and Thurtell into bursts of unnecessary anger and railing against the gods who withheld from them their hearts' desire.

"You're not the only ones that's worried," shrugged Probert. "If I don't pay Wood some of the back-rent soon, I'll be in the street; and I've got a larger family than yours to maintain, Joe. But it's no good putting on a sour face about it. The means of escape are in our own hands and we must take em."

"Ay," said Thurtell. "If it's true that the bastard always carries his cash with him——"

"It's well known," murmured Probert. "Everybody knows it. Weare don't trust banks."

"And if the sums are as much as they say," continued Thurtell, "there should be four or five hundred pounds apiece in it for us; and that's no bad thing."

"No," said Probert, "it ain't, it's just about what I need, just the sum to get me out of my present difficulties."

"I've never handled so much money in my life," sighed Hunt; then with a half-hearted attempt at joviality which failed because it sprang from no jovial heart, "There's not that much money in the world," he said.

The three men remained silent, eyes blank as though they were tranced amongst the shouting and the clink of metal and earthenware and glass about them in the Cock. They did not see the other drinkers, their thoughts turning inward, contemplating the rich fruits which a few hundred pounds could bring. A new suit of clothes for Hunt, clean linen, good food and expensive wines, and the chance to appear at some important theatre to prove his genius before applauding multitudes. For Probert, it would mean a certain freedom from debt—he could not conceive complete freedom from debt—and, at the least, about two hundred strange women to investigate at their leisure and his comfort. To Thurtell alone the money meant little. He scarcely considered it, save to think that it would be pleasant not to have to worry about what he had to spend and to be able to awe St. James's with his prodigality; his thoughts were concentrated on the killing of Weare and on the bloody splendour that afterwards would follow him through life. The deed would soon become known as his, of course. Except from the traps, he did not want it hidden. No, let him be recognized as Weare's killer, the demon whom it was dangerous to disturb, the man who carried death in his fists.

Then, by God, he felt, he could be happy. Often now with Probert did he drive to Elstree, surveying the fields and lanes and coppices, seeking the perfect murder-spot; but never once did he glimpse Caroline. Around the major's property he prowled, watching to snare the man he hated; but, like his betrothed, Wood did not appear to be killed. On earlier occasions, he and Probert, at Wood's invitation, had shot on these grounds, stuffing their bags with birds and rabbits only, while the one at whom they should have fired had stalked at their side and refreshed them afterwards with claret and cold chicken. No longer were such invitations offered to Probert or any visitor at Gill's Hill Cottage. The major presumably had vanished, although Thurtell learned at the Artichoke that he had not yet left the district.

"O, he's still there," said the landlord, slow-speaking but sharp-eyed Robert Field who rarely talked but was always listening, "but seems he's got a terror of burglars, so he's moving to Aldenham; ain't that so, John?"

A tall, shambling, toothless labourer seated on a low stool raised his dirty face from the rim of his mug.

"Ay," he said, "got mantraps laid. I says to him the other day, I says: 'These here are dangerous things, major, to have lying about.' Says he: 'That's why I have em, cause they're dangerous.' 'You never know,' says I, 'they might snap off the leg of some poor fellow's dog,' I says. 'They ain't there for dogs,' says he; and he wouldn't say nothing more. Ain't that so, Dick?"

"Ay," said the labourer at his side, a man as ragged and dirty as his friend. "Never does say much, he don't; talks at you as though you was the army and him the colonel. Shouts at you, too, even when you ain't deaf. But a terrible foe he'd make if he didn't like a man. There won't be no poaching in those woods, no more."

Thurtell raised his eyebrows and glanced at Probert who gave him a scarcely perceptible wink.

"Probably got somebody's wife hiding with him," chuckled Probert, "and don't want any husbands nosing about."

The labourers laughed, glancing knowingly at one another. On the bar, the landlord leaned, seeming to take great interest in a flyblown poster pasted to the wall, advertising Old Tom for sluicing the kidneys.

"Don't know about wives," giggled Dick after Thurtell had ordered gins to be tipped into their ale, "but I knows a woman what works in the major's kitchen. You know her, Mr. Field; Jem Freeman's old woman, the one that has rheumatics and fell down the well."

The landlord took no heed. As though enrapt, he stared at Old Tom's announcement on the wall.

"Course he knows her," said the other labourer. "Don't he have to throw her out every week-end after she starts hitting Mrs. Merle over the head because she can't forget what she saw her husband doing with her the night the rick caught fire and she found what was happening between em in the ditch?"

"This Mrs.—er, this lady, she works for the major?" asked Probert.

"Ay, that she does," said Dick solemnly, "and she's the one what's seen this young woman there. I ain't seen her myself, but . . . What you making faces at me for, Mr. Field? I ain't done nothing yet."

Whatever faces the landlord might have been making at him, they were no longer to be seen when Thurtell and Probert looked at the bar. Robert Field remained impassive, apparently spellbound by Old Tom's message of good will to kidneys.

"Of course," groaned the other labourer. "Your gob was always too large for anything but lushy, Dick. So shut it now."

" What the hell have I said? I was only saying about this young woman at the major's. . . ." Gradually, his chin drooped, his eyes grew round, and in consternation he looked from his friend to the landlord, to Probert. "Must have been another young woman," he muttered. "That one wouldn't have acted so shameless, even if she did think herself alone with her fancy man. No, it was someone with the same face as her, only it weren't her, if you know what I mean . . ."

His voice stumbled to nothing and he sought refuge in his pot, drinking very slowly to conceal his face while his friend mumbled about bloody fools what couldn't keep their mouths shut. Only the buzzing of a lazy bee was heard beating against the light glimmering through the thick twisted glass of the jalousied windowpane, until Thurtell suddenly set down his glass on the bar and strode out on to the road.

"There! look what you've done, big mouth," Probert, hurrying after Thurtell, heard the landlord growl. "Sending good custom off with your slack-jaw. Time you got to work again, cleaning the bloody roads. . . ."

With long strides, Thurtell was pacing up and down the grassy plot before the tavern. His face was dark as a gipsy's when he turned to look at Probert with murder in his little eyes.

"That was her," he said, his voice trembling. "Her that was so bloody high and mighty, touch-me-not, and all that, like something at the Surrey Theatre or out of some damned ladies' magazine, and playing the whore with him, that coward! ay, teasing me and singing cock-a-doodle-do once I was away. Women . . . ah, how can you trust em! shameless! with peasants like those in there sniggering over her doings! Has she no shame whatever?"

"You don't know . . . it's only talk. . . . Mightn't have been her at all," clucked Probert, worried at seeing Thurtell's hatred being again diverted towards less remunerative ends.

"Of course it was her! Don't you start trying to defend the bitch!" So furious, almost lunatic, was the flame in Thurtell's little eyes when he turned on him, that Probert went back a step. "She'll not get away with this!" Thurtell shouted. "I'll let her know I ain't deceived by her pussy-lying! I never did trust the woman."

"It mayn't have been her. . . ."

"Don't come that over me, you fool," snarled Thurtell. "Who else could it have been? It stands to reason, don't it? She's going to marry the cove, ain't she? Think he'd risk having other females about the place with her nosing about? And if she ain't living there, where is she living? Tell me that."

Wearily, Probert shrugged. "She's with her aunt," he said.

"And where's her aunt live?"

"I don't know. I'll find out. . . ."

"Ay, find out quickly. I'll call on her one night with a razor up my sleeve and I'll beg a farewell kiss. And when she lifts her chin for me to lip, I'll up with my razor. 'How'd you best like to die?' I'll ask her; and before she can say she don't like the idea at all, I'll slide it across, quick, and watch her eyes to see what a woman looks like when she's croaking. . . . If I leave a letter for her, will you see she gets it?" he demanded suddenly.

"Of course, of course, old man. . . ."

"Good. I'll have some ripe things to say to her, by glory!"

Mental composition of that letter gagged Thurtell for the remainder of their walk back to Gill's Hill Cottage; and after dinner, he sat alone in the wilderness at the back with paper, pen and a bottle of ink, tearing up and cursing page after page, to Probert's distress. Watching him from the window, biting his nails, Probert calculated the cost of each sheet thrown away, and he could not keep still as the sum began to mount. The way the fool was going on, there'd soon be no paper left in the house; although, he sighed, that would probably be the best thing, after all, as he had no intention of forwarding whatever the fool wrote.

Thurtell must have suspected this meditated treachery, for when at last he had penned a missive to his satisfaction, he gave it to Anne Noyes to deliver. She had strolled from the house and stood beside an over-grown rose-bush with twined boughs like green thorny snakes in and out into a giant knot which no one could have unravelled. Without her bonnet, her black curls gleamed in the sun with a bluish gloss, and her skin was faintly freckled. At first sight of her through the bushes, he had thought her Caroline and had begun to tremble, then she had raised her head and he had seen that wrinkled skin over the right eye which, to his taste, made her repulsive, like a witch.

"Writing poesy, Mr. Thurtell?" she asked in her faintly jeering, yet sweet voice. "Ah, what it is to be young and handsome and a man with all the ladies at his feet!"

As usual, she was jeering at him and he wriggled uncomfortably under the mocking smile. Of course, the bitch knew that Caroline had maced him over the major, and now she crowed her petty feminine triumph in pride of her sister and her sex. The letter he had been about to ask her to deliver to Caroline, he slipped into his pocket.

"I am no writer of poetry, ma'am," he said gruffly. "And I am neither very young nor handsome, and if ladies fall at my feet, which they don't, they have only themselves to blame if I trample them. You have a sour velvet, ma'am, and a cat's lick on a man's feelings. This was a letter I was writing to your sister."

"To dear Caroline!" said Anne with a deep sigh that raised her bosom to show its shape through the thin cloth; and Thurtell was surprised to note its beauty. When a woman had only one ogle a man was liable to notice nothing else, which was scarcely fair, although natural enough. Poor bitch, he thought, she'd never get a man: was that why her tongue was gall; and she so well-shaped, too, with pretty velvet curls on her sconce. . . .

"Would you like me to deliver it for you?" she asked, turning aside from his intent scrutiny. "Let me play Cupid, sir, although . . . I give full warning, my sister, being the beauty of the family, has a . . . well, let us say she is a little vain, a little too too feminine, but doubtless, and naturally, that is what you most admire in the dear puss. I will see that she takes it into her own hand."

Yes, he could trust her to do that. She had no love for Caroline. How could she, one-eyed jealousy in the family of Venus?

Watching her one eye carefully, he drew the letter from his pocket and placed it in her hand. She would read it, of course. That was to be expected; but he was not ashamed, indeed, he was proud of what he had written and it might tickle her spinster's heart to be loved by proxy, if only in words.

"Pray," he said, "do not show it to Mr. Probert."

"I will show it to no one," she said, "other than to my dearly beloved sister. I promise you, sir."

"Is—is she living with—is she marrying Major Wood?" he muttered. "I heard talk in the Artichoke."

"Then you had best ask the Artichoke, Mr. Thurtell," said she, smiling with pale lips.

"Excuse me, ma'am," he mumbled, "but I must be going;" and with an abrupt bow, he pushed past her back to the house. Behind him, he heard the rustle of her gown when she moved and he knew that she had turned to watch him with her gimlet-eye; and he wondered whether he had been right to trust her. . . .

He felt extremely proud of that letter. His first attempts had been merely abusive; through ink he had expended much of his rage until, becoming calmer, he had been able to realize that insults would never bring a girl into his arms, nor would they even worry her. More likely she would accept them as flattery, as proof of her feminine witchery that she could drive a man demented. Better, he decided, to write to her with dignity, with passion and a faint reproach that might touch her cruel heart to pity and regret at her scatterbrained refusal of so noble an admirer.

"Dear Miss Noyes," he had written, after long cogitation deciding against both the familiarity of "Caroline" and the manly honesty of "Bitch."

"Dear Miss Noyes, I have this morning suffered a deadly blow and had I not feared to spread the scandal further by chastising the clown I would have killed him for it, for pausing with my good friend, your brother in law, William Probert, to partake of refreshment at the Artichoke in Elstree I was struck all of a heap to hear your fair name discussed infamously in this public place. The clowns were unworthy of my whip or I would have whipped them. For they said—— No, I will not soil this virgin page by writing on it what their vile lips said about you as a permanent resident, an unhallowed partner, in the abode of Major Wood, the serpent. That this was voluntary on your part I cannot believe but I am burnt to the soul that you should, even when unconscious, drugged or hit on the head, have allowed his infamous designs to be . . ." Unable to recollect how one spelt "consummated," he hurriedly, as though to pin the word down with his pen, had added "culminated," hoping that it meant the same thing; and had concluded with, "your obedient, unhappy and surprised servant, J. Thurtell, Esq."

When in the evening he drove back to London through the twilight beside Probert in his gig with the big bay horse, Thurtell's blood was cool again, his rage having been diluted into ink, and with a certain pity he contemplated Caroline's consternation when she read his letter and found that her incontinence was known and had become the jest of country clowns in taverns. Almost could he pity her, seeing her in his imagination crumple the letter in her hand as, weeping for shame, she slid in a swoon to the floor. Well! she had only herself to blame if her reputation stank. He had behaved honourably towards her, there was nothing for which she could reproach him. When she opened her eyes to what she had done and realized how she had ruined her future hopes of heaven and dishonoured her name forever on earth, he hoped she would not act too rashly. Roses, after all, can have a second flowering, and repentance can bring renewed innocence even to the most fallen female. Death was so damnably final, and she was too choice a bit of muslin to do herself in while she was in her prime and he was prepared to forgive her if she married him and let him use her money.

Such magnanimity of spirit on his part kept Thurtell in good humour with himself and the world for a day or two while he awaited Caroline's reply. Whenever he saw the blue-uniformed postman, he stiffened with pleasurable anticipation; and when by the third day he had received no answer, he felt furiously assured that Anne Noyes had betrayed him. He wrote again—even more indulgent and forgiving this time—and he inscribed it with her name in a disguised hand and gave it himself to the postman when at five o'clock he came, ringing his bell.

The following day he received his answer by the hand of Probert's boy, and, lounging back in his chair, his knees against the table, he split the seals. Out dropped two letters. Two sealed letters. Two un-opened letters. His unopened letters.

Dazedly, he looked up, staring at the beams across the ceiling, and blinked. Then suddenly he saw Mary watching and he knew by her intent expression that she had been watching him for some time. She had seen the letter arrive, had seen him seize it eagerly from the boy, tear it with his thumb, letting the enclosures fall, and then search furiously for a message that was not there. A slow malicious smile was on her small, pursed lips, and he knew that she was humming to herself, exulting over his disappointment, for, being a woman, she would have guessed by his agitation that he must have expected either

I

a love-letter or some money. The letters falling to the floor, their
seals intact, would have told her the truth, or sufficient of the truth to
assuage her jealous heart.

He would not be cheated of his revenge. He would write again and
again, and Caroline's woman's curiosity must in time succumb to
temptation until she would be impelled to read what he had written
to her. Her womanly curiosity, however, seemed made of iron.
Back came, intact, each of his further letters.

His rage and disappointment at this insult, this contemptuous
silence from a woman lost to all shame, abandoned to the arms of a
doubtless profligate major, ruined of womanhood and innocence . . .
his rage, the more he considered such behaviour, became almost un-
controllable. Forgotten was his hatred of Weare, almost forgotten his
intention of murdering the man; he could think of little beyond this
faithless, abandoned creature, this worse than whore, and of ways
whereby he might exact revenge on her or on her keeper.

Moody, dangerous to disturb with ordinary conversation, he was
like a caged lion with ginger on its tail, everything save his feeling
of being wronged forgotten; and thus, to Probert's despair, would
he have remained had not a tipstaff from the court run with a
warning one afternoon in the Cock. Thurtell had slipped the man
money to keep him primed about any proceedings that might
be brought against him; and it was fortunate that he had taken this
precaution.

Days of dreaming were over. Here, unavoidable, came the hour to
action. An indictment for the fire conspiracy had been found against
him and Tom, the man said; and the officers were on their way to
lumber them.

When Tom heard, he trembled, his face like dough between the
chestnut whiskers, and he could not speak. Hunt gaped, ready to do
whatever he was told by Thurtell, and Probert sat grimly nodding his
head with an exasperating I-told-you-so air.

"We've got to clear," cried Thurtell. "At once."

"That's all right," smiled Probert. "I've got it all arranged. I'll
mention no names here, there are long ears at the bar, but come with
me. Both of you. I know where you can hide out."

"I must get my clothes, my stick, my gloves——"

"I'll fetch em later," said Probert. "The traps'll be here any
moment now, and then it'll be too late."

"Yes, yes," cried Thurtell, "come, Tom! Come, Joe! Let's mizzle quick. Thank God I paid that cove to give me the office when the traps were coming!"

Pushing back his chair, he squeezed around the table after Tom and bumped into Mary.

"What are you doing?" he snarled. "Get back behind your bar."

"Not until you tell me where you're going," she said.

"Get out of my way——"

"I'm not getting out of the way, Mr. Thurtell, not until I know where you're running off to. I heard that cove. He said that the traps are after you; and about time, too; but before you go, I want to know what's going to happen to us and the Cock."

"I don't care a damn what happens to you."

"You'd better care, you'd better bloody well care," she said.

He blinked at her, not understanding what she meant. "Get out of the way," he growled again, "or I'll give you one."

"I'll give you more than one, you flat, you!" she cried, her voice rising to a scream. "I'll tell Mr. Beaumont what you done. Why should you leave me and Bill here to starve and face the bums while you sneak off with our cash? You've drunk the tavern into liquidation, you and your dirty friends, and now you're leaving us with nothing but bad debts."

"I'll send you money——"

"You was always good at promises, the great John Thurtell, Old Flare, the good fellow, the dirty, rotten, cowardly rooster! That's what you are, John Thurtell!" she howled. "All wind and bellowing. The things you promised me! I was going to have my own carriage, wasn't I? I was going to have a dozen footmen and ride in the Park? Yah! Froth and bleating, lies, all of it! You Swell Yokel, you, you always were a flat and you've been the bad joke of St. James's and the Garden; and you've ruined me, took me from Norwich where I was queen and brought me down to this! I'll not keep my velvet quiet. Why the hell should I!"

He struck without meaning to. Something within him, some force within his arm, sent his fist against her jaw and tumbled her over in a froth of skirts and petticoats, chairs and tables toppling about her as she fell, coves and their covesses darting off and holding their drinks high lest they spill a drop.

"Y-y-you f-f-fool!" wailed Tom. "No-no-now she'll go to B-b-beaumont!"

"Come on, for the love of God!" Probert gripped Thurtell's arm and dragged him towards the door. "You've done enough damage," he growled. "You don't want the traps to get you, do you?"

With a blind stare in his eyes, Thurtell squared his great shoulders and glowered about the room.

"I'm here," he growled. "I'm here if anybody wants a battle with me."

Nobody answered. Behind the protection of the bar, Mary's husband slunk back, while on the filthy sawdust Mary lay, faintly moaning.

"I'm here," said Thurtell again, his voice rising. "Swell Yokel, am I? Let any cove call Old Flash a swell yokel to his face! Come on, now! Who's the first what's going to be killed! I'm waiting for you."

Still, nobody answered. Nobody moved. With a toss of his head, Probert, Tom and Hunt dodging at his heels, Thurtell turned towards the door, shouldering through the drinkers who shrank back, heads down. With deliberately slow steps, so that anyone might have the opportunity to challenge him before he left, he walked to the open door, the noisy street outside.

"Sw-sw-swell . . . swell bloody yokel!" rasped a woman's voice.

Fists up, Thurtell swung round; and he saw Mary droop before the bar, her metallic hair straggling down her white cheeks, and her bosom heavily panting, while she held her jaw.

"You always was a flat," she jeered; "and you always will be a flat because you think you're clever, don't you? The Swell Yokel! that's all you are, still a bloody yokel, plucked raw by clever coves like Bill Weare. You deserve what you've got and I hope they hang you for it."

The blood vanished from Thurtell's cheeks, leaving them chalky white, and with difficulty he breathed. As though about to answer her, he stepped forward; then he shut his mouth and abruptly turned on his heel.

Into the blinding sunlight he stepped, Mary's shrill voice following him, crying: "The Swell Yokel! the bloody yokel, Jack Thurtell, the Swell Yokel!" and he wished that she had been a man so that he could have returned and killed her then.

CHAPTER TWELVE

THE BAIT IS SWALLOWED

FROM Regent Street to Bond Street ran Conduit Street and on the corner of Conduit Street and Mill Street stood the Coach and Horses. Here gathered the riffraff of the sporting world, legs and rooks and dismissed jockeys and bruisers with puffy faces, slitted eyes and ears like deformities. Nearby, on the corner of Conduit and George Street, was Limmer's Hotel, a down-at-heel Tattersalls where nothing, day or night, was heard save the lingo of the turf, and where men with not very clean hands made up their books. It was one of the grimiest hotels in London; but in its gloomy, comfortless coffee-rooms might be seen members of the rich squirearchy who visited the city during the sporting season. Frequently, the place was so crowded that even Lord Midas found it difficult to hire a couch; and if a bed was not to be had, there was always, for consolation, heaped plates of old English fare, beef or mutton, boiled or roasted, with excellent wines and a famous gin-punch.

The nearby Coach and Horses served as a sort of tap to the grand, if dirty, splendour of Limmer's. While the gentlemen put up at Limmer's, their coachmen and grooms met in the Coach and Horses to argue matters of horseflesh and the ring in language equally as outrageous as their masters'. And here it was that Probert had arranged for the Thurtell brothers to hide while the traps sought them at the Cock and in their other haunts. The landlord, Mr. Charles Tetsall, was an amenable man, if well paid to keep his mouth shut, and he asked few questions of his lodgers. "Gemmen want to keep out of the way for a short time," had been Probert's explanation when he produced these new lodgers; and Tetsall had gravely nodded, asking no questions but shaking the Thurtell brothers' hands without troubling to inquire whether they were wanted for theft, perjury, forgery, arson, rape, manslaughter or murder.

Here they would remain safe from anything except betrayal or their own bravado. Tetsall could be relied on to keep a good look out and to deny knowing them should any questions be asked. In two upstairs rooms, each containing two beds, a small table, two small

133

chairs, a fireplace, and a window opening on to Conduit Street, the brothers glumly settled and called for rum punch to console them in misfortune. At this sudden fall from freedom and all the lushy he could drink without having to pay for it, John Thurtell felt vicious and resentful. He sulked, lying most of the time, day and night, on his bed with his coat and boots off, glaring at the ceiling and occasionally cursing in a slow, unemphatic way as though the curses were merely a part of his breathing. Tom slouched about the rooms, unable to sit down for long, often sighing and groaning and drumming his fingers exasperatingly on the table.

Here, time stood still. Day or night did not matter. They could not venture out, save with lapels pulled high and hats pulled down, and neither man was ever talkative, even when they felt gay. Even at meals they rarely spoke and, in silence, they passed each other their snuff-boxes without being asked for a pinch, as though words were not needed in their mutual understanding.

From the street they could hear throughout the day the clop of horses' hoofs, the creak of carts and the clink and whine of harness, with men shouting, laughing, cursing, jesting, greeting one another with affectionate insults and talking all the while of horses, hounds, fighting-cocks and bruisers. This was the Thurtells' world, and they felt cosily at home in such an atmosphere, liking the stinging reek of horses' urine and the sweetness of golden manure spangling the air. Only now they were shut out from it all, prisoners above a rowdy paradise, dreaming of a golden key miraculously falling into their laps and opening the door to lost freedom.

That Tom did not abuse him rankled with Thurtell. He would have preferred an open quarrel to this accusing silence that left him in a misery of self-torment. He should not have struck Mary and thereby turned her into an enemy. Should she give evidence for the County Fire Office, as perhaps she might in her vindictiveness, they had no possible hope of escaping conviction on the conspiracy charge of burning down the warehouse. She knew everything that had happened in Watling Street. Fool! at the time, he had trusted her, he had talked openly in front of her, laughing with her at his cleverness in rooking the insurance company. And now, for them to make certain of winning the fight, he would have to kill, not only Barber Beaumont, but perhaps Mary as well. The roll of his future victims seemed to lengthen every few days.

Who first? Undoubtedly, Weare, although Thurtell would have

preferred to have tackled Wood; but to open and to carry on his campaign of murder, a certain capital was required. Only Weare could supply that capital. Once possessed of his swag and their most dangerous debts settled, he would feel encouraged to kill Beaumont and Mary. Then, he could turn on the others who had turned against him. But first, decidedly, had to come Weare who carried a fortune hidden in his clothes. With his blunt, they could put up the bail and be given time to act in their own defence.

Such little money was needed for his peace of mind. Less than a thousand, all told. Yet even this small sum his damned fate grudged him. Now that he had learned all the tricks of the town, he could have amassed a fortune in no time, if only someone, fate or Caroline or Weare, would have given him the capital with which to invade Jermyn Street and its citadels of sharpers. And because fate denied him this one small favour, he was being forced to kill to learn a living, dammit! . . . And poor Tom; poor, innocent Tom and his two little girls would have to suffer with him. That was not fair, by God!

"Tom," he said suddenly, "I've been thinking. . . ."

Wearily, Tom raised his head from his hands and looked with dull eyes at his brother.

"I've been thinking, Tom . . . I've not done right by you, I haven't. I shouldn't have spoken my mind to Mary and smashed her one. I've got to put that right; and I will. Don't you worry. Leave it all to me."

"I-I-I've al-al-always left everything to you," groaned Tom, "an-an-and look where we are now!"

"It's not for long. Only till I can raise the bail."

"Y-y-you raise the bail!" cried Tom; and he laughed.

That mocking laugh surprised and disappointed Thurtell. Never before had Tom made the faintest criticism of his conduct; always had he unquestioningly followed him, accepting his superior judgment on any question. But now he mocked at him. . . .

"Yes," he cried with sudden energy, "I'll raise it! I know a cove where I can get it from."

"If-if-if you mean by mur-mur-murdering Weare," scoffed Tom, "you're the one that's l-l-likely to be murdered! W-w-Weare's no flat. Y-y-you thought I didn't know what you was plotting wi-w-with Pr-pro-Probert and that lit-lit-little bastard, Hunt——"

"Joey's all right!"

"J-j-joe'll see you swing yet, Jack. He'd peach on his mother if-if-if'd save his own neck. You-you-you're the flat, you fool."

Thurtell gaped at him, and felt his cheeks blaze. Too astonished to speak, he could only gape at his brother, as though not believing that he had heard correctly.

"Yes, a f-f-flat," said Tom with a certain smugness. "Mary was right: you're only a s-s-swell yokel and l-lo-look where you've landed us!"

"I'll not be angry with you. I'll keep my temper." Half-choking, Thurtell managed with difficulty to jerk out the words. "I can see I've been much to blame," he said, "and you're right to be annoyed with me. But a man's luck don't always run downhill. We've just been unfortunate, that's all; our luck's bound to change soon. When things seem black one should always look to the future. You can't say I haven't worked and schemed; I have; and what I'm going to do next to fill our pockets is going to be done by me on my very own. I'm not having you mixed in it."

"Th-tha-thank you for once," sniggered Tom.

"No," said Thurtell, very seriously; "it may be all dickey with us at the moment, but don't lose heart. I'll raise the wind before we're much older, ay: I'll be coming back one night with a swag to make your heart turn to ginger. I know I shouldn't have slapped Mary; but she shouldn't have said what she done. I made her what she is, didn't I? Now, it'll serve the slut right to start walking the piazzas again and get rid of some of the lard that's grown on her in the Cock. And if she thinks she's going to turn evidence against me . . . she'll have to learn to talk through her throat after I've sliced it open."

"O, sh-sh-shut up," groaned Tom. "You and that Hunt cove al-al-always t-ta-talking about cutting throats and being Tur-tur-Turpin lads! I-I-I'm sick of it. Y-y-you couldn't kill a mouse."

"Tom, you don't know what you're saying!" Aghast to hear his own brother say such things, Thurtell sat up and looked sadly at him. "I've been a soldier," he cried, "I've seen death and have never flinched from it. I've told you before about the storming of St. Sebastian's; that was bloody warfare, cut and thrust, man to man, up and down the streets that was slippery with gore. I spied a Polish officer—I've told you this dozens of time—and how I seen him leaning on a wall, wounded all over and out of breath. I thought by the look of him he must be a man of rank, thought I, and must have some blunt about him; so I stuck my sword into his ribs and settled him; and I found a hundred and forty doubloons on him; and damned good booty that was!"

"I—I—I don't believe a word of it," said Tom.

"What's that? what's that? you don't believe it!"

"You ne-ne-never was at St. Sebastian, you ne-ne-never sniffed a battle in all your bl-bl-bloody life," sneered Tom; and, with an air of deep satisfaction, he took a pinch of snuff.

"If you weren't my brother," howled Thurtell, "I'd do you for that, by God!"

Tom shrugged, tightly smiling, and took refuge in a most insulting silence.

"By God," groaned Thurtell after a long pause, shaking his head, and looking indignantly at his brother, "I never expected this of you, Tom! I thought I had a real friend in you, I did, even though you was my brother; and after all I've done for you!"

With a bitter laugh, he lay back on the pillows. After this, he felt, no treachery could ever surprise him. To say that he hadn't killed the Polish officer at St. Sebastian was the final blow that knocked him for the count. Of course it was true; he had not killed the man, nor had he been at the storming of St. Sebastian; that was beside the point. True or not did not matter when his word stood in question. Tom told lies, all men told lies, but it was an accepted, unwritten rule amongst gentlemen that each accepted the others' lies and never openly doubted a word.

He closed his eyes and lay as though dead, scarcely seeming to breathe; but under the closed lids he was very much alive, watching a hateful version of the past, a madman's dance to death, hopes reached and lost, love put by and the future resting in a dice-box. He'd not repine. Despite all the hell he had suffered, his had been a good life, a life of action, of taking and giving, and to hell with tomorrow! From boyhood had he been a scamp, leader in mischief when at the grammar school. Learning he had found tiresome and, to this day, his spelling and orthology were not always of the best; but a man was not judged by his grammar or the number of his "Gs" that went into "mulligrubs" when everybody understood that it meant that you wanted to spew.

Heavy-hearted with sorrow and indignation that his own brother could so unjustly have misjudged him, he lay throughout the afternoon and evening, pretending to sleep, until he heard Hunt and Probert noisily enter. Let Tom do the entertaining, he thought angrily. Let him be the leader of the Thurtell brothers for once and see if he could manage any better on his own.

"Well, Jack," cried Probert in a doleful voice, looking down at the still figure on the bed. "I've come to tell you that it's off."

"What's this?" All pretence of sleep was flung aside. Thurtell sat erect with a jerk. "What's this you say?" he cried.

"It's off: that's all." Gloomily, Probert sat on the end of the bed and, with the spoon, scraped what dregs he could out of the punch-bowl. "I've got to get out of Gill's Hill Cottage any day now," he said. "A pity! You couldn't have picked a better spot for a job like that if you'd searched all England. Whatever's done there need never be found out. I told you that I kept a private jigger there once, and it wasn't ever discovered."

"What the hell do you mean?" shouted Thurtell. "Why is it off?"

"You've waited too long, that's what it is." Probert spoke sadly yet without reproach. "I've got to get out or I'll have the bums in. Bloody Major Wood's moving and he's sold the lease to that bastard Heward of Hatton Garden. I've known him for years; and what's worse, he knows me."

"Where the hell's Wood going to?"

"He's taken everything to a house he has near Aldenham, near Watford. Needs a bigger place for his bride, he tells me."

Trembling, Thurtell sank back on to the bed. So the rogue was going to marry Caroline, after all, and it was true that he had a house near Aldenham? Previously, he had tried not to believe it, but he could no longer shift from the truth. Fear of him had driven from Elstree both the girl he had loved and the man he hated; and fear of him had driven them into each other's arms.

"When have you got to go?" he asked in a low, rasping voice.

"Next week," groaned Probert. "If I'm lucky."

"Next week? but you can't!"

"I have to," said Probert, shrugging. "Heward's after me for back-rent, and he's worse than even bloody Wood ever was. . . . Ain't you got no more booze in this roosting-ken? I'm thirsty."

"I'll have to see Bill Weare at once," said Thurtell, sliding off the bed. "Where's my boots? my coat?"

"If you really think you can do it," said Probert dubiously, "I'll try and hold Heward off a bit longer, though it ain't easy. You'd better make it Friday night, if you can. I'm usually down there

Saturdays and Sundays, and if I show myself to the neighbours, no one'll think it unusual for visitors to be about."

"All right, all right," grunted Thurtell, pulling on his boots, "I'll try to make it Friday. Depends on what he has to say. I'll run and see if he's at Rexworthy's now. . . . You'd better wait here. No, Joey can come with me. . . ."

"As you wish," said Probert, sighing towards the empty bowl. "But you'll have to hurry. Don't forget this is Thursday."

"I've not forgotten . . . tomorrow night . . . I'll make the bastard do it."

Now that action had been forced on him, a feeling as of liberation made Thurtell almost happy. Lying down, doing nothing but drink, had left him unarmoured to the harpies of fear and self-doubt. Once action was taken, an aim resolved on, the horrors went and his confidence in the future returned. Besides, he had to prove to Tom that he was no idle boaster. And not only were there Tom's mutinous misgivings to be stilled, Mary remained a scoffer, an enemy, jeering at him as one who talked of what he feared to do. Did others, men as well as women, also scoff at him behind his back? laughing at Old Flash, the Bully, as the Swell Yokel who had been milked by city sharps?

Such a thought was unbearable. Thurtell shuddered from it, the spirit cringing in the lion's pelt as he shook the monstrous idea away.

And then he thought of Caroline and was astounded that he had forgotten her. Wood had left Elstree for Aldenham to give his bride a finer house. That bride must be Caroline. Nobody else, nobody. . . . She was Caroline. No longer at Elstree, which seemed suddenly empty without her presence, was she living, but a married woman at last, and married to that little ramrod! she would be at Aldenham.

Quietly, he laughed to himself, shouldering his way forward through the crowd. He laughed because he found that the thought of her in Wood's embrace no longer galled him. And he laughed because she would be living on hot coals of fear, each tap of the wind against her window turning her to jelly lest it be Jack Thurtell knocking. Wherever she went, she would be looking behind her, looking for him; whenever Wood left the house, she would tremble like a dried leaf, wondering if he'd come back with all his limbs to his body. This was no rosy bed she had married; a nettle-bed that would keep her wakeful, robbing love of indolence, making her aware, even under her husband's kisses, that Jack Thurtell had sworn their death. Had he plotted it, he could not have devised a more apt revenge. Not that she

would escape him. Eventually, he would strike; suddenly when her
defences were down and she thought herself and the major no longer
in danger, then would he kill the man in front of her face before he
taught her the final lesson, that he was no lover to trifle with, by
snicking a knife into her supplicating throat. But that must wait. . . . He
would have to start with Weare.

By thunder, he had forgotten one most important point! He had
no weapon with which to kill the fellow. The borrowed air-gun
disguised as a stick was practically useless, untrustworthy in its
mechanism, and he would have to buy a pistol. Let damned Probert
pay for that, egad! let the rogue fork out at least that much towards
their common investment. Then there was also the chaise to be hired:
but that could be left till the morning. No use ordering one tonight
when he was not certain whether he would find Weare in his usual
haunts.

But Weare was not difficult to find. After passing safely, un-
challenged, through the dark streets with never a bailiff to bar their
way, Thurtell and Hunt reached Spring Gardens and entered Rexworthy's; and there was Bill Weare in his shirt-sleeves playing some
flat at billiards for half-a-crown. Not wishing to interrupt the game,
Thurtell merely nodded to him and settled into a seat to watch, Hunt
sidling in to sit beside him.

Smaller and very much leaner than Hunt—but strong: all sinew
and muscle, no fat on that agile body—Weare walked briskly about
the table, chalking his cue and taking careful aim . . . then, click click,
the ivory balls rolled smoothly, sedately towards the red, or they
cannoned with a gentle kiss into the pocket into which he had intended
them to fall. Not the kind of sharp to be easily caught off his guard;
a man who calculated every shot before he tried it, quizzing along the
length of the cue that moved slowly, as though alive, back and forth
between the fingers and thumb of his left hand over the green cloth;
and when a ball ran untrue, Weare did not curse. He took up the cue
and slipped it into the rack on the wall and took down another which
he hoped might serve him better.

At last, the last ball rolled into its pocket and the flat's half-a-crown
was passed to Weare; then before they could start another game,
Thurtell stepped up to Weare and whispered:

"Will tomorrow do?"

"I've a lady to see tomorrow," said Weare slowly. "I'll be with
her all day. Can't get away till late."

"That don't matter," said Thurtell, and he could have grinned with relief. He had been wondering what explanation he might give to suggest their travelling in the dark.

"All right," said Weare. "Will Cumberland Gate do you? About half-past five to six?"

"Ay," said Thurtell, "that'll do me all right;" and he wondered why the other could not hear the loud beating of his heart. "I'll await you with a chaise. Bring the rhino and your backgammon board. . . . Goodbye till then."

"Goodbye," said Weare coldly, watching him as he turned away with Hunt.

"What you doing with the Swell Yokel, Bill?" grinned Rex-worthy, sidling up against him. "You can't skin him a second time; he ain't got nothing now; and the traps are after him."

"That's all right, Rex," grinned Weare. "He's got a flat for me; somewhere in Herts; and I'm going down with him tomorrow to do a little shooting there."

"Be careful, Bill. I don't trust the fellow, I tell you. Make sure you ain't the target when he tries a little shooting."

Weare laughed, a dry rustling in his throat.

"Gammon!" he said. "I'm fly to anything he tries. He's got the brains of a louse. Anything he might think of doing, I'll have thought of it ten minutes before him. It'll be Mr. Mutton-Head who'll get it, if anyone does. . . . Shooting! I'd go a hundred miles for a bit of shooting; no sport like it in the world, my friend." He laughed, balancing the cue in his hand. "Poor Old Flash," he chuckled, "I suppose some day I ought to give him the opportunity for his revenge. I did rook him for a lot, you know."

CHAPTER THIRTEEN

DEATH ON A SHOVEL

TWENTY-FOUR hours to go; a little less, perhaps. It was now nine o'clock Thursday evening; by this time tomorrow night, if there were no slip between, Weare should be a dead man. Drink was not needed to keep Thurtell in a state of exaltation, and he was proud to notice that he was not afraid, that he could contemplate the murder calmly as though it were some everyday commercial transaction, an unpleasant one perhaps—but so was borrowing money or calming creditors an unpleasant business that had to be faced if one wished to keep out of jail. Besides, there was satisfaction in the thought of killing Weare, the meanfisted little swaggerer, and he was almost looking forward to the moment when the bastard awoke to the realization that he was about to be murdered. Thurtell hoped that it would not be too dark. Darkness was needed, of course, lest some wayfarer tout on him, but he would like a scrap of moonlight here and there to sparkle on the terror in Weare's eyes and to show his ashen cheeks where the whiskers did not spread. He would like to watch him while he died.

"I'd like to get drunk tonight," he said, striding through the dark Haymarket on the opposite side to the Cock.

Brightly shone the windows of the Cock, trellising with gold the pavement and turning passers-by to ebon shadows. Outside the theatre, in the shadow of the pilasters, Thurtell stood with Hunt, frowning, glaring at the tavern which he felt should still have been his property. Instead, he had to skulk away in Conduit Street, paying good money for everything that he ate and drank; and he was thirsty. Bottles. Bottles ranged like soldiers at attention behind the bar; and barrels in the cellar. Mary and her boneless husband could drink till they fell, drinking his wine, his spirits, his ale and beer, while he remained locked out with a palate like unbleached calico.

"Let her make merry tonight," he growled. "Her time'll knock if she thinks to peach on me to Mr. bloody Beaumont; but I don't believe she'll do it when it comes to the pitch."

"Hell hath no fury like a woman scorned," said Hunt in a low voice, and he sighed as though recalling some unpleasant memory.

"I ain't scorned her," said Thurtell. "I just told her I wouldn't bear malice if she wanted to marry some other cove. That was handsome of me, letting her go like that and having him to work with her for me in the bar, and both of em dipping their fingers into my till. But I've not met a woman yet who knew what it was to be grateful. They want you always to be carneys with them, fondling em and telling em how crummy they are and how you love em. All right at first, but . . . well, a man has other interests."

"He has only one interest," said Hunt in a suddenly solemn tone. "Gold. When you've a pocketful of gelt, you can take what you like, whether it's a bottle of bingo, a handsome coat or the prettiest high-flier who drives her chariot down Rotten Row to show her blubber to every Corinthian and swell that's got eyes to see her. That's all that's needed, Jack: rhino; then your worries are over."

"And I'm going to get some," snarled Thurtell, glaring at the bright windows of the Cock, hearing women's laughter and excited screaming, seeing the prancing shadows of cocks and hens inside dancing behind the bottle-glass. Nearby, standing beside a post, he saw two men watching, the capes of their box-coats pulled high to ward off the night's chill; and he wished that he had his shooting-stick with him, if only the damned thing would work, so that he could have taken swift and silent revenge on those two traps waiting over there to lumber him.

"Come on," he snarled. "Mary'll get what's coming to her before very long."

A seemingly endless night to be passed through now. With his body tensed for action, Thurtell dreaded the thought, but he had insufficient money to drug his angry thoughts to sleep with floods of gin or brandy. What little he had to waste he spent with Hunt, drinking in small dark taverns because the traps would not have thought to look for him in such places which usually he never visited. Again and again he and Hunt went over the morrow's events. He would leave the Coach and Horses first to meet Weare at Cumberland Gate. Half an hour later, Hunt would start in Probert's gig and catch him up, if he could, before Edgware, going ahead to await his and Weare's entrance into the narrow Elstree lanes near Gill's Hill Cottage. Then when he pulled up, feigning surprise at meeting him and Probert in that lonely place, all three would rush on Weare, shooting out his brains before he could scream.

"Shouldn't take more than a minute," he said.

Hunt's dark eyes glowed, his breath came sharply, quickly. "I've never done anything like this before," he said, "but there's a kind of relish in the thought, ain't there?"

"Aw, you soon get used to it," shrugged Thurtell. "The first one or two might make you want to bring your breakfast up; but after that, you think no more of it than smacking a fly. And you're right, Joe. There's relish in it if you hate the man sufficiently to love such work."

"I hate quite a lot of people," said Hunt, eyes narrowing.

"We'll make em all pay," grinned Thurtell with a benevolent sweeping gesture as though offering his friend the riches of the bar. "I've got to get Beaumont and Wood first: that'll satisfy me for a time; then we'll set to work on your lot."

That night he could not sleep. He dozed, moaning, to awake with sweat in his stiff hairs. He had not had enough drink, blast it; but tomorrow night . . . tomorrow night, he would be at Elstree with thousands in his pockets, and he would have a banquet in Gill's Hill Cottage. He hoped that Caroline would be there to see him in his greatness, clinking her glass with his, and never realizing that the hand that stroked hers was newly washed of blood that might yet show, perhaps, crusted under the fingernails. Weare's blood. Then, shortly afterward's, Wood's blood. Then Barber Beaumont's. . . . So many to die that he might live in power and comfort, king of St. James's with a house in Jermyn Street, not lurking in a thieves' haunt like this Coach and Horses and listening anxiously to every knock on the door.

Despite his broken night, he did not feel tired when he dressed in the morning. His spirit upheld him like a song in his blood and he greeted Hunt cheerily when he arrived for breakfast. Only Tom remained glum, in the bitter mood in which all yesterday he had sulked.

"I-I-I'm tired of this," said Tom, gulping hot tea and chewing buttered toast. "I-I-I'm g-g-going to see about my bail."

"The traps might get you," growled his brother.

"Th-th-they're c-c-coming here, to r-r-raise the money."

"Who's coming here? The traps?"

"You w-w-wouldn't know em. They-they-they're respectable people, f-f-friends of mine, to-to-to raise my bail."

"Be careful, Tom; you don't know who you can trust."

"I-I-I've dis-dis-discovered that already," said Tom, leering at him.

Only Tom's ill-humour and sulky antagonism marred Thurtell's pleasure that morning. But he bore his brother no ill-will. When the day after tomorrow, or tomorrow night, he showered a few hundred screens on the table, Tom would quickly forget his rancours. No man could remain bad-tempered in the face of gold.

He had scraped together every penny he could find, taking a few shillings from Tom's pockets while he slept, and had now a little over four pounds; and with these coins to jingle, he felt unafraid of anything that fate might think to throw at him.

First, there were the pistols to be bought and these, after gazing into many shop-windows, he and Hunt purchased from a pawn-broker called Bow in Marylebone High Street. They were new pistols and small enough to fit neatly into a man's pocket and, together with a key and a mould, they were priced at one pound seventeen. Even browns being precious in his barren world at the moment, Thurtell haggled for minutes with the shopman, until eventually he beat two shillings off the price; and satisfied that he had made a bargain, he counted out the money, piece by reluctant piece.

Being now close to dinner-hour he and Hunt returned to the Coach and Horses and dined on saddle of mutton and onions; and the plentiful food with a bowl of rum punch oiled away some of Tom's stiffness until he was able to smile again without seeming to crack the skin.

Too late to be invited to the table, Probert thumped up the stairs, and Thurtell was pleased to note that again the bowl was almost empty and the scoffer at the feast could find little more than a drip or two of the liquor left. Disappointed and angry though he must have been, having an insatiable thirst, he smiled and made no complaints while, rubbing his hands slowly together, he watched with fatherly interest Thurtell melting some lead on a fire-shovel at the grate.

"Warmish day for a fire," he said, as though he had not understood what Thurtell was doing. "Yet October's a dangerous month, I suppose: usually more winter than summer."

Hunt grinned at him from where he crouched beside Thurtell. Lying back in a chair, a glass in one hand, a bottle of Madeira on the floor beside him, Tom lounged in a corner, making it clear in his posture that he dissociated himself from whatever nefarious work the others might be up to.

They were making bullets. Probert had realized that in a glance; but

K

like Tom, he wished to be both inside and outside the conspiracy, to know what was going on and to benefit by any possible results, and at the same time remain aloof lest he find himself lumbered should the adventure miscarry.

The fierce fire, crackling and spitting sparks, showed redly the faces of Thurtell and Hunt. Lit by hell's glare, thought Probert amusedly: having a lick on earth of what was coming to them afterwards. Like a pair of devils they crouched, like wizards brewing dark spells, while the lead ran in spiky globules when they moved the shovel, rolling it around before letting it flood the mould placed in readiness on the hob. One bullet. Two bullets. Three bullets. Four. . . . As they cooled, Probert gingerly picked one up, licked his fingers, then tossed the round ball in his hand.

"A little thing like that, a silver pea," he mused, "to kill a man! You've made it too small, me lads. That'd never kill a man on the spot."

His lips twisted into a smile that was half a snarl, Thurtell leered up at him, rolling the last of the lead on the shovel.

"You'd be damned sorry to have one of em through your head," he muttered, "small as they are. I can tell you, if you had one of these in you, you'd not get back to Gill's Hill Cottage in a hurry."

Probert chuckled, still tossing the shining ball of death, watching it dance and flare in the firelight. "You know best," he said. "You've been in the war, you've been trained in these things. Anyhow, I'm sure that damned air-gun of yours wouldn't kill anybody unless close to."

"I know that as well as you do, Bill," said Thurtell, trying to speak patiently, "or why the hell should I have bought these pops, if it wasn't because I don't trust the air-gun? Aw, I was a bloody fool to go all the way to old Harper at Norwich to borrow that damned thing; but I'll take care not to miss bloody Weare with this . . ." He cocked the pistol towards the ceiling, ". . . as I did your low-bottomed friend, Master Wood."

Probert laughed again, lolling in the chair, determined, if possible, to keep his friend in this amiable yet truculent mood; and he bent his thumb into his fist, the bullet on the nail, as though he would play marbles with it.

"Ay," he chuckled, "you made a bad business of that, Jack, for I expected Wood'd have been dead and you'd have had the girl long before this."

At the mention of Caroline, a spasm like a tic twisted one side of Thurtell's face, red in the firelight, making him look a demon, a devil-headed bird of prey crouching over the hearth.

"Well," he said at last, staring into the flames as though he saw Wood roasting in the coals and would not have spat to save him, "you shall see what sort of a mess I'll make of Weare before the night's out. And after him comes Wood and two or three more than you know."

"I hope you'll do your business well," murmured Probert, eyes down, "and your friend's got plenty of money with him."

"There's no fear of that." Thurtell smiled, then sank back into the shadows from the fire that glared redly along his boots and trouser-legs, casting belly and chest into shadow, his face a dim shape between the points of the collar. "He thinks I'm taking him into the country flat-chasing!" The smile widened, and he took a deep breath, basking under Probert's laughter like an actor before applause. "It'll be pretty flat-catching," he grunted, "for I'll lay the swine flat enough before I've done with him. This time I'm taking no chances with these blasted barking-irons. Pass me the other fellow, Joe."

He took the other pistol in his hand, fingers closing lovingly around the butt, the first finger caressing the trigger, while, kick-kuck-kick, he drew back the hammer.

"Damned thing's stiff," he muttered, frowning. "Too new. Never been used."

He pulled the trigger and winced at the effort until the hammer clicked down.

"Joey," he said, "slip out and get some oil. Here's half-a-bull. Keep the blasted change." And he spun him a half-crown from his thumbnail.

"Get some booze, too, while you're about it," said Probert. "I've got sand in my bloody throat."

"Get it yourself," said Thurtell, eyeing him steadily. "Run off, Joe: take no heed of Bill." He waited until Hunt had danced off down the stairs; then, still watching Probert as though he expected him to vanish if he so much as blinked, he said: "You've as much to gain as any of us, Bill, in what we're going to do; and you risk the least."

"What do you mean?" Probert returned his glare, thick quizzical brows raised, lips outpressed petulantly. "I'm taking more risks than any of you," he said. "Ain't you taking him to my place?"

"*I'm* taking him near there, yes. I'll be seen meeting him, driving with him, if I'm unlucky, and I'd not be surprised if he ain't told Rexworthy of our jaunt. Rexworthy don't like me and I don't like Rexworthy. But he's thick with Weare as only a couple of thieves could be. And what risks are you taking? None. You'll be with Joey, you'll be in Elstree with him before me; who can prove you even knew I was coming or what happened to my companion in the lane? No. You've got the clean end of the stick, and now you won't even buy us a drink."

"I can't. I've got no money."

"You never do have money when someone wants to borrow it. Ain't you a friend of Tetsall's? can't you tick up with him?"

"I—I can try. . . ."

"Well, go on: try. Go on."

Not until Probert had shuffled from the room did Thurtell relax. Then with a grim smile of satisfaction he sat back in his chair, pleased with himself for having shown his mastery. It was time he asserted himself, he felt. Damned Probert thought that because his smooth talk could make fools of women it could make fools of men, too. Because he was a few years the elder—how many years? about five, little more—Probert thought he must be the superior. He was going to learn differently, and the first of these lessons was being made to pay for the morning's drinks.

Pleased at having asserted his power, Thurtell glanced at his brother for approval, and was startled to see that Tom was watching him almost with dislike, head down, chin pressing against the stock.

Before that unblinking regard, Thurtell shifted uncomfortably. Embarrassed by his stutter, Tom rarely spoke, but he had been his brother's shadow, ever at his heels, under his heels, the uncomplaining slave, entering whatever projects might be suggested and never objecting even when his hopes proved ruins. And now the slave was rebelling. With sulky eyes, Tom stared at him as though he hated and despised him.

"What's the matter, Tom?" asked Thurtell, forcing a laugh. "You ain't yourself these days. There's nothing to be a-feared of. I'm handling this with Joey and Bill. All you've got to do is stay right where you are; or, it'd be better perhaps if you showed yourself downstairs to have as many as you can get to swear you was miles away when it happened. I'm only thinking of your own safety. I'd never face poor mama again if you got into any trouble."

Tom laughed or, rather, he neighed; but he did not speak.

Flushing at such insolent noise, Thurtell bit his lip, determined not to lose his temper.

"Come, lad," he said, cajolingly, "I love you more than anybody in the world, 'cept dad and mama. Put your hand in mine. What I do is done for your sake and your kids' sake." He stretched out his hand, and Tom made no attempt to take it. "Why do you bear me this ill-will?" he whispered in a coaxing voice. "Brothers should always stand together. I know you're down at the moment, Tom, thinking of those poor girls of yours, of course. But if they're going to have any future we have to make money for em so that we can give em dowries and see that they marry honest husbands. It's a kind of sacred trust which we must obey. Not for ourselves: for those dear girls' future we must work, no matter how dangerous the tasks to which we set our hands."

"Yo-yo-you can talk big," jeered Tom, "but th-th-the only one you c-c-carney is yourself. Yo-yo-you can't g-g-gammon me. Thin-thin-thinking of my kids, you l-l-liar. Yo-yo-you only think of yourself and you al-al-always have."

"Tom!" cried Thurtell in notes of deep horror; and he sprang to his feet, wringing his hands in supplication. "You can't mean that, you can't! What have I had from life? Nothing, nothing. I've worked for you and the dear girls, trying to make a fortune for all your sakes more than money for my own. What do I care for money! I throw it away when I have it; and my blood runs cold at the thought of killing a fellow-man. But I must be Cain for both our sakes—the outcast Cain; and you my good and honest Abel."

"C-C-Cain k-k-killed Abel, did-did-didn't he?" scoffed Tom.

Thurtell shuddered and sank into a chair, his hands shielding his eyes. That Tom could possibly say such things hurt him to the heart; but, he groaned, he was becoming inured to ingratitude. Nobody had ever tried to understand the generosity behind his motives. Nobody. Tom whom he had made a city gentleman, saving him from the muck of a rural existence with pigs and other beasts and teaching him the glorious temptations of the town . . . he blamed him for it!

The return of Probert with two bottles of claret roused him from his melancholy; and fast on Probert's heels came Hunt with oil for the pistols.

"Here," said Probert merrily, setting the bottles on the table, "here's nectar for our Ajax. Find some cups or glasses, will you, Joe? We must drink success to the great enterprise."

"To the Turpin lads!" cried Hunt, and he crowed like a cock.

Glumly, Thurtell accepted the full glass passed to him, and took a gulp of the cheap tart wine.

"How we going to manage about your old woman?" he demanded suddenly, watching Probert: "stopping her looking out, I mean."

"O, never fear," smiled Probert, settling his great bulk into a small chair that squeaked beneath him. "I've worked out a plan to get her to go to bed."

"What are you going to do about it? Besides, there may be other women, mightn't there? her sisters, for example?"

Probert shrugged, pretending not to understand the point of the question. "Anne'll be there all right," he murmured. "I can't be certain about Carrie, of course."

"Of course," growled Thurtell, dripping the oil carefully on to the triggers and hammers of the pistols. "But what you going to do about it? I'd like you to say, so that we'll all know how to act when we get there."

"Well," sighed Probert, sipping his wine and rolling his eyes as though the near-vinegar were ambrosia, "Hunt must sing us two or three songs. That's all. After a little of that, the old woman'll get sleepy." He did not smile, nor did he look towards Hunt drawing himself up indignantly to his full height. He added: "I can then say that, having my friends down, I must sit up with em to keep em company, and as we mean to enjoy ourselves, she and Anne had better go to bed, I'll say. When they find we're determined to sit up, they'll be glad to get off and leave us to it."

"That's up to you, Bill," smiled Thurtell. "Now this is what I've planned. Listen carefully, Joe. We can't afford to make mistakes: our necks depend on it. . . ."

Away from the three leaning their heads together in front of the fire shifted Tom, not wanting to overhear their talk, and trying to pretend that he did not know that they plotted murder.

"You two must get ahead," whispered Thurtell, watching their eyes. "Start about half-an-hour or three-quarters of an hour after I leave here; but not later. Half-an-hour should be enough. By then, I should have got to Cumberland Gate and picked up Weare, even if he is a little behind time. Get ahead quick and don't stop even to have a drink until you're at the Artichoke. When you see me pass, come after me, but don't catch me up. That'll block the lane in the rear and if you hear anybody coming, you can give me the office. I'll run past the cottage until it's out of hearing of a pistol-shot. Then, while Weare's sitting next me in the gig, I'll give it to him."

"That's it, Jack, that's it!" cried Probert, clapping his hands. "You're the lad, Jack! by glory, you are! There's no one like you when it comes to planning! Wonder they never made you a general in the marines, being such a master of strategy!"

"O, I left before I had any real chance for promotion," muttered Thurtell. "Besides, the life didn't appeal to me."

"A pity for England's sake," groaned Probert. "Nelson wouldn't have had a look in if you'd taken to it seriously. But to come to our muttons. . . . Lookee, if the fellow has any suspicions about that lane being so untended, you can tell him you think that you've lost your way. Then when you get to a convenient spot, you being the driver, you can make some remark and point his attention to make him look to the left. Directly he turns his head, that's your time to shoot him, and Joe and me'll run to help."

"Ay, ay," said Thurtell, nodding his head and thinking how he had misjudged the fellow. Probert wasn't as bad as one might believe at first; and he was clever. No doubt of that: he was clever.

"After you've done him, we'll push the body in a sack and bring it to the cottage," continued Probert in a hoarse whisper. "We'll toss it into the pond next door. We'll do that together and leave Joe to keep the women and kids amused to stop em asking questions. . . . Now, what about dinner?"

"Dinner? Yes, yes," cried Thurtell. "I suppose it must be dinner-time! Run down and see Tetsall and tell him to send up four dinners, and a couple more bottles of wine. . . ."

Thurtell lay back in his chair, stretching his legs to the fire, his hands behind his head, while Probert refilled the glasses and Hunt rattled downstairs to order the meal. Anger had fled Thurtell, leaving him in a state of peaceful lassitude, and he smirked under Probert's admiring look, pulling back his shoulders and swelling his chest that the man might note how strong he was and how unconcerned he was about so trivial a matter as a mere murder. Yes, Probert wasn't a bad fellow at heart, so long as he didn't rattle on about women and how none of them, beautiful or plain, rich or beggars, could resist him.

Putting all that carney aside, at bottom Probert was a fine fellow and what Probert might lack in bloody enthusiasm would be fully made up by the ambitious Hunt who, while Probert talked of women, talked of little beyond slitting up wealthy folk or anyone who had offended him.

Such a combination should prove irresistible: himself giving strength and leadership and courage; Probert his low cunning; and Hunt his artistic fervour. Ay, thought Thurtell complacently, nodding by the fire, they could not fail, a trinity like that.

CHAPTER FOURTEEN

ANOTHER DRINK . . . ANOTHER . . .

AFTER dinner, with a bowl of hot punch following the wine, Thurtell and Probert settled into chairs to belch or snooze in comfort either side of the fire. Glumly silent, Tom sat away from them, like a deaf and dumb man unable to understand what was being plotted or why uncharged pistols should be cocked and fired in a flurry of sparks until the triggers moved at a touch and the hammers fell sound-lessly. Hunt had been sent off to make some last purchases and arrange-ments. A six-bushel sack would be needed, he had been told, and a hank of cord. He was also to go to Probatt's stables at the White Lion, Charing Cross, to hire a horse and chaise; and on the way back he was to call in at the Cock and see if he could manage to entice Mary to surrender Thurtell's coat and the red shawl which he had draped over his head when he had waited to murder Wood in Manchester Build-ings. And Tom had asked him to call at Cribb's in Panton Street to bring back the box-coat he had left there.

With difficulty had they forced Hunt out of the room when he heard Probert order another bowl of punch.

"It's not for us now," Probert had hurriedly explained. "I'm ordering it for later. We'll need something to drink before we start and it's best to order it directly."

Unconvinced, licking his lips, Hunt had stood with lowering looks like a small boy ordered to stand in a corner while his elders enjoyed themselves.

"Be off with you, Joe," Probert had cried, half-rising out of his chair, "and get those things for Jack. We've got to stay here about three-quarters of an hour after he's gone and we'll have some punch together then."

Once Hunt had left on laggard steps, the punch was carried up by the waiter, Probert and Thurtell drinking greedily, Tom, without a word of thanks, accepting his portion; then they had settled them-selves for a snooze. Only Thurtell had snoozed. Seated stiffly in a corner, seeming to exude a miasma of moral disapproval which depressed his brother, Tom remained, while Probert nodded in his chair betwixt sleep and waking, listening for Hunt's return, listening on the chance that the two brothers might whisper secrets not meant for him to hear. The opening of the door roused him from his thoughts and he looked up to see a waiter enter.

"Some gentlemen to see Mr. Thomas Thurtell," said the waiter.

"A-a-ay," said Tom. "S-s-send em in."

"One moment!" Thurtell was broad awake, awakening quickly like a dog at any unaccustomed sound. "Who are these gentlemen?" he asked.

"F-f-friends of mine," growled Tom, with a weak attempt at dignity. "I-I-I a-a-asked em to come about my-my-my b-b-bail."

"Damn it!" cried Thurtell, springing to his feet, "this is too much! Today of all days you must have these people here! Dammit, Tom! I've stood a lot from you, but this is too much, too much, indeed!"

"Th-th-they are m-m-my friends!" cried Tom, his face darkening. "and I-I-I *will* see them, I tell you; I-I-I w-w-will see them." Trembling, he stood erect and faced his brother. "I-I-I'm g-g-getting out of this," he muttered. "I-I-I'm starting anew. I-I-I've had enough of-f-of this, I-I-I want to be c-c-clean for my-my daughters' sake. Th-th-these are all friends of mine."

"Tell the gentlemen to wait," said Thurtell to the waiter. "I'll send for them when my brother's ready."

"N-n-no! bub-bub-bring em up!"

"Tell them to wait," repeated Thurtell quietly and he tossed the man a shilling. He did not speak again until after the door had closed and he heard the waiter's footsteps retreating down the stairs. "What do you mean," he asked, "about starting afresh, Tom? You're in everything with me; you're in over your ears."

"I-I-I'm not; y-y-you cac-cac-can't prove it!" In his rage and excitement, Tom choked, his face turning purple, yet he managed to spit out a few further words. "I-I-I wasn't t-t-there when the fi-fi-fire broke out. I-I-I'm clean. M-m-mary will stand b-b-by me, and t-t-to hell with you, J-j-jack! Y-y-you brought mu-mu-me to this, and I-I-I'm gug-gug-going to s-s-save my ch-ch-children. I-I-I'm g-g-going to make a-a-a co-co-composit-it-ition with m-m-my cre-cre-editors. Th-th-that's why th-th-these g-gen-gentlemen are here. So-so-so get out!" He ran to the door and flung it open. "S-s-send up th-th-the gentlemen!" he shouted. "Now, g-g-get out, you!"

With a look of rage and pity, Thurtell pushed by his brother, Probert following quickly, and strode into his own bedchamber.

"My God, Bill," he gasped. "Is he mad?"

Probert shrugged and closed the door. "Got virtuous," he said. "It sometimes happens when a man's afraid. He's like an old trot who takes to religion because she's too old for any more of the game. He's frightened and a frightened man's best left alone. They can be damned dangerous sometimes, like madmen who don't know what they're doing. You don't think he'd peach, do you?"

"Not Tom!" cried Thurtell; yet he felt uncertain, astonished and unable to understand this new, this rebellious Tom. "He'll get over it," he said with an attempt at light-heartedness. "And if he can make some arrangement about his debts, all good luck go with him, if only for his girls' sake. But why should he have chosen this of all days!"

"Probably didn't," said Probert, thumbing his chin and frowning doubtfully, not liking this interruption of their plan. It seemed no good omen for the night's adventure. "Probably fixed it before we knew what you were up to; or they may have fixed the time, not him."

"I don't like it, Bill," muttered Thurtell, striding the floor, "I'm damned if I like it."

Probert also did not like it but he knew better than to agree with Thurtell lest he depress the man's mercurial spirits.

"It'll be all right," he said; "perhaps it's for the best. Who'd think you were planning what you are on the day when your brother fills the place with visitors, lawyers and respectable men of commerce? . . . No, I think it's for the best!"

"Do you really think so?" Thurtell stood, frowning down at his feet, his shortish hair drawn forward to make his puckered forehead seem even lower than it was. "Yes, perhaps you're right," he said. "It does give a kind of a—of an air of respectability to things, don't it?"

"It decidedly does," agreed Probert, sliding into the only chair in the room. "What about another wet?"

"Wait till Hunt comes . . . I think that's him." Thurtell slowly opened the door, peeped out, then stepped out. "Wait there, Joe," he hissed, "did you get what I told you?"

"Ay," said Hunt who could scarcely be recognized under his parcels, the red shawl being about his neck, the sack over one arm, and a length of rope twined about the other. "Only couldn't get Tom's coat," he said. "Cribb weren't at home."

"Don't matter about that," said Thurtell, leading him into the bedroom. "Come in and we'll have some punch."

"That sack looks damned small," growled Probert, taking it from Hunt's arm and shaking it. "I'm sure it's not a six bushel. It won't be large enough for him, Jack. Just look at it!"

"Never mind," shrugged Thurtell; "we'll make a shift with it. We've got no time to lose, dammit. What a bloody fool my brother is to have a parcel of people here at a time like this!"

"Ay, it was foolish," said Probert lightly, "but I'm sure he didn't expect anybody today; and as they've come to serve him about his bail, he couldn't deny himself."

"Well," said Thurtell, attempting to toss his gloom aside with a twist of his neck, "let em stop and be damned. I'm off. . . . You go in there, will you, Bill? I don't want to interrupt their bloody dignities. Get me Tom's drab great-coat."

While Probert hurried off to obey, he took the red shawl from Hunt and tied it around his neck; then, when Probert returned, he slipped on Tom's coat, annoyed that Hunt had failed to obtain Tom's box-coat with its capes, the coachman's dress which was warm and more concealing than this tighter-fitting gentlemanly wear which he was forced to don in its place.

"Now I need some money," he said. "Give me back the ten quid I lent you to take up that bill a few days ago."

"Ten quid!" cried Probert. "I haven't got ten bob, let alone ten quid!"

"Well, I've got to have it," growled Thurtell. "I can't go with Weare unless I've got some blunt in my pocket. We might stop for drinks, you never know, and I can't afford to let him suspect me, not having more than a brown or two."

"I—I haven't got it, Jack!"

"All right," said Thurtell, beginning to peel off the coat. "Then the deal's off. You'd better run down to Cumberland Gate, Joe, and tell Bill Weare I can't get there in time."

"No!" cried Probert, sweating in torment between avarice and the hope of booty. "I'll tell you what I'll do. I'll have a word with Charlie Tetsall. He might help us."

"That's the lad," said Thurtell. "Get as much as you can out of the dog. Tell him he'll be paid without fail in the morning."

Smiling maliciously, he watched Probert slouch out of the room; and when the door closed behind him, he turned and winked at Hunt.

"That's the way to treat Bill," he said. "Give him half a chance and he'd eat and drink you out of house and home, cuckold you in the process and carry off your money-box. Everything for nothing's his motto. Why shouldn't he do something to help?"

"You're right there, Jack," said Hunt, ferociously nodding his head and brushing out his coal-black whiskers. "Don't let him take you for a flat——"

"No one takes me for a flat!" cried Thurtell ferociously, the tiny eyes like diamonds in their hollows when the light flicked over them. "He dies, if he does."

"I didn't mean it that way, Jack. No one'd take you for a flat unless they was mad or drunk. You're the sharpest of the sharps in all St. James's." Hunt's voice sank to a cooing, almost feminine murmur of adulation. "Look at them muscles on your biceps!" he cried. "See how they swell up when you fold your arms like that! Bet you could crack a man's skull if you caught him in there, in the crook there, and squeezed hard. Like iron. That's what you are, Jack: like iron!"

"I flatter myself I'm in training," said Thurtell with a smirk. "Always in the pink and ready to put up my mitts against any man: the bigger he is the better, for then the further he has to fall to smack his nut. I've had a royal academician stop me in the street and beg me to be painted by him because of my Greek anatomy, he said."

"Why didn't you? You could have had a print of it made."

"I'm not a pugilist," said Thurtell, tossing his head: "I'm an amateur, and I don't want my mug put up in shops and taverns. . . . How long's that fool going to be?"

"He's coming," said Hunt. "I can hear him."

With bowed shoulders and an unhappy look on his dark face, Probert slouched in and slowly counted five sovereigns into Thurtell's hand.

"All he'd let me have," he moaned.

"That'll do." Thurtell scooped up the money and slipped it into his trouser-pocket. "Now," he said, "I'll be off; and don't you be too long."

"About three-quarters of an hour," said Hunt.

"Make it a little less. Pass me so that I'll know you're on your way, but don't look as though you've seen me. Then wait for me at Gill's Hill. Probert knows the spot."

"Ay," said Probert, "I know it."

"All the luck of the world go with you, Jack," cried Hunt, clasping his hand and looking lovingly up into his eyes, "and our prayers, too.

And my wife's prayers and my children's and Tom's children's prayers."

"Amen," said Probert, swinging away to conceal the scornful twitching of his lips.

"You can rely on me," said Thurtell, a sob in his voice. "Goodbye, good fellows. We meet at Gill's Hill. Watch for me at the Artichoke, then follow the gig. And then, heigh ho, we'll have a merry evening! Don't forget to bring some rum, will you?"

With a cheery wave of his arm, he strode out of the room, softly shutting the door behind him; and they heard his confident step going down the stairs.

"He's gone," sighed Probert, sinking into a chair and wiping his forehead; then he stared at his hand, astonished to realize that he had been sweating. As yet, he could not fully believe that the adventure had begun, that Thurtell should be now settling into the chaise which Hunt had hired for him.

"You hired that chaise all right from Probatt?" he asked with sudden anxiety.

"No," said Hunt, sighing as he settled into a chair, "couldn't get one. Went to Charing Cross and he had nothing that was any good, but I borrowed a fine roan horse from him——"

"What's the bloody good of a horse without a chaise, you fool!" howled Probert.

"O, I got a gig from Cross's in Whitcomb Street; better than a chaise for two people." Hunt looked at him almost angrily. "Finelooking gig, too, painted a deep green. Told him I was driving to Dartford. . . . What about that punch you promised me?"

"All right, all right. Tell the waiter to bring it up."

Sighing, Probert settled back into his chair, feeling exhausted. Having to encourage others to take action could be, he groaned, as tiring as to take action oneself. Now, for a while, he could breathe again, like a swimmer rising into clean air; and if only Hunt would keep quiet, his placid strength would soon be back in full. But he knew that Hunt would be unable to keep quiet.

Eyes closed, he lay back in the chair until the waiter brought the punch.

"Mr. John Thurtell'll pay when he gets back," he growled. "Put it on his bill. . . . Come on, Joey. You should need a drink."

Into the bowl they dipped their glasses and drank quickly, gasping with relish and rubbing their bellies as the warm liquor set alight to their entrails, calming their fears and doubts, and making the future appear a delectable land to which they alone held the key.

"He'll not have got to Cumberland Gate yet," chuckled Hunt. "We might have time for another bowl."

"We might," smiled Probert. "Anyhow, there are taverns enough on the Edgware Road. . . ."

It was nearly an hour before they heaved themselves out of their chairs and strolled into the gathering dusk to clamber into Probert's gig in the yard.

"There's a butcher's in Oxford Street," said Probert, "that always has prime cuts. What do you say to a loin of pork?"

"I'm no Hebrew," said Hunt. "Pork let it be."

With the loin of pork tossed under the seat, they continued until they reached the Edgware Road where they pulled up at a tavern and had some brandy and water to keep out the cold. Starting again, feeling merrier and warmer, they were bowling briskly along the Edgware Road when suddenly Hunt clutched Probert's arm. In his alarm, Probert dragged on the reins, and the horse, head swung back, slithered and almost fell.

"Don't do that, damn you!" cried Probert, wrenching his arm free.

"Shh!" hissed Hunt. "There they are! Drive by and take no notice."

Not far ahead, Probert saw a gig with a deep green body jolting slowly along. The two men seated in it had their heads close together as though they whispered secrets they didn't want the horse to hear. Thurtell with a brown topper—he had decided against the grey as being too easily seen at night—and Weare in an olive-coloured coat and black topper, a carpet-bag across his knees, they looked the best of friends, two gentlemen off to the country for an evening's sport. Hunt pulled up the lapels of his coat and pulled down the brim of his castor, Probert hunched high his shoulders, as they trotted briskly past.

"He's got him!" cried Hunt, gleefully bouncing up and down. "O, my heart and liver, my tripes and bowels," he chanted. "He's got him, Old Flare's got him! he'll Turpin him; we'll Turpin the bastard! I'll cut his throat till his head drops off. O, Bill, it's good to be alive!"

"Better than being dead, at any rate," nodded Probert. "I feel like a drink, blast it, but we'd better not stop for fear Jack notices; although we might. . . . It's getting dark. . . . What do you say if we have one outside Edgware?"

"I object fiercely," cried Hunt, and whooped. "Dammit," he howled, laughing like wind in a chimney, "I want more than one!"

More than one! They had twice more than one; then thrice more than one to keep the others company. Probert lounged, grinning, against the bar, watching Hunt's antics as though he were a beggar with money. Then he had almost to drag him into the dark and push him into the gig.

"The Bald-Faced Stag's next stop," he chuckled. "Know it?"

"Know it!" wailed Hunt. "Cut my throat, Bill! don't go there!"

"Why! how much do you owe em?"

"Don't owe em anything. Only I've forgotten to give em back two horse-cloths I borrowed."

"Then get out and walk," laughed Probert, pulling the horse to a stop. "If I don't have a drink soon I'll bust."

"I'm not going to bloody well walk."

"Then come into the Stag with me."

"All right," muttered Hunt. "I'll walk."

Grumbling and cursing, he slipped out of the gig and stumbled in the ruts.

"Don't be long!" he howled.

Probert did not answer. He tickled the horse to a start and Hunt saw the gig sway on and draw up outside the lights of the Bald-Faced Stag; and he howled blasphemies at finding himself left with his thirst while, in the warm, Probert would be seizing the opportunity to swallow double portions which he did not have to share with a friend. A rogue, this Probert, a sly mean cheating rogue, to leave a pal outside and drink by himself! That's why he'd chosen the Stag so that he wouldn't have to dip into his pockets to pay for two, for he knew that Hunt dared not show his nose inside.

So tremendous was Hunt's rage at such treachery that he had to dance to find relief.

This tavern had evil memories for him, for the horse-cloths he had taken had brought only a few shillings at uncle's; and on the occasion when he had slipped off with them, Thurtell had started a brawl with three farm-labourers. Triumphant, if bloody and tattered, Thurtell had staggered off, the victor. "Look what I got," he had whispered to Hunt, showing him a watch. "Hooked it out of his pocket while I was punching him." That watch had brought twenty-five bob when they had popped it in London; and like a true gentleman, Thurtell had shared the money with him, half and half, just as Hunt had shared what he had got from the cloths. Very different from this mean-gutted Probert; but Thurtell was a gentleman, his father was an alderman or something, and, of course, he knew how to treat a gentleman.

Panting, Hunt reached the White Lion in Edgware, and was about to enter when he heard the rattle of a gig behind him and swung round to see Probert draw up. At the same time, from the opposite direction, a tall fat man ambled towards him, and Hunt recognized the landlord of the Lion, Bill Clarke.

"Well met!" he laughed, clapping Clarke on the back. "Welcome, mine host, to your own inn!" And he turned, glowering, on Probert who was wiping his mouth on the back of his hand. "Took your time about it, didn't you?" he sneered.

But, facing a warm fire, with warm brandy and water in his hand, Hunt could not maintain his indignation. Soon he was skipping and laughing, chuckling and chaunting bawdy verses, and all the customers were laughing with him.

"You're good company tonight, Mr. Hunt," smiled the landlord.

"I'm a Turpin lad!" Hunt chirruped. "Give me your gelt or I blow out your brains! Bang bang bang! You're dead! And I'll dance on your teeth when you're down! heigh ho, a-dancing we will go!"

"What spirits!" sighed the landlord, nodding his bald head. "I do declare, he's got the spirits of a little boy!"

"Some of a little boy's bad habits, too," grinned Probert. "Give him another drink."

More brandy. Hunt drank as though he were a fowl, lifting his chin and smacking his lips after each sip. Then he took a newspaper from the bar and would have shaped it into a cocked-hat had not the landlord snatched it from him.

"That's today's," he said reproachfully. "I ain't read it yet."

"One minute! Hey, Bill, look at this." Gently, Hunt took back the paper and pressed his finger on a small paragraph. "Says here that Mr. Lemming's still at the Queen's Arms at Margate."

"What of it?" shrugged Probert.

"Nothing; but it explains why Thurtell ain't had much of the blunt lately. Think he's quarrelled with Lemming?"

"If he's quarrelled with Lemming," scoffed Probert, "he'd have been hit on the head or had his throat cut long before now."

"Ay, I know that," said Hunt, putting on a solemn countenance to impress these yokels with his intimacy with the sporting world of sharps, legs and bruisers. "But no one'll ever kill Jack. He's like me, a Turpin lad! Let's drink to all Turpin lads!"

"You've had enough," said Probert and seized his arm and dragged him into the street.

Back in the gig, jogging through Edgware, he took no heed of Hunt's threats and cajoling. Hunt had had enough for the time being, and resolutely, to the fool's wailing protests, Probert passed taverns and inns; and he pulled up only at a chandler's because he had to buy some corn. While he was in the shop, Hunt shivered in the night, his body warmed with spirit protesting at the ice in the wind; and while he sat, bouncing on the seat and hugging himself with both hands under his armpits, he heard the clot-clot of a horse's hoofs, the clatter of wheels, and turned just in time to see an olive-green gig whirl past, two men seated in it, one man in a brown castor, the other in a black castor, one man big and burly, the other slimmer and small; and this second man clasped, as though he loved it, a carpet-bag across his knees.

"Just gone by," he hissed at Probert when Probert staggered out under a sack of corn which he tossed into the gig: "not a minute since. Suddenly I turned round and there they was, racing past like a couple of turtle-doves. We'd best hurry if we're to pass em again."

"We'll do that easy," grunted Probert. "Gimme the ribbons."

He took the reins and shook them, clucking his tongue, until the horse wearily started again to trot.

The coldness of the air, now that the sun had long since gone, nipped at Hunt's body and brains; and he felt drowsy, shaking from side to side, swinging against Probert, then almost swinging over the rail into the road. His coat was ancient and worn and patched, his trousers had a large patch on the seat and were shiny over the knees, and only his waistcoat, being mainly concealed, looked clean except for a crust or two of dried soup down the front. Such garments were no protection against cold. But the excitements, long drawn out, of that day, and the amount of drink he had consumed, turned Hunt drowsy, and through half-closed eyes he watched trees, houses, bushes, and further trees and houses, bob past him against a heavy sky, while the gig dipped and rose amongst the ruts like a ship at sea.

"Where—where are we?" he gasped, staring around him when the gig pulled up before bright windows.

"At Elstree," chuckled Probert, jumping down. "At the Artichoke;

and we passed our friends again a long way back. Time for a little wet before we get down to business."

"Ay, ay, always time for bingo," mumbled Hunt, scrambling from the gig that swayed under him; and, had not Probert caught him by the arm, he would have fallen on his face, his legs seeming as stiff as wood.

Groaning, he hobbled after Probert into the warm bar, rubbing his hands and blinking at the oil-light.

"Bingo," he growled, shivering: "that's the nectar for a dead man. Hey! don't drown the poor thing! brandy can't swim, you know."

The landlord chuckled at the ancient joke, but Hunt's wits were not yet thawed and he could think of nothing better to say while he yawned, stretching his arms before the fire.

Quickly, the brandy warmed him. Liquid fire flooding under his skin and making him blink and shudder pleasantly. Only he didn't feel like murdering anyone at the moment. Much of his enthusiasm had been dozed away in the gig, and he would have liked to have taken a short nap before starting on the important work before them. Hitting people over the head and cutting throats seemed an enchanting occupation when you didn't have to do it yourself, but the time must be very close when he would have to show that he was no mere babbler and he would have to join Thurtell in killing, stripping and hiding a fellow-man who, at this moment, was breathing like himself and who had no conception of his doom ahead while he jolted beside his future murderer through the night.

"Give me another drink," he cried in a harsh voice.

A glance at his face with the greenish tinge in what skin showed between the luxuriant growth of hair was sufficient to stop Probert arguing. Without a word, he had Hunt's glass refilled; nor did he protest when Hunt asked for a third brandy.

It was while Hunt had this third glass to his lips when he stood before the fire that he heard the sound of approaching wheels. Probert looked up. He, too, had heard them. Swiftly, Hunt tossed the brandy down his throat, and shivered, listening to the rattle drawing nearer, the clump-clump of horse's hoofs, the whine of springs. . . . Nearer it drew, seeming to sound like a rush of wind through trees; then it passed, flitting its green body through the light from the tavern-windows flickering on it a moment, showing two men upright in their seats, one swinging a whip negligently, the other slouched inside his great-coat. Clearly seen, lit up as on a stage, they were; then into darkness they went, and the rattle of wheels and the clop-clop of hoofs grew gradually fainter in the distance.

"There they go," whispered Probert, staring into Hunt's eyes. "Now we must be after them."

With a shaking hand, Hunt took the glass of brandy and water he offered.

"Never mind," said Probert, beginning to smile, "we'll have time enough; and we can't waste brandy when it's a shilling a glass. Their horse's a hired one and he must be nearly knocked up by now. Ours is fresh. We'll soon overtake them."

Dumbly, Hunt nodded, thanking him in a glance; and with a jerky movement, he lifted the glass and was about to drink its contents; then he lowered it. . . . Better to drink slowly. . . . This must be his last drink before . . . before they left. . . . O! he must prolong its pleasure! . . . Soon, very soon, they would catch up with Thurtell; as Probert had said, his horse, being a hired one, must be blown while theirs was still fresh, a good horse. . . .

They might even have time for another drink. . . .

Cautiously, timidly, Hunt looked up, then smiled with relief to see the understanding acquiescence in Probert's eyes.

"An-another drink?" he asked, and shyly smiled.

CHAPTER FIFTEEN

AT LAST

AFTER eternities, riding through hell, round and round over the same damned lanes, the same damned hedges scratching him as he passed, Thurtell feared that he was going mad. Round and round, mazed, bewildered, he drove, wondering where he could have missed damned Hunt and Probert. Or had he taken the wrong road? No. No. This was the road to Radlett. No. It was the road to Letchmore Heath. But two roads ran to Letchmore Heath, and Gill's Hill Lane ran, or wriggled, between them. Or was it the way to Aldenham? or to Watford? to Shenley? or was he turning back to Elstree and towards Edgware? No. Of that he was certain. He'd have remembered recrossing Medbourn Bridge, the way it humped in the middle and gave one a jolt. Absurd. He was on the right road, the same road, going round and round the same damned road, with never a sight of Hunt or Probert.

There shone the lights of the tavern, the Artichoke, with a gig tied to the fence outside, the horse lazily cropping the grass. This was the second time he had passed it, and he wondered why Weare had made no comment about this damnable-go-round in the country. Of course, in the darkness, to a stranger, all country-roads looked alike, but he must by now have begun worrying over the time they had taken. Deliberately Thurtell had dawdled on the way to give the fools the opportunity to rattle ahead, and twice had he passed them on the road. Were they already drunk? or were they scared? For all his great body, Probert had the heart of a mouse; and you could not expect courage from poor little Joey Hunt; but he could not believe that Hunt, his noisy champion, would have deserted him on the brink of action. Probert he had never trusted. Something greasy about Probert; that false smile and jovial amiability would deceive nobody except a woman. The man was capable of any treachery; but not Hunt, not gay little, tragic little Joey Hunt dancing and singing to hide the tears in his voice and the misery that urged him to lie down and die. Never would Joey let down a pal.

Yet where the devil was he, blast him? and where was Probert? Even the moon was in hiding, but he was glad of that. He didn't want to have even Oliver's eye to watch what he must soon do, what he must, dammit, do alone. Alone. A peasant in a dirty smock passed, rising a moment near the gig as though springing out of the earth, then passing as quickly as he had been seen. Nobody else. Over a deserted earth, through tunnels of darkness, he drove, on, on, around and around and around.

Where in God's name were Hunt and Probert!

Beside him he felt Weare shuffle, easing his bottom on the seat, and he heard him yawn.

"Damn my eyes, Jack," Weare chuckled, "here's a pretty place to cut a man's throat if you want to get rid of him."

The prescience of that remark so startled Thurtell that he almost dropped the reins, and he found it impossible to say anything in reply. Did those near death really feel their death approaching? were there guardian angels to shout warnings which human ears could hear only dimly? Why else had Weare said that? A pretty place in which to cut a man's throat if you wanted to get rid of him. . . . A dark place, a dank place, stinking of rotten vegetation, a place to which the clean sun rarely penetrated and which was therefore always damp, the earth retaining puddles long after the water had dried on the fields: a place, as prophetic Weare said, for a murder. After all, that was why he had chosen it.

But where the hell, God blast them, were Hunt and Probert?

Suddenly fearing that Weare must be beginning to suspect, he cleared his throat and said in a casual manner: "I must have missed the lodge gates, blast it. Only been here once before and it's a dark night. We must have passed em."

Now was the moment. Now before Weare's suspicions should grow strong and warn him to raise his fists in self-protection. Now . . . now, even though he must do it alone, without those deserters, Probert and Hunt, to help him. Should he race round a third time, Weare was certain to become suspicious, recognizing perhaps the Artichoke, the gates of Mr. Phillimore's Lodge, or some other feature of the landscape; and once he grew suspicious, it would mean a fight. Thurtell did not want a fight. Easily, with his superior strength, should he be able to master this small creature, but in every fight there was the possibility of a wild blow causing damage, giving a black eye or a swollen nose, and such marks would be difficult to explain should the traps come asking questions. Besides, Weare might scream; and a scream in this still countryside, not a mouse squeaking, not a bird chirruping, would sound for miles. Quickly must he be slain, cleanly, without noise of fighting.

Slowly, finding a more open space, he turned the horse round.

"Must have passed it, dammit," he said. "Beautiful country round here, Bill; worth looking at again."

"If you could see it," grunted Weare.

"The moon'll soon be up. Look, over there! you can see her . . ."

Now. Now. This was the way that Probert had suggested. Make him look away from you, Probert had said, point something out to him, then clap the pistol to his head, and fire.

"I can't see no moon," growled Weare.

The damned pistol was caught in his pocket, the hammer catching in the lining. With a quick tug, Thurtell had it out.

"There! can't you see it!" he cried, pointing with his left hand, while with his right he pressed the pistol to Weare's head and pulled the trigger.

Sparks whirred, the hammer clicked dryly down. That was all.

"What's this? what's this?" cried Weare, and he sprang from the gig. "Would you kill me, Jack?"

"Ay," cried Thurtell, and he leaped down after him.

"For God's love, Jack," wailed Weare, stumbling in the furrows when he tried to run, "don't, don't!"

Thurtell pulled back the hammer and fired again. This time the hammer fell with force, the oil beginning to work, and the explosion startled him almost as much as it startled Weare, who screamed.

Out of the trees, whirring their wings and lashing the leaves, birds sprang, squealing, into the clouds. Then the night, lit for a moment, closed down again.

"No, no!" screamed Weare. "You can have all I won off you, every penny, Jack, if only you'll spare my life!"

"Damn you!" cried Thurtell and sprang on his back.

Who would have thought this lean man could have had such strength! Weare twisted, writhed and kicked; he punched and bit and scratched, rolling under Thurtell's hands. For a wild moment, Thurtell feared he would topple over and his enemy might get on top; but Weare's agility, spurred by terror, was no match for Thurtell's strength and hatred. All the time, he kept on screaming, begging for mercy, offering wealth, fortune, everything if only Thurtell would not murder him. God's curse on the dog! Someone, even in the dead countryside, must hear such screaming in the night.

The knife. That would be quickest. With his left hand trying to keep his victim steady, Thurtell fumbled for the knife in his pocket, found it, opened it with his teeth, and struck with it and plunged the blade into the ground, Weare suddenly squirming aside as it fell.

"Damn damn damn," sobbed Thurtell.

"Pity! for the love of God, Jack, Jack, take it all, don't kill me, you can't kill me!"

"Damn you," growled Thurtell, feeling for the jugular vein. He thought he had it, but his fingers slipped when Weare twisted and tossed him, and he cut only into flesh, then found himself under his enemy.

"Damn and blast you," he groaned, and he felt the knife jar on a rock when he struck with it, the blade snapping off. With the broken blade, he sought again for the jugular and began to saw into the flesh; and suddenly, to his horror and disgust, the blood fountained and rushed into his own open mouth. Almost he fainted, feeling his stomach retch, and in rage at this sticky deluge, he picked up the pistol where he had dropped it and, with all his rage and strength, rammed the barrel into Weare's head. Again he rammed it, and again, and he had the satisfaction of hearing the bone crack when he bored in, twisting the barrel.

Even after that Weare did not lie still. He moaned and his limbs twitched while Thurtell staggered to his feet and wiped his face with the red shawl he had brought with him. There must be blood on his great-coat, damnable stuff to wash off. . . . He'd have to say he had been in a fight: no! that he'd had a tumble, that was it! the gig had been upset!

In this tunnel of greenery little moonlight penetrated and Weare was only a dark shape, still groaning, at his feet; then soon the groaning ceased and everything became still. All was now silence save for a creak from the gig and the munching of the horse cropping grass under the hedge. It was only a moment since, it seemed a hundred years ago, Weare had been alive. Now he lay on the earth, leaking blood, an empty carcase that must be concealed from the world.

Leaning on the wheel of his gig, Thurtell vomited to rid his mouth of the salt taste of blood; and he shook as though feverish. This would not do, this womanish spewing and shaking. He was a man, dammit, a marine, he was Old Flare whom nothing could unnerve. Besides, he must find the rascal's money.

Now that the excitement was passing, rage against Hunt and

Probert for having failed to be on time began to leave him, and he felt proud that alone he had managed to kill this man. The wretched pistols had failed again; but his hands had not failed even though the knife, like the pistol, had rebelled and snapped its blade. Now he must have his reward. Quickly, before Hunt and Probert stumbled on him. Why should he split the winnings with them when they had done nothing, dammit? All the work was his, the plotting and the act itself; therefore should the rewards be his, and it could scarcely be said that he had bucketed his pals if he pocketed most of the proceeds.

As though the dead body retained something of its late master's malicious spirit, it would not be obedient to his fingers. It slipped and slumped and rolled always the way he did not want it to roll, as he sought to unbutton the waistcoat, then to undo the flannel shirt. Here, against the skin, ay! it was here!

With shaking hand he ripped the tape that held it about the body's neck and drew out a leather case which he opened to see notes and gold. This was not for the others. No, this he would keep, all of it. At least a thousand pounds must be there, and they were his. Exultantly, he pushed the packet inside his shirt and rebuttoned Weare's shirt and waistcoat; then, with more leisure, he set to search for lesser booty.

A gold watch in a handsome double case, and a gold chain attached, hanging from his neck. Handkerchief. A penknife. Spectacles, for reading. Snuff-box. Betting-cards. Dice. Ay, as he expected, they were loaded! Another handkerchief, a fine yellow silk one. Loose change, silver and copper. A silk note-case containing twenty pounds. That he might put back and let Probert find. Also the brown silk purse holding three sovereigns. There was also the gun and the carpet-bag and the backgammon-board in the gig. Altogether, not a bad night's work.

But he could not leave the body lying there for any chance wayfarer to stumble over. Coldly, without repugnance now could he turn towards it, and, tying his red handkerchief around its neck, he dragged it to the hedge, then into the hedge and through the hedge into the open ground beyond. There, panting, wiping his brow, he stood in the cool wind, his face stinging from thin bramble-scratches, and for the first time, under moonlight, could he see his victim plainly.

The handkerchief concealed the cut throat and Weare lay on the side that had the hole in the head, so that he looked like any sleeping man, the legs drawn up and one arm flung out over the grass. He must not be left here; but for the moment, this field would have to do. Later, he would return and, with Probert and Hunt to help, carry him to some secret place where none should find him.

He was too tired for further effort. Pushing into the dead man's pockets those things he did not want, while keeping purse and secret-case, he pushed his way back into the road and looked about him for the exploded pistol and the knife, neither of which in the darkness could he find.

Later. He would come back later. Probert could bring a lantern and they could clean the place, wipe away the blood, see that no tell-tale signs remained. . . . For the moment, he wanted to rest, to get away out of this damned darkness. Leaving the horse to crop the grass, feeling that he needed to walk, he stumbled down the lane towards Probert's cottage, then saw a dark figure rise before him.

"That you, Bill?" he whispered. "Where's Hunt?"

"Hulloa!" cried Probert, standing still in his surprise. "Didn't see you coming, Jack. What a bloody night!"

"Bloody, indeed!" said Thurtell, and began to laugh.

"You've done him? have you done him?" Hoarsely, Probert whispered, shuffling closer. "I left Hunt waiting for you near Philli-more's Lodge. You know the place."

"I don't want him now," said Thurtell, "for I've done the trick."

"And the rhino? how much did he have?"

"I've not looked, not properly. Go and get Hunt. I'll wait at your place."

"The women are there."

"What! Carrie?"

"No; Carrie ain't there."

"Never mind, never mind. I'll wait for you at the stables. Find Hunt. You know best where you left him."

Pleased to be alone again he stumbled around the corner towards the cottage, hearing the dogs bark and rattle on their chains, guiding him forward until he saw the lighted windows twinkle through the greenery. In a way, he was relieved that Caroline was not there to-night. To play the courtier with pretty phrases would have been no easy task after what he had recently done. Something of the elation of the deed remained with him, keeping him light-headed as though a little drunk, and he did not want to lose this feeling of near-ecstasy by having to talk to others. Yes, it was like being drunk, as though he walked on feathers and everything about him, himself as well, was all slightly larger than life, brighter, more richly coloured, more deeply perfumed. A feeling like being in love. He had thought of that before at some time. To kill was like making love, a release of dammed energies bringing not so much delight as a freedom from pain, a tightening of the heart-strings in an ecstasy that was almost beyond bearing. . . . Now the relief, the blissful peace of the freed spirit, making him feel both drowsy yet alert.

Gently he opened the gate and stepped into the neglected garden. No one, save the howling dogs, heard his step when he tiptoed to the shadows of the stable and leaned against its door, taking deep breaths of the air flavoured with manure and horses' stale. As yet, he could not believe that he had slain his enemy. That was a dream, something he had imagined, and not true. When he got back to London, he'd see Bill Weare waiting for flats at Rexworthy's, the same cat's grin on his phiz. Yes, things would be no different. He felt no different, apart from a certain elation, so why should other things be different? The killing had been a dream; yet he shuddered and felt sick at the memory of blood, and he spat to spit away the taste.

Men, and women, too, had best be careful what they said to Old Flare in future. You can hang for only one murder, so what difference did it make if you killed a million? Not that he was likely ever to hang. Not for killing Weare, at any rate. Rexworthy possibly knew of their meeting, but he would call him a liar in his teeth. Who else, apart from Joey and Probert? His brother, of course; but Tom would never betray him. Nobody else. Someone in the street might have recognized him while he had driven with Weare, such unlucky chances usually did happen, but that would be no proof of murder. Here, in the thickets of Hertfordshire, on an unkempt path which almost nobody used, a path that led to nowhere, merely linking two unimportant roads together, who would think to look for a city-lover such as Bill Weare? Only one fear seriously troubled Thurtell, lest Weare's howling and shrieking had been heard, for sounds carry far in the night.

That was the only danger. Some damned inquisitive woman might have been woken up by the screams and tomorrow she would mag about it until the tale was rattled all through Radlett. They would have to get up before dawn and clean away any suspicious marks. Let Probert and Hunt do that. He had done enough for this night. But he was not sleepy. He remained alert, ready for action, for hard drinking through the night.

If only he could get this damned taste of blood from his mouth. He spat and spat, yet it remained. A drink might clear it, and food. . . . He shuddered. Idiotically, he felt that never would he be able to eat again, so dry was his mouth, and he feared that everything he bit might taste of blood.

At last, slowly down the path came his gig, Probert at the reins, Hunt crouched beside him.

"You there, Jack?" piped Hunt in a shrill voice, then he sprang to the ground and ran to where Thurtell stood outside the stables. "How could you have passed us?" he wailed.

At sight of Hunt's distress, Thurtell smiled, yet he remained annoyed that he had been left to do the work alone.

"It doesn't matter where I passed you," he said coldly. "I have done the trick. I have done it!" Then, seeing Probert approach, he added: "Why the devil did you let Probert start lushing at his damned public houses when you knew what was to be done?"

"I made sure you were behind us," cried Hunt, dancing in his disappointment; "else we'd never have stopped."

Slowly, Probert descended from the gig.

"Take the pork into the kitchen, Joe," he said, "and tell the cook to dress it for supper. You'll find it in my gig."

"I'm sorry, Jack," he said gloomily, watching Hunt scamper from the stable to the house with the parcel, "but I'd have sworn you never passed us."

"You'd swear away your mother's life," said Thurtell. "One day you'll swear yourself into the rope and it'll be too late to swear yourself out again. You intended I should do it alone, didn't you?"

"Good heavens, no!"

"Well, I did do it alone. It's the first killing that's difficult, Bill. You've heard me say that, haven't you? And it's the truth. Having done it once, you can easily do it again. Everything comes easier with practice, even murder."

"Of course, of course. You shouldn't fail with the major now."

"Nor with somebody else, perhaps."

"Ay, with bloody Barber Beaumont neither."

"Nor with anyone," said Thurtell ferociously, "who lets me down or talks too much of what I've been doing. I'm a good friend, Bill, but I'm a damned bad enemy, as Bill Weare's found. I hope that'll be an example to others. Old Flare don't stand for traitors nor for any man who thinks to make a fool of him. Remember that."

"Of course you don't," cried Probert in his most cajoling voice. "No one'd dare try make a fool of you, Jack."

"They'd better not try," growled Thurtell. "Now let's go in to Joey."

In the kitchen they found Hunt explaining to the slatternly cook the exact way in which he liked his pork chops grilled.

"Come on, Joe," said Thurtell. "Meet the ladies."

Thank God, Caroline was not there! In his present tensed condition, with his clothes ruffled and doubtless bloodstained—the bloodstained great-coat he had left in the gig—he would have feared her sharp eyes; but there were only Mrs. Probert and her one-eyed sister, Anne, to greet him. Thurtell kept far from the lamplight while Probert introduced Hunt to the women, saying:

"This is my friend, Joseph Hunt, of whom you've so often heard me speak as being so good a singer; now I've brought him down to entertain you."

Very much the gentleman, Hunt bowed low over each lady's hand when he kissed it.

"Come, Joe," said Probert suddenly, "let's leave the ladies for a time. While supper's getting ready, my love, it'd be better if we men got out of your way. We'll go to the stables and see to the putting up of the horses."

Back to the stables they went, Probert leading the way in the dark. Hung from a nail in a post a lantern in the stables showed the youth, Dick Addis, rubbing down the horses.

"Leave em for a time," said Probert. "See if you're wanted in the kitchen. I'll call you when I want you."

No longer angry, his pride every minute growing the greater at the realization that alone he had killed Weare, Thurtell put his fist to his mouth to conceal the smile that kept plucking the corners of his lips, while he awaited his comrades' congratulations. He had not long to wait. They drew closer to him, gazing up at him in the feeble light as though he had become a stranger, a being of different flesh and bone, to be adored and feared; yet, at the same time, he remained their friend, Old Flare, Old Flash; and that was something they could not fully realize as they looked with wonder at his great hands.

"Well," sighed Hunt, "you really done it!"

Thurtell nodded and shrugged. "I told you I would," he said, "but I didn't expect the trouble I had to kill him. I never had so much trouble to kill a man before in all my life, and at one time he nearly had the best of me; for after I'd discharged the pistol at him he jumped out of the gig and run. I followed and he fought with me till I had to knock him down with the pistol; and he then struggled with me with great resolution and actually got me undermost. . . ."

Quietly, modestly, he spoke as though telling of some everyday affair, but his blood quickened in the telling, beating through his limbs, suffusing him with a glow of pride and excitement. Again he could feel Weare panting against him, under him, over him, while they wrestled on the earth. Weare screaming and his knife digging into his throat.

"While I was in this situation," he said, watching the others' eyes in the flickering light, "I took out my penknife and cut his throat, and in so doing I broke the blade. The blood rushed from him in large quantities, some got down my throat and nearly choked me. . . ." He could still taste it, salty, hot. He shivered and spat.

"At last, when his strength failed him by the loss of blood, I got up," he said. "He lay still and groaned for a short time, but I soon stopped that by tying my large red handkerchief round the bastard's throat and dragging him through the hedge. In the struggle unfortunately I lost my penknife and the pistol, and we must try to find em. Otherwise, someone might pick em up and start an alarm."

Without a word, as though stupefied by the horror of that recital, Probert unhooked the lantern from its nail.

"I took his purse," continued Thurtell. "It'd only got two or three sovereigns in it; but I'd no time to search thoroughly, of course."

"Of course," repeated Probert, raising the lantern and glaring into Thurtell's eyes. "I don't expect we'll find much else," he said and turned and walked out of the stable.

In the darkness that closed around him with the going of the light, Thurtell stood, his fists clenched for murder. The damned insolence of Probert to suggest that he had bucketed his pals when he, the drunken idler, had dallied in taverns to keep his hands white from blood, was almost too much for him to tolerate. That Probert's suspicions were correct did not mitigate the insult. Probert who had never worked in his life, a gross caterpillar feeding on silly women's bounty, for him to dare to sneer! Alone, deserted, he had had to work dangerously for them all; and this was his reward! Probert openly hinted that he suspected there would be no money on the corpse because it had been already frisked. . . .

At the moment, it would be absurd to quarrel. Until the body was hidden and they were safely back in London, private angers must be held in leash. Disunity could ruin them all. . . .

Quickly, he hurried after Probert, Hunt skipping at his side. There was no need to go round by the road, the body being on this side of the hedge, and they saw the twinkle of Probert's lantern dancing before them as he stumbled over the ruts. The earth, turned by the plough, was hardening, and thistles, nettles and other weeds were beginning to sprout amongst grass. Up and down, as though on the tail of a boat at sea, the lantern rocked in Probert's hands as he moved cautiously forward, and it was not long before they reached him. He said nothing; he did not look up. Head bowed, he trudged on, taking no notice of the others.

Suddenly the moon escaped from the clouds and all became light; the earth showed golden brown and the trees took shape with gleaming leaves, shining as though with frost, and there were stars once more in the sky. Under this soft light, on the edge of the purplish black shadows of the hedge, Weare lay as Thurtell had left him, slightly on his side, one leg bent, as though he slept. The red shawl tied about his neck concealed the face, as sleeping men will hide from the moon in fear of being struck lunatic.

"Take this," said Probert, forcing the lantern into Hunt's fingers. "I'll hold him, Jack, while you frisk him."

Easily in his powerful arms Probert raised the body, gripping it under the armpits, and the head lolled forward, shaking off the shawl. Little of the face could be seen under the mask of blood, yet Weare did not appear to be dead. The way the creature moved in Probert's grip, lurching like a drunken man, nodding forward, nodding back, made Hunt giggle, so ridiculous the body looked.

"He wasn't carrying much," muttered Thurtell, quickly running through the pockets while Probert watched him. "Damn little, the dog! Why! there's only four screens! twenty lousy quid!"

Neither Probert nor Hunt spoke. In that uneasy silence, Thurtell continued busily searching the dead man, knowing what the others were thinking, Probert, in particular, being no fool. A traitor himself, such a man would expect treachery from others. But to hell with him! Thurtell was sorry that he had to bucket Hunt—later he might slip him a pound or two—but Probert, that fat and lazy bull, deserved to be cheated.

"Give me the sack," he said.

Still silent, Probert passed him the sack which Hunt had bought and the three managed to shuffle the body into it; then Thurtell sat back on his haunches and looked up at his companions in the moonlight.

"Now," he said, "what are we going to do with him? Can't leave him here."

"You're not taking him to the cottage," said Probert harshly. "I'm not having him in my house."

"If he stays here, he'll soon be found in the morning!"

"He's not coming into My House," repeated Probert firmly.

"There's that pond next to the cottage," suggested Thurtell.

"Too close to My House," said Probert. "I'll not have it."

"O, hell," growled Thurtell. "He can't stay here and we can't take him there. The best thing's to leave him until the women have gone to bed."

"Then what are you going to do with him?" quavered Hunt.

Wiping his hands, Thurtell rose slowly to his feet. "We'll take the horse to carry him," he said. "Then we'll throw him in the pond."

"You won't. Not in my pond," growled Probert.

"Only for a while, Bill. Just to get him out of the way until we have a chance to bury him."

Probert did not answer, but it was plain by the stiff way in which he held himself that he disapproved of the plan. He said nothing, however, but trudged back towards the cottage, Hunt with the lantern showing the way, while, for the second time, excitedly Thurtell began to tell about the murder and the unexpected difficulties he had encountered in trying to kill one man.

"By God," he cried suddenly. "We've forgotten about the gun! and the knife!"

"No good looking for em now. . . ."

"But if somebody finds them! And there's blood everywhere!"

"Hardly anybody uses the lane," said Probert. "And if they did, they'd see nothing in the dark. I'll go early in the morning and find em. Better for me to look for em. I'm known hereabouts and there'd be no talk if I was seen in the lane. I'll take the dogs as an excuse."

"Nobody uses the lane? You're sure of that?"

"Why should anyone use it? It don't lead anywhere except to my house and I'm not expecting visitors."

Uneasily, Thurtell looked back over his shoulder. In the shadow of the hedge, Weare's body lay unseen and the night was quiet under the stars until the dogs, hearing their approach, began to bark in Probert's yard. So peaceful was it that even he could scarcely believe that murder had recently been done; but when he plunged his hand inside his shirt, the fingers closed on a bag, on a bag he dared not play with lest it jingle or betray the unmistakable rustle of banknotes to the sharp ears of Probert trudging silently before him. Probert suspected; and be damned to him! Scornfully, Thurtell looked at the big man, at the great body on the shortish legs, and he smiled with closed mouth. Let Probert think whatever he liked. He was not afraid of the man's malice or even of his hatred. There was nothing Probert could do to hurt him, for was he not, as an accomplice, as guilty as the murderer himself and equally as liable to be hanged?

CHAPTER SIXTEEN

SHADOWS IN THE NIGHT

MRS. PROBERT could not sleep. The hour was late, past twelve o'clock, yet she did not feel drowsy, and that was surprising for she had drunk many glasses of wine and, later, of rum; and she was not a drinking-woman. Fear kept her wits sharp, driving off sleep; for she was inexplicably afraid.

Downstairs in the parlour she could hear the men talking, and there sounded Mr. Hunt's laugh, a braying noise that did not seem quite human. What were they doing? When she had suggested that the two men might sleep in Anne's bed, Anne sleeping with the children, the offer had been graciously refused. He and Hunt, Mr. Thurtell had said, would sit up together, snoozing on the chairs or sofa if they felt tired. They were keeping her husband up with them, although that was not unusual. While anything remained to be drunk, Mr. P. could be relied on to stay until all the bottles were empty. Yet something was wrong . . . something . . . but what?

She fingered the thin gold chain about her neck. At first when Mr. Thurtell had offered it to her, she had refused to accept it. He had insisted, sighing and saying that it had belonged to a woman he had once loved at Norwich, but now he wished her to have it. After that, it would have been discourteous to deny him and she had bent her head while he had clipped it about her neck. Why should this gift, no very valuable gift, make her afraid, suspecting . . . yes! she did suspect it! . . . that they had been robbing somebody.

Unable to remain still in bed, at last she slipped out of the sheets, pulled on her slippers, and, in her flannel nightgown, tiptoed to the door. She opened it carefully and stole out on to the landing.

No women's voices. She'd have detected the faintest whisper of a female. The men were alone, clinking glasses, and it did not seem that they talked about women.

Over the balusters she leaned, but they spoke in such low tones that she could not untangle the words. They were saying something about trying on clothes. There sounded Mr. Thurtell's voice. "I think it'd fit you very well," he said; then his voice lowered again, and she heard Mr. Hunt giggle. Then sounded rustling, like papers being moved on the table; then, a hissing and a rattle of the poker. Something was being pushed on the fire. Those papers, perhaps?

Exasperated by her inability to hear, her nameless fears growing stronger every moment, Mrs. Probert tiptoed back to her bedchamber, not wishing her husband to catch her listening; and in the darkness on the bed she sat and shivered, wringing her hands. It was not knowing that was so exasperating. This being kept out of a secret maddened her because it started her worrying, imagining the most dreadful things, judges and juries and even hangmen in the dawn. Mr. Thurtell seemed a threatening person, now that she considered him. He was strong and quiet and one could not tell what went through his mind. And her husband was so easily led astray; that was why he had so many women: the hussies tempted him, he was such a fascinating person, and he hadn't the will-power to say No to them.

What were they doing downstairs? Again, restlessly she stood up and padded to the stairs to listen. They were going out. Yes. Chairs were pushed aside, the door into the garden was opened.

Quickly, she darted back to her bedroom and, parting the curtains, peeped out into the night. They were walking to the stables, her husband holding a lantern. In the bright moonlight they were clearly seen, the two big men, Mr. P. and John Thurtell, and portly Mr. Hunt bobbing about them. Round the corner they went, apparently to the stables, and soon returned, leading a horse through the yard-gates. A horse? What could they want with a horse at this time of the night or, rather, of the morning? Her mind still running on her husband's fancy pieces, she pictured amazons waiting round the corner; but this cold dead hour was scarcely the one for love-play?

Shivering, she waited, fearful yet knowing not what she feared, until she heard the men return, the horse being led in again with something across its back. Something. She peered into the night, trying to make out the shape, yet knowing, while not confessing that she knew, that it was the shape of a man. Of a dead man. Only a dead man could have lain so loosely, head down, arms swinging. An accident? No. No. This was why they had been so excited at supper; this was why Mr. Thurtell had been unable to eat. Murder! They had made a murderer out of Bill, or an accomplice in murder. They had killed somebody and were bringing the dreadful body to Her House.

Now they were dragging something after them. A sack. They were dragging it along the Dark Walk. She could see them clearly when they stepped into moonlight. Whatever it was they dragged, it was large and heavy: something large and heavy in a sack. Then they were gone again; but she still heard the dragging noise until it stopped somewhere to her left. Silence. Suddenly a splash sounding like a heap of stones thrown into a pit. They had thrown the sack, and the body, into her pond! a pond that was shallow and in dry weather could conceal nothing. They must have been mad! Any chance passerby might see the thing lying in the mud and drag it out. In her pond! Dear God, did they want them all to be hanged!

They were coming back, speaking in hushed voices, but she caught one remark of Mr. Thurtell's. "We must say there was a hare thrown up on the cushion of the gig. Say that somebody made one of us a present of it as we came along. We must tell the boy so in the morning."

Whispered Hunt: "We had better be off to town by four or five in the morning."

"No," said Mr. Thurtell, "we'd better not go before eight or nine."

The door slammed and she heard no more; but she had heard and seen sufficient to terrify her. Murder. Bloody murder. And in her own house! They had killed and robbed some man and had brought the body to Her House! Poor foolish Bill to have let them do such a thing to her; but he was always weak, weak with men as well as with women.

Sobbing, she slid to her knees and began to pray, imploring God to protect her and her Billy; and she was kneeling thus, head on the bed, when Probert entered the room.

"Hey," he cried, "what's this? why aren't you abed?"

She could not speak. Dumbly, she stared at him, still leaning on the bed, a grey blur in the darkness.

"What's this?" he cried again. "You'll catch cold, my duck."

"What have you been doing?" she quavered at last. "You and those dreadful men. . . . There was a dead body. I saw it. It was put into a sack and thrown into Our Pond."

"You're dreaming," he growled.

"I wish to God I were," she said. "O, Bill, what have you done? You can't leave it in Our Pond. It'll be found at once. Particularly now that we're leaving and the new tenant's sure to start poking around. Why did you do it?"

"It's not for long. I told Thurtell I'd not have it, and it's only for the night."

"Then it *is* a dead man! I knew it."

"It's not a dead man. It's . . . it's some property that Thurtell wants kept out of the way for a time. Now, get to bed."

"I'll never sleep again," she moaned. "A dead man in Our Pond! Pray God, poor Annie knows nothing of it."

"Nobody knows anything; you wouldn't if you'd gone to sleep as you should have done. Don't take on, I pray you, my duck. What's done is done and we must make the best of it. Above all, not a word to Anne or your brother. Not to anyone."

"O, God," she said, "to think that I'll soon be a hempen-widow!"

"Don't be a fool, woman! Nobody's getting hanged so long as we keep our heads. It's always like that. The traps can do nothing if nobody talks. That's what they always work on. Talk, talk. If you start blabbing, you'll have us all hanged."

"I . . . I'll not say anything," she sobbed, "of course I won't. O, Bill, Bill, why did you have to do it!"

"I've done nothing. Dammit, woman, they can't do anything to me. I wasn't even at the murder! It's all Thurtell's work. Me and Joe never had a hand in it; so how can we be hanged?"

"They don't reason like that, those lawyers. They'll say you did it and they'll hang you for it. It's only your word against the law."

"Shut up! I'm tired. I'm going to sleep."

Muttering to himself, he sat on a chair while he unbuttoned his boots and pulled off his hose, then took off coat and waistcoat. Watching the man emerge from his clothes, a big huge-chested man with long arms and belly like a soldier's cuirass, thick hair on his chest and running below the navel, Mrs. Probert felt an uprush of pity mingled with adoration. Beside his powerful masculinity she felt weak and easily hurt, soft-fleshed, fat where he was muscled, and she hoped that he would love her tonight as once he used to do. But their loving days were over, alas, she was growing old, being much older than he, and she dreaded unlacing the garments that held her in a fashionable shape. More the mother than the wife to him was she these days, and he needed cherishing, being on occasions as foolish as a boy, as a cruel, unthinking boy who did not understand how he could hurt her with his infidelities.

"Aren't you ever going to bed, dammit?" he growled, pushing her aside that he might crawl under the blankets.

Moaning a little as though ill, she kicked off her slippers, and crept in beside him; and for a time she dared not speak. But at last she could keep silent no longer and she whispered:

"Bill, you're not going to let em stay here, are you?"

"Don't be a fool. They're going in the morning but they're coming back in the night."

"I don't want them here again."

"You want to get rid of the corpse, don't you? They're coming tomorrow to get rid of it."

"How?"

"How the hell should I know! For God's sake go to sleep! I'm tired."

Timidly, she shrank away as he tossed on his side, turning his back on her; and she lay, eyes open in the dark, trying not to weep lest she anger him, and afraid to sleep lest her dreams prove more fearful even than her thoughts. Never again, she felt, would she be able to sleep; waiting always for a knock on the door, she would remain poised in terror, seeing the hangman's shadow wherever she looked.

Exhausted though she was, when dawn came, she rose and dressed; then in her slippers she tiptoed downstairs to the kitchen and stirred the embers in the fire, putting on new sticks and a handful of small coal. Quietly she worked, not wanting others to hear her, particularly not wanting the men to hear her. She had always admired Mr. Thurtell as an upright, manly gentleman, but now he possessed a dark aura, becoming a saturnine monster in her mind. Hunt she despised. His shabby gentility disgusted her, making her feel ladylike, although he had a pleasant singing-voice. Nevertheless, he did not seem quite respectable. Stage people never were respectable, she believed, the women as shameless as the men, and her father would never have approved of her keeping such low company; but the dear man was dead, and weak Bill was no judge of honesty; anybody could deceive him.

While she waited for the kettle to boil, she strolled into the yard and patted the dogs chained near the stable; but no matter where she went or what she did, her thoughts were always on that horrible thing concealed under water. Almost without her intending it, she found that she was strolling past the cottage towards the long pond; and on its edge she paused. The morning sun danced over its slow ripples when a fish, a carp, flicked by under the surface, and the wind rustled in the reeds. No sign of a body there. Near her, the reeds had been trampled and lay bent: that must have been where the men had stood while throwing their dreadful burden from them. Yet who would have suspected evil under this placid water? Difficult was it to believe, last night seeming now only a dream, that a man, a once living man, was lying in a sack down there. . . .

Hurriedly she turned and sped back to the cottage. Its quietness soothed her and after sitting a few moments on the stool she felt sufficiently composed to begin brewing the tea.

"Why, ma'am!" cried Thurtell, springing from the chair at her entrance into the parlour, "you are a fairy undisguised. Of all things I desire, a dish of tea comes first."

With red-rimmed eyes, Hunt gaped at her, then rolled off the sofa, tossing aside the blanket that had covered him.

"Thankee, ma'am, thankee," he yawned.

With a low bow, Thurtell took the tray and, looking into those small yet gentle eyes, Mrs. Probert could not believe him to be a murderer. Hunt, perhaps: he was dirty and ill-dressed enough to be anything, but Mr. Thurtell . . . no, he was too kindly, too well-mannered a man. . . .

"I'll tell Mr. P. you're up," she said, and hurried off, regretting that she had not taken care with her appearance. Not having washed or painted, her hair greasy and uncurled, and her loose dressing-gown torn and stained, she felt suddenly as bashful as a girl.

"Here, Joey, take a gulp of this," said Thurtell, handing Hunt a cup.

"Wish it was bingo," grumbled Hunt, taking the cup. "Or even beer. This is cat's lap and gives you the mulligrubs."

"We'll have a drink later, on the way back."

"Wish we were going now. I wanted to clear out early but you wouldn't have it."

"Have some sense. We don't want talk. And running off like that would start the women and servants gossiping. Everything's got to be as usual."

"It never will be usual again," moaned Hunt, burning his lips and cursing when he tried to drink.

Thurtell shrugged from him and drank daintily. It was going to be a fine day, he was pleased to notice through the window. A good day for a shoot: Weare would have applauded it. That gun of his was of Manton's make and should bring at least a tenner. The watch should fetch anything from twenty to thirty pounds. And there was the backgammon board, the cards and some loaded dice, the penknife and some fine clothing. Hunt could take the clothes. The poor devil was almost in rags and they should fit him. The rest they would share equally, while he would keep that fat package, gold and notes, of which the others knew nothing. For him, at any rate, the expedition had proved lucrative, and there was no reason why they should ever be suspected of the murder. Weare was not a man of regular habits and his house-keeper would have been told that he was going to spend some days in the country. Days, perhaps weeks, might pass before his absence would be noted. Then Rexworthy might mention when last he had seen him and they would come with questions. He knew nothing, Thurtell would tell them; and he smiled at the prospect of baffling the traps.

"Come on, Joe," he said suddenly. "Fresh air'll do you good; besides, we ought to have a look for that knife and pistol. Don't want em left hanging about for anybody to stumble on."

Groaning, Hunt staggered to his feet, sought and found his hat tossed into a corner, then lurched after Thurtell into the light. To his London night-crow's eyes, the glare was blinding, the green too green, the sky too blue; and he shivered. Birds were singing, and he didn't like birds. They made him think of cages and cages made him think of prison. . . .

"Hey, Jack," he cried, "what's the hurry!"

Thurtell paused impatiently for the man to catch him up, then he strode on through the garden into the lane. It was a curving lane and it was not until they had turned the first bend, that they heard voices. Thurtell held up his hand and they went forward carefully, softly. Men were talking; and their voices sounded from the opposite end of the lane, close to where Weare had fallen. Country voices. Could they have found the gun? could Weare's screams last night have been heard, bringing searchers with the dawn?

Hunt looked at Thurtell and Thurtell looked at Hunt; both their faces were white and haggard as though they had suddenly grown old.

"They can't have heard anything," Thurtell muttered, "they can't have."

"Then why are they here?" whispered Hunt.

Squaring his shoulders and striding out and trying to whistle, Thurtell swung round the corner. Two labourers were standing with spades and mattocks and sickles heaped at their feet; and when they looked up, Thurtell recognized them as the two men with whom he and Bill had talked the other day in the Artichoke, the men who had hinted that Caroline was Wood's mistress. They were standing beside a heap of stones and staring at a puddle in the ground; and Thurtell felt that his heart missed a beat when he saw that the puddle was blood.

The two men looked up and watched him and Hunt approach. There was no suspicion in their eyes; they stared with the indifferent interest of countrymen watching a city-interloper in their world.

"There, Joe," cried Thurtell, forcing a wild laugh. "That's where I had that spill last night I told you of. Lucky it didn't break the nag's leg. Ay, and there's some of my own blood. Strange to think you can lose so much blood yet not feel it in the morning!"

From Thurtell to the blood, the labourers looked; and still they did not speak.

"Cleaning up the road, are you?" asked Thurtell, determined to be friendly.

"Ay," said one of the men. "Been complaints about it. Now that Major Wood's sold the cottage, the new owner wants this cleared. Mr. Probert was always complaining about it, too. You can tell him that we've started work today."

"You . . . you're . . . you're starting work . . . here, today?"

"This very minute," said the labourer, "ain't we, Dick?"

"That's right, Johnny," said Dick.

Wildly, feeling he was going insane, Thurtell gaped at them. That they should have decided to start work today of all possible days seemed such monstrous injustice on fate's part that he could not speak for fully a minute. He knew, to his rage, that his face was turning white and that he was exposing his guilt before these men, but he was no longer able to control his feelings. This blow was so unexpected that it dazed him.

At last, he managed to stutter, forcing a sickly smile: "Had a spill here last night, me and my pal, might have dropped a few things out of the gig, nasty fall. If you find anything—keep it for me, will you? You'll be suitably rewarded. . . . There was a penknife, and a handkerchief. . . . Come, Joe, we mustn't keep the ladies waiting at breakfast."

He turned upon his heel, taking such long strides that Hunt had to trot to keep up with him. Nor did he speak until in the garden of Gill's Hill Cottage they saw Probert standing, patting his two dogs that romped about his legs.

"What is it now?" Probert gasped, seeing the terror on their faces.

"We've got to get," muttered Hunt, "they'll be on us any moment now. It's not safe here."

"What do you mean?" Probert gripped him by the lapels of his coat and swung him round. "You yellow little cur," he snarled. "Spit it out. What's stung you now?"

"Let him alone," said Thurtell quietly. "He's right, Bill. There's danger ahead, dammit. Why didn't you tell me that Wood had sold the cottage?"

"Tell you? Of course I told you. That bastard Heward's bought it and the land from Wood. What's it matter?"

"It matters this much," cried Thurtell. "The new landlord's having the bloody road repaired. Do you understand that? He's having Gill's Hill Lane cleaned up. Those two country fellows we saw at the Artichoke the other day, they're there with spades and things."

"With spades?" Probert's face went white. "What bloody luck," he whispered.

"Bloody enough to hang us all," said Thurtell grimly.

"Well, you don't expect us to kill them, too, do you?" almost shouted Probert. "One blasted corpse's enough to have about the premises. But they mightn't notice anything. They're clowns, simpletons. I'll go and see. . . . No, better wait a while. Don't want to make em suspicious by going too soon after you. After breakfast. . . . O, hell, blast it. And here's me being going over the place looking for a likely grave. Come round here. . . ."

Behind the shrubbery he led the way, breaking through the brambles with his stick.

"Here," he said, stopping in a small space in the weeds that was hidden by trees and shrubs. "Make as neat a grave as ever you'll find, wouldn't it? When you come back tonight, Jack, bring a new spade, will you? My old one's not fit to use. Leave this to me, I know more about digging than you do. Damn those labourers! Well, whatever they find, it can't prove nothing; and I'm damned if I leave here before everything's stowed away in safety."

"Spoken like a true friend and a good man," said Thurtell, shaking him by the hand. "So long as we keep our courage up we're safe. My pistol's out there, and the broken penknife. But they prove nothing, nothing whatever. So long as the body's hidden, we're safe. Without it, they can do nothing."

"They'll never find it," swore Probert. "But we'll have to have our story ready. We'll bury him here and cover the grave with nettles. That's the only kind of wreath the bastard deserves."

"Ay," said Thurtell, pressing up his chin. "While we stand together, we're safe. It depends only on us. Let them suspect, let them investigate, ask questions—but unless we talk, they can do nothing."

"They'll never get me to talk," grunted Probert.

"Not if they put hot pins under my fingernails," cried Hunt. "Not if they beat me with nettles and put me in the Tower, I'd not talk, I wouldn't, especially on a pal."

"Your hands on that," cried Thurtell, and he felt tears prickle in his eyes to think he could have inspired such loyalty as this. Didn't the Bible say somewhere that there was no love like the love of man for man, surpassing far the love of women?

Here was proof of it. Two friends, their hands linked in his, forming with him a chain, an unbreakable human chain locked together in loyalty and blood. Yet he shivered. A blue-grey cloud was over the sun, bringing a sudden chill to the young day, and it made him shiver as he looked up, tightly gripping Probert's hand, Hunt's hand, in a unity of trust and love.

CHAPTER SEVENTEEN

A RUM COVE

ONLY once on the drive back to London did Thurtell pull up, taking compassion on Hunt's thirst. The fellow's skin had retained its hint of green, like decomposition, and anyone seeing him would at once have suspected him of being either very ill or very frightened. At a public house near Edgware they drank brandy while the horse was baited, and the spirit brought a hint of natural colour back to Hunt's face—or what could be seen of it around the lush whiskers—and the fleshy nose began to thaw, turning a gentler red. More important, the drink brought him courage; some of his usual jauntiness seeped back into him and the whites of his eyes did not look quite so muddy. Still, it was plain he was a frightened man. The excitement that had led to murder had evaporated; like a lover driven near madness to possess his mistress who awakes, tired and disappointed after success, the reaction that must follow any high emotion had caught him and left him miserable and afraid.

But in his pocket Thurtell had the magic with which to transform his misery to joy. Back again in the gig, cosily warm within as the brandy brought contentment and disposed of nervous doubts, he suddenly pushed into Hunt's hand a paper packet.

"Hey?" cried Hunt. "What's this?"

Thurtell chuckled, watching his friend from the corners of his eyes while he whipped up the horse. "Just a little something I forgot to give you last night, Joe," he said. "A hundred flimsies."

"A—a hundred pounds!" Hunt could not believe it. Hands trembling, he opened the package; then, tears in his eyes, he gazed lovingly at his friend. Never had he possessed so much money in his life. It was too much for any one man to spend. Nobody could spend a hundred pounds! not unless he gambled with it, of course. . . . But a hundred! a hundred canaries on paper! and all of them his!

"God bless you, Jack," he whispered in a husky voice, being close to tears; "you are a true friend, indeed."

"I don't forget my pals," said Thurtell complacently. "But I didn't see why bloody Probert should have a share of what I worked for. I know it weren't your fault, Joe: you've got the heart of a lion, even though you may be a fat fellow; but there's Probert, big as an ox, and he ain't got the heart of a mouse! Thinks he's clever, too! thought he'd be cunning and leave all the hard work to me; but I know his game. Them that don't work, don't get paid. You're different, Joe: I know it weren't your fault you was late. But Probert! . . . And now he wants me to do for some cove what's been hard against him and won't let him have his discharge. Fellow called Holding. Know him?"

"I know him; and I heard Bill asking you to croak him; had something to do with Bill's bankruptcy or something. Are you going to croak the fellow?"

Thurtell shrugged. "I think I'll do it for him," he said after a minute's thought. "Bill's not a bad fellow; only he's a coward, but he can't help that. I've paid him out, though. He got only six quid while we have the rest of the swag! Yes, I'll see to this fellow Holding if he wants me to."

"I thought you was going to do that bastard Mountain for me," said Hunt in a sulky voice.

"Don't worry, pal," grinned Thurtell. "I've not forgotten. That makes it—Holding, Mountain, Barber Beaumont, Wood, Graham and Kelly, if Lemming gives the office, and Springfield—that's the Norwich attorney who turned me bankrupt—and anybody else what interferes in my business. I've knuckled under too long. From now, I'm going to show em I'll be stood on no longer. Weare's only the first."

"What's it feel like," whispered Hunt, watching him hungrily; "I mean, what's it feel like, killing a man? I mean, when you're doing it?"

"Why, nothing," said Thurtell, after thinking hard. "Just like doing anything else. Nothing more than chopping off a chicken's head, only a man's got more blood in his carcase than a fowl. There's a certain pleasure in it, a satisfaction as if you had the whole damned world under your fists and was paying it out for all it's done to you. Only I was unlucky last night. You and Bill . . . I'll say no more about that! But those poppers not working right: that was a nuisance; and I never thought a little man like that could have had such fight in him. Honour bright, Joe, there was a moment when I thought that he was going to murder *me*!"

Hunt laughed at the absurdity of such an idea.

"I mean it," said Thurtell. "It's wonderful what getting murdered can do to a man. He was like a giant with the strength of ten. Only, dammit, if those poppers had worked or you and Bill'd been there as you should have, I'd never have left that mess behind and lost my knife and pistol. I don't like those labourers poking about there this morning."

"Probert'll see to them."

Dubiously, Thurtell shook his head. "I've lost faith in Bill," he sighed. "He should have known about those workmen coming."

"Well, he ain't friendly with his new landlord, is he? He says so himself. And if Woody's going to marry his sister-in-law, I don't suppose he'll want anybody like Bill on his property, living like gipsies and never paying no rent."

"He'll not marry the girl," said Thurtell, the cheekbones seeming to rise as he set his teeth. "He only think he's going to do it, and there's many a slip 'twixt the ring and the bed. He's next on my list."

He did not speak again nor, to Hunt's disappointment, did he stop at further public houses. Not until they had reached Oxford Street did he pull up.

"I'm getting out here, Joey," he said. "I don't want to get lumbered about that blasted fire. Take back the horse and gig and see me at Tetsall's."

"What about these?" asked Hunt, kicking the carpet-bag, the backgammon-board, the gun and Thurtell's bloodstained great-coat in the bottom of the gig.

"Take em home with you, hide em for a time. Upson's got a warrant against me, as you know, and I don't want him turning up suddenly to frisk me. If he found those things in my room, he might start to ask questions. They'd be safer with you."

"I'll look after em," said Hunt, calculating what they should bring when he carried them to uncle's. "See you in half-an-hour."

Thurtell waved goodbye and, choosing lanes and side-streets, made his way back to Conduit Street and was relieved to notice no sign of traps watching the tavern.

Tom was in his room, lying on the bed and reading the *Weekly Dispatch*; and he looked up cheerily at his brother's entrance.

"I—I—I've done it!" he cried.

"Done what?" said Thurtell, startled by this echo of the words himself was eager to shout.

"Made a com-com-composition with my cr-cr-creditors; at le-le-least, I'm out of trouble," chuckled Tom. "They was a bit-bit-bit nasty at first, but in the end we had some gr-gr-grog and everyone was f-f-friendly. I'm going to start ag-ag-again, start fresh, get-get-get a home to-to-together if I can, find some honest wo-wo-woman to look after me-me-me, have the gu-gu-girls back, give em a ch-ch-chance in life. . . ."

"You've forgotten about the fire," said Thurtell harshly.

"The f-f-fire's nothing to do with me. Th-th-that was all in yo-yo-your name."

"So you'd let me stand the racket," said Thurtell slowly. "I'd not thought that of you, Tom. I've always been a friend to you as well as a brother."

"I-I-I'm sorry, J-j-jack, b-b-but what's the u-u-use of both of us getting n-n-nabbed?"

"All right," said Thurtell, sinking wearily into a chair. "You're right. You've got the girls and we have to think of them. It don't matter about me. What if I get transported? There ain't nobody to grieve but myself. You'll be all right while I go away botanizing. . . ."

"D-d-don't talk like that, p-pup-please!"

"It's all right, Tom. I understand." Thurtell stood to his feet, finding it impossible to remain still, and began to pace the room. "There's another reason why you should keep away from me," he said.

"You d-d-did it? you d-d-did what y-y-you was talking of!" cried Tom, sitting up and staring, white-faced, at his brother.

"Yes, I said I'd do it and I done it." Thurtell sat down again, able to relax now that he was opening his secret. "I've got to tell you because you suspect it anyhow," he said, "and I don't want you to say something you shouldn't without knowing what you were talking about, if you understand me. I've been after Weare for some while, as you know, ever since that time at blind hookey when he wouldn't lend me even a brown afterwards when I asked him. He's at Bill's place now at Elstree. In the pond there."

"D-d-does anyone suspect?"

"That's what I'm afeared of. Bill and Joey let me down and I had to do the job myself; and it weren't easy, I can tell you, and there was a hell of a lot of gore; and I lost one of my poppers and my penknife. I'd broken the knife in him, I think. If they dig the bit out and put it against the blade, they'll know where it comes from. Wouldn't have mattered, nobody ever uses that lane, but Wood's sold the damned place and when I went back this morning, there was a couple of johnny raws clearing the lane up! Would you believe it!"

"So you did-did-didn't f-f-find the g-g-gun or th-th-the knife!"

Gloomily, Thurtell shook his head. "That's what's worrying me," he groaned. "And he sang out so loud when I went for him, someone must have heard."

Again, he had to stand up and walk, sitting down becoming impossible.

"O-o-o, h-h-hell!" gasped Tom.

"It'll turn out all right," said his brother with a quick smile. "None of your business anyhow. Tom. You were here, talking things over with your creditors, while I was doing it. But I only wish I could trust Bill Probert."

"He-he-he'll not let you down?"

"I pray not," sighed Thurtell. "If he does, I'll kill him. Who's that?"

He sprang round, fists up, as the door-handle turned; then the door opened and Hunt sidled in.

"Hullo, my Turpin lad!" Hunt cried. "Here's a fine day for a throat-cutting or a ballum-rankum! Never felt so well in my life and only wish I had two bellies to accommodate the bingo I want to cool my throat. What are you doing up here when the bar's downstairs?"

Slowly, Thurtell smiled again. In the presence of Hunt, he could not be afraid. The silly fellow worshipped him and therefore he had to prove that worship justified; Hunt's weakness gave him strength.

"Don't mag too much, Joe," he smiled. "You might let something slip."

"Not me!" laughed Hunt. "Come on! My belly thinks my throat's cut. Let's to the lushy, boys!"

Yes, it was better to sit in the taproom with company than to remain with the devils of fear. Thurtell smiled and put his arm around Hunt's shoulder; and when Tom stood up, he put the other arm about his shoulder; and he hugged them both.

"We're pals," he said huskily. "Thank God, I have some pals!"

"Ay," giggled Hunt, "we'll all hang together!"

It was a pun in poor taste, but Thurtell did not complain. Smiling like a father at his son's antics, he followed Hunt downstairs into the bar, Tom at their heels.

Usually, when entering a bar, Hunt sidled in with an air of apology, as though asking to have his presence excused before somebody threw him out; but this morning, he took long strides and he shouldered aside the other drinkers with a strident: "Make way, make way, for Dick Turpin, or I'll do you; I'll stick you! Three brandies, Mr. Tetsall! and don't be faint-hearted with the bottle. Fill em up."

"You're in a ripe good humour this morning, Mr. Hunt," smiled the landlord, filling the three glasses carefully.

"Who wouldn't be after cutting throats!" laughed Hunt. "Bang bang bang! That's got him."

"You?" scoffed one of the drinkers, "you couldn't shoot an owl by daylight."

"Then you'd better stay at home, young fellow," said Hunt, "because you're a night-bird, too, if I can judge by the rings under your eyes."

He passed two glasses to his friends, taking a deep drink from his own.

"Hey, Tom, you're not looking well today," he said suddenly.

"N-n-never fe-fe-felt better," grinned Tom.

"If you're pressed for rhino, just give me the hint," grinned Hunt, thumbs under his armpits. "Would twenty quid be any use to you? A bit more if you need it."

"Twenty quid!" laughed one of the drinkers. "Where did Joey Hunt ever get twenty quid from!"

"I've got more than twenty," cried Hunt, dragging a heap of notes out of his breeches pocket.

"Rot my soul!" gasped a drinker. "Where'd you get that? been cutting throats, or what? or robbing the bank?"

Hunt saw the warning look in Thurtell's eyes, the frown pencilling between the eyes, and quickly he pushed the money back into his pocket, and laughed uneasily.

"Worked hard for that," he mumbled. "Ain't that so, Jack? Been drawing game in the country, netting some fine birds. . . . Why! did you think I stole it? If we wanted to, we Turpin boys could do it, for a-murdering we will go."

"You're drunk," said Thurtell. "You shouldn't drink in the morning."

"That's it, that's it, I'm drunk," cried Hunt, his enthusiasm wilting under Thurtell's dark glowering. "I was only joking. You all know Joey Hunt and how he always talks of murder. It's by way of a joke with me, always has been. Fact is I've been killing game with Bill Probert holding the bag."

N

"Here, Joe." Thurtell drew him aside, tightly gripping his arms. "Stow magging, can't you?" he whispered. "I want you to do something for me. You know Gray's, the pawnbroker in Fleet Street? He's got a suit of clothes I left with him in pawn. Told him my name was Price and he wrote it on the back of the note. Here's a fiver and the duplicate. Take em to Gray and bring me back the change."

Relieved, he watched Hunt hurry off. Amusing though his chatter might be, it was also dangerous. Soon when Weare was found to be missing, remarks such as he had made would be remembered. How the day after his disappearance, Joe Hunt was displaying large sums in the Coach and Horses and talking of Turpin and murder. Impossible, however, to be angry with him, so boyishly enthusiastic was he, but he must learn to keep his tongue quiet if he didn't want to get them all hanged.

Suddenly, Thurtell felt tired. Last night in that uncomfortable chair he had had little sleep and now his body needed rest, yet there was still much work for him to do. Telling his brother to call him when Hunt returned, he climbed upstairs; then, taking off his coat and easing his collar, he lay down.

When he lay down and closed his eyes, his mind sprang awake. Under the lids quickly passed scenes of violence, and he sweated as again he fought Weare in the dark and again felt the hot blood in his mouth. Ugh, he groaned, and spat into his handkerchief. Again, he lifted the body, lifted it on to the horse, carried it to the stable, towards the pond, and tossed it into the pond. The noise of its fall, the crash of water, echoed to him again like a tocsin in his ears. That splash. Weare's screaming in the lane. Could they have been heard? They must have been heard. And the pistol and knife—had they been found? Had the labourers found them? or had Probert?

Now he would have to kill Beaumont. That was essential. If the rogue persisted in having him boned for fraud, he was asking for trouble and his slaying would be justifiable. Once Beaumont was out of the way, the insurance company's case would fail for want of evidence and, like Tom, he could start again, having the capital provided by Weare with which to set about accumulating a fortune. Yes, had it not been for Probert's laggardness last night and the dropping of that knife and pistol, he would have had nothing to trouble him. But every time he sought to sleep, thought of those lost weapons stung him awake again; and it was with relief that he welcomed the return of Hunt who darted in, lugging a large parcel, Tom following with glasses and a bottle of brandy.

"Came to three pound eight bob," said Hunt. "Here's your change."

"Keep it," said Thurtell, slashing the string with a knife. "These are the breeches I've always liked best," he smiled, drawing out a pair of leather breeches and two long gaiters. "Just the thing for riding or a day in the country. . . . What o'clock is it?"

From his fob he dragged Weare's gold watch and looked at it. "What!" cried he, "twelve o'clock already! and I'm peckish as a pig. Ain't had a bite since breakfast."

That meant a return to the bar for further drinks and for some beef sandwiches to calm the stomach before dinner. Thomas Noyes joined them and Thurtell glanced at him sharply to note whether he had heard anything from Elstree. Apparently not. He was, as usual, melancholy, suspicious and quick to take anything that was offered; and they bought him what drinks he wished while Tom tried to cajole his brother into making him a present of Weare's watch. But Thurtell was extremely proud of that watch, more proud of it, indeed, than if he had paid money for it, and he would not give it up.

During dinner, they bickered friendlily over its value; and, still with the watch in his fob, after dinner, Thurtell carried Hunt out shopping. Close to where Hunt lived was an ironmonger's in Warwick Street, Golden Square, and it took them a full half-an-hour in the warehouse over the shop before Thurtell could decide which of the spades he preferred. Having at last found one weighted and balanced to his liking, he paid for it and sent Hunt to conceal it at his lodgings round the corner.

After that, they continued drinking; into the night, they continued drinking, Thurtell determined to stun himself asleep if there were no other way of finding rest. Until he returned to Elstree and learned what had been happening there, he would not sleep, he knew. Better would it have been to have been boned, he felt, than to remain in this vacuum, not knowing what was happening and aware of approaching danger without being able to tell what shape that danger might take.

For supper, he and Hunt ate oysters until they felt sick, and when Tom strolled into the parlour to join them in a glass of wine, he found them twisted with laughter.

"Joe'll be the death of me," gasped Thurtell, gripping his belly.

"I'm going to buy a theatre for him, and if he don't make a fortune, I'll eat my best castor."

"Let's have a bottle on that," cried Hunt, "nothing else'll do me now! Got to drink, Tom, only protection for a husband. The old woman was in a precious rage with me this morning for stopping out all night. But when I pulled out the money she was satisfied. The only way to stop a woman magging, fill her to the back teeth with gold. I gave her a sovereign and told her to get a pair of fowls and a piece of pickled pork."

"Why?" asked Tom. "You ain't been home all day."

"Bought em for her," said Hunt with dignity. "That woman has an appetite; I do declare that she's in a chronic state of triplets which never get born. She'll have eaten all them, bones and all, and be hungry for more by the time I get home. Can't satisfy her, nothing can satisfy her. Give me another drink."

He drank, and Thurtell drank with him; and it was only when after midnight that Tetsall told them that he was going to close the tavern that he was inveigled into leaving. Thurtell took a bottle of rum to bed with him and drank it in long gulps; and when next he blinked awake he found that it was Sunday morning.

The day was a fine one, a surprisingly fine one for late in October, and he felt that that should prove a good omen. A soft spring light shone on the windows of the houses opposite, glancing off the glass and making the dull bricks seem newly baked and washed in oil.

Quickly, he dressed, pulling on the leather breeches and buttoning the gaiters which Hunt yesterday had redeemed from the pawnbroker's. Then with only his drab waistcoat with a double row of buttons over his shirt, he hastened across the street to be shaved at Collis's. A hair-dresser's shop could often be more instructive than any newspaper, and to Collis's went most of the Bond Street sporting-world to have its hair clipped and its whiskers trimmed. This would be one of the first places to be tickled by any rumour; and while he awaited his turn, reading an old number of *Bell's Life in London*, Thurtell listened carefully to the buzz about him. No mention was made of any corpse having been found in any pond; no talk of any murder at Elstree; no questions of where Bill Weare might be. . . . So far, so very good.

With better heart and cleaner face he returned to breakfast at the Coach and Horses, after finishing his toilet and putting on a bright blue coat. Then, with the white castor on the side of his head, he paraded in the bar while Hunt and Tom applauded.

"Ho-o-how f-f-fine my bro-bro-brother is today!" cried Tom lounging against the bar; and Tetsall nodded assent.

When dressed in his best, as now, there was no doubt that Thurtell looked a swell. His fine, powerful shape was not concealed by the tight clothing but was rather enhanced by it; the great shoulders, the deep chest, flat belly and muscled thighs and shapely calves in gaiters, made him a figure which any artist would have been proud to paint. Not only was it the perfect physique that caused you to look at the man. The haughty chin upthrust by the points of the collar emerging from the stock, the broad cheekbones and the bright eyes glimpsed only when he lifted his head, the supercilious swelling of his mouth and the quizzical eyebrows—one lying flat, the other lifted inquiringly as though in scorn of the world—made of him a figure not easily passed in the street without a second glance. And his hard training in the marines had given him an upright carriage and a swagger in his walk.

Strong and refreshed though he felt, when it came to breakfast he found he could not eat, the lees of last night's wines, oysters and spirits turning sour in his belly. Tom, too, felt queasy, and they contented themselves with a cup of tea each and a glass of brandy.

Tom Noyes joined them; then Hunt; and after half-a-dozen more drinks, Thurtell began to feel strong again. There wasn't room in the gig for them all, he explained, so Noyes decided to walk ahead; then Tom, saying that he needed a stroll, left them, asking to be picked up on the way; and eventually at about half-past ten Thurtell and Hunt, merry and laughing, jumped into the gig.

Standing at the door to watch them go, Tetsall noticed as they placed some beef and clean linen in the gig that it also contained a spade or a shovel, obviously as yet unused, and he raised his eyebrows at a friend lounging beside him.

"What the devil can they want with a shovel on Sunday," he said from behind his hand, "when they're going on pleasure bent?"

His friend did not answer. He picked his teeth and closed one eye as though aiming an invisible gun at the horse.

"Look at the way Hunt's dressed," continued Tetsall with a grimace. "His coat's dirty and torn under one arm. His small-clothes are torn up all one side near the pocket there."

"Judging by the back of it," murmured his friend, "seems the wheel of the gig must have been scraping against it. He's not even washed, and look how shabby he is! Even a singer don't have to look as bad as that."

"No," agreed Tetsall, frowning and shaking his head; "if I were Thurtell I wouldn't ride with a man in that condition; I wouldn't."

"Nor me," said his friend, and spat. "They're up to no good," he added. "I'd swear blind to that. They're up to no bloody good."

"Thurtell's all right," shrugged Tetsall; "only got a gentleman's troubles, a few I.O.U.s and the bloody insurance after him: might happen to any of us . . . but that Hunt! He's a rum cove."

"Ay," nodded the other, "that he is. A very rum cove, indeed. We'll see him hanged one of these days."

"I'd not be surprised; and it's Thurtell's own fault if he finds himself mixed in something real shady, forgery perhaps, or even murder."

"Ay," agreed the other, "I'd put nothing past that Hunt fellow. Any man what dresses like that ain't got no respect for himself. He's capable of anything, he is!"

"That's true," sighed Tetsall. "We're going to hear a bit more of him before he swings. Thurtell ought to have more sense than to mix with a cove like him. . . ."

CHAPTER EIGHTEEN

BEAUTY UNDER A MASK

WHEN Joseph Hunt came prancing down the stairs into the parlour everybody in the room looked up and gaped at him, for the moment not recognizing the chaunter in such splendid toggery. This was a new Joe Hunt, a very different man from the scarecrow in torn clothes, seams showing down the sides, lining pushing through the elbows, who had arrived at Gill's Hill Cottage that morning with the Thurtell brothers and Tom Noyes. He had butterflied into a gentleman and the approving murmurs of Mrs. Probert and Anne Noyes with the chuckles of the men at his descent excited him like the clapping of an audience when he performed on the stage. By cutting the back of waistcoat and breeches he had made of the dead man's clothes a passable fit and with white collar and stock and deep blue coat with yellow big-buttoned waistcoat, tight breeches and polished shoes, never had Hunt looked so like a gentleman, his vast whiskers standing out and his coal-dark hair perfumed and brushed into a thick, curling mop over his right ear. Without a smile, as though he were being presented at court, he bowed low to the ladies, right hand above his heart.

"How smart Mr. Hunt looks today!" cried Thurtell merrily, head to one side, watching his friend with amused affection.

"How smart of you to have made him appear smart, Mr. Thurtell," said one-eyed Anne Noyes who was standing beside him next to the door opening into the garden. "For did you not supply that exquisite coat and those inexpressibles which suggest a manly calf? I am rather partial to a piece of calf myself," she smiled.

Blinking uncomfortably, Thurtell looked down at her. This young woman always tantalized and rather frightened him because he could never tell whether she spoke seriously or whether she quizzed him. This remark about her being partial to a piece of calf, for example. . . . It could mean very much, or it could be nonsense. Many an elderly high-flyer had he seen in her carriage driving slowly along the Mall or Rotten Row that she might indulge her feminine fancy by quizzing the men's muscular legs, and it had amused and titillated his masculine vanity, his own legs being strong and shapely. But those had been abandoned females or great ladies who cared not what lesser folk thought of their foibles. That this demure-looking woman far from the West End should confess to a similar interest he could not believe; and also he found it difficult to believe that she could have been so feather-pated as to leap inconsequently from human to animal flesh. Or was she merely laughing at him?

That accursed flat ogle—why didn't she wear a patch to cover it? —always baulked him. The other eye, a bright brown, seemed merry, and her small pursed mouth smiled faintly, the nostrils wrinkling at the sides: impossible to tell what such a woman meant when she rattled so irrelevantly.

"Really, ma'am," he muttered. "Boiled or roasted?"

"I'm not a cannibal!" she cried, raising both hands in protest. "Really, Mr. Thurtell, you do say such odd things!"

Then she had meant that she was partial to male calves! There was nothing extraordinary in such an interest, only very few women, particularly unmarried and genteel women, would ever have confessed to it.

"I don't know," he said, trying to dance to her coquetry, "I've met females I wouldn't mind taking a bite out of here and there."

"Sir! you do surprise me! La, to bite a lady! I have too great a respect for my poor sex, sir, to ask what part of the female anatomy excites your cannibal interest. I was not thinking of eating anything, except with my eyes . . . with my one poor lonesome eye."

"Why don't you wear a patch over it?" he asked.

"A female argus is at a disadvantage in a world of two-eyed women. They not only see more than I do," she sighed, "they are also more seen, more looked at. Like our dear Caroline!"

Thurtell flushed and shuffled a little away, not wanting to be reminded of Caroline. Yet every time he looked at Anne, he thought of her, they were so alike, save for that lost right eye: only Caroline was more high-spirited, quicker to laugh or to dance. Anne had something of a scornful devil inside her which looked out on the world, one-eyed, seeing through pretence and being amused at human antics. A kind of woman he disliked. He wanted his women to be clinging and passionate yet humble. And, even had she had two ogles, this Anne Noyes would never be the clinging kind, nor would she be humble, although he could detect passion in the pinching of the lips, the shadows under the eyelids, and the occasional twitch she gave as though she were suddenly cold. Altogether, whether one-eyed or two-eyed, he did not like her because she frightened him.

"Excuse me, ma'am," he muttered. "There's something outside I wish to attend to."

With a lift of eyebrows, a swelling of the lips, she mocked him in a curtsey; and he hurried into the garden oppressed by the feeling that he had made a fool of himself with that hurried excuse so unimaginatively worded.

To the devil with the woman! He did not want to think of women when all the time he was worried about Probert. Some hours ago, Bill had set out to visit a neighbouring farmer, George Nicholls, that he might with casual talk discover what was being said in Elstree about the murder-night and learn what had happened to the knife and pistol. And every minute that passed was growing torment to Thurtell wondering what Probert could have learned, whether he had been nabbed, and conjuring a dozen disastrous scenes that urged him to run to his gig and drive with all speed back to London.

Scarcely ruffled by the faint wind lay the pond before him. He stood on its edge and stared into its depths. Now that damned Wood had sold the cottage, new residents would soon be coming, and what more natural than that they should go fishing? Not a carp but a sack might they drag out of there and that would mean his ruin. Yet, he swore, he had no regrets. Were the deed to be done again, again would he do it, and he would delight in doing it. Weare had not deserved to live. He had sat on his money, spending nothing. A spider feeding richly and never disgorging so much as a brown even in charity. Such men were better dead; but, curses on it, they could not be made to vanish from the earth. Behind them were left memories, mementoes, a home containing hounds to keep the neighbours awake with whimpering for their master, a woman to come each day to clean and mend and cook; and the sharps and flats in Covent Garden and St. James's would wonder where Bill Weare had got to, while a woman in Kensington waited for her lover who would never steal to her again. Worse even than these tongues were the inanimate things the man had left behind, the knife and pistol, the blood and the marks of a struggle in the lane, the suit of clothes that fitted Hunt so neatly: all these silent things spoke loud of murder.

A sense of failure, of mighty efforts done for small returns, made him feel savage and weary. He looked about him at this desolate place, bushes and trees and weeds growing without help of man, intertwining and making the ground mushy and stinking with rotten leaves. Over the treetops ahead he saw the slanting roof of Gill's Hill Cottage with tiles fallen to show the rafters, and the brick chimneys out of shape, ready to tumble in a high wind. Yet, in the hands of one who loved it, this could have been an idyllic spot, the bushes tamed, the grass clipped, the weeds shorn from the water's rim, and the wretched pergola to his right, creepers now tumbling over the thatched pointed roof, propped up again, swept and given new tables and benches; ay, a man could be very happy in this small kingdom if he loved it.

Behind him, suddenly, he heard a rustling in the grass and he spun round to see Anne Noyes watching him with, surprisingly, a sad expression on her face; but when he turned, the sad look changed to one of mockery. In that pale light her dark curls shone as though oiled, and her complexion was white as milk although her hands were brown; and her muslin dress was simple and clean and suited her well, showing off her body's excellent, womanly shape.

"Why have you followed me?" he cried.

"La, sir!" she trilled, "what a vain monster have we here! *I* follow *you*, my man! Rather should I ask why you intrude on my favourite walk. Every afternoon, once the heat of the day declines, I walk here to read poetry in my romantic pergola or to look at the fishes and wonder what lies at the bottom of that pond."

"Why! mud lies there," said he, forcing a smile, "and frogs' spawn and leeches, no doubt, and eels and newts: I know not what else besides."

"Have you never heard of mermaids and their husbands, the mermen?" she whispered, "and of a lady in a lake in Scotland? and perhaps of men down there, too? Who knows what can lie in the depths?"

He did not like such fancy palaver. As usual, uncertain whether she spoke lightly or with hidden meaning under her words, whenever he found himself alone with this woman, he wanted to run away.

"There is nothing in that pond, man or woman," he said harshly.

"And yet I dreamed. Do you believe in dreams, Mr. Thurtell?" She drew a little closer, smiling archly. "I don't mean day-dreams," she whispered, "not those silly stories we make up to please our vanity in which we are always beautiful and wise and beloved and so sweetly revengeful to those who've hurt us. I mean night-dreaming. These night-dreams, they say, go by contraries. If that's the truth, there's a living man deep under that pond."

"A living man? what do you mean?"

"Why! this . . . I dreamed that a dead man lay there. So, if dreams go by opposites, he must be a live man, mustn't he?"

"A live man in a pond!" He tried to laugh but could not, feeling chilled and afraid, while her one bright brown eye held him entranced. He found that he could not look away from her while he strove to interpret her thoughts. Mischief, he read in that clear pupil, mischief, ay, amusement and, unexpectedly, tenderness, with a touch of pity.

"I dreamed I could not sleep," she said, watching him closely. "It was the very night before last. I dreamed that I heard my sister in her bedroom next to mine sighing and walking up and down as though in jail, in a jail of her own terrors; and I dreamed that I, too, stole from my little maidenly bed and, for some odd nighttime reason, peeped out of my window. Shall I tell you what I dreamed I saw then? Three live men with a dead man in a sack!"

He sweated and could not speak. Nothing he had done that murder-night seemed secret any longer. This woman also had watched when he had thought she and her sister too well dosed with rum and wine not to have slept in heaviness. Yet no one, except the children and the servants, it seemed had slept at Gill's Hill Cottage that night. And what of the servants: the boy, Dick Addis, the woman, fat Susannah Woodruff? Quickly he turned and looked up at the attics where they slept.

"They didn't dream like me," smiled Anne, interpreting that look. "I talked to them in the morning, spoke of my weary night. They were logs in bed, it seemed. Neither knew nor suspected anything. Tell me, Mr. Thurtell, what was his name? I mean the name of . . . ?" With a genteel shudder, she pointed into the pond.

"You must be mad, or you're still dreaming!"

"Yes," she said, drawing a step nearer, "the same dream. . . . Ah, poor Mr. Thurtell! I have frightened you."

"Nothing can frighten me!" he cried.

"Of course nothing can frighten you. You're big and strong, you're a man. Fears are only for women who are forbidden to act. They must remain like children, mustn't they—do whatever they're told, conceal their thoughts? I am weary of being a woman," she sighed, her shoulders drooping. "No," she cried, raising her chin, "I am not telling the truth. I should have said: I am weary of being myself, of being Anne Noyes, one-eyed Annie! Annie on the shelf; and all because when I was a child a bramble cut this eyeball."

"So that was it?" Suddenly he felt deeply sorry for her. To be a woman and to lose an eye! Here was a tragedy he could understand and with which he could sympathize. "Why don't you wear a patch?" he asked.

"Again you are impertinent, sir! You should not ask women questions, never personal questions, for we are all, even the one-eyed ones, vain of our person which we must bear through life. I would to God," she cried, "I were a man that I might pity women who are deformed or ugly or . . . or one-eyed."

"I couldn't pity you," he whispered. "You are too bold, too certain of yourself."

"And I don't want pity," she cried, snapping at the air as though to bite off her words. "In my fashion, I am happy as I am." She laughed, a thin wicked-sounding laugh. "When you are out of the race," she said, "there's much amusement to be found in watching others puff and blow, scratching with claws and tongues at their rivals, and all for a prize that will probably beat them, take their money from them and most certainly will deceive them with chambermaids and other drabs."

"Poor little girl," murmured Thurtell, seeing unexpected beauty in her face, even in the flattened eyelid that told of suffering.

Almost she spat as she cried: "I told you, I want no pity, damn you!" Panting she stood back and he watched her sadly, seeing the pallid skin a little flushed, her mouth wet and parted, and her bosom shapely when in rapid breathing it showed its contours under the cloth. An impulse to take her into his arms and to kiss that poor eye grew strong in him, but he feared to act, fearing her anger and, far more, fearing to be repulsed as her sister had repulsed him.

"You are right," she said after a pause in which slowly she regained her breath. "I should wear a patch. There is a vanity so strong that it refuses to be vain. To wear a patch would mean I was ashamed of this eye, that I was giving in to the censure of a world that despises a woman for what she's not to blame for. I thought I would be bold. To look at the world one-eyed so that I could show my contempt for what others thought about me. Yes, I was wrong . . . I will wear that shade, Mr. Thurtell."

"Then you would probably look very beautiful," he said.

She flushed like a very young girl and looked down at her hands and sucked in her lowerlip. No longer the teasing minx defending herself with her wit against female mockery and masculine pity or aversion, she had momentarily lowered the mask that he might see into her tortured heart. Perhaps, the surprising thought occurred to him, perhaps no man had been sufficiently compassionate to flatter her, to make love to her; and that was strange. What did so small a blemish as a lost eye matter when otherwise the woman remained young and shapely? A tiny flaw it was that might have looked enchanting had her pride permitted her to wear a patch.

"For my sake," he said, "I beg of you, do wear a patch."

"For your sake! You mock me, sir!"

"No, ma'am, I am no mocker. My feelings towards your sex has always been respectful; and towards one such as yourself, something . . . how say it? . . . something deeper than respect."

"There! you're pitying me again!" she cried and swung away that he might not see her tears. "I'll not have your pity," she cried, "do you understand! And I will not wear that patch, I won't, ever! It is detestable of you to speak to me of it. I am fully aware of my deformity and need no reminding of it at every word."

Bewildered, he watched her back and saw her shoulders rise and the black curls shake on the nape of her neck while she wept; and he did not know what he should do. Whatever he said seemed only to hurt her; and never had he suspected that that cynical scoffer, Anne Noyes, could have a heart to be touched. Poor girl, writhing within because she was always passed by, suitors pursuing the hoyden, two-eyed Caroline; while even her eldest sister, fat Mrs. Probert, had found a mate. And she of the three was left alone.

The anger he had felt for the world and the pity he had felt for himself trapped in circumstances not of his begetting but the result of Probert's pusillanimity, made him see clearly how this woman suffered. Helpless before the malice of fate robbing her of an eye, she was, like him, repudiating others' sympathy and insisting always on her independence, and her happiness in remaining unloved.

He heard the woman sob and he trembled at the sound. The casual iniquities of fate, of God or of the devil, seemed to him diabolic, without reason. Why should this young woman, good-looking, well-shaped, a fountain sealed with the love curdled in her breast, why should she have been robbed of one bright eye by some indifferent thorn? And why should he, young, vigorous, strong and brave, be left the toy of fools and enemies, betrayed by others' cowardice or stupidity? They stood both very much alone; yet they need not remain alone. . . .

"Miss Noyes," he muttered, clearing his throat, "I am deeply sorry if I have offended you. I can only assure you that that was very far from my intent. Whether you wear a patch or not is of little matter, after all. It is the soul we love, and not its envelope."

Timidly, fearing he mocked her, she turned and peeped at him over her fingers covering her dead eye; and with the one eye showing, the dark curls above falling along her temple, she looked indeed beautiful, mischievous and wary. Had she two eyes, he thought, she would have been most beautiful, the superior of Caroline.

"Fie! sir," she trilled, her voice high-pitched, "that is not the way of a gentleman to tease a poor girl. You think me a goose who'll swallow any pretty lie; but I can assure you, sir, I have had my admirers, however you might think me disfigured."

"I did not say you were disfigured. . . ." The mention of other admirers made him retreat, and quickly she saw it, noticing the dulled look come over his eyes and the tightening of his lips.

She said, sobbing: "No, you would not say such a thing to a woman. I have misjudged you there and ask your forgiveness. I forget that with you there is no need for me to lie and for all my poor little defences to go up and my claws to go out, as they do when I smoke pity. Pray, sir, forgive me. I promise I will wear that patch."

"It does not matter!"

"Yet I will wear it," she said firmly. "Too long have I pretended, flaunting this socket as though I were proud of it, and pretending not to be a woman. And it has made me hateful, spiteful on occasions. See! I am being very honest with you, sir, and I pray you will not mock me."

"Mock you!" he cried. "By heavens, I'd kill the man who tried it. I am strong, Anne, and my strength is given me to protect the weak. It is yours for the asking."

"Thank you," she whispered and looked away. "Words are poor things," she sighed. "I say 'Thank you' a hundred times a day and I rarely mean it. This time when I do mean it, I have only the same silly words to use."

"You have nothing to thank me for," he said and he felt tears under his lids with the longing to protect her, to bring her courage in an embrace and pride in his loving. This was the kind of woman whom since boyhood he had wanted. Not the high-flyers like Mary; not the tantalizing flirts like Caroline ever dancing out of reach; but a quiet, loving girl who craved affection and who would be grateful for the least caress a man might offer. Foolishly, he had despised the woman, eyes only for her calculating flirt of a sister, not even considering her a woman with a beating heart and a queenlike shape simply because she had lost an eye. Brute had he been: blind, stupid, callous, obsessed with outward beauties that he might flaunt his capture before envious friends, while not realizing that what a man truly needed was not a peacock-mistress but a gentle mate, one who would thank him for his love and show herself more nutty over him than he was over her. A wife such as this . . . yes, such as this Anne Noyes would prove, pale-skinned yet passionate, with dainty nose and minikin mouth that had never been kissed save by relatives who had no tang to their kisses; for he did not believe her little boast of having had admirers. Vanity had demanded that lie.

And what did two eyes matter when the soul was beautiful, as Anne Noyes's soul, he felt certain, must be beautiful; and he was amazed that for so long he had remained blind to her attractions. Dazzled by Caroline's practised tricks and body-undulations, he had not realized that true beauty, soul's beauty, dwelt in her sister hiding behind a mocking smile and a tongue of self-protective venom.

Gently he took her hand and she made weak resistance, tugging a little, her face averted; then suddenly she let him take and kiss the hand; and he saw, with a rush of delight, how her shoulders shivered, elbows tight to her sides, as though her ecstasy were great. To please her at that moment, he would have gone on his knees, such being his mood. Instead, he turned her slowly towards him and dragged down the other hand that shielded the blind eye; then he kissed her on the mouth. From head to toe she trembled, as though transfixed, and she sobbed.

"No," she sobbed, "no, you don't mean it, sir;" and she tried to squeeze her lips aside.

He would not let her go. Her weakness—he could feel her ribs under the cloth and her arched spine—excited him; and when he felt her lips open, all fight leaving her limp in his embrace, he held her tighter, swinging her off the ground in a mingled longing both to crush and to cherish her; a confusion of desires he could not understand, before unknown to him, blinded him and he gripped her fiercely, all else forgotten. And she did not complain, although doubtless in his strength, he hurt her. Sighing, moaning, she pressed up under his kiss.

Probert's voice. Hunt's voice. Probert asking where Thurtell was, sounding shrill, agitated, muttering:

"We are undone, undone. . . ."

With all her strength, Anne clung to him as though to hold him from the dangers outside her arms.

"Don't go," she hissed, "don't leave me;" and, for once, forgetting her disfigurement, she looked straight into his eyes.

"I must go," he said. "I'll not be long."

"You'll never come back," she moaned. "I knew it. I was a fool. There is no happiness in this world for me."

He kissed her again, more hurriedly, and smoothed the hair back from her forehead.

"I'll not lose you now," he whispered, "now that I've found you;" and he kissed the eyelid that was soft under his lips.

Despairingly, she unloosed him, letting her arms fall, and moved away on stiff legs.

"Jack! where the hell are you, Jack?" shouted Probert.

Away from him she walked, the hem of her muslin gown, soaked by the grass, clinging to the underskirt, and she did not look back at him. Into the wrinkling pond she stared as though she hated it.

"Coming!" cried Thurtell, and, turning quickly, he pushed his way through the shrubberies to the garden.

In that small clearing where he had suggested he might dig the grave, concealed from the house, Probert stood with Hunt. On both their faces, terror showed. Had he not been leaning against a tree, Hunt might have fallen, so feeble and desperate he looked; while Probert walked up and down, slashing the thistles with his stick, his eyes quick and bloodshot watching all corners as though expecting the traps suddenly to spring on him.

"O, there you are!" he cried. "Come closer. . . . We're smoked, Jack," he said, "we're done for."

Thurtell felt his knees weaken. In Anne's embrace he had almost forgotten the peril in which they stood; now, after the excitement of those precious minutes, his lips yet warm and wet from hers, full horror sprang again behind his eyes.

"What's happened?" he snarled.

"Listen," hissed Probert. "I went to Nicholls and there were two or three other fellows there, friends of his, and one of em told me he'd heard a pistol go off about eight o'clock on Friday night. Another fellow ups and says he'd heard two shots; and Nicholls says he'd been told in the village that people had heard dreadful groans and cries of murder and someone calling for help and saying: 'O, John, for God's sake, spare me, and I'll give you all the money I robbed you of,' or something like that. And he says to me, he says: 'I suppose it was done by some of your friends to frighten each other?' While they was all talking, I had a glass of gin and water in my hand. I was so agitated, I can tell you, and got in such a trembling that I feared I'd drop it. No doubt I should have dropped it if I hadn't sat down. Dammit, I was so agitated they must have noticed me, but it came as such a surprise when I weren't ready for it."

Thurtell's face had grown as white as the others' while he listened.

"Then I'm baked," he groaned in a low, shaking voice.

"It's certainly a bad job," babbled Probert. "Mr. Nicholls seems to know all about everything. I'm damned sorry it ever happened here. It'll be my ruin, just because I was obliging to you."

"Never mind," growled Thurtell, darting him a contemptuous glance. "They can do nothing to you."

"I want that body carted away, and carted away damned quick," cried Probert, the sweat, although the day was cold, running down his nose. "I'm not having it in my pond any longer!" he almost shouted. "Take it away at once."

"I'll see to it," said Thurtell coldly. "After you've gone to bed, Joey and I'll take it out and bury it."

"Not here, you won't! That'd be just as bad, worse perhaps, to have it in my garden."

"I'll bury him," said Thurtell quietly, his voice shaking, "where you or no one else will ever find him."

He turned and strode away. And he strode in the wrong direction, into the parlour, while all his longing was to hurry back to Anne beside the pool; but he did not want Probert to suspect his suddenly aroused feelings for the woman.

"Bill," whimpered Hunt, "they can't do nothing to you and me, can they?"

"Only hang us," snarled Probert.

"Even if they did find out, neither of us was at the murder."

Probert stared at him, his thick brows almost meeting over his nose, and was about to speak; then he shut his mouth and a lightness as of hope began to glimmer in his eyes.

"No," he murmured at last, "we weren't there, were we, Joey? No one was there but Jack. At a time like this, it's every man for his own skin. You're right, we didn't see it done. . . . Shh!"

O

Finger to fleshy lip, he nodded his head warningly as his sister-in-law, head down in dreams, walked by on the other side of the thistles and weeds, apparently not seeing him.

"I wonder," he murmured, "where she's been hiding. . . . Little girls sometimes have quite long ears."

CHAPTER NINETEEN

ALAS, TOO LATE...

THAT night they were a merry party at Gill's Hill Cottage, if noise can be taken for proof of merriment. Even Thurtell was lifted a little out of his customary gloom and smiled tolerantly at his noisy friends. When first he had heard it, Probert's warning of an aroused country-side talking of pistol-fire and of screaming in the night had come as an almost paralysing shock, for a moment bringing a threat of panic; but now as, food and wine in his belly, he sat in the candlelight and was able to watch Anne, noting how rosy and young-looking she had become, Thurtell could not remain afraid. His sudden discovery of love gave him stronger self-assurance as though he felt that even fate would not dare strike when he was beginning to believe that there might be some happiness in living.

Probert was glum. Sunk in his chair, he drank steadily and grunted rather than spoke when anyone spoke to him. The more he drank, it seemed, the more despondent and bitter he became, while the wine and spirits drove away Hunt's fears, turning him to a laughing mounte-bank jesting and dancing, or making him solemn while he sang some sentimental ballad about true hearts or broken hearts. Smiling at his antics, Tom had played with his daughters, caressing their curls, until they had been packed off to bed; since then he had crouched on a cushion on the floor, remaining happy in the thought of his children's love while dreaming of a peaceful future with his creditors appeased. Even the usually melancholy Tom Noyes had been stirred to song and action, making the ladies laugh when he waltzed with Hunt—Noyes the gentleman, Hunt with an old sheet wrapped about him the affected, simpering, squeaking lady with rolling eyes. Earlier in the evening, cards had been produced but Thurtell had frowned on them as being a bad example to the children on a Sunday; but once the children, kisses all round, had trudged laggardly upstairs to bed, they were again brought forth and Hunt and Tom Thurtell played against Mrs. Probert and her brother, leaving Probert to sulk over his rum and Thurtell to whisper to Anne.

After the fading of his initial astonishment in the discovery that he could desire such a woman, Thurtell accepted Anne as though they had been affianced for years. Something of the wonder remained but complacency was gradually congealing it, and he could already consider their future more or less dispassionately. After all, it was only taking one sister in place of the other, and he believed that he was getting the better of the bargain, despite the loss of an eye in his beloved. With Caroline, he would never have been happy. Her high spirits would have jarred on his reserve and he did not like women who laughed too often, particularly at things which to him appeared perfectly sensible. When a man decided that it was time he settled down, he didn't want a lady-bird for lawful blanket, nor any leery, pert piece like Caroline, nor some peep-o'-day woman of quality who would yawn in his face after nights at cards; no! he wanted an honest, comfortable, quiet, affectionate female such as Anne. That Anne previously had been on occasions even more pert than her sister he graciously overlooked. In those days she had been frustrated and un-happy and had had reason to resent life which seemingly neglected her. Now that she was loved, she would soon flower in gratitude, he was certain. And she was a good woman, not a flash thing like Caroline who would prefer a pretty gown or a piece of jewellery above a husband's peace of mind. They would be happy together.

No matter how Probert objected, he intended to dig a grave in the wilderness at the back and, with Hunt's help, to have transported and buried the body before dawn. Although the end of supper would mean the departure of Anne to her virgin-bed, he was impatient for everyone to go that he might set to work; and nobody seemed inclined to go. At the table, Mrs. Probert muttered to herself, clawing at the cards and the money while abusing her partner who sat stiff in his chair as though the discarding of unwanted cards were some kind of a religious rite which had to be pondered and solemnly performed. Hunt was noisy and reckless, a Croesus who had no need to trouble about the size of his losses and who thought either to win or to lose of equal unimportance so long as he was able to laugh and jest. Tom was in a similar mood. Although never one to talk because of his stutter, this friendly evening with the presence of his daughters overhead and the expectation of reaching a settlement with his creditors, had made him gay and good humoured, no matter his losses at cards.

It seemed that they would sit up all night. And Probert, hugging his glass, glared at the floor, drinking often and quickly. The quiet satisfaction Thurtell had felt in Anne's presence was beginning to leave while he considered the passing hours and the labour that was to be his before dawn. Delighted though he was to lie back and bask under Anne's loving glance, sensing her watching him, grateful and tender and passionate, he would rather have been digging up the garden, burying his past with his enemy. Then tomorrow he would have felt free, prepared to begin a new life beside Anne. She had suggested travelling with him in the morning to London, and he was delighted at the idea. This, if he managed well tonight, should be the last time he ever saw Elstree and he wanted her with him in town. Let Mrs. Probert tattle or Caroline hear of their love and scoff at her sister for a wanton—he did not care. They would be liars, whatever they said. Anne was too good a woman ever to be a wicked one; and should he in his love permit his animal nature to over-rule his principles and betray her before marriage, he would hate himself and, possibly, despise her. This was to be a sacred love, a love for always. When she wore an eye-shade, she would appear attractive and he'd not be ashamed then to present her in any company as his Mrs. Thurtell.

Were they never going to bed, the devil snatch em!

But at last even Mrs. Probert began to weary of cards when the luck started to run against her; and, yawning, Tom stood up to stretch his legs. Noyes sat silent, glowering, while his sister abused him and told him what cards he should have played.

"Where are we all sleeping?" asked Tom.

This was, indeed, a problem. Beds were few, and so were bed-clothes. In the attics slept the two servants; below them was the Proberts' room; another room ran beside this where, it was decided, Tom Thurtell and Noyes could sleep together; a third room was a little lower than the others and had a slanting roof: here Anne could bed with the two girls. As before, Thurtell and Hunt would have to sleep downstairs, here in the parlour.

After these details had been sorted out, everyone bade everyone a sweet goodnight, and Thurtell could do no more than squeeze Anne's hand. "Till tomorrow," he whispered, gazing into her happy eye. Tightly, she squeezed his fingers, and with a languishing glance over her shoulder, she walked prettily up the stairs, raising her skirt to show her ankles and a little of her calves in white stockings.

"Remember," growled Probert, slouching to the stairs, "you've got to get rid of that fellow for me."

"He'll be out by morning," said Thurtell loftily.

At last, they had gone; all of them had gone. Thurtell could hear them moving around upstairs like dogs before they settled; and the murmur of their voices came to him in the parlour where he sat and drank while Hunt whistled to himself and gathered old blankets for bedding on the sofa. Would they all never settle in bed! Tensed for action like a boxer before a bout, he waited, arms loose, and flexed his muscles. This would not be pleasant work tonight. By now the body would be soaked, and clothing always became a drag once it had been in water.

"You're not going to bed yet, Joe," he said. "So don't take your boots off."

"It's late, must be past midnight, and I'm tired," growled Hunt, ruffling his mop of black hair.

"You'd better shave tomorrow," said Thurtell suddenly. "Take all those whiskers off."

"What!" Hunt spun round and gaped at him. "Take off me whiskers!" Gently, he stroked them, listening to them purr. "What the hell do you mean?" he shouted. "I'm not taking off these whiskers for no man, so there!"

"You'll take em off," said Thurtell, "if you don't want to get hanged. From what Bill tells us, they've snuffed our trail. They'll be asking questions next about strangers seen in these parts, then they'll be tracking gigs back and forth to London; and there's one fellow who could never be mistaken. Hundreds of people will say—Ay, a seedy-looking chap in torn toggery with whiskers as black as your hat: seen him Friday riding down to Elstree, boozing at the Artichoke, friend of Probert's, a stranger to these parts. . . ."

Trembling, Hunt sat down on the sofa and caressed his whiskers. "It'd kill Mrs. Hunt," he moaned, "if I lost em. Fair dotes on em, she does."

"Better for them to kill her than for you to be hanged by em, ain't it?"

"I'm not the only fellow in England with whiskers!"

"You're the only fellow with whiskers like that that I've ever seen."

"I suppose you're right," sighed Hunt. "They are unique."

"If you'd only shave your head you'd be taken for a Turk. So off they come, Joey, off they come tomorrow."

"Tomorrow," he quavered, "yes, I'll take em off tomorrow. They've been the pride of my life, Jack, and the joy of Mrs. Hunt's precious heart, they have. I've treated em like a child, pomades and hog's grease and sweet-smelling fats and macassar oil, all have gone on my nob. Why! it took me years and years to get it to grow as I have done."

Never before had Thurtell seen Hunt so pugnacious. That the fellow was a Narcissus about his hair was evident. Often had Thurtell smiled to notice how he could not pass a mirror without tossing his head, and how he liked to manœuvre you in front of glass so that, while he talked, over your shoulder he could grimace at his own reflection. Always a comb was in his pocket, and every few minutes out it would come to be drawn quickly under the waves, while, with his other hand, he embraced the back of his head lest the hairs there be disturbed by his jerking. This feminine vanity Thurtell had always despised, for he wore his own hair like a pugilist, cropped comparatively short, and he disdained even the adornments of large whiskers, shaving his chin and cheeks almost to below the lobes of his ears. In his present angry mood, he watched Hunt's distress with a sardonic pleasure, then he shrugged and said mockingly:

"If you like your head above your neck, that's your concern. Thought I'd warn you: that's all."

"But they can't hang *me*!" squeaked Hunt, with shaking hand fondling hair and whiskers. "I never killed the cove."

"You don't have to kill a man to get hanged," smiled Thurtell. "Why, they can hang you if you hunger after a leg of mutton or for preferring somebody else's property to your own; they can hang you for a rape, if a man's fool enough to try it; or for putting somebody else's name on a banker's draft; for taking anything above one bob's worth that don't belong to you. . . . O, yes, they've got you whatever you do, so long as it ain't too honest. They can hang you for a heap of things, from concealing the death of a bastard to cutting other fellows' throats. And one of the things they hang you for is being party to a murder; just knowing about it's enough to get you scragged."

"That ain't right!" squeaked Hunt, sitting up straight, face ashen and great eyes staring; "that ain't justice!"

"It's good law, all the same," said Thurtell with a grim smile. "I know what you and Bill have been thinking. You think you'll beef on me, don't you, and not get nubbed yourselves? It just won't come off, young fellow. Have a try at scarpering and the traps'll pounce on you at once. No, Joey boy, you're in that pond with me and Weare as deep as can be."

The false optimism which, with rum, had kept Hunt skittish through the evening suddenly evaporated. He saw himself helpless and alone in the shadow of this dangerous giant, Jack Thurtell, the man whose strength and pitilessness he had once adored and whom he had encouraged to kill so that he might know vicarious excitement; and no longer did Thurtell seem to him a god whom nothing or anybody could harm This blundering murder had revealed him as being altogether too human. Everything there had gone awry. The prolonged and noisy killing, and the blood, and the pistol and the knife left on the spot. . . . And he had believed Thurtell's tales of many murders satisfactorily and safely executed, of rivals and faithless women despatched quickly and without risk; now, blasphemously, he doubted those tales. The man, like himself, was probably an amateur at the game; doubtless he never before had killed anybody.

Hunt longed to insult him, to call him a liar, a counterfeit-villain; but he dared not do it. Thurtell was so strong and big and, having committed at least one murder, might think a second murder a mere trifle or even a pleasure. The lying braggart had deceived him and Hunt felt that he had been cheated; and he did not like being cheated.

"You sweet on that mort with the single peeper?" he asked suddenly.

When Thurtell swung round, fists clenched, and in two strides was over him on the sofa, Hunt cringed and began to sob in terror.

"No, Jack," he whined, doubled up as though to hide behind his legs and arms, "I never meant nothing! I was just talking, conversation-like. Ain't no harm in that. She's a lady, a very pretty woman and virtuous, I'll swear, and having only one lamp won't make her any the less loving. No, you can't hit *me*!"

Thurtell let his arms fall and stared down contemptuously at the man writhing on the sofa. This spineless creature was not worth the thrashing. And he had thought him to be a pal . . . but Hunt, after all, was weak and could not be blamed should he turn coward.

"I won't hurt you," he growled, moving back to the door that led into the garden. "Get the spade from the stable and help me dig."

Hunt dared not disobey. Off the sofa he rolled and limped after Thurtell into the garden. The moon was up and it was a cold night, but the few flowers with the weeds breathed odorously about them. The windows in the house now were dark and shuttered. All the world slept, it seemed, save for these two men taking deep breaths and shivering in the night; and passionately Thurtell wished that he had never embarked on the adventure.

While Hunt scuttled off to bring the new spade they had bought, he waded through the weeds, holding high his arms that his hands might not be stung by nettles, and he watched the stars as though their twinkling brought peace from the torment in his mind. On such a clear, bright night it was impossible to think of corpses and murder. This was a night for love: quiet, cool, and soft underfoot. All nature seemed an open bed, sweet-smelling, springy and bathed in a pellucid violet atmosphere that would have smoothed even a drab's skin into beauty. A night for love; yet for him, it was a night for death; and he shuddered at the thought of raising that body out of the pond.

Panting in his eagerness to prove how servile he could be, Hunt pushed through the wilderness and reached Thurtell where he stood beside the bare patch under the trees. This was the place which he had that day chosen and which Probert had refused to allow being used. To the devil with Probert! The rogue took too much on himself, doing little himself and quarrelling because the others did not do more.

"Give me the spade," said Thurtell; and gladly, Hunt surrendered it to him and stood back to lean under the tree.

The earth was soft on top, being damp and away from the sun; but after he had dug a few inches, Thurtell found that he struck stones and clay, and the work grew harder. Muscles on his back began to ache. Strong though he was, he had developed muscles mainly on belly and shoulders, neglecting others which digging now brought into play; but, in front of Hunt, he could never confess to weakness. Sweating, he continued, stabbing in the spade, stamping on its shoulders, then stamping on its arm to kick up the clay. Hard he worked and the result was maddeningly small. To dig a grave of even three or four feet in this soil would take hours, and dawn would catch him at the work.

"O, Jack, you're strong," sighed Hunt from the shadows. "I don't know how you do it, I don't! Got the guts of fifty men, you have! If you'd taken to the fancy, you'd have floored even Spring; I swear it! The muscles on you! a very Goliath or a Hercules himself."

Suddenly Thurtell saw Hunt stiffen and raise his arms as though to ward off a blow. Down the man sank, whimpering, his eyes seeming too large for their lids; and with a shaking hand he pointed towards the cottage.

Expecting to see the traps approach, Thurtell leaped out of the hole and in both hands lifted the spade to strike with; then the spade shook and slid out of his hands when he started back.

A white figure, transparent figure it looked, a flutter of greyish lace, shapeless, edgeless, seemed to float towards them, pressing down the weeds on either side as it approached. Not until he heard it sob when the nettles stung, did Thurtell realize that this was not Weare coming in a mist from the pond to haunt them. This was a woman in a linen nightdress with frilled collar, wide sleeves gathered into a cuff buttoned at the wrists, and wearing a white lacy cap on her dark head. It was Anne Noyes.

"Anne," he gasped. "You startled me."

"It—it's a woman?" Cautiously, Hunt peered at her over his arm. "It's flesh and blood! O, my heart and liver, ma'am, I—I thought you . . . I don't know; I didn't know what you was!"

"What are you digging?" demanded Anne, standing erect before Thurtell, the moonlight shading her skin delicately and sparkling on the one bright eye.

"Nothing to concern you, my dear," he muttered, beginning to breathe easily again and wiping his brow with his sleeve while he listened to the thunder of his heart. "Never expected to see you," he said. "Joe and I were just talking about the big fight. You know, Tom Spring and Jack Langan. Joe's putting his money on Langan, the fool. He's not got a hope against an artist like Tom. Being an Irisher, he's sure to be only a miller. They always are. Plenty of fight but no science."

"What are you digging here?" she demanded again.

"A hole," said Thurtell, staring into the narrow pit as though he had noticed it for the first time.

"A grave?" she asked. "You wouldn't be so foolish, Jack! not here!"

"It's Probert's place, ain't it?" he growled, shifting aside from the unblinking stare of that accusing eye. "Serve him right if it's found here."

"If it's found here," she said coldly, "you'll all be hanged; Mr. Hunt will be hanged; and Bill will be hanged: all our family will be ruined. And I am not going to have that."

Nothing of the weak, adoring little woman about her now. Erect, defiant, she stood, bosom outthrust and chin up, her shoulders back.

"No," said Hunt, "it might be dangerous. You're right, ma'am. These new tenants might like a garden and start digging."

"That is common-sense," cried Anne. "Thank you, Mr. Hunt. Surely, Jack, you can see that! At any hour, there's so much talk in Elstree, they might come searching here; and if they found the soil turned, they'd dig at once and find what you've hidden."

"I'll have left here by then. . . ."

"Where will you have gone to?" The impulse to shake him was so strong that Anne had to keep her hands clenched behind her as though she would sit on them as on a swing. "Look, Jack," she said softly, "I've thought of something . . . but I must tell it to you alone."

"Joey," said Thurtell, not turning while staring into Anne's eye. "Leave us. I'll finish this by myself."

Reluctant to leave them to their secrets while delighted to escape the horror of having to help dig and fill that grave, Hunt rose to his feet, brushing leaves and mould from his backside, and with a bow to Anne, walked sedately back into the house. She watched him go; and, not until the parlour-door had closed behind him, did she turn back to stare at her lover.

"We must leave here," she said, "as quickly as we can. I talked to Susannah while we prepared supper tonight. Sue's a slattern and a fool but she knows what's tattled in the village. They've always talked about us there. And now . . . they heard . . ."

"I know, I know," he snapped. "They heard the poppers go off; they heard him sing out; they've found a popper and a broken knife and broken leaves, but they've found no body. . . . They've not found a body, and they won't find one."

"Jack," she whispered, timidly touching his hand. "Should you bury . . . it . . . here, in the garden, they'll only find it. Here'll be the first place they'll look. You must think of something better than this."

"Well, Tom—my brother, I mean—he did suggest taking it to Manchester Buildings," said Thurtell dubiously.

"Yes, yes; what then?"

"Well, he says that it's the head that's the trouble. Tom may have a stutter but he's no fool. He says to cut off the head and bury it somewhere, then take the body to Manchester Buildings and hide it there until we have the chance to throw it into the Thames."

"That would be excellent," she cried, "excellent! Brave Tom!"

"Yes, it's not a bad idea," agreed Thurtell, beginning to think that it might work, after all. "If it floated, no one would recognize it without a head, would they?"

"That's the way!" she said, seizing his arm and pressing against it. "Let us do that, Jack."

"Us?" he repeated wonderingly, looking down into her shining face with its violet shadows in moonlight.

"Yes," she said passionately. "It's us, we, from now on, my beloved. Whatever the dangers, I am sharing them with you."

"I'd never let you——"

"You'll not stop me! Listen! today I heard this Hunt creature and Bill talking. They didn't know I listened, but I heard a word here and there, enough to tell me that they're going to betray you when they're caught."

"I'd expect it of Bill," he cried, clenching his fists, "but not of Joe. Bill's selfish and might be dangerous."

"He is selfish and he is dangerous," she said, pressing his arm against her bosom in her fury to convince him. "I know him better than you. I've seen how he's treated my poor sister. Not a woman, not the foulest hag is safe when he's in the mood. He has no loyalty, no love for anything other than himself. He'd betray you and think he was clever to do it."

"If I was sure," said Thurtell darkly, "I'd break his neck and tear out his bloody tongue. I know he's a mace-cove, but to betray a pal . . . They'd hang him anyhow. He's in it as deep as me."

"Not if he turned king's evidence," she said. "They've got to give him a full pardon before he can swear against you in court. And he would do it. I know him. He'd do it."

Yes, it was possible. Never had Thurtell really trusted Probert with the wheedling tongue, the blarney in his eyes. So puffed up was the dog with his success over silly women that he thought he could diddle anyone with his talk.

"Yes," he whispered, "you're right. Now I shall have to do him!"

"No, no!" she sobbed. "There has been killing enough, too much. Had you not done this thing we could have been happy, married and happy by now."

"We will," he said, "be married and happy yet."

"Not if we go on like this. We must leave Elstree. Leave as soon as we can. This moment, if possible."

"What!" he cried, looking down at her in amazement. "You expect me to mizzle and let Joe and Bill stand the racket!"

"Why not? they'd do it to you! They're going to do it to you if they get the chance."

"Old Flare's no nose, by God. You misjudge me, girl. I have no pretence of being an honest cove, but there are some things I'd not do." Proudly, Thurtell raised his chin, his mouth tight-set. "Talk no more of it, my duck," he growled.

"But I have the money," she cried. "You know when papa died he left his money to be divided amongst us all and most of it's still in chancery . . . I don't understand these things, but I'll be rich some day. Tom was a fool, he realized what he could on his, and lost it all; Bill did the same to my sister's. But Carrie and I were careful. We've spent nothing, and soon it'll all be ours. Within a few months, the lawyers tell me."

"Too late," said Thurtell in a dead voice.

Too late. . . . Had he known of this months ago, and had he then been wise enough to have seen the treasure in this woman's love, Weare would have been still alive; he could have satisfied his enemies, have bought his discharge from bankruptcy, and perhaps have been able to keep Barber Beaumont quiet. Now it was all too late. Money could not save him now. He knew it with a blinding horror that made him shudder and which set his teeth on edge. Too late, because the traps soon would catch him. Money, the will-o'-the-wisp that had danced out of reach before him so long, money had become dirt. There was nearly a thousand pounds of Weare's now under his shirt, and he would never live to spend it.

"It's not too late!" Anne sobbed, shaking him in her exasperation. "If we got to France, we'd be safe."

"For a while, perhaps, if they let me go. As soon as they heard I'd bolted—and Probert would be quick to tell em—the ports would be watched. They'd nab us at the docks."

"We could hide somewhere in the country. Go north. Or to Ireland. Or to Scotland. Anywhere."

"No matter where we went," he said, "they'd find us."

"Not if we wore disguises. I'll dye my hair and you can wear a wig. I'll dress like a gipsy or a harlot. I'll stain my skin a dirty brown as though I was bred in the sun. I'll take my fiddle with me—did you know that I could fiddle?—and you'll come with me as my dancing bear and we'll take pennies from the people. What will money matter, darling, when we are together!"

Half-weeping, half-laughing, quickly Anne talked as though with a gipsy-dream to blot away the truth; and she clung to him, squeezing his great hand, her tears staining his shirt, while he put an arm about her and held her tightly.

"It is getting cold," he said. "The mists are rising."

"I am warm. I feel nothing," she cried and, timidly, then excitedly, she kissed his throat, his neck, his ear; and all the time she babbled.

"I am weary of living this lie," she said. "You don't know what it is to be a woman jailed in a skirt. I've had only books till now, and songs and dreams; and often I've dreamed of freedom on the highway, a Maid Marion with her Robin Hood."

"Not nowadays," he said, smiling sadly; and, pushing his hand under her lace cap, fondling her hair, feeling the round skull underneath, such tenderness shook him, such pity and such love of her, that almost he wept. "They'd ask questions if you went begging; and questions . . ." He shrugged. ". . . you know where questions would lead. . . ."

"I was but jesting," she said, and tried to smile. "I'll have my money soon. Then you wouldn't need to work."

"How can we ever marry? Banns must be called . . ."

"I . . . I wouldn't care!" she cried, gripping him furiously. "What would it matter when I love you! No one will know. We'll be two strangers in front of strangers; and so happy together, everyone will envy me!"

"You forget . . ." he said; then paused, not knowing how to put the thought into words and at the same time not hurt her. "You forget," he said again, "that there'll be descriptions of us sent throughout England. We can disguise ourselves a little . . . but . . . there are some things. . . ."

"My God," she moaned and, shuddering, drew away from him, her hands over her eyes. "I had forgotten," she said. "For the first time in my life I had forgotten it. Of course, you're right and I am mad as a child with dreams. Wherever we went, I'd give you away. They'd seek the one-eyed mot, the argus doxy, and they'd soon find me. This is one thing nobody could hide. A patch would only draw attention to it. It . . . it doesn't seem right, does it, that I . . . that I who'd do anything for you might innocently cause your betrayal . . . ?"

"I love you," he whispered, and tried to draw her to him. "That's all that matters. I love you."

She did not answer to his touch. Away from him she stood, hands over her eyes, too sick at heart to weep.

"I'll not sleep tonight," at last she whispered.

"Nor I," he groaned.

"We could get married soon," she cried. "There are special licences, aren't there? You get them from a bishop, I believe."

"I'll find out; and if we've time——"

"Time, time, time!" she cried. "Let us not wait, my love! There may be no more time for us. You may go away, and I will never . . . might never see you again!"

"Have no fear of that. . . ." He tried to laugh. "Come to London," he cried, "with me tomorrow, away from this damned, haunted cottage."

"Too late," she whispered. "I knew it would be too late."

He kissed the back of her neck, lifting the black curls that he might kiss the dazzling skin.

"Leave everything to me," he whispered. "Now! off to bed with you. I must fill this in before dawn. In the morning . . . London!"

Uncertainly, her back towards him, Anne stood, as though unable to make up her mind. Then, hearing him take up the spade again and spear it into the earth, she began to run away; nor did she stop, heedless of nettles and thistles tearing her nightgown, until she reached the kitchen-door. There, one hand on the latch, she paused, as though thinking he might yet call to her. But he did not call; and, face covered in her hands, choking back tears, she stumbled indoors, half-falling up the stairs in her eagerness to reach her room where she could weep at ease beside the sleeping children, some other, luckier woman's children, lying in innocence upon her maiden-bed.

CHAPTER TWENTY

A PROMISE OF LOVE

IN THE morning, after breakfast, amongst trampled weeds and broken thistles in the wilderness, the three conspirators, Thurtell, Hunt and Probert, stared down at the sunken hollow, the earth in it stamped hard. To them, Tom Thurtell strolled, wiping the egg from his chin, and lounged beside them. For some minutes, no one said anything. Each deep in his thoughts, they stared into an empty grave. Tom was the least interested. This murder had nothing to do with him; that night he had been with his creditors and he was therefore safe from arrest, nor did he believe that the others stood in any serious danger. Many were the perilous corners into which his brother had been driven before this; and always, after smothering from the blows of fate, out Jack had come with fists up ready to fight on, his hat forever flung with a challenge into the ring.

The other three could not feel a similar confidence. Probert was plainly uneasy, sweating, starting at any sounds, and his eyes were bloodshot from over-drinking and lack of sleep. Hunt watched Thurtell like a dog prepared to take on its master's mood; but he, too, looked uneasy, his large eyes wary, shifting their glance around the garden as though fearing to see traps behind every thistle. What Thurtell thought could not be detected in his eyes. Calmly frowning, he stood, mouth pressed out, the eyes' expression hidden under the jutting brows.

Then, clearing his throat and spitting, Probert said: "I want him out of here. I told you that. I'll not have him in my garden or in my pond. You put him there. You take him out again."

"I've told you already," said Thurtell in a weary, angry voice, "I tried to bury him here, and I'd have done it and to hell with you. But the blasted dogs were barking all night and I thought someone must be prowling about. Wasn't that so, Joe?"

"Ay," said Hunt, bobbing agreement: "that's the truth."

"Thank God you couldn't do it," snarled Probert, his eyes red-rimmed and sparkling with liverish anger. "Now take him away before the traps come."

"Don't upset yourself," sneered Thurtell. "Joe and I'll come down tonight and take him far away; and that'll be the better for you altogether."

"Take him where you like," snarled Probert. "Only—take him away from here."

"Y-y-you kno-kno-know what I th-th-think," shrugged Tom. "T-t-take him to Man-man-manchester Bub-bub-buildings."

"You're right, Tom!" cried his brother, clapping him on the back. "Last night I thought over your plan. It's the best. First, we've got to hide the head. Joey and I'll see to that tonight. Then we'll carry the rest to Westminster and give him up to the fishes."

"That's it," said Probert, "get him out of here. And there's that damned boy, sharp as a ferret he is. God knows what he's seen and heard. If the traps come asking questions, I can't promise he'll hold his mag."

"That's all right," said Thurtell. "We'll take him with us to London, tell him we'll find a situation for him there."

"Anything," said Probert. "Only get him out of the place. And get that thing over there out, too; and get it out damned quick."

"What are you so shaky about?" growled Thurtell. "What have you done? not a bloody thing except start howling before you're touched. Leave everything to me. . . ."

"That's what I've done and now look what a mess we're in!"

Thurtell stepped towards Probert, fists clenched; but his brother caught him by the arm and drew him back.

"D-d-don't be a fool," he stuttered. "We-we-we can't qu-qu-quarrel."

"No," said Thurtell darkly, dropping his arms. "None of us are ourselves today. The strain's been great, but soon it'll be over and in the years to come we'll laugh at this."

"Pray God, you're right," said Probert in a melancholy voice.

"Come, now," said Tom, "it's time we were off. You'll not be long, Jack?"

"The moment Miss Noyes is ready," said Thurtell, "I'll follow you."

As though eager to escape from this dank and tangled garden, Hunt began talking loudly, gaily, while he moved off with Tom towards the stable where young Addis waited beside the gig and horse.

With their going, Thurtell and Probert found themselves swaddled in a suffocating silence which neither knew how to break. The last couple of days had turned Probert into an elderly man; his usually erect bearing gone, he stooped, his long arms hanging, and his dark hair seemed lifeless. Nothing about him now of the arrogant Lothario, the leerer at women in the streets, the confidant of barmaids and whores and shop-girls, the swell who liked to lounge about the West End to watch the fashionable and often titled ladies pass and repass up and down Bond Street from two to five o'clock in the afternoon. He had become haggard and old; and, Thurtell noticed with sardonic amusement, in his worries he had forgotten to dye his hair and whiskers and the grey in patches was beginning to show. Yet the conceited mutton-monger could have been only thirty-four or thirty-five years of age, a mere five or six years his senior.

Slowly, Probert raised his head and looked at Thurtell. With twitching lips, he tried to smile and to put on his usual jaunty, superior manner, but he could not do it. His clothes seeming too big for him, he stood with ape-like arms and with a twisted, wheedling look on his phiz, his head to one side as though he were already hanged.

"Sorry, Jack," he whimpered in a jerky manner, "but that damned thing's getting the top of me. Can't forget about it! Swear I ate him with my egg this morning. That's why I had to leave the table. suddenly. Had to vomit. Damned good egg wasted."

"Play the man, for heaven's sake!" said Thurtell, his lip curled. "You've nothing to fear. Joey and I'll be back tonight, honour bright we will, and we'll take him where you'll never hear of him again. Anyhow, you're leaving the place, aren't you?"

"That's half the trouble. To leave here and have that damned thing in the pond for strangers to find . . . it makes me shiver just to think of it!"

"Only one more night," said Thurtell. "You've got enough chink left for a couple of bottles of rum, ain't you? That'll keep your courage up like good old Captain Macheath's."

"Anne's waiting for you," mumbled Probert suddenly; "and her brother, too. What's she going to town for?"

Thurtell swung round and saw Anne standing with her brother outside the parlour-door. She had drawn a dark cape over her shoulders to keep out the cold and she wore a bonnet trimmed with flowers; but these things he did not notice. Over her blind eye she had placed a semi-circular patch cut from black velvet and held there by thin black cord which vanished under her curls.

There was something that she wanted to say to him. He could tell it by the puckering of her mouth and by the anxious flutter of her lashes, and doubtless she did not want to speak before her brother or Probert. Plainly, she was agitated, although striving to conceal the agitation, and anxiously she glanced at Probert walking towards them from the wilderness.

Moodily, sullenly, the man stared back at her, and Thurtell noticed the frank enmity in his glance. Being left with the body in the pool while they gallivanted to London had plainly enraged him. Thurtell smiled. The scoffing Probert with his superior airs had become a frightened man; and that, Thurtell felt, he thoroughly deserved.

"Come on!" called Noyes from the stables; and, with a heavy sigh, Anne turned and walked towards him, Thurtell at her side.

Plainly, she was oppressed by some secret on her tongue, although she attempted to be gay when in the gig she sat pressed between Thurtell with the reins and her moping brother leaning on the rail. Jolted from man to man, she lurched with the gig as it bounded through ruts along the lane; and when she swung towards Thurtell, heavily, lovingly she pressed against him as though to reassure herself that he was with her still. Past the spot where Weare had fallen they swung and pretended not to notice the group of people, men and women, inspecting the broken hedge. The men took off their hats and Anne was forced to return them a slight bow; and she paled to see amongst them Mr. Clutterbuck, the magistrate, talking to Major Wood.

Thurtell drove on, chin high, the grey topper of the fancy on the side of his head, and he managed to smile as though he were at his ease and had no cause to fear the suspicions of any man. Even the major's presence could not anger him. Why should it? Rather now did he pity the devil who had the spiteful Caroline for wife or mistress while he, the luckier man, possessed her sister for his love.

"What are they all looking at?" asked Noyes, turning to stare behind and seeing everyone, men and women, watching them in baleful silence before they swung away from them into Watling Street. "You'd thing there'd been a murder there or something," he said. "Never seen so many people in that God-forsaken spot before, never!"

Neither Thurtell nor Anne answered. With her hands in her lap, Anne sat, her face concealed within her bonnet, and Thurtell seemed intent only on tickling the horse into speed.

Anne almost spoke, but seeing the set look on Thurtell's face, the mouth pressed out pugnaciously, the heavy chin swollen with the pressure of the cravat and high-tipped collar, she settled into silence, darting a weary, angry glance towards her brother. Yet speak she must, and soon. With mounting desperation she watched the milestones flicker past. London was getting nearer with every quick pad of the horse's hoofs; London was sweeping on to her, stealing into the country, turning villages into miniature towns, and taking her too quickly into its busy heart. And she must speak to Thurtell before they reached there and parted with only a shake of hands.

When they trotted into Edgware, she felt that she could continue no further without speaking. Less than eight miles to go to Oxford Street where she would have to say goodbye. That thought was unbearable. After leaving Thurtell last night, she had not slept, but had lain, tossing, near to tears, on her bed while plotting ways of seeing him alone. All those plots had proved useless when the time came. Not for a minute had she had him to herself; and she grew to hate her brother who, she felt, should instinctively have recognized her wish and have given her the opportunity she wanted.

"Pray, Mr. Thurtell," she whispered, laying her kid-gloved hand softly on his arm, "would you pull up here? I feel . . . a little . . . indisposed."

"That's the good sister!" cried Noyes, for the first time showing animation. "Right outside a pub! There, Jack! the Chandos. Wasn't this the village where Eclipse came from? Greatest horse that's ever been! Here! stop! the Chandos. . . ."

"You are not well?" whispered Thurtell, anxiously gazing into Anne's furtive eye.

"I am well enough," she said, licking her pale lips, "a little giddy . . . it's nothing. . . . Only the motion of the chaise upset me a little. . . ."

Outside the Chandos, an ancient public house of oak and rotting plaster, Noyes scrambled out of the gig.

"Come on," he shouted and ran through the open door.

"Jack . . ." Tremulously, Anne put her hand on his thigh when Thurtell was about to rise. "Jack, there's something I want to say. It's not easy. O, I'm well enough, that was a lie to get rid of Tom, but I felt that I had to talk to you, I just had to."

"What is it, duck?" he asked, watching her tenderly.

"You know," she whispered, looking down at her hands on her lap, "what we talked about last night? I mean about us getting married? . . . well, I've been thinking. . . . This is not easy to say! . . . but I was thinking, it might take days to get that licence and you have to wait three weeks, don't you, for the banns to be read out? . . . O, Jack, don't you understand! I don't want to wait."

Stonily, he looked at her, and that cold look terrified her.

"I know what you're thinking," she said in a low, gasping voice, hiding inside her bonnet, "but it's not what you think. I . . . I am not a bad woman. I have been good. All my life I have been good. It's only . . . it's only that I'm afraid."

"Of what?" he asked in a flat voice.

"Of losing you. It would kill me if I lost you now. O, the things you force me to say! You make me ashamed, and I am frightened; I couldn't sleep with thinking of it."

"Thinking of what?"

"Of you, and us, and marriage and the future and of how fate's never been kind to me. Never. Until now. And that makes me afraid. I feel it can't last. That's why I don't want to wait."

"You mean," he said, "you think I will get hanged?"

She could not answer. She plucked the tips of her gloves, breathing in deep gasps, her cheeks burning her.

"That's what it is!" He laughed, a low chuckling laugh in his throat that did not open the lips. "Well, I'll disappoint you there, duck," he said. "You'll not make a hempen-widow. I give my oath on it."

"Yet I'm afraid," she whispered.

"Do you think I'd accept such a sacrifice?" he said scornfully. "I am a bad man, I've not been kind to women in the past, but I'm no mutton-monger like your Bill Probert. I don't go seeking to plunder good women of their reputation, then leaving them to hate me. Not I! The women I've known have been able to look after themselves right enough. You're different. You don't know what you're asking."

"I do know, Jack. I do. I've thought and thought about it, and I know what I'm doing. I have the dreadful feeling that the sand's running out. . . . Look at me, Jack."

She raised her head and stared full at him, a shy smile on her lips that trembled, puckering the small chin; and her cheeks were red and there were tears on her eye-lashes.

"Shamelessly," she cried, "I ask you now. Come to me at Castle Street tonight. At midnight. I'll leave the front-door unlocked."

"I go back to Elstree tonight," he said. "I promised Bill to get rid of the thing."

"You are going back? Of course . . . I had forgotten." She gulped, as though swallowing tears. "There will be other times," she said, forcing a smile, "please God. Tomorrow night? I'll be waiting then."

With affectionate pity he gazed at her, feeling humble before such unselfish love. He understood what had urged her against all maidenly terrors to this womanly sacrifice. She was certain that he would be hanged and wanted a rapturous memory to support her through the lonely years ahead. This was an offering too great for any man to accept; his self-respect alone forbade it; yet Thurtell was deeply grateful for the honour she would have given him and he was proud to know that she could love him to such madness.

"No," he said. "You don't know what you're saying, my duck."

"O, God," she cried, staring at him with a kind of greedy tenderness, her mouth loose and her eye dim with yearning. "O, God," she cried, "last night I went on my knees and prayed and prayed and thought and thought until I feared that I'd go mad. Of course I know what I'm saying! You have kissed many women, women who, no doubt, meant little to you and didn't love you as I love you. Then how can you deny me who in the sight of heaven is your wife?"

"We must think of the future. . . ."

"I am," she cried, "I *am* thinking of the future!"

"There's not only ourselves to think of," he muttered, "there are your relations."

"What do I care what they think!"

"And, have you thought, have you reckoned the risk——"

"Of course I've thought of it. I've thought of everything. I only pray that what you fear should come about. He—or perhaps she—would give me something to live for if . . . if . . ."

"If I were hanged?" said he and softly laughed. "I'll disappoint you there," he said. "I'll not be hanged."

"Tomorrow night at Castle Street?" she whispered. "You'll not disappoint me?"

He took her gloved hand and kissed the palm. "Do you really know what you're suggesting?" he asked.

Quickly, watching him, she nodded and her hand gripped his fiercely.

"All right," he said. "Tuesday."

For a moment he thought that in the morning-light, before the inquisitive villagers, she would kiss him. A blissful smile on her lips, her eye showing happiness and, yes! gratitude, she swayed towards him, her grip so tight on his fingers that she hurt.

Then Noyes shouted from the tavern: "Aren't you two ever going to have a drink?"

Hastily, Thurtell pushed Anne back into her seat and waved his hand. "Not at the moment," he cried. "Anne's got over her vapours and it's time we went on."

"Aw, come and have one!"

"No," said Thurtell, taking up the reins, "I want to get to London. We've wasted time enough here."

Grumbling loudly, Noyes lurched back to the gig and hauled himself in, viciously jerking his hipbone against his sister's as he sat down. Anne made no protest. Within her bonnet, her face could not be seen by the men on either side of her when Thurtell whipped up the horse, but passers-by were startled at the joy that seemed to glow through the skin, parting the pale mouth in a faintly dimpled smile, of this lady in a gig with a patch over one eye.

Thurtell did not look towards her, nor did Anne take heed of him. The promise had been given and there was nothing further to be said, but he remained troubled and had not Noyes been there he might have begun protesting again. Her argument rested purely on the prospect of his getting hanged and that seemed a callous excuse for a woman to make so that she could forget her natural modesty. Or had he misjudged her? under her modest mask was she a gallivanting piece like her sister? No. This girl was honest, too honest, and she was fortunate he was not some flash cove like her brother-in-law who'd have leaped at such an opportunity to ruin her.

He caught his breath suddenly as though he had been punched. Probert could never leave a woman alone. Once he had caught him tickling Caroline and had been amused when she had slapped the rogue's face. Beyond argument, he must also have essayed Anne, and the idea infuriated Thurtell.

Not for a moment did he believe that Anne had ever been the dog's mistress. The girl was chaste; the simplicity of her proposal to him to visit Castle Street was proof of that. An experienced woman would have shied around the question, leading him from excitement to excitement, with veiled and lewd suggestions until the proposal had been forced out of him so that, before submitting, she could boast her virtue and make him appreciate the greatness of the favour she was giving. As open as a school-girl, Anne had not bargained, not even protested a squeaking modesty. Nevertheless, he was certain that Probert could not have left her alone, and the mere wooing of such a man somehow degraded her, even though she had rejected and been outraged by his handling.

That was another mark to be scored against the fellow. Never again would he allow Anne to return to Gill's Hill Cottage alone. Until they married, and that would be as soon as it could be arranged, she would remain in Castle Street under her brother's protection; although he distrusted Castle Street. An unsavoury quarter of thieves and down-at-heel Cyprians, it was no setting for a jewel as chaste as Anne. Once Weare had been safely disposed of and there was no further risk of his being lumbered on a murder-charge, he would hire lodgings for her or take a small house in Kensington or Marylebone or Paddington, somewhere close to London; and there with a duenna she could lodge until the banns had been called and they could be married. Probert would never get at her, by God.

"La!" said Anne suddenly. "I do declare there's Mr. Hunt!"

Thurtell jerked himself out of his brooding and saw Hunt bowling behind them in a chaise along the Edgware Road. Quickly he pulled up and waited until Hunt had reached them.

"What are you doing round here?" he cried.

"Been to see my mother," said Hunt gloomily, "about Tom's bill. More trouble, more bloody trouble."

"Wait there." Thurtell tossed the reins to Noyes. "Farewell," he said, squeezing Anne's thigh because he dared not squeeze her hand or kiss her mouth. "I'll see you tomorrow."

"You'll not forget!" she cried, her face white. "Promise!"

"I promise," he said, smiling, as he leaped into the street. He waved his white hat and she turned round to flutter her handkerchief when her brother whipped the horse. Then, quickly, she put her fingertips to her lips and blew Thurtell a kiss.

"What a difference that patch makes!" said Hunt. "She's the real bon ton now, egad! Wish she carried a broom for me."

"She carries a broom for no man," said Thurtell, frowning as he leaped up beside Hunt in the chaise. "I'd have you know, that lady is soon to become Mrs. John Thurtell!"

"Congratulations!" cried Hunt. "You've picked an out and outer as I always knew you would. A nice little dowry goes with her, too, I hear."

"I am not marrying her for her money," said Thurtell stiffly; "and

I don't want this mentioned, Joey. We're keeping it secret until after we're man and wife. So not a word."

"Cut my throat," said Hunt, "but I'll not tell a lie."

"Now," said Thurtell, "what's this about more trouble?"

"It's not your trouble," groaned Hunt, "it's your brother's for a change. When we got down this morning, Tom quitted the chaise at the corner of Maddox Street and sent me to his attorney to find if his bail had been accepted. So I drove to Clement's Inn but the fellow was out, and I went back to Tetsall's. Tom was waiting for me, reading the newspaper, and when I told him what had happened he asked me to go to my mother's to see if there'd been any inquiries there about him. I told him he was silly to ask it, but he insisted, so off I trotted. When I saw my mother, she was furious that her name had been used by someone she'd never even heard of before, and she swore she'd not stand bail. Well, that's all. I was on my way to Tetsall's when I saw you."

"So Tom's not out of the wood, after all?"

"He'll be all right. I warned him that mother don't like her name being used without being asked; but she'll get over it. Everything all right at Gill's Hill?"

"Everything," said Thurtell with a decisiveness that he did not feel. "After tonight there'll be nothing whatever for us to worry about."

"I hope to God you're right," said Hunt, and groaned.

Thurtell frowned at him. Even to himself he could not admit the possibility of their being nabbed, particularly now when his future for once showed brightly with a wife who not only adored him but who carried with her a small fortune which would set him free of debt at last, forever.

CHAPTER TWENTY-ONE

FRIENDSHIP ON EDGE

THAT night, damn it, there was a moon. Had strangers passed they would have clearly seen Thurtell and Probert at work; but few were the strangers that ventured down Gill's Hill Lane even in daylight; and since the tattle of firing pistols and of blood on the earth, even the most courageous stayed away and locked their doors at sunset. No one was there to see them yet they were plainly to be seen under moonlight bright as day, although the morning was many hours ahead.

Cursing softly, Thurtell looked down into the white face of the man he had killed. Water had not changed him, only now he was stiff and could be rolled as though he were a carving in wood. Open were the eyes, dull as glass, staring at their murderer; open the mouth, the jaw fallen, as though the tongue cried silently. There lay what had been a man, a wicked avaricious cruel man, but nevertheless a man, dead now, with water running out of the mouth which curled back to show the greenish teeth.

Out of the pool had they drawn this damned thing, this haunting enemy, and even now they were not certain what was to be done with it. Probert refused to allow it to lie in his garden; they had no time in which to dig a grave in hard and frosty earth; and Thurtell did not relish a journey to Westminster with this thing in the night. That might be dangerous. There might be an accident, the gilt-buttoned patrol in Edgware Road might become suspicious and call on the gig to halt. Perhaps this cottage was already being watched. Yet something had to be done, some place had to be found where this thing could lie till doomsday and not be disturbed. Hunt had told him during the journey that night that his brother, when driving that morning with Hunt and the boy Addis back to London, had pulled up over a small bridge near Edgware. Pointing to the water, he had suggested that that would be the place to use. As good as anywhere else, Thurtell supposed: ay, they would carry the damned thing towards Edgware.

O, he was weary of the name and sight of Bill Weare! bone-weary of the whole accursed business which he wished he had never begun.

"Better take off his toggery," said Probert. "Probably got his name on it somewhere. Anyhow, his laundress or somebody might recognize some of it, and we'd best make sure."

"Ay," said Thurtell and knelt on the damp grass. Between them the stiff figure lay outstretched, and quickly they set to work undressing it. This was no easy task. The joints would not bend without difficulty and the accursed thing kept rolling and slipping from their hands. Finally, they had to use their knives and slash the cloth. Like a pair of madmen who would murder a man already murdered, they struck and ripped, tearing off the coat in pieces, dragging down the sleeves. The waistcoat. The shirt. The breeches, the stockings. The shoes. China silk small-clothes—the dainty rogue! The leather braces. . . . All had to be ripped off and destroyed.

Panting they sat back and wiped the sweat from their faces with pieces of the shredded cambric frill from what had been the linen shirt.

"You must get rid of this stuff," said Thurtell.

Probert did not answer. Crouching on his haunches, he flashed at him a glance of hatred, then looked again down at what had been Bill Weare. Without his garments, pitifully small and white he looked, the ribs showing on his surprisingly hairy chest, and the legs, without the top-boots he had usually sported, seeming to be sticks.

"I'll cut em into little pieces," he said at last, "and burn the bloody lot. You can't burn a body. At least, not without being caught doing it. I wish to God you'd done this job in Westminster."

"Well, I didn't," growled Thurtell. "And I'm sick to death of your puling and whining. We're all in this. Remember that."

"Do you think I can forget it! It's well enough for you to gab but you haven't got a family to support."

"Don't be funny," said Thurtell with a mocking laugh. "*You* support anyone or anything except your own fat belly! You've run through your wife's money, you've swindled everybody you've met, even your own friends, and now you talk about having a family to support! Which reminds me . . ." Suddenly he became serious, dangerously serious, as Probert realized when the man leaned towards him, peering into his eyes, the open clasp-knife in one hand. ". . . There's something I want to ask you," he said. "It's about Miss Noyes. Miss Anne Noyes. . . ."

"A good girl," said Probert hurriedly, flinching before the knife, "an honest, hard-working girl. Pure as snow."

"How do you know she's pure as snow? Did you test her?"

"Before God, no!" he whimpered. "You can't believe all what

women say. You know that, Jack. It flatters em to think that every fellow what looks at em is after em . . . I swear I've not tried the girl. My own wife's young sister! D'ye think I would?"

"Yes," said Thurtell, "I know you would, you bastard."

"It's not true. For the love of God, Jack, listen to me. She's like my own sister. I may be rather low but I ain't as low as that. Damn it, I never wanted her that way, anyhow. Not that she ain't beautiful, of course she is, but that lamp of hers . . . Put away your knife, you fool!"

"I'll put it in your dirty giblets, that's what I'll do with it, and remember this, Bill Probert. If I find you sniffing round her skirts you can start saying your prayers, if you can remember any of em."

"I give my Bible-oath," he quavered, "I've not laid a finger in love upon her. I ain't done anything to her. Ask her yourself. She'll tell you the same if she's got any truth in her female heart."

"What's the good of asking her?" laughed Thurtell softly. "As you said, Bill, it's no use asking a female anything. They can lie with smooth faces. Only, I'm just warning you. In future, leave her alone."

"Of course, of course," he stuttered, "whatever you say, Jack. I'd not touch her with a barge-pole. She's all yours, lad, all yours . . . but I thought it was Caroline you was after."

"It was," said Thurtell, shutting the knife and slipping it back into his pocket, "but I've woken up about her. Let Wood have her and her fancy ways, and I pity the fool. I'm going to marry Anne."

"Good, good," gasped Probert, wiping his face on the rags. "You'll be one of the family then! That's prime, Jack! Mrs. P. will be proud."

"I don't want her told yet. I don't want anybody told."

"As you say, Jack: anything you say. . . ."

"It's all been sudden and things aren't certain yet, and I want to find out how the wind's blowing before I marry her and bring shame on her as my wife. Once we've got rid of this fellow here and all's fair ahead, I'll announce it. So keep your mouth shut till then."

"I never tattle," cried Probert. "You can rely on me, Jack. And I can tell you, this makes me a very happy man. If there was one fellow in the world I'd like to have as my brother-in-law, it's you. To hell with Carrie! Anne's the girl for you!"

Slowly they stood up and without a glance at the naked body oozing mud and water into the grass, they trudged back to the house where they had left Hunt to amuse Mrs. Probert. To their relief, she had discreetly retired to bed and Hunt was alone, sitting miserably over a bottle of rum. At the sound of their approach, he leaped up and ran to the foot of the stairs under some wild idea of fleeing and hiding should this be the traps or Weare's ghost approaching. When he saw that it was only Thurtell and Probert he cringed forward, seized the bottle in shaking hands and poured himself out a large dose.

"Don't take too much of that poison, Joey," said Thurtell. "There's work yet to be done."

"Do you think I'm drunk!" Hunt cried pugnaciously, almost knocking over the bottle. "Could drink you under the table, any night."

"That's all right, Joey," said Thurtell with an amused smile. "We only came back lest Mrs. Probert was wondering where we were."

"Gone to bed," muttered Hunt. "Said she was tired and left me. And what's this work you want me to do?"

"The same work," sighed Thurtell, "the same damned body. . . . But this is the end. After tonight, we finish."

"Finish?" repeated Hunt, looking dully at him. "There's some things that are never finished. Who'd have thought that doing a low-down fellow like Bill Weare would cause such bother! Nobody ever liked the cove."

Resting his elbows on the table and running his fingers through his heavy black hair, he mumbled: "And I've got to shave because of him! Well, I'm damned if I'll do it. Damn you, damn him, damn the constables, damn the bloody world! Life's not worth living when you can't sleep unless you're drunk. I've had enough of it. I'm clearing out and leaving you to it."

Thurtell could never sustain anger towards Hunt. Towards him he felt fatherly and accepted his tantrums as a father accepts the screaming of his child. And, impatient though he was to have the task over, he felt too happy, in his knowledge that Anne waited for him with open arms, to be seriously annoyed with this sad fool. Towards Probert he felt differently. Probert had slimed Anne by attempting to seduce her. Besides, he was a boastful animal, carrying with him in the curl of lip and loose carriage an insulting aura of superiority; although that was now gone in the frightened animal cowering in a chair and with shaking hands lifting a glass to its lips.

Contemptuously, sadly, Thurtell looked at his comrades in adventure and he was amazed that he had been fool enough to accept such as his equals in courage. And they were the true inspirers of the killing. Suddenly, he realized that. With shame and disgust, for one moment he saw himself as a dupe, a puppet pulled by Probert's flattery and urgings towards murder, and by Hunt's resentments that he should remain a broken-down singer while his brother had sung at Covent Garden Theatre and was now playing in Ireland. Their failure, not his failure, had spurred him on to act.

No sooner had that appalling thought shocked him with the fear that he had been the weakest of the three, the gull, than in horror Thurtell flung it from him. Without him, without his will, his strength, these two would have been nothing. He was the only one who had dared to act while they, shivering behind the protection of alcohol, had left him to work alone. Yet now, it seemed, they were ready to betray him because they lacked the courage to stand erect.

"All right, Joey," he said quietly. "You can leave us. You can run away as far as you like. I'll leave you to it. . . ."

"By God," cried Probert, springing to his feet, "you're not leaving us?"

"Hunt's going. He says he's clearing out. Then so am I." To show how steady was his hand, slowly Thurtell poured himself some rum. "I've carried you both long enough," he said pleasantly, "and now I get the blame for it. Here's the pair of you both thinking how you can put the cross on me. Then go and do it. I'm tired of the whole damned business."

"You—you'd not leave us, Jack," whined Hunt, bravado gone. Incredulously, yet fearfully, he gaped at Thurtell. "You couldn't let a pal down, Jack, could you?"

"I'm not having that thing left here!" cried Probert, starting to his feet. "If you're going, take it with you, or—or——"

"Or what?" asked Thurtell, smiling. "Come on, Bill: or what?"

Back into his chair slumped Probert, wiping his forehead with a shaking hand; and he did not speak.

"You almost said it, didn't you, Bill?" jeered Thurtell. "I'm not surprised at Joe, he never was no hero, but you, Bill Probert, you talked big; you'd killed many a man in your time, hadn't you, you said? O, you was afraid of nothing; yet a dead man in a pond can turn you into a girl. . . . A girl! Good God, no! Girls have more spunk than you. There's . . ." He bit his lip to hold back Anne's name. "You've grumbled at me, hated me, you've plotted to go to the traps," he growled, "each of you waiting your chance. Well, I've thought about it, too. . . . King's evidence means that you can't be hanged, don't it,

Bill? That's what you're thinking. Well, you ain't the only one who can mace on his pals."

"No," gasped Probert, "you couldn't do it, Jack! not on your own pals."

"You mean, you mean," stuttered Hunt, "you mean you'd lie to the traps and have us hanged?"

"Your wits are working well tonight, Joe," smiled Thurtell. "I was thinking of Ruthven. You know the Mercury of Bow Street, George Ruthven. . . . He's by way of being a friend of mine. A little word dropped in his ear, mention of a pond, perhaps——"

"No, no, no," screamed Probert, "no, Jack!"

"Mention of a singer what nobody wants to hear and how he's got some bon ton toggery without having had to work for it. . . . Just a hint. That's all a fellow like Ruthven needs. . . ."

Slowly, he drank, chuckling and grinning; and there was silence in that room. As he knew, as Anne had warned him, both Probert and Hunt were alert to turn king's evidence and escape hanging. It was well, he thought, to warn them that this was a game at which three could play. Amusedly, he watched them: Hunt staring at him with great eyes of horror, Probert shaking and mumbling, unable to speak.

"So I bid you good night," he said; "and to hell with both of you."

No sooner had he slapped his topper on his head and turned towards the door than Probert and Hunt both found their tongues. They shouted, leaping to their feet, calling on him to think again, swearing that they were his pals, that he could trust them to the death.

"I've had enough," he said. "I'm finished."

On to his knees slid Hunt, spittle dribbling from the corners of his mouth, and he raised both hands in supplication; and Probert put an arm around Thurtell's shoulder, clasping him as though he loved him while wheedlingly he whispered:

"Don't take it like that, Jack. I'd cut my throat rather than let it blab a word against you. You can trust me, you know you can. Of course I'm worried. I've got the wife to think of and there's such talk in the village. And if the damned thing's left here . . . well! . . . it won't look good for me, will it? But you've no right, Jack, to say I'd turn nose. I'm with you to the hilt."

"So long as somebody else uses the knife, eh, Bill? No," said Thurtell softly, "I've learned my lesson. A man can trust only himself. As I said, I didn't expect much from Joey; but you, Bill Probert, you damned mutton-monger! I've stood enough from you, blast you, and I hope you hang for it."

From that madman's glare, Probert shifted aside and walked as though he were blind back to his chair into which he sank.

"I ask nothing for myself," he whined. "A man can only hang once. I'm thinking of others——"

"And about time, too!" jeered Thurtell.

"I'm thinking of my old woman and her family. The Noyes are proud of their reputation." He groaned and brushed the greasy greying hair from his brow. "I'm a man," he said with false heroism while watching Thurtell from the corners of his eyes. "I'm prepared to take what's coming," he said. "A hanging's as good a death as any other. Better than most. It's quick and it don't hurt, they say. But there's my old woman; proud of her name, she is; and her sisters, too; and what the newspapers'll say about em. You know what newspapers are. It won't matter to me: I'll be dead; but my poor bloody wife, and Carrie . . . And Anne, too!"

"What about Anne!" snarled Thurtell.

"Nothing," sighed Probert, flapping his hands. "Ain't nothing to do with her. We all know that. But she'll be dragged to court like the others, put into jail like a criminal with the robin redbreasts at her day and night, always at her, the bastards. But I suppose it can't be helped. . . ."

Thurtell said nothing and he no longer smiled. Fiercely he glared at Probert, wondering what the trick could be, and he knew that the rogue, trying to soften him, had produced Anne as his trump; but he also knew that the trump would win, that should the body be found and Probert arrested, everybody who had lived in this house would be questioned and perhaps sent to jail on suspicion.

"Aw, Jack," whimpered Hunt, "you don't mean this. We're pals, always have been, always will be. I'd never give you away, not if I saved my own neck by it."

"Shut up!" said Thurtell and raised his fist as if to hit him.

But a blow would not break a way out of this dilemma. Never had he intended to desert them—that was not the way of Old Flare!—he had wished only to frighten them back into submission; but Probert's sly mention of Anne's name had made him realize that in this he was not acting alone. Now he had become two, and in all decisions he must consider that other half of himself, his future wife. To run off and leave Probert to hold the corpse would not save Anne from smirching. On the murder-night, she had been in this house; and to save his skin, Probert was fully capable of taking revenge by denouncing her as the inspirer of the plot. Never had Thurtell really liked Probert. Now he hated him with such hatred that he would have killed him had he known what to do with his body afterwards. And all the time, there was that other body. . . .

"We shouldn't quarrel," he said, forcing a smile. "I thought to frighten you a little to give you some of your courage back. Old Flare has never let down a pal. We're in this together; and so long as we stand together, we're safe!"

"Of course, of course," gasped Hunt. "We're with you, Jack. Whatever you do, we're with you. You know that. You can count on us."

"I was thinking of my old woman," muttered Probert; "otherwise, Jack, I'd be with you all the way. By God, I am with you, wife or no wife! We men must stick together."

He thrust out his hand but Thurtell took no heed of it.

"All right," said Thurtell slowly, "I'll stand by you for the time. But I give full warning . . ." His small eyes, scarcely seen in the hollows, moved from Probert to Hunt, then back again. ". . . I give full warning," he repeated, "if I think that either of you are going to do a put-up on me, I'll break your bloody necks; and if I can't do that, I'll turn king's evidence——"

"You, you can't!" cried Probert. "You're the principal."

"That's what you've been thinking, both of you," grinned Thurtell, "but look at it, my friends, as though you were clear of trouble. Who knows anything about me except you two? No one saw me and Weare together. You was both making yourselves swine-drunk at the Artichoke—the landlord'll swear to that—then you leave, then almost immediately afterwards a cove's heard screaming, and there's pistol-shots. Just think it over, pals. You asked me down here, Bill, because you wanted to put the blame on me. I'll talk, and I'll tell what I think they ought to know."

"But there's Rexworthy. He must know. Weare must have told him."

"Weare was never a cove to talk; and if he did, that's too unlucky for me, ain't it?" Thurtell grinned into their frightened faces, and he was happy. These rats, to think that they could out-trick him! "Anyhow, what Rexworthy can say is small compared to what's against you two," he laughed. "And Tom'll swear to anything I ask him."

Q

"O, God," groaned Probert, tearing at his collar. "Why talk like this! Nobody's going to blab. . . . It's only to get the damned thing out of my pond!"

"That's what I came to do," said Thurtell. "Now I'm beginning to think. . . ."

Afraid to speak lest they anger him, Probert and Hunt sat gaping like dogs hoping for biscuits. For fully a minute, Thurtell let them roast in their terrors, then abruptly he said:

"All right. You don't deserve my help, either of you, but I'm not one to scarper from trouble. Come on, help me carry the bloody thing."

So quickly did Probert spring to his feet that he stumbled and almost fell; and fast behind him came Hunt, skipping into the night, behind Thurtell who, without one backward look, strode through the weeds and bushes towards the stable. Under the glimmer of the lantern, he fumbled in his gig until he had found the new sack and the cord which Hunt had bought. Then carrying these, still not speaking to his companions, he walked through the wilderness, kicking aside the weeds, until he reached the pond.

With face upturned the dead man lay there, naked as a worm beneath the moon.

"Pick up his clothes, Bill," he said. "You, Joe, hold this sack open. Hold it steady."

Swift to help, Hunt took the sack and opened it wide while Thurtell lifted the corpse by gripping it under the armpits while he pushed its head into the gaping mouth.

"Don't shake the damned thing," he snarled, while he tried to shuffle the body down and in, Hunt at the same time working the sack upwards.

Weare had been a smallish man, but now that he was dead, his weight seemed to have multiplied. Only by exerting all his great strength was Thurtell able to guide the body, knocking aside the flapping arms, into the waiting sack which reached a little below the dead man's waist.

"There," he said, letting his burden fall to the grass. "The rope, Joe."

Teeth chattering, Hunt passed him the rope and around the body's waist he knotted it, then cursed and unknotted it.

"Damn and blast," he growled, "we'll need some weights. Get some stones, Joey."

Slowly, muttering curses, he dragged off the sack and saw once more the white thing which he had hoped never to see again. No element would accept this wretch, it seemed. The earth had proved stubborn to the spade and now out of the water the thing had come. A killing should have been a simple matter; and simple it would have been had not these two damned villains deliberately loitered that night that his hands alone might dip in blood! From the beginning, everything had gone awry, and it was not his fault, groaned Thurtell.

As though the corpse were to blame for all this bungling, he glared down at the white face glaring up at him, and he wished that he had never met the man. Had not Weare cheated him, he would never have hated the fool; had Weare not been avaricious, he would not have believed his tale of the country pigeon. No, the rogue had brought his death upon himself and he deserved his end. But the evil of the man lived after him, frustrating all attempts to conceal his death. Even when Weare had been alive, Thurtell had not hated him so much as he hated him now that he was dead.

"Come, come," he muttered, "hurry;" and he seized the stones which Hunt brought, tossing them into the sack. "More," he cried, "more."

More stones rattled into the sack. Then the sack was again upheld by Hunt while, again, head-first, Thurtell pushed the body in and tied it about the waist that it should not slip out. And to the ends of this rope he tied one of the largest stones which Hunt had brought. The remaining stones he heaped into his pocket-handkerchief and tied to the lifeless ankles. Now Weare was heavy enough, almost too heavy to lift. To the bottom at last would he go, never to rise again.

"Give us a hand, damn you, Bill," gasped Thurtell. He weighs a ton."

Probert put down the pieces of clothing he had been gathering and took the dead man's legs, Thurtell caught the creature under the shoulders and Hunt supported it in the middle. Thus, slowly, stumbling, they carried it through the brambles and weeds and thistles, a slippery weight which grew heavier with each step, until they reached the garden-gate leading to the stables.

"Drop him," said Thurtell.

Into the nettles the white weight sank and Probert and Hunt looked up into Thurtell's sweating face, waiting for orders.

"Stay with him here, Joe," said Thurtell. "We must get what's left of his clothes. Come on, Bill."

"No-o-o!" squeaked Hunt. "You can't leave me by myself with him. He's dead."

"Why!" scoffed Thurtell: "so he is, poor fellow! But he won't hurt little Joey—will you, Billy Weare? There! he won't do nothing to you. He's a pal."

Shivering, Hunt shrank into the shadows, away from the corpse, while Thurtell and Probert returned to the pond to gather the pieces of cloth and leather which Probert had collected. With these, they returned, and Hunt gibbered up at them, raising his white face into the moonlight.

"Thank God," he groaned, "I thought you was never coming."

"Not three minutes away," said Thurtell. "Now, into the gig with him."

Through the bushes they lurched until, reaching the stables, with difficulty they forced the body into the front of the gig. Then as Hunt and Thurtell fitted the dead man into place and tossed a dirty blanket over its bare legs, Probert came with an armful of the rags that once had covered the creature's nakedness, and he would have tossed them in had not Thurtell caught his arm.

"We're loaded enough as it is," said Thurtell. "You'd better leave the clothes here, Bill. We've no room for em."

"No room!" gibbered Probert, choking on the words. "I'm not having em left here. You take em with you: go on!"

"Get up, Joey," said Thurtell, springing into the gig.

"I tell you, I won't have em here!" howled Probert, dancing in rage and terror. "What do you think I'm going to do with em!"

"Eat em," said Thurtell, cracking the whip and laughing at his repartee.

"With salt and pepper," giggled Hunt, "and horse-radish sauce!"

Off went the gig, starting so suddenly that it almost knocked Probert down. Cursing and dropping pieces of cloth, he sprang back, while Hunt turned to make insulting noises through pursed lips.

"Serve him right," said Hunt, settling comfortably into his seat as the gig rocked out of the garden into Gill's Hill Lane and swung to the left. With every beat of the horse's hoofs bearing him from the dank and haunting threat of that gloomy cottage and its wilderness, his spirits rose. "Hope the traps catch him with the stuff," he chuckled. "Always was a bully; and I don't like the way he talks about the fair sex. You and me, Jack, are not particularly pious fellows, but there's some things what are sacred. Woman's one of em, ain't she?"

"Ay," said Thurtell darkly, but his thoughts for the moment were on a different pursuit. In a moment, now, round that bend . . . ay! there, towards the end of the lane, that was the spot where he had struggled with Weare. So much and so swiftly had happened since that night that he could scarcely believe that it had been only last Friday . . . last Friday! while this was only Monday! Three nights ago! And the blasted body was still with them, rocking now under his feet in its sack.

"I don't mean all women," continued Hunt. "There's women and women."

"If I thought he'd laid a finger on Anne," growled Thurtell, "I'd break his neck!"

Hunt smiled tightly, giving him a sharp glance from the corners of his eyes.

"That's the spirit," he said, "give him hell, the old goat. I'd not trust him with my own grandmother, I wouldn't. They can't keep a servant, not a woman servant, anyway, and it's not only because they don't ever pay em, the women just get sick of him always after em. Poor Mrs. P.! My heart bleeds for her, it does; 'pon my honour, it does."

Thurtell's jaw had tightened, the underlip pushing out, while he glared over the horse's ears into the night.

"I don't trust him," he growled. "Thinks he's clever, thinks I'm a cake; but I'm going to learn him. He'll be next, before even Mr. bloody Barber Beaumont."

"It'd be safer to do him," murmured Hunt. "Apart from his lowdown way with silly women what don't know no better, he's not a trustworthy cove. It'd be a blessing in disguise to poor Mrs. P. if he were suddenly to kick the bucket; and it'd be a merciful deed to all the other poor deluded females waiting to be ruined. And, Jack, it'd be safer for us. He'd peach on us tomorrow to save his own dirty neck."

"Ay," said Thurtell. Probert was a danger and should be killed, but, to his own surprise, he found that his enthusiasm for killing was gone. He wished that he had never opened this dangerous sport and he wished, desperately he wished it, that he could turn the page of his life and begin again with Anne as his wife. That, alas, was impossible. Once done, a violent act could never be dismissed. Bill Weare lay dead, but the memory of the man remained and he had become somehow even more substantial as a ghost than he had been when alive. Then he had been merely a sneering, conceited sharp whom one forgot after he had left the room. Now he had become omnipresent and could not be forgotten or escaped.

At Thurtell's feet, under his feet, the sack bobbed and bounced as though the thing tied in it struggled to break free; but this empty body was unimportant, merely something that had to be hidden. Beside the inescapability of Weare's ghost, it did not matter. This ghost which he could not exorcize rather than any suggestion from Hunt confirmed him in the belief that Probert must be killed. And after Probert? . . . Hunt, too? No, he could never hurt Joey! . . . Together, they would be safe. Only Probert must be silenced.

Suddenly he began to chuckle, and Hunt turned smiling to him, eyebrows raised.

"I was thinking," said Thurtell, barking his amusement, "of the poor bloody fool having to sit up all night cutting Bill's toggery into little pieces, then running about the countryside dropping a bit here and a bit there. I'd like to see him at it!"

"Me, too," squealed Hunt, kicking his heels and trampling the sack. "You can see the traps smelling at the bits next day, and following where they lead to and ending up in Gill's Hill Cottage. Do you know, Jack, I'd even pay to see that cove hanged!"

"No need to pay," chuckled Thurtell. "You can sit down, Joey, in a comfortable seat and watch me do it. . . . Now, where the hell's this stream you said Tom thought'd do us?"

They were on the road to Elstree and had passed Cobden Hill, and no one watched them. The few distant cottages were dark and the moon shone with such brightness that nothing remained hidden. They were alone in a bright landscape of black and purple shadows, and the sound of the hoof-beats and the rattle of the wheels were the only sounds to be heard, even owls being apparently asleep.

"There we are!" cried Hunt, clutching Thurtell's arm. "There's the bridge."

The bridge was low and slightly humped. Sitting in the gig, Thurtell peered down and he could clearly see pebbles under the slowly moving water.

"If Tom thought that was a good place," he growled, "he must have been seeing double."

"That ain't it," said Hunt. "Go on a little. There's a pond further on what feeds this. That's the place Tom picked."

The pond was not deep, Thurtell groaned to discover. Tom and Hunt must have been drunk to have chosen it. Yet it had advantages which a river or deep pool might not have had, he slowly decided, after wetting his boots on the spongy grass when he climbed from the gig to inspect it. Yes, it might be used. No one would trouble to examine such a muddy fishless marsh in which the water, at its deepest, could not have been more than about four feet deep. Tom was not such a fool, after all. . . .

"Come on, give me a hand," he said, dragging the sack from the gig and letting it fall to the road. "Weighs twice as much as he must have done when he was alive and kicking. By God, I'll be pleased to see the last of this!"

Hunt took the legs, Thurtell took the shoulders, and on the edge of the pond they stood, slipping in the wet and mud, the body swaying between them.

"Now," said Thurtell. "One . . . two . . . Three!"

Out and up whirled the body, then it fell to sink with a terrifyingly loud splash towards the centre of the pond. But there were no cottages near, no passers-by or poachers to watch them at work. Under the starry sky, on a silent earth, they seemed alone, and they were almost happy to think that at last that damned body was out of their hands, and that Probert did not know where it was hidden. Now they were safe, the secret theirs; and, light-heartedly, they turned back to the gig.

"I could do with a drink," sighed Hunt.

"Not till we get to London," said Thurtell. "The less we're seen the better for our necks. Thank God that's over."

"It'll be Bill's turn next," chuckled Hunt. "Think we ought to throw him in there to keep Weare company?"

Thurtell did not answer. Back in the gig, he took up the reins and clicked his tongue in his cheek to command the horse to pull. No longer did he want to talk of killing. His thoughts were all on love, on a placid future, children at his knee, and Anne at his side: a happy world in which there would be no need for further murders, and which at last, it seemed, might be possible.

Tomorrow night he had promised to visit her. . . .

Dear child, to abandon modesty from silly fear lest he be taken from her by the traps; but she'd not suffer for her love's recklessness, he swore. Even though she did become his mistress, he would never forget that the sacrifice had sprung from love with the fear of losing him and not from any carnal wickedness. She would not suffer for that. Whether she quickened or not, he'd stand by his word and would marry her. Ay, he would keep faith and never would he remind her, no matter how they might quarrel as married couples, even the happiest, always quarrelled—never, by God, would he remind her that she had been the temptress while he would otherwise have shown himself a man of honour, respecting her until the church gave its blessing to their union. That she should trust him so utterly put him on his mettle to prove that her trust was not mistaken.

Always—it was his proudest boast—Old Flare stood by his pals and never let them down, no matter which their sex might be.

CHAPTER TWENTY-TWO

WHAT GOES ON?

LONG after midnight they parted, Hunt staggering from the Coach and Horses and singing to prove that his heart was carefree, while in his narrow bedchamber Thurtell dragged off his clothes, and after a long tussle pulled off his boots; then he flopped into bed to sleep soundly for the first time in weeks. With the throwing away of Weare's body, he had thrown away his fears, it seemed, and contentedly could he snuggle into slumber after an exhausting day and a perilous night. His worry over the small amount of water in the pond had been soothed by his brother when, back in Conduit Street, he and Hunt had told him of their adventures. "It-it-it's not th-th-the wa-wa-water that matters," Tom had explained, "it-it-it's the mud." And, as usual, Tom, of course, was right. Droughts might come to empty the pond, cattle drinking might kick up the body, small boys might stumble on it seeking tadpoles or leeches: any casual accident might suddenly reveal its secret.

Should Probert talk, he and Hunt could give him the lie in his teeth and of what use would be his accusations when he did not know where the body lay? Besides himself, only Hunt and Tom knew that, and both could be trusted. Let there be panic at Elstree and Radlett, let the yokels thereabouts howl and chatter of blood on the ground and of screams for mercy heard at night. Sounds at night, even blood on the ground, were not evidence. There must a corpse for the coroner to sit on.

Half-asleep, Thurtell smiled in the darkness, imagining some fat coroner seated on the wet body of Weare. And he smiled again when he recalled the bugaboo tales he had read of murderers being driven insane by the memory of their deed. Apart from a gnawing doubt at the back of his mind, an incessant nagging about something, something, he could not tell what, that he had left undone and which might point him out as the slayer, he was at peace with himself. Weare had deserved to die, so why should he repine that he had made him die? No, only he felt that, after all, the deed had not been necessary. Nearly a thousand pounds did he now have in his reader, and about half of this he would give to Tom to help bribe the witnesses against them in the coming conspiracy trial. But, all the while, had he thought of it, he could have earned far more money in a far more pleasant way by having married Anne.

That dancing witch, Caroline, had dazzled him, blinding him to her elder sister's fascinations. Because the poor girl had lost an eye and used a pert tongue to protect her from impertinence, he had not considered her desirable or even attractive. Now, under his love, this jewel was shining; for love can bring beauty, adding fire to eyes and provocation to a smile, making even once clumsy movements graceful. Miraculously since yesterday had Anne altered, her very body seeming to have grown, to have become plumper, the skin clearer, whiter, and the dark curls to shine more glossily.

By God, he did believe he loved the woman!

Thought of the morrow's night excited him as he had not been excited since boyhood at the prospect of some little girl's embrace. At the same time, he would have preferred delay. This hole-and-corner loving in a drab lodging-house was degrading when their love was not merely a satisfaction of immoral longings but a fulfilment, a unity of two spirits finding joy in mutual adoration. As soon as it could be honourably arranged, he would marry the woman, perhaps take her to Norwich to receive his parents' blessing; then he would settle comfortably into commerce, financed by the proceeds of Weare's murder and Anne's dowry. And it seemed to him that there should be no reason why they should not live happily together ever afterwards.

Refreshed after a sound sleep, in the morning he awoke, washed, shaved and dressed, and, with Tom, ate a large breakfast of mutton chops and tea and toast. As in his youth after a night of love, he felt pleasantly lazy yet alert, his blood calm and nervous tension eased, and he yawned while he read the newspapers and discussed with others in the bar the forthcoming fight between Spring and Langan. Boxing was the only sport Thurtell genuinely loved. Others, horse-racing, cocking, card- and dice-playing, coursing, bull-baiting, cricket, fives, fencing, and such, he liked, but they could not excite him in the way a pair of boxers in the ring could excite him. Then, when two strong men, stripped to the buff, stood knuckle to knuckle while thousands, whipped back from interfering by hired pugilists, shouted for claret, he always felt light-headed with sheer joy. Skill and muscle against skill and muscle, and skill was usually the master unless the other should land a lucky blow. Ay! give him skill, give him brave

Tom Spring of Herefordshire against any miller in the game! Langan was a Patlander and therefore certain to be more or less a miller. What was it that sharp Jon Bee had once said?—"An Irishman fights before he reasons; a Scotchman reasons before he fights; an Englishman is not particular as to the order of precedence, but will do either to accommodate his customers." And damned true that was! All his spare money would be on Tom's strong back.

Although there was little betting, the morning passed not only pleasantly but instructively with discussions on past fights for the belt of the champion of England, that lion's skin with a lion's head which only a hero could wear. Thought of the coming mill between Tom Spring and Langan made sportsmen impatient of witnessing it, but they had to wait until the stakes were raised and an open ground chosen where the law would not interfere.

Meanwhile, in Tetsall's bar there was satisfaction in recalling old fights and in boasting of the great men of the past. Once he married and was settled at Norwich, Thurtell decided that he would spend his profits, and make a fortune with his knowledge of the game, by backing fighting men. Had he not backed Gas in his memorable battle with Neat? That was the life! To drive to all the fights in an open barouche, bruisers about him like the bodyguard around a king ... Ay! and unlike most day-dreams, this did not seem an impossible one to attain.

Almost had he forgotten the murder, yet, under his mind, like the body in the pond, lay that shadow, the chance of discovery. Again and again in his thoughts he ran over the events and could see no flaw that could bring him into the dock. Suspicion, yes, there would be more than enough suspicion. Doubtless, Weare had told Rexworthy of the appointment and it was not impossible that they had been seen together in the gig on the road to Elstree; then there had been the shots fired, the screams, the blood on the road, the finding of pistol and knife. But nothing else. Suggestions, hints, all pointing towards him and Gill's Hill Cottage, but so long as he, Bill and Joe kept their heads and their tongues, the traps need never learn the truth. The body was sunk well over a mile from the scene of the killing, in a place where no one would ever think to look. All depended on keeping silent. Hunt he could trust; but Probert . . . For his own skin's sake, surely Probert would not dare mace on his pals?

No! he was safe and could relax and consider that future with a devout wife and a home in Norwich, sighed Thurtell.

During the afternoon, Hunt appeared and at first glance remained unrecognized. Without his great whiskers, he looked almost boyish and very plump, and Thurtell clapped his hands appreciatively on seeing him.

"Feel naked," muttered Hunt with an apologetic grin, ruefully rubbing his bare chin. "And damned cold, too. Every blasted wind freezes my chops. Give me a hot drink, quick."

Much of his truculence had gone with his whiskers. A pasty Samson, he seemed lost and frightened without their disguise and he no longer had the wit with which to retort to the laughter of the Thurtells. Feebly smiling, he sat, drinking deep of what was placed before him and looking furtively from side to side as though expecting to be pounced on and ejected as an impostor.

"There's something we'd like you to do for us, Joe," said Thurtell. "Tom wants you to go to Probert's and arrange about bringing up his children tomorrow. He'd go himself but he's got to see his damned creditors. And I don't want to show my nose there. Bill's fond of you but he don't like me. Thinks I maced him over the swag."

He chuckled and Hunt laughed with him, two knowing coves sniggering at having made a flat of Probert.

"All right," he said. "When do I start?"

"Soon as you like," said Thurtell, returning to the bar to continue the interminable arguments about the merits of this and that pugilist which the call to dinner had interrupted.

Into the afternoon, the argument continued, mainly because nobody listened for long, each man all the time considering what he hoped to say and seeking a pause into which he could thrust himself. One man swore that if Molyneaux hadn't been cheated he'd have beaten any white man, and that Cribb was never no good nohow; Thurtell argued that Tom Spring was the nonpareil; another insisted that Spring would never have beaten Oliver if he hadn't been the taller un with a longer reach; while a fourth offered to fight anybody as proof that Belcher could have eaten the lot of em with one hand tied behind his back; and when somebody piped up about Josh Hudson, he was howled down that Josh was like Gas, only a miller; and although the infuriated Joshite screamed in an attempt to be heard that although Josh might have been a miller at first he weren't one no longer, nobody troubled to listen to him.

When the argument was approaching the point at which it might end in a brawl and Tetsall was looking apprehensively at his bottles lest they be seized as weapons, Hunt sidled in. At sight of his white puffy face and huge, dark, haunted eyes, the smile fled Thurtell's lips and he shivered as though in a sudden draught.

Quickly, he seized the fellow and hustled him upstairs to his bedroom and shut the door.

"What is it?" he whispered.

"We're done," gasped Hunt. "I wish we'd never done it, O, I wish we'd never done it!"

"For the love of God," cried Thurtell, shaking him, "what's the trouble?"

"We're done," moaned Hunt, "that's the trouble. No! don't strike me, Jack! I'm trying to tell you, but my poor heart! Give me a drink."

"I'll give you a drink," said Thurtell, "when you've told me, and not before."

Yearningly, Hunt looked towards the bottle of brandy on the table, but seeing the implacable anger in Thurtell's eyes as he towered over him, he restrained his hand from seizing it.

"It—it's like th-th-this," he stuttered at last. "I got to the Artichoke, thought I'd call in for a taste on my way, and God be thanked that I did! Otherwise . . . O, I don't dare think of it!"

"If you don't tell me, and quickly," cried Thurtell, "I'll beat your silly brains out. Now, come on."

"Well," said Hunt, shivering while he talked, "I went into the Artichoke like I told you, and there was a hell of a lot of people there, all mag-magging. I took no heed at first till I heard em speak of murder. Bloody murder. That's what they said. And they talked of a body drowned in a pond, they did. They said it was a woman, but I suppose they hadn't looked close enough to make sure."

Thurtell swayed, the blood running from his cheeks and his hands turning clammy. Such horror seized him that he could barely stand. Panic, as in some nightmare when you run and run, the demon at your heels, made him both giddy and sick. He grasped a chair-back and slowly sank on to the chair itself. In an instant, all hope had fled and he knew that he would never escape the hangman.

"You must tell Tom," he whispered. "Call him. He's in the parlour."

With Hunt out of the room, he could lower the mask, he could let terror show in his eyes and not fight against his limbs' shaking. How the body had been found remained a mystery. No one had watched them last night. Of that he was quite sure. No one, save himself and

Tom and Hunt, knew where the body lay. Of that also was he quite sure. And as he and Tom had not talked, it must have been Hunt . . . but that was impossible. To whom could Hunt have talked?

With an effort, he forced a smile and stretched his legs and arms to control their shaking. Then carefully he poured himself a glass of brandy and drank it at a gulp. These fears were madness. Nothing had been found. The cowardly fool of a Hunt had heard the villagers gossiping in the belief that some murder had been committed; but that they should believe that a woman and not a man had been killed was proof that they knew nothing. It had been the shock of the revelation coming when he had felt secure, flushed with spirits and pugilistic arguments, that had momentarily unnerved him.

When Hunt returned, a frightened Tom at his heels, Thurtell was able to look up and smile, on the surface, himself again.

"Joe's been seeing blue devils," he laughed. "Too much bingo on an empty stomach. Take more water with it in future, Joey."

"I tell you I heard em magging in there, old Field going it, too. He never did like us," said Hunt in an aggrieved voice, the brandy Tom had given him beginning to calm a little of his agitation. "Don't know why; we was always polite when we was in the Artichoke, weren't we? Probably it's Bill he didn't like and we got blamed for it, being his friends."

"Wh-wh-what egg-eggs-exactly did they say?" asked Tom, running his fingers through his hair.

"I told you," growled Hunt. "About a woman having been found drowned in a pond."

"If it was a woman," said Thurtell, "we're safe. Either you or they are imagining things, or somebody put a knife into a woman just about the time we was doing Weare. But we must find out the truth. One of us'll have to go down and ask Bill."

"I'm not going again," said Hunt with a shudder. "The bloody robin redbreasts are probably already there, waiting to nab us."

"I'd better not go," mused Thurtell. "They know me. They know I was down there at the time."

Both men turned towards Tom who shuffled and flushed under their anxious glare.

"I-I-I can't go-go-go," he said. "I'm your bur-bur-brother."

"It's different for you," said Thurtell wheedlingly, forcing a smile as though he had not a fear in his heart. "Joe's right. They know us."

"Th-th-they know me, t-t-too," muttered Tom. "E-v-ev-ery

week, y-y-you know that, I-I-I go do-do-down there t-t-to see the gug-gug-girls."

"That's the very thing!" cried Thurtell, slapping his thigh. "They often see you down there with your kids, they're used to you going for innocent reasons; and as Bill's doing a fly-by-night, ain't it natural for you to go and arrange to bring the girls to London? But if Joey or I go there and get nabbed, what excuse are we to give?"

"I d-d-don't like it," muttered Tom, "but I-I-I sup-up-uppose I'll hav-hav-have to do it, d-d-damn it."

"Thanks, Tom," said Thurtell, sighing relief. "You're a real out-and-outer, ain't he, Joe? A trump, if ever there was one, and I'm real proud of you, Tom."

Tom did not answer. Muttering to himself, frowning and glaring at the floor, he strode off; and the sound of his steps on the stairs echoed up to them in the room.

"What do you think about it?" whined Hunt, gazing at Thurtell as though expecting him to work a miracle. "I could have dropped dead, I tell you, when I heard em magging like that at Field's."

"I'm not thinking about it," said Thurtell quietly. "Get the cards and let's have a game."

"I couldn't play, Jack, I couldn't. Not with this hanging over us. I wouldn't know a knave from a king, I wouldn't." With trembling hands, Hunt poured himself more brandy while from under his heavy, jutting brows Thurtell watched him contemptuously. "I can't think of nothing but him in that pond and traps dragging for him. Murder will out, they say; and I don't like it, I don't."

"Nobody likes it," said Thurtell, "but that don't do no good. You'll only worry yourself into a fever and start saying things you shouldn't. There's nothing against us so long as Probert don't blab."

"He'll talk. You can't trust him. If ever there was a mace-cove it's Bill Probert. We should have killed him, too. Once the traps have him, he'll open like an oyster in front of a fire." Moaning, Hunt sank back in his chair and covered his naked face with his dirty hands. "I wish we'd never done it," he sobbed.

Such pusillanimity gave Thurtell strength. Scornfully, he lounged to the carpet-bag under the bed and pulled out a pack of cards.

"Those were Weare's!" squealed Hunt. "Burn em!"

"What do you mean—burn em!" Opening the pack, Thurtell placed it on the table and spread out the cards for a game of patience. "There are hundreds, thousands of cards like these in London," he said. "You can buy em at any stationer's. They don't smell of Weare, do they? Now, shut up. I've got to concentrate."

To finish the game, he had to cheat, such was the confusion in his mind, but he had never quibbled about a little cheating, even of himself; and it kept Hunt quiet. All the time, however, while his eyes were on the coloured pieces of pasteboard, his thoughts were at Elstree, and he counted each passing minute, riding in the gig with his brother, until he knew exactly where Tom must be on the road. At the turnpike at Tyburn Gate, then along the Edgware Road. Maida Hill. Kilburn. On, on. On to Edgware. The flicker of the wheels spun with each card. He heard the beat of hoofs, the crack of the whip. On, on.

Out of his fob he drew Weare's watch, dragging the lining with it, and Hunt shuddered at the sight, while he placed it on the table before him that he might watch the minutes click past. Not yet at Edgware. Would he stop at the Bald-Faced Stag or some other public house? Unlikely. He would want to reach Gill's Hill as quickly as possible to be rid of his anxieties. No. Tom wouldn't pause. Yes! he must be at Edgware by now, or going through Edgware. Not long before he would reach Medbourn Bridge, passing the marsh which, if tales of ghosts be true, should now be haunted, and over Cobden Hill. Then the road to Batler's Green, and the lane to Gill's Hill Cottage turning off it to the right.

Batler's Green? He wondered how it had got that name. Could there have been a battle there in the past? There had been a battle not so far away at Barnet, he vaguely remembered having read somewhere; and hadn't there been another at St. Albans? Or it might have been a real battle, a bout of fisticuffs between some earlier Tom Spring and some other Jacky Langan.

Thinking of fighting, Thurtell tried to concentrate on Spring and Langan; but not yet having seen Langan come to the scratch, he could not maintain that fantasy for long. But Tom Spring was worth thinking of. Who could feel afraid once he had shaken the fist of that amiable giant? Remembering him in his mill with Bill Neat on Hinckley Down near Andover last May, Thurtell began to smile; and amazed, Hunt watched that smile, praying that he might have found some trick whereby they could escape the traps.

"What the hell are you grinning at!" screamed Hunt suddenly, leaping to his feet. "I can't bear to watch you grinning like that!"

"I was only thinking about Tom Spring and the battle with Bill Neat near Andover," said Thurtell, astonished at the outburst. "Did you see it, Joe? Ay, two such big fellows going for upwards of half-an-hour and no mischief done, that gave the heart joy, I tell you! It was beautiful! And most of the money was on Neat. You should have seen the sour faces when he went down! They all thought Spring'd be smashed and nothing else but smashed. One hit was to have spoilt all his science; two was to have taken the fight completely out of him; and the third was to be the coup de grâce. But he never could break through Tom's guard. There's true boxing for you! He never landed a real effective hit in the whole battle. He said he broke a bone in his hand in the fourth round, but that's all Mars in a band-box. Tom had won before he'd really started. Even Randall never done so well as that. You should have seen the Bristolians. Some of em went mad and others swore it was a cross. It was no cross, I'll bet a hundred——"

"Shut up!" cried Hunt, leaping to his feet and dancing on the floor, hands over his ears. "I'll go crazy if you keep on magging about fights that ain't nothing to do with us. Where's Tom?"

"He'll have just about got there," said Thurtell, glancing at Weare's watch. "It takes roughly an hour, don't it? No; he should be on his way back by now, just about passing the bridge nigh where we put him last night. Can't you sit still? Have a drink, blast you!"

Hunt's impatience, his wriggling and moaning, his wiping his face with his hands every few minutes, his darting at the brandy-bottle and gulping of the spirit, his leaping suddenly up and walking about the room, bumping into the bed and kicking the chairs, was beginning to irritate Thurtell. Trying not to lose his temper, he poured himself a drink; and again fear closed about his heart.

Tom Spring was forgotten. The green world of the ring was insubstantial against the ghost of Weare. Damn and blast the fellow. His wet presence seemed with them in that room, brought to them on the reek of Hunt's sweating terror, and it could not be dismissed by memories of brave men and the exhilarating clap of knuckles against flesh and the crack as of a broken neck when the defeated went down with a snapped jaw, such as he had heard on many an occasion. Those now were the phantoms beside the reality of that damned dripping ghost bringing with it the tart odour of decay and foul water and rotting vegetation. Would to God he had never met the man; would to God Probert had never suggested the security of Gill's Hill for the murder; would to God this sweating shaking coward of a Hunt had never urged him to the deed. Would to God, above all, that he had recognized his love for Anne long before now.

R

That night—almost he had forgotten—he would be climbing the stairs to the second floor of 35 Castle Street where in the darkness sweet Anne Noyes would await him. How could he go without first hearing from Tom? But Tom would return all right. He should be back in . . . well, give him another twenty minutes, twenty-five minutes. He might stop for a drink or to bait his horse. Madness to become worried when there was no need to worry. What was there for him to fear? Tattle: nothing else; and some woman's body found in a pond, if Hunt had not imagined that. He had killed no woman. That was something they couldn't say against him. Never in his life had he killed a woman.

Sighing, Thurtell shuffled the cards and began to deal himself and an invisible opponent hands as though for a friendly game of double-patience when suddenly Hunt leaned forward and swept the cards to the floor.

"What the hell!" Thurtell was on his feet in an instant, fists clenched, his usually sallow face dark with fury; but he could not hit this cringing child wailing and sobbing and begging his pardon.

"Pick up those cards," he growled; "and for God's sake, be a man."

Whimpering, Hunt went on hands and knees, trying to gather up the scattered cards.

"A bold Turpin lad you've turned out to be, by God," jeered Thurtell.

"It's this waiting, this damned waiting," sobbed Hunt. "I could stand anything, anything, but not this waiting. What do we know what they're doing down there? Ruthven or Upson or some of their mates might be coming to nab us. And think of what they'd find here! There's Bill's own watch ticking in my face, and there's all that stuff under my bed in Golden Square, and my poor old woman—it'll drive her mad!"

"To hell with your old woman! You should have thought of her before."

"I never dreamed things would go like this. I thought you'd manage it and no one'd suspect."

"You've only yourself to blame for that," said Thurtell. "If you and Bill hadn't stopped to booze on the way, the three of us could have settled him without a squeak."

"It weren't my fault . . . I swear it, Jack!"

"Aw, shut up," snarled Thurtell, sitting down and pouring himself more brandy.

Tom should be back soon. It seemed hours, ages, ago since he had left, and already night was closing in. Strange how one's fears intensified in darkness! Couldn't see what was happening outside, of course: that was why. A black uncurtained window made one think of devils peeping in; and what devils could there be so dangerous as traps? He'd fight a dozen bogles rather than one robin redbreast with the handcuffs under his coat-tails. Damn Hunt, it was his terror that was making him shake and sending him to peer through the window, after wiping clear the damp glass, to see only the wet street and the lights from the Coach and Horses glinting on the dung and the sheen of a waiting pony's flank. Neither day nor night, the dead hour before the West End woke up to the bobbing of the ball at rolly-polly—that new and increasingly popular French game sometimes called roulette—in the hells of St. James's, to the free food and wine—the more wine drunk the better for them, smirked the proprietors—to the shuffling of cards in rouge et noir, to all the other games played to fleece flats while croupiers raked in the ivory counters. They were making ready, the vast London army of sharps and whores and bullies, shuffling and cutting cards, cogging the dice, hitting and pocketing the balls with cue or mace. Only now Weare would not be sidling amongst them seeking whom he might devour.

"The bottle's empty," quavered Hunt.

"That means," scoffed Thurtell, "I suppose, that, like Macheath, your courage is out. Wait here; I'll get some more."

"I'll go. I'd like to go!"

"Stay where you are!" cried Thurtell in a terrible voice, and Hunt slid back into his chair.

Strange to believe, Thurtell felt, when he re-entered the cheerful, noisy bar that at that very moment, perhaps, some magistrate was writing out a warrant for his arrest. Pah! these were fantasies at which he would laugh in the morning. But certainly, Tom should have been back before now.

Yes, he should have been back long before now. . . .

No sign of his worry showed on Thurtell's sallow face and his voice did not tremble when he bought a bottle of brandy; and, with cheerful nods to acquaintances, he strolled back up the stairs to Hunt and the smell of fear in his bedchamber.

Hunt seized the uncorked bottle and gulped down some of the liquor before Thurtell could stop him.

"Th-tha-that's better," he spluttered, coughing and hitting his chest. "It's the old woman I'm worried about," he said. "I've still got that damned great-coat of yours at home. You can't clean the blood off it. I tried, but you can't. Then there's his dressing-box and his double-barrelled gun, and his shooting jacket and drab breeches and his gaiters and leggings and Hessian boots, and I don't know what else."

"Burn em," said Thurtell coldly.

"Where can I burn em? I've only got an ordinary grate and it'd stink the place out. What the hell am I to do with em!"

"For God's sake, shut up!" roared Thurtell, striking the table and sending bottle and glasses jiggling.

"All right," muttered Hunt sulkily; "only I wish to God Tom'd get back, blast him!"

No argument about it now. Tom was late. Every minute ticking away on Weare's watch told Thurtell of approaching danger. Even had he paused for a drink, and he'd not have lingered over it, Tom should have been here before now. No ordinary accident would have stopped him. But . . . an accident! Had the gig overturned, a wheel flown off, the traces snapped?

Anything, ay! anything might have happened. But argue though he did against his mounting terror, trying to keep sane and to think clearly, Thurtell felt his heart's beat growing faster and his temples begin to throb as though all within him was working at double-speed and reaching towards a crescendo which his mind would not be able to sustain.

Slowly on the indifferent dial the hands jerked forward as though they were alive, Weare's watch jeering at him, while the minutes ticked into hours, the hours to further hours; and yet Tom did not come.

CHAPTER TWENTY-THREE

NIGHTMARE AND DAYMARE

BEFORE dawn, Thurtell awoke. He awoke, feeling not only physically sick but with such a weight of horror on his mind that he tried frantically to escape back into sleep, but could not. He was ill, not only in body but in mind. And he prayed that he might be ill unto death, although he knew that fear and a night of heavy drinking alone were the causes of his misery. In time, damn it, he would recover and be strong again. And he did not want to recover and have to face life and his accusers with only the treacherous Probert and the wretched Hunt to stand beside him. Far better death. Far better to cut his throat or blow out his brains than to undergo the indignity of a public trial and, later, a public hanging. In that cold hour before dawn when life itself seems suspended between the death of the stars and the rise of the sun, he could see no reason in trying to continue to live when fate always fought against him. And fate was an opponent which even bold Spring could never have floored.

Had Tom returned? Thurtell could not remember. Last night came back as nightmare, the slow, clammy realization that something had detained his brother at Elstree or on the road back, leaving him poised in suspense, not knowing what to do, while frantically Hunt had watched him, expecting from his strength some miracle. But he was only a man and, like all men, he was fallible, liable to make foolish mistakes, slips of memory, acts of carelessness on which the traps could pounce and denounce him for a villain. There was still much to be done before he could hope for safety, but he was unable to move. Sweating, shivering in alternate fits of heat and cold, iced one moment, grilled the next, he lay in bed in his dark room, trying to summon the will to force his brandy-soaked body into action. And it could only roll and tremble and sweat, while he groaned to think of justice closing in.

Last night . . . He must try to recollect everything that they had done last night. When the constables came for him they would start asking questions, the magistrates would ask questions, the judge would ask questions, the jury and counsel would ask questions, if what he

261

feared should prove to be the truth. And he must be ready with his answers.

Last night . . .

At Hunt's lodgings. 19, King Street, to the east of Golden Square. A street come down in the world, if it had ever been far up in the world. The houses scabby, dirty, with unwashed and often uncurtained windows, yet some there were that still maintained, with curtains and paint and washing, an air of more than gentility, of even a lick of splendour, like old courtesans, painted and patched, who refuse to recognize the bedraggled company which they are forced to keep. Close to these unhappy dwellings stood fine houses, large shops, clean streets; but the clustering lanes and alleys also concealed thieves and such riffraff behind façades of poverty. Here, in this part of London, dwelt wealth and poverty, honesty and crime, cleanliness and squalor, as though the district could not make up its mind whether to sink into night's misery or to rise to the sun with a clean face. The square itself seemed to have forgotten why once it had been built. It slunk, it lurked, it hid behind narrow and often filthy streets; it plainly did not want to be recognized and few Londoners knew of its existence unless they blundered on it by chance or were called there in the way of business. Even during the summer it wore a dull and dingy look, a furtive air, although maintaining a pretence, like some draggletail landlady, that it had once seen better days.

The kind of semi-respectable, lurking bolt-hole in which you would expect a man like Joe Hunt to live. There, last night, Thurtell remembered the hurry with which, after sending Mrs. Hunt off to redeem one of her husband's coats pledged to a pawnbroker in St. Martin's Lane, they had set to to destroy whatever incriminating evidence they could find. Drinking brandy from the bottle, in the fluttering light of a tallow candle, they had attempted again to wash the blood from the sleeves of Thurtell's great-coat. Finding this to be impossible in the time, they had cut off the sleeves. These Hunt had thrown into the privy in the yard at the back. The remainder of the coat they had tossed down an area somewhere in Marylebone. Weare's hat they cut into small pieces and dropped them, bit by bit, along Maddox Street. His white-handled razor and strop they let fall on the pavement in some dark street facing Maddox and Bond Streets. Scarcely had they dropped the damned things than they had been picked up by a stranger strolling by. The tortoiseshell comb and hairbrush were tossed into the middle of the same street and a housewife, still containing needles, thread, pins and scissors, was dropped behind the railings of somebody's house.

What was there left to get rid of? Not a great deal. The dressing-box—it had no name on it—and the double-barrelled gun, the shooting-jacket, and other of the dead man's clothing, and his carpet-bag. Hunt had sworn to get rid of them before morning. What else? did he have anything left here that could be associated with Weare?

The effort to think was painful but it had to be done. Laboriously, Thurtell burrowed back into the past few days and nights, trying to remember whether he had forgotten anything that might prove incriminating. Some of his clothes had bloodstains, but they could have come from anybody's blood, his own, the result, he would say, of shaving. Anything else?

The watch!

For a moment, he remained stiff, scarcely daring to breathe; then he relaxed and smiled again. He remembered now, thank God! Down a deep privy in the yard of a tavern he had never entered before, a tavern somewhere in Warwick Street, he had let it plomp, although he could have wept at hearing it fall. In the Coach and Horses that afternoon when he had consulted the dial, a Jew had offered him twenty-six guineas for it, and, luckily, outraged by the smallness of the offer, he had scorned the petty sum. A beautiful box of minutes like that! worth every penny of sixty quid, at least! and he had had to throw it away. . . .

Then what had they done? They had drunk, of course; they had drunk enormously. Without a bellyful of spirits he had feared he would not sleep; and he had slept only to be now woken suddenly, heart hammering like a fist in his chest, his body drenched in sweat.

Groaning, he crawled out of bed and in the milky dawnlight found a bottle and raised it to his lips. The raw spirit made him vomit and he reached the window and threw it open just in time.

The sky was lightening, pearly clouds beginning to glow, and the ridged roofs and countless chimney-pots could be seen in outline. The street below was empty. Even a Charley on his beat was not to be glimpsed. Even the slaveys had not yet woken up to start the fires and to set the kettle on the ashes bustled to life with a bundle of sticks. Nobody stirred in all that silent world, save he. Alone, he looked down into the mists of the streets and up into the sky breaking into shreds of pale blue. From somewhere in Soho a rooster crowed and was answered by a rival nearby, other roosters joining in to cockle-doodle-do defiance; then a dog began to yap, setting other dogs yapping and barking, while, in the distance, a donkey brayed. Sounds only. No life, as yet, until, belly close to the pavement, a grey cat sped past, fleeing from a tom-husband's revenge on the tiles. A few birds tried to sing and the chimneys began languidly to smoke. Slowly, life was coming back to this city of ghosts, and soon the shops would open and men on the way to work would call at public houses for a warming drink to stir them back to activity.

With the rising of the sun rose Thurtell's spirits. The webs of horror began slowly to dissolve in his mind; and, mixing it with water, he was able to drink and retain a little of the rum.

Tom? Had Tom come back? He could not remember for sure. Late last night there had been a third with him and Hunt in their drinking. Yes, there had been somebody else. It must have been Tom! Who else but Tom?

With sudden joy he ran from the room into the next room along the hall, Tom's room, and saw a shape under the bedclothes. Sobbing with relief, sweating and ready to cry, he leaned against the door in the brightening light, cursing himself for having been a fool and a coward; and last night's frenzied attempts to get rid of Weare's clothes and property now seemed a comical and foolish frolic; and he regretted the loss of the golden tattler. Worth sixty quid, too! ay, every penny of sixty quid!

Something in the shape of the man under the bedclothes stiffened the smile on his lips and, beginning to feel cold again, he tiptoed forward. This was not Tom! No, no, this was not Tom. . . .

His surprise and horror at the discovery kept him stiff as though frozen. Of course, he remembered now! and he groaned at the memory. Tom Noyes had called at the Coach and Horses and they had welcomed him with bowls of lushy. Too drunk to leave, they had rolled him into bed in the early morning, laughing and thinking it a jest. A jest, indeed! Tom must be still at Elstree, unless injured in some accident, and that meant that he was probably in the hands of the constables.

Almost falling, Thurtell tottered to a chair and, seeing a bottle of rum on the table, seized it and drank great gulps of the raw spirit. With reviving consciousness it brought greater misery until he wished that this were the morning of his death and he was waiting for Jack Ketch and not for a Bow Street runner to come and handcuff him.

Noyes had come last night with damnable news. Slowly memories seeped back and he could see again, could see a little, of what had happened. He could remember Noyes, already drunk, swaying and whispering and almost biting off his ear while he whispered.

He had called at the Cock, Noyes had said, and had found that Mary was no longer there. Asking discreet questions from the temporary landlord put in by the creditors, he had learned that she had moved to a garret in Windmill Street where her dandiprat of a husband had returned to his old trade of tailoring. That did not matter. What did it matter what the bitch was doing or where she was living? He had laughed in Noyes's red nose; but the laughter had swiftly changed to rage. Not content with deserting his public house, she had taken her woman's vengeful spite to Barber Beaumont and had told the dog everything about the fire; and she knew everything, having been living with him as his wife at the time and helping with her own accursed hand to set flint to steel. . . .

Must she choose this moment when fate had cornered him to drive at his heart another blow? Woman, faithless woman. . . .

And not only Mary! Dear God, not only Mary Dobson. . . . Of course, of course! . . . When Noyes had staggered into the Coach and Horses late last night he had cursed the sight of him because, while drinking with her brother, he would be unable to steal off to Castle Street; and after that, he had forgotten the appointment. . . .

He had forgotten! Drink and worry, the torment of waiting and of doing nothing until the constables were prepared to nab him, had drowned even that promised joy. In her bed, trembling at every sound, Anne would have waited in the darkness, listening, listening and weeping, and thinking that he did not love her sufficiently to answer her brave proposal. Swine. Swine. He had remained here drinking until he had collapsed into bed. And all the time, that darling girl had waited in her bed, had waited, listening . . . listening for his step on the stairs which now she would never hear. Would never hear! He, fool and villain, had failed her as all his friends and the woman he had thought he had loved were failing him. There was no truth left in the world; there was nothing worth living for. . . .

In that state of dumb misery he remained, drinking and shuddering in the morning light until the door quietly opened and he looked up to see the Bow Street officer, George Ruthven, sidle into the room with an artful smile on his fair, unhandsome face.

"Jock, my boy," he said friendlily, "I want you."

No longer afraid, almost with indifference, Thurtell looked up at him.

"What do you want, George?" he asked as though this were merely some casual visitor, or a servant, smiling at him.

"Never mind," said Ruthven, shrugging faintly. "I'll tell you presently. . . . Who's your friend there?"

"You don't want him, George," sighed Thurtell. "He's nothing to do with the fire."

At mention of the fire, Ruthven cocked an amused eyebrow at Thurtell as though sharing with him a private joke, both men knowing that he had called about nothing so unimportant as arson or the cheating of an insurance office.

Tiptoe, Ruthven went to the bed and peered down; and at the same moment, Noyes opened his eyes and started up in terror.

"Wh-wh-what do you want?" he gasped.

"Not you, Mr. Tommy Noyes," grinned Ruthven, head to one side like a fowl about to peck at a worm, "not yet, Mr. Noyes. How's the wine-trade nowadays? Not too good? That's bad, that's very bad; but don't you go playing with fire like some naughty boys, will you?"

He winked at Thurtell who stared back stonily at him while, with trembling hands, Noyes pulled on his boots, having, by great good fortune, fallen fully clothed into bed the previous night.

"Now, Jock, my boy," said Ruthven after the door had slammed behind Noyes, "you and I must have a little talk together. This ain't your room though, is it? I'd like to have a look through your things, if you don't mind."

"Do what you bloody well like!" snarled Thurtell.

"Now, now," clucked Ruthven as though at a naughty boy, "I'm only doing my duty, Jock, and you know I always treat my friends right and fair so long as they treat me honest. I bear you no malice for making me work when I'm tired; and I hope you don't bear me no malice for just doing my duty. . . . Now, let me have a look at them hands of yours."

Languidly, Thurtell stretched out his arms and, with the quickness of much practice, Ruthven had the handcuffs around the wrists and the key turned before he fully knew what had happened.

"Eh, George!" he cried indignantly, slowly standing to his feet and brandishing the linked wrists, "there's no need to do this to a pal."

"Honour bright, Jock, my boy, it breaks my heart having to do it, but them's my orders." Woefully, Ruthven shook his head and sighed. "Now, do you mind if I just have a quick look through your room?" he asked, not shrinking, not showing a blink of fear as those steel wrists swung above him.

"Whatever you want, George," said Thurtell wearily, letting his arms fall.

What use was there in trying to fight? Ruthven was only doing his job. And no longer did it seem of great importance to Thurtell that he might be hanged. That was as good a way out as many others, better than most, when life had lost enchantment and Anne would be shivering with shame, hating him, reviling herself, alone in her cold bed in Castle Street.

CHAPTER TWENTY-FOUR

IN SEPARATE BEDS

IN FRONT of Ruthven and those who came to peep at him as at a squirrel in a box, Thurtell maintained an imperturbable unconcern after he had been lodged and strongly guarded in the Essex Arms Inn, Watford. Nobody gave him a hint about what was happening outside the four walls of his room, his jailors shrugging and professing ignorance whenever he asked them. This, he knew, was the usual treatment of a suspected criminal, the authorities wanting him kept in ignorance of any evidence that might be produced against him in the hope that, under examination, he should be trapped into some damning admission from which he would later find himself unable to wriggle. Of his own stoical courage he suffered no doubt. Let them pry and question as they liked, they'd get nothing out of him, he swore; but what of the others? Tom, undoubtedly, had been taken yesterday. Hunt he had seen on his arrival at Watford, for he had been driven down independently by Ruthven's fellow-officer of police, Jack Upson, in a gig that had followed his and Ruthven's; and Thurtell had been deeply relieved to find him of unexpectedly high courage. Asking Ruthven to fetch some brandy and water, he had clasped and conspiratorially pressed Hunt's hand to give him courage, at the same time winking and merrily crying: "Give us a song, Joey;" and Hunt, God be thanked, had piped up without a tremor, *Mary, list awake*.

That was the way to baffle the rogues. Grin or whistle in their teeth, sing them *Mary, list awake* or even, mockingly, some thieves' chaunt, and never let them know that the worm of fear was in your heart. If only Hunt could keep up this bravado, they would be safe, for Tom would not talk, and none of the others, apart from Probert, knew anything seriously damaging, whatever they might suspect. On Probert alone, on that untrustworthy hair, were their lives suspended, and it was exasperating not to know what the villain might have already confessed.

The boy, Addis, doubtless knew a little, and the serving-wench, Sue Woodruff, and Mrs. Probert; but Mrs. Probert could not give evidence against her husband. Everything therefore depended on

Probert; and Probert was the one whom Thurtell did not trust. Should he split . . . O, that did not bear thinking of! But of what was he to think, caged in this small room with a pair of stupid constables watching him as if, handcuffed though he was, he could suddenly without any weapon murder them both, the fools?

Other matters pressing on his mind, he dared not ponder. His parents . . . No! his poor dad, respected in Norwich, a good man, an honest man, and his devoted mother. . . . Not of them. No. Of whom then? Of Anne? Of Anne he dared not think. No. More tormenting even than the possibility of being hanged was thought of her in her misery believing that he had abandoned her, forgetting his promise and scorning her noble offering of selfless love.

On this worry, Ruthven took pity. Bringing Thurtell's supper and a bowl of rum punch, he set the tray on the table and told his captive to be of good cheer, for he'd known of worse cases, he said.

"It's not about the trial," said Thurtell, while the runner unlocked his hands that he might eat, "that don't worry me—well, not much, seeing that I'm innocent. It's about a lady."

"Hem?" said Ruthven, raising his thick eyebrows.

"Lookee here, George," whispered Thurtell, glaring at the constables by the door, "we're friends, ain't we?"

"Of course we are, Jock, my boy, never liked a cove more of all I've nabbed. You're a gentleman and don't give no trouble. If there's anything I can do for you what don't go against my duty, you understand? I'll do it and be proud to be able to do it; but I'm afraid . . ." Mournfully he shook his dark head. . . . "'Taint allowed, not these days it ain't, my boy. Downright cruel it is, unnatural, I grant you, but these are unnatural times. In the old days, I'm told, they was more free and easy, more human about poor fellows in your lonely situation——"

"What the devil are you magging about?" cried Thurtell.

"Why, only about what you was asking," said Ruthven, looking pained. "About smuggling some sweetheart of yours in here."

Thurtell laughed. "Don't be a fool," he said. "A man in my situation's got no time to waste on that sort of thing. He's got more important matters on his mind. Now what I was asking you, George, as a pal, is if you've heard anything of a young woman called Miss Anne Noyes? Bill Probert's sister-in-law."

"O, her?" said Ruthven, plainly disappointed. "We nabbed her, all right."

"What the hell do you mean! She's got nothing to do with all this! You leave her go this instant, damn you!"

Thurtell was on his feet, almost knocking over the laden table in his rage, and although his knife had no edge to it, it could have performed unpleasant work in that strong hand.

"Hold your horses!" said Ruthven, shaking his dark head reprovingly. "It ain't got nothing to do with me. You know that. And no harm'll come to the lady. I give you my word on't. She's at Mr. Clutterbuck's now. And he's a good man is Mr. Clutterbuck. A magistrate, too, and he'll treat her kindly."

"But what the hell did you take her for!"

"I never took her. Now, calm yourself, Jocky boy. It was Simmons what brought her down here. He's a local constable, but not such a bad fellow for all that. A bit slow in the head, that's all."

"What are they doing with her at Clutterbuck's?"

"Now, Jock, if you won't keep calm, I'll tell you nothing. Have a go at your grub. Strike me! if it ain't veal! and tender as a babe unborn! Now, get it down, like a good fellow, and put some strong belly-tinder inside you, and I'll talk while you eat."

"Then talk, for God's sake," snarled Thurtell, sitting down at his table and glaring at the food. No wonder they had given him veal! Against a knife as blunt as the one they trusted him with, any solid food would have rebounded like iron. "Well?" he growled. "Out with it."

"There's little to tell," said Ruthven, looking sadly at him. "You mean the one-eyed lady, don't you? Now, there's no need to get angry! I meant no offence. As good-looking a lady as ever I've set lamps on 'cept . . . well, as good-looking as one could hope for nowadays. She was taken, as I told you, by this here Simmons in her lodgings in Castle Street, Leicester Square, her and her sister, Mrs. Elizabeth Probert. They was brought to Watford in separate post-chaises, Mrs. Probert being in the custody of Bishop, a Bow Street officer like myself, and a brave, honest man into the bargain. They got to Watford at about twelve o'clock at night and lodged here in the Essex Arms——"

"Here!" cried Thurtell, and dropped his knife and fork, "and you never told me!"

"I never knew . . . I'd have told you. Course I would if I'd known! Besides, she was in Bishop's care. . . ."

"Here, in this bloody inn; all the time here!"

"Not all the time!"

"And me here wondering where the hell she was! Nobody telling me a bloody thing. And all the while, she's here and I didn't know it!"

"Now, you can't blame me, Jocky boy," said Ruthven, deepening his voice and speaking cajolingly. "If only you'd have told me, just given me a hint, O, dear! I'd have done anything to help you, Jocky boy, I would."

"Can I see her now? Bring her to me here."

Sorrowfully, Ruthven shook his head. "'Taint allowed," he sighed. "I'd do it, I swear on my own Bible, I would, I'd do it and be damned to the magistrates; but I can't, Jocky boy, 'cause she ain't here any longer."

"If they've put her in jail . . . !"

"Of course she ain't in jail. I told you, she's with Mr. Clutterbuck, and he's a true gentleman if ever there was one, is Mr. Clutterbuck. Why, no one'd harm the poor lady. The distress she was in! Ah, it broke one's heart just to hear her howling."

"Howling? why?"

"What am I telling you? I don't know, but the poor dear soul, she did take on so. She was far more affected than Mrs. Probert. There's a deep one for you, Jock, my boy. No tears from her blessed eyes; but poor Miss Noyes now, it were terrible to hear her. She cried almost incessant and was greatly depressed." Ruthven groaned sympathetically and, taking up Thurtell's glass, drank from it in an absent-minded manner as though not knowing what his hand was doing. "They had some tea in the same compartment as the officers," he continued, wiping his lips on his sleeve; "then they retired to rest in separate chambers—without the officers, need I say, Jocky boy?—and they were locked in all night."

"O," sighed Thurtell, settling back into his chair, relieved to discover that, even had he known of her presence in the inn, it would have been impossible for them to have met.

"Ay, that was the way of it," said Ruthven, belching softly. "All by their lonesomes, they was, and that was what troubled your Miss Noyes. Didn't like the idea, she didn't. Seemed to fear to go to bed without company . . . I don't mean what you think! so don't you look at me like that, please sir! I'm only telling you what I was told. But the horrors the poor maid did have about being shut in by herself, and the clack she set up! nobody knew what to do, for nobody could get a wink of sleep."

"I heard nothing," said Thurtell suspiciously.

"The other side of the house," explained Ruthven, "and they locked the door on her. There was nothing else the poor fellows could do. She entreated em to let her have a light——"

"And they'd not give it to her, the rats!"

"They daren't! You know that right enough, Jocky boy. It weren't that they was hard-hearted, poor fellows, but how could they have done it? She weren't eggzactly under arrest. Held for questioning, I suppose you might call it. And if they'd given her a light and she'd have set fire to the curtains or something and burnt down the place, where'd they have been?"

"In hell," said Thurtell, "where they belong."

Ruthven laughed as though he believed Thurtell had spoken in jest. "Ay," he said, "and that's where they'd have been if the magistrate had heard of it. But they could do nothing to help the bonny lass. When they told her she couldn't have no light, the poor lady asked if she might have a chambermaid to sleep with; but, consequent of there being so many strange men in the house, the chambermaids weren't going to have that, I can tell you; and pretty some of em are, too, I'd perhaps be thinking if I wasn't a married man already."

"So she slept by herself?" said Thurtell, staring at the food growing cold on his plate and seeing Anne's white face staring back appealingly at him.

"All by herself," said Ruthven, slapping his thigh. "I can swear on the Bible to that, Jocky boy, so set your mind at rest. All by herself she was in the dark without even so much as a female to bear her company. They do tell me that when they unlocked the door this morning, she was half-dead with fear, being in the dark and too timid even to crawl into bed by herself, but had her bonny phiz pressed to the window and she on her knees there as though praying."

"I don't want to hear any more!" groaned Thurtell. "And take that grub away. I couldn't eat the stuff."

"O, come now, Jocky my lad!" coaxed Ruthven, speaking as though he were a lover, and languishing at him, "good grub like that, made special for you 'cause of the knife! Ah, well!" He eyed the veal with cocked brows. "If it's all holiday at Peckham," he said, seizing the plate and rising to his feet, "I'll take this out of your sight. Anything you want before I go?"

"More bingo, damn it," cried Thurtell. "And, George! If you can see Miss Noyes, tell her . . . tell her that I couldn't get there; it weren't my fault. She'll understand."

"Anything to oblige," said Ruthven, hurrying off with the plate. "I'll see Miss Noyes for you. Have no fear," he added.

Certainly, he must see the woman, not having suspected before that she might have anything interesting to tell. But Thurtell was so worried, so eager to hear of what his moll was doing, that his curiosity was piqued. She might even know where that damned body lay hidden. . . .

That poor Anne had been distressed and sleepless both troubled and pleased Thurtell. This sounded like proof that she still loved him and was in a state of nervous exhaustion after her disappointment the other night. So long as he knew that she loved him, he felt that he could face anything, even Jack Ketch himself, without fear.

Ruthven having told the prisoner so much, the constables became easier in their manner, particularly after Thurtell had asked them to share his punch and brandy and seemed prepared to sit up all night and buy drinks. But soon he realized that they did not know a great deal. The mystery of Tom's disappearance was, however, explained. On arriving at Gill's Hill Cottage he had found a magistrate there and Probert and his wife being questioned while the pool was dragged by Field of the Artichoke in the hope of fishing up Weare's body. He had, of course, been immediately taken into custody, then orders had been sent to Bow Street to have Hunt and himself detained.

The other prisoners had quickly followed, Anne and Mrs. Probert and her brother, Tom Noyes, after Tom had scurried out of Ruthven's clutch to be caught in Castle Street; and there were, the constables alleged, warrants out for others; but who they were they did not know, although they had heard that Mr. Tetsall, the landlord of the Coach and Horses, was in custody, while Probert's servants, Dick Addis and Susannah Woodruff, had been questioned. Also the landlord of the Bald-Faced Stag in Edgware Road, and Probatt, the landlord of the White Lion in Charing Cross, together with his servant, Steve March. . . .

Wide had the net been cast and unexpected fishes had been brought to land, but Thurtell did not despair. Indeed, having learned that Anne was in torment and unable to sleep, he grew almost contented after the fading of his anger; and as they apparently had not yet discovered Bill Weare's whereabouts, he even began to hope that the case against him might collapse. Everything depended upon Hunt keeping his damned mouth shut; and having seen him in such high spirits on his arrival at Watford, Thurtell believed, and prayed that his belief

S

might not be a cheat, that the fellow had regained his courage for good.

Nevertheless a great deal had apparently been found. Mary, blast the woman, had produced the air-gun he had left at the Cock; and investigation of Probert's cottage and garden had produced more than suggestive details. Bloodstains on the sofa which must have come from his damned coat. The bloodstained sack in which the body had first been carried had been dug from under a heap of dung, and some of Weare's shirt saturated in blood had also been recovered. . . . There was nothing, however, to damn him in any of these things.

Then one of the constables let slip that the inquest was being held that night, indeed, that it was already under way.

"How can you have an inquest without a body!" roared Thurtell, springing to his feet. "It ain't legal!"

One of the constables dragged a large pistol from his belt and waved it menacingly.

"You sit down, Mr. Thurtell," he said, "and behave like a gentleman. Ain't our fault you've been nippered, so behave yourself."

"But an inquest and no body! and to tell me nothing of it! to go behind my bloody back, this is too much!" He strode the floor, waving his handcuffed wrists and cursing. "You can't have an inquest when you don't know whether a cove's been killed or not!" he shouted. "How do you know Bill Weare mightn't walk through that very door there any moment, alive and kicking! I'll have justice, if I have nothing else. As an Englishman, I have my rights, and I insist on em!"

At the sound of the key turning in the lock, he started furiously round, and saw Ruthven stroll in smiling.

"George!" he roared, "what's this about an inquest tonight and me knowing nothing about it!"

Ruthven darted a furious glance at the constables, but he continued smiling.

"Don't get excited, Jocky boy," he said, "I know it don't seem right. Thought so myself, to be honest on it; but what's it got to do with me? You tell Mr. Clutterbuck what you think, don't tell me."

"Then it's true!"

"Ay," said Ruthven with a grave nod, "it's true, Jocky boy. Though it ain't eggzactly an inquest: it's an inquiry. That's what I've come up here for, to take you down to them."

With a strong effort, Thurtell mastered his fury and, taking his glass in both hands, the metal links jingling, drank it empty in a gulp.

"Now," he said, "escort me to the bastards."

The dining-room in the inn had been cleared and at one end behind a long table sat two men, the magistrates, looking as solemn as mutes at a funeral. Few others, save some officials and constables, were present, and a clerk to write down whatever was said. Without jury, without the public to watch, at about eleven o'clock at night, Thurtell stood to be questioned and he managed to look scornfully around the dark-panelled room which even the light of three candles could not fully illuminate so that the clerk had to strain forward over the paper and pen while he wrote.

At the table, close to the magistrates, stood a man whom Thurtell recognized as a Mr. Noel who had once been Bill Probert's solicitor. The fellow was well known in the hells of St. James's, having last year been taken to Bow Street with about twenty others on a charge of gaming in a house near Pall Mall. With such a sharp in charge of the questioning, it seemed that he might indeed literally have a friend at court.

This hope soon fluttered down when, with no glint of recognition in his eyes, Noel began to question him. These were more or less questions of the kind which he had been expecting and had ready the answers to give; but Noel put them to him in a sharp, insulting voice that made him flush with annoyance.

Briefly, he answered. No, he said, he had had no appointment with any gentleman to go down to Elstree on the night of October 24. No, he'd taken no gentleman up on the road. No. No. No. Almost at every question his answer was: No; given sometimes with a shrug, sometimes with a weary smile, sometimes with an emphatic shake of the head. He was almost beginning to enjoy himself, having these men watch him steadily and the clerk all the time busily writing as though every word were precious.

No, he'd never told anyone he'd taken em for a day's shooting. On Saturday he'd walked with Hunt and Probert in the lane for about ten minutes. They all had black hats on. Yes. No, his clothes and boots hadn't been so dirty as to need a great deal of brushing on Saturday morning. The scratches on his hands? They'd been partly caused by brambles while he was out shooting; and these marks there? . . . The bite of a dog. No, he never said anything to Mr. Hunt, nor to anybody else, about his hands being scratched. Why should he?

Noel's sharp, sneering voice did not alter but something in the twist of the lips and the glint of the eyes warned Thurtell that the moment of danger was close; and his instinct was correct. That damned unused pistol he had foolishly kept for Ruthven to find at Tetsall's, forgetting that it was the twin of the one lost in Gill's Hill Lane, was suddenly produced. This needed thought to explain. He had found it, he said slowly, near Mr. Probert's cottage.

"Now, Mr. Thurtell," said Noel, abruptly genial, smiling, thumbs under his armpits, "you have said that you found this pistol near Probert's? What would you say when I tell you that I can produce the fellow to it, found within a few yards of the same spot?"

Thurtell shrugged as though disinterested, swelling out his thick lips and looking sullen. "I know nothing about that," he said.

From the table, Noel took a small bundle of paper and began slowly, deliberately slowly, unwrapping it, while Thurtell watched, holding his breath, wondering what was to be revealed. Then suddenly he saw, crusted with blood, Weare's hairs sticking to it, that other, the damning pistol, in Noel's hand.

For one moment, his iron control snapped. For one moment, he gazed with haggard face at that damned damning thing which he should never have lost and which had returned to kill him as surely as it had killed Bill Weare. His complexion, naturally sallow, turned deadly pale, while he shuddered and stepped back.

The other pistol, the pistol Ruthven had found at Tetsall's, was placed beside the bloodstained pistol, and both were passed to the magistrates who shrank from the disgusting one. Their shrinking—and certainly the sight of it was enough to have appalled a perfectly innocent man—returned Thurtell some of his sang-froid.

"You will see," Noel was chattily explaining, "that on both weapons the maker's name is the same. 'Hill, London.' You will see it engraved, here. In the make, ornament, and every part, they exactly resemble each other . . ." Suddenly he swung round on Thurtell and said sharply, almost accusingly: "I can tell you, Thurtell, Mr. Weare is not to be found."

With difficulty did Thurtell suppress a smile. Until then, he had been troubled whether Hunt might have talked; now it was plain that these men knew nothing positively. They were questioning out of the dark and hoping for him to bring them light.

"I am sorry for it," he said; "but I know nothing about him."

After a glance at the magistrates, Noel turned to the constables and said briefly: "That will be all, gentlemen. Where is Hetherington? . . . Ah, there you are, Hetherington! Come closer, man."

From the shadows at the other end of the room, a labourer shuffled forward, and Thurtell's heart almost seemed to miss a beat when he recognized the fellow. One of those to whom he had spoken in Gill's Hill Lane that morning when he and Hunt had set out to recover the gun and knife. They had kept the man there, half-hidden from him, that he might watch and swear to his identity. . . . But the identification proved nothing. He had never denied having been at Gill's Hill on Saturday morning.

Head high, he returned with the constables to his room and sat down at the table, regretting that Ruthven had carried off the supper. After his ordeal, he felt empty within and thought of the veal brought water to his mouth; and even drinking could not fill that void. Back over the questions Noel had asked he went carefully in his mind, seeking to discover how much the authorities really knew. Damned little he was certain. Otherwise they would have charged him before this. And Noel had said that the body remained undiscovered. Although that might have been a trick, it seemed a purposeless trick. No, the more he considered it, the more convinced Thurtell became that Weare had yet to be found; and his spirits rose with the rum that he sank.

A knock on the door summoned him back to the magistrates. In that brief pause, surely they could not have learned a great deal more? The labourer could have had little to tell; but, of course, there might be other, unexpected witnesses, strangers to him, anyone. . . . Nevertheless, Thurtell felt safe, and mockingly he bowed to the table, then with an insolent smile, left eyebrow raised to a circumflex, turned again to Noel.

"Thurtell," said Noel solemnly, "we have brought you here again to consider carefully all you have told us. Is there nothing you wish to alter in your deposition?"

"Nothing," said Thurtell with a snap of the jaw.

"You persist in saying that you have not seen Weare since Tuesday?"

"I do. I have not seen him since Tuesday."

"Not on Wednesday? Not for one moment on Wednesday?"

"Not for one moment on Wednesday."

"That will do," said Noel wearily, shaking his head. "Take him away."

Thurtell did not want to go. He felt that, the moment he turned his back and left this room, damning revelations would fly out against him. What these men had discovered they kept concealed and he was not the kind of flat to tumble into their net by talking too much. Yet if only he knew what they knew!

Out of the room, who would take his place at that table? what creature, someone perhaps whom he had never seen but who, hidden, had seen him, would perhaps step from darkness to tell of this or of that? Yet who in the world was there to speak truth against him? No one. No one could possibly have seen him and Joe toss the sack into that pond beyond Medbourn Bridge. The moon had lit the landscape brilliantly, offering no hiding-hole even for any dirty tout spying for lovers on the grass. . . . Clear as day and twice as beautiful. . . . Nobody could have watched them.

Yet fear like ice remained about his heart, an intolerable growing fear which fed upon itself and was bred in loneliness. If only he were able to talk; if only he could have been left for a while with Hunt or with Tom and could have talked and laughed with them and thereby have wrought his courage back to iron! But he was alone amongst enemies, amongst unscrupulous enemies, and lost even to the woman he loved who, so Ruthven said, had wept all night in the threatening dark amongst phantoms of terror and untapped desire such as haunted his own bed and, he feared, would never let him sleep again on earth.

CHAPTER TWENTY-FIVE

UP IN A SACK

UNTIL late the following afternoon, Thurtell remained perplexed, a little frightened, but on the whole assured about his eventual freedom. No one, it seemed to him, had slept last night, except the constable left on guard who had flopped, snoring, on to a chair with his legs out to straddle the door. Tiptoeing to the window and pulling wide the curtains on the street, Thurtell had seen many people clustered talking, some staring up and others pressed against the lighted windows below, peering in at some unusual activity. With the greying of night and the opening of a dull, drizzling dawn, more people gathered, filling the street, and the sound of their voices came to him as a confused murmurous noise from which few words could be untangled. But the word most often spoken was the word: "Murder." He could also hear "Weare" and "Thurtell" and "Hunt" and "Probert," and, occasionally, "Clutterbuck" and "Mason," the names of the Watford magistrates before whom he had been taken last night to be questioned. Men and women, boys and girls, they stood in the rain, bright-eyed, excited because murder had been done and, it was said, the murderers captured.

This night-long activity downstairs was worrying. Of course, it was to be expected that the sensation-loving curious should gather in awe to gape at living murderers, thereby showing the baseness of human nature; but why should the magistrates have sat up until dawn when they might have closed the proceedings at any hour they wished? Could the witnesses have been so many? They had not taken long with him; and the others, had they any sense, would say as little as they had to say. Mrs. Probert, being a woman, might be difficult to shut up, but fortunately she had no proofs with which to support whatever she might tell without incriminating her husband; and it had always faintly surprised and amused Thurtell to notice that she seemed genuinely fond of the goat. Anne Noyes would say nothing. Even though he had insulted her unforgivably by failing to visit her the other night, hers was not the heart to nourish hatred of a man she loved. Shrewish Caroline would damn him with poison if she had any poison to spit;

and Major Wood would certainly hurry to accuse him of having tried to murder him; but again, no proof, and anything he might say would be irrelevant to the charge of killing Weare with which the magistrates were plainly concerned.

Over and over again Thurtell examined all possible facts that might be brought against him, and again and again he failed to find anything dangerous, so long as Probert, Hunt and Tom didn't talk. There lay the fear that itched him whenever he sank into complacency: Probert. That big-bodied, short-legged man with his fulsome geniality remained the danger-point. Resentful over his small share of the takings, a coward in a braggart's skin, a giant only in a lady's chamber, he was the kind of man to creep into treachery in hope of pardon. But unless the body were found, even he could do nothing; and neither Hunt nor Tom would have been fools enough to have told him where it lay.

Ruthven had sworn that Anne was safe and in the care of Mr. Clutterbuck, and Thurtell trusted Ruthven, not having yet snapped him in any lie; but it seemed to him strange that a magistrate, a stranger to her, should protect a woman who was supposedly implicated in a capital crime. If Ruthven were lying, it meant that Anne might still be somewhere in this inn. She might be in the next room to his, beyond this wall he touched, and he not know it. Useless asking these damned hobbledehoy constables any sensible questions. Obviously they had been severely rated by Ruthven for having told him of last night's investigations, and any questions he now asked were met with a cunning leer or a shrug. There was nobody whom he could ask anything. Only Ruthven. And now he did not come. Even after the breakfast plates had been cleared away and Thurtell sat quietly drinking and smoking his pipe, Ruthven did not appear.

The constables, of course, pretended not to know where he was. They might have been dumb foreigners for all the use they were to Thurtell, and the only English they appeared to understand was an invitation to have a drink.

Slowly, time passed, exasperatingly slowly. At every step outside the door, Thurtell became tense, expecting Ruthven; but Ruthven, damn him, did not appear. Dinner arrived and was cleared away. And still no Ruthven. That something of great importance must be happening in the town was evident by the shouting and occasional cheers outside; but he, the most interested party, was left shipwrecked from the world, the guards refusing even to send out for the newspapers. That Probert had betrayed him in some way appeared evident to Thurtell: but in what way? what was there for the man to tell that would not implicate himself?

At last, early in the afternoon, the key turned in the door and Ruthven strolled in, slapping his gaiters with one hand.

"Dirty work," he grumbled, "damned wet dirty work on a cold day."

"What's that!" cried Thurtell. "What's dirty work?"

"My work," said Ruthven, strolling to the table. "Ah!" he said, "I see you've stoked in your dinner. May I?" He raised the bottle.

"Of course, of course," said Thurtell, sinking back into his chair and hiding behind a cloud of tobacco-smoke. If Ruthven thought to worry him into a confession by idle talk, by driving him into desperation with half-statements, suggested revelations, he had better think again. Two could play that game.

"Wet day," he said carelessly. "Warm in here, though."

"Ay," said Ruthven, smacking his lips at the tang of brandy. "You've had the best of it in here, Jocky my boy," he said, yawning. "They don't never think that a police-officer ever wants some sleep. Forgotten when I slept last, I have, you've led me such a dance, my boy." He smiled and nodded his head reprovingly at Thurtell. "Now, if fellows like you," he said, "fellows with a head on em, only troubled to use their canisters, they'd save us a lot of trouble and it'd be better for themselves in the end; but you will look on us as though we was your enemies. We ain't, you know. If it weren't for you, we'd all be out of work; and anyhow, I've always liked to see a fellow with some spunk in him. Most of em I have to nab . . . why! Jocky lad, you'd be ashamed to own em, you would! Shrimps what have blotted their napkins, young devil-may-cares what are too feared to load the guns they point at you. They got to be in a pack, they have; and then it's twenty to one and boots in and knives out; or they think it sport to upend some poor servant-girl what they'd be feared to kiss if they was on their own with her in the light. . . . Don't talk to me about my work, 'cause there are times, Jocky boy, when it makes me sick, it does. Then I come across a fellow like you, a real out-and-outer; then it's different and I feel right proud of my job."

"What!" grinned Thurtell. "Proud of getting me hanged!"

"Not if I could help it! they wouldn't hang you, they wouldn't. They'd give you a medal and a public house for wiping off a thing like

Bill Weare. Never did like the cove. Had my eye on him for years hoping to see him trip, but he was fly, I'll say that for him." Slowly, Ruthven drank a little more brandy. "Burns the cold out of you," he said. "I can feel it like watered fire through my very bones."

"What have you done with Miss Anne Noyes?" asked Thurtell suddenly.

"Me! I done nothing with her!" cried Ruthven, giving him a hurt glance. "I told you, old Clutterbuck's given her a talking to as though she was his own daughter what's stayed out late at night. You can trust old Clutterbuck. He might like em young but his wife's got a fist like a slab of mutton; won't let him keep a servant what's under ninety. And of course, being a magistrate and a gentleman, he's got to behave himself and be an example to all other poor husbands. Ay, your lassie's safe enough under him."

"I wouldn't suspect Mr. Clutterbuck――"

"Wouldn't you!" chuckled Ruthven. "Then you must know him better than his own Mrs. C. knows him."

"This is no jesting matter," said Thurtell, putting down his pipe and turning earnestly to the police-officer. "You don't know what it's like, George, being shut up here and not knowing what's going on out there. I'm not worried about myself. You can't do nothing to me. But when I think of poor Miss Noyes, my heart bleeds! I tell you, it bleeds! Can't I speak to her for a moment?"

"I'm sorry, Jocky," said Ruthven with a sympathetic groan. "You know I'd do it if I could; but it just can't be done. You ain't supposed to talk to nobody. Even I shouldn't be talking to you; but, there!" He shrugged, pouring himself more brandy. "I've got a soft heart for them what I like and what treats me fair," he sighed. "It's a great handicap, Jocky, in my business, but a fellow can't help how he was born, can he?"

"So you won't let me see her?"

"Don't say that, Jocky! Please, don't say it. It ain't *won't*, it's *can't*. I just *can't*, Jocky boy, and I know what love can do to a fellow, what it means to be separated from her what has your heart while you have hers. Hell, ain't it?"

"Aw, shut up!" snarled Thurtell.

"That's not the way to talk to a pal!"

"Go to hell! And stop drinking my booze!"

Appalled, Ruthven stared at him, then, shaking his head mournfully, slowly he stood to his feet.

"I'd never have believed it," he groaned. "Strike me with a marrow, who'd have thought it! And here I've been all morning on your business! getting wet to the skin, broken to the bone——"

"Hey," cried Thurtell, "what's this about my business?"

"It's too late now, my boy. No, I feel it too deeply to want to listen to anything you say. You don't trust me, you don't like me——"

"Don't be a fool!" roared Thurtell. "Come here and have a drink."

"After what you said, never!"

"I'm sorry, George, I'm sorry. Hang it all, you've got to give some consideration to a man in my situation, even if I am a little short of temper at times."

"Say no more, Jocky, say no more! Spoken like a gentleman," said Ruthven, hurrying back to sit at the table while Thurtell refilled his glass with brandy and water. "I'm never one to bear malice," he said. "And, between ourselves, there's been some coves I've lumbered who've used far worse language at me than ever you have. Enough to give you the horrors, some of em! And the things they tell you about their women, particularly after they've half-murdered one of em——"

"I don't want to hear about that," said Thurtell. "What was it you were saying about being out on my business?"

Immediately, Ruthven became again the official, turning solemn, his bright blue eyes losing their sparkle.

"Bad business, Jocky," he murmured, "bad business. The more you keep your gob shut the worse it'll be for you, you know. If you don't talk, there's others what will. I'm telling you as a friend."

"Probert!" cried Thurtell, and hurled his glass to the floor. "I wish I had him here," he cried. "I'd trample his teeth back into his dirty, lying throat, the traitor."

"Probert?" said Ruthven. "It weren't Probert. It was Hunt."

"Hunt!" Thurtell gaped at him. "Hunt told on me!"

"What can you eggspect, Jocky, taking up with fellows like him!" Sadly, Ruthven shook his head over man's folly in trusting anybody. "He's a little, frightened, wicked fellow without the bottom to hit back, even if he was pushed in the face. I know the kind. Meet em every day in my business. They're the fellows what get some bold spark to do something they're afraid to do themselves, then they squeak when they get frightened. All talk, they are; like that little old Boneypart that was always going to have a go at us but daren't cross our Channel. All bluster, boil and bubble; and the first to run away when it comes to a fight."

"But Hunt! He was my friend." Thurtell seized the bottle and drank from the neck. "I can't believe it yet," he said, shuddering as he put down the bottle; "I thought of Probert, but not little Joey!"

"Little Joey's got a big mouth," said Ruthven. "Not that I don't agree with you about Bill Probert. He's lucky not to have been hanged afore this. I've had my eye on him for some time. But, no, he ain't said nothing agin you. It was Hunt what done that."

Still, Thurtell could not believe it, although he knew that it was true. Hunt, the merry-andrew, the bustling, jolly, sing-you-a-song and let's-have-a-drink-and-be-damned young sharp, Hunt to turn nose and mace a pal! It was as though a son had bitten his own father, as though a devil had worn friendship's mask . . . yet all the while, Thurtell recalled that he had known doubt at which affection had always snuffed, refusing to believe that the loving roisterer, that jack of hearts ever with a jest or a song on his lips, the bandit's whiskers framing a cherub's dial, could have turned traitor. . . .

"My God," he said, "I can't, I don't believe it."

"Last night," said Ruthven slowly, looking at the floor, "after the beaks had done with you, they had Mr. dirty Hunt in and showed him the pistols, same as they showed em to you; but he didn't have your gumption, laddie. One look at em and he near spewed; then that lawyer-fellow—Weare's lawyer he is—Mr. Noel, he had a talk to him, pointing out the criminal errors of his ways and telling him what was coming to him; then he sent him out. Wouldn't listen to him, he wouldn't, told him to go and think it over before he talked any more. Weren't as long as before you could spit and pretty Joey was wailing to be heard and he'd tell the lot, everything. . . ."

"No," groaned Thurtell, writhing in his chair.

"I'm afeared he did, had it all wrote down, too, and signed it and swore to each bloody word." Contemptuously Ruthven spoke, with all an experienced officer of police's dislike towards the informer and the coward whom he nevertheless must use in his work. "Told about you having a talk with Bill Weare at Rexworthy's and getting him down to Gill's Hill on the hook of having a pigeon for him to pluck. Course he says he had nothing to do with it. Said you wanted to pink Weare's eye out—and I don't blame you for that, Jocky; he was a bad un, was Bill Weare——"

"He swindled me of three hundred quid at blind hookey," said

Thurtell, his lips swelling with rage at the memory; "then when I asked him to lend me five of what'd been my own, 'Go and rob for it as I do,' he tells me; 'go and rob for it as I do,' says he. . . ."

Suddenly he realized that Ruthven was listening to him with more than sympathetic interest, and he added quickly: "Not that I'd have done the cove for a little thing like that."

"I heard all about it," said Ruthven, sadly shaking his head, "heard about it at the time; and last night Joey Hunt put it down in writing."

"Damn and blast him!"

"Just my sentiments, Jocky boy," nodded Ruthven. "But those are the kind of coves about today; and who the hell are you going to trust! And they're always the ones who get away with it, pardoned for turning nose. I'd hang em first, I would; and mighty quick, too. Ay, he told us all about you. How you bought them pistols in Marylebone High Street when they was marked one pound seventeen and a tizzy, and you gave only one pound five for em. Then you let him have one pound ten to hire a horse and chaise with, which he done from Steve Probatt at the White Lion. Course he says he done nothing to Bill Weare. Him and Probert went ahead, he says. Probert told him, he says, that he didn't like driving by himself at night, and kind-hearted Mr. bloody Hunt's good enough to say he'll bear him company down to his cottage at Gill's Hill near Elstree. . . ."

He paused to take a long pull of brandy and water; and over the rim he glanced at Thurtell and was pleased to note the tightness of the muscles over the jaw, the strain in the outthrust chin and the blank anger in the eyes under the shadows of the brows, the left brow up, the other down, the left suggesting surprise, the other fury.

"You, by the way," continued Ruthven, "he says, tells him you had to meet a gentleman at Cumberland Gate, telling no names. That's all he knew about it, he says. Him and Probert boozed on the way, stopping at the White Lion in Edgware and ending at the Artichoke at Elstree; and it weren't until the two poor innocents get to the cottage and find you there, and out of the moon you tells em: 'I've settled that bastard what robbed me of three hundred quid!' you say. 'I've blown his brains out,' you tell em to their horror, and Probert begins to say: 'You wouldn't do such a thing to me, would you, Jack? Right here,' he says, 'near my cottage where my character and family'll be ruined for ever,' he says, 'shame on you, Jack Thurtell. I can't believe you'd be guilty of so rash an act. Here, Mr. Hunt,' he says to Joey—so Joey says—'here, take in this here loin of pork what I bought and kindly desire the cook to get it dressed immediately.' He takes the pork, Joey says, and he looked at you with his heart in his mouth. 'You are jesting about killing a man tonight?' he says to you as though he was on at the Surrey Theatre. 'Ay, but I have,' say you, with an oath, 'and no one else but Weare,' you say, 'what robbed me of my three hundred quid!' you say; and they shrunk from you as though you was a leper. Then Probert, he ups and he says . . . Wait! I've got some notes I made. These are the very words what Bill Probert says to you, according to Hunt. He says: 'John,' he says, 'you have taken such effect on me that unless we retire and get some refreshment, my senses will totally leave me.' . . . Perhaps I'm a bit deaf, but I ain't never heard Bill Probert talk like that when he wanted a drink."

As he raised the bottle to his lips, Thurtell's hand shook so badly that he spilled the brandy over his chin and chest; but Ruthven pretended not to notice.

"Next thing, he says," he continued, "was that you all had a drink and pork chops together, only you couldn't eat nothing. Said you was sick or something, so they wolfed the lot. Then you take em outside——"

"I have heard enough!" said Thurtell in a choking voice. "I want to hear no more."

"Come now, Jocky," cajoled Ruthven, "I'm only telling this to help you. I could lose my job, telling you all this, 'cause they're going to take you downstairs soon and they want to spring it at you."

"Let them spring what they like at me!" cried Thurtell. "It's all lies, I tell you, all lies."

"Course it is," agreed Ruthven as though to a fretful child. "I certainly couldn't stomach the way he made Probert talk, like a young woman what you read about in books who gets nabbed by the villain in a dark wood. The trouble is, Jocky, it don't matter what you and me believe but what Clutterbuck and the likes of him believe. They talk like that themselves sometimes when their wives are about. But putting all this aside, whether Hunt thought he told em the truth or was putting on a cross, he did know where Bill lay, and he took me to the place this very morning. Pool they call Hill Slough, about a mile this side of the Artichoke, on the left-hand side of the road. Field—you know, the landlord of the Artichoke: he don't like you nor Probert for some reason, that cove—well, Field provided a drag and some country-fellow threw it into the water, then they drew it out without finding anything. . . ."

Slowly, Thurtell shifted and looked at him, light gradually returning into his eyes. "You found nothing?" he whispered.

Ruthven continued as though he had not heard him speak. "Hunt was in the chaise with me," he said, "and I had my hand on him, you can be sure, and he hollas out: 'It ain't there. Further that way,' he says; and he points to one side of the water. So in they threw the drag again, and this time it hooked something; and with a heave-O, up he come in a new sack. We hauled him out, laid him out pretty on a ladder with all the women goggling, and carried him to the Artichoke. It was Bill Weare, right enough. I'd know him even without his toggery. His head and the rest down to his navel was pushed into a sack, the body having been thrust down head foremost; the feet was roped together with a piece of cord to which was tied a snotter filled with flint stones which must have weighed an easy thirty pound. There was another cord over the sack, tied around Bill's waist, and to this there was hung a great big stone. And I forget to tell you, there was a great number of other stones in the sack, must have been put in just before the late corpse."

"I told you, I don't want to hear any more!" roared Thurtell, glaring at him as though with hatred. "It's lies, bloody lies, all of it! I wish I could get at Joe Hunt, just for a minute, just to get at him once. I'd need no more than a minute!"

"I'd very much like to oblige you in that," said Ruthven; "I felt like doing it once or twice myself, I don't mind telling you. I suppose him and Probert went to the Artichoke that night in the hope of proving an alibi. That weren't fair and handsome. It weren't right."

"Do you think they'll let me see Hunt?" asked Thurtell quietly.

"I'm afraid, Jocky, they won't," sighed Ruthven. "But they'll be wanting to see you soon. Have you thought of what you're going to say to em?"

"I know what I'm going to say," said Thurtell; but that was not true: he did not know what he would say.

Through long hours he sat after Ruthven had left him, dazed with anger, trying to think, and he regretted not having kept Ruthven that he might have listened to the whole of Hunt's story and known how to answer it. But then, how did he know whether he could trust Ruthven? No longer had he a friend in the world, Hunt now betraying him, and even his brother he began to doubt, even Anne's love he doubted. . . .

In this state of savage despair, the constable escorted him back to the room in which he had been the night before to face the same magistrates and Noel; and he heard the evidence against him read in a sleepy, unemphatic voice by the clerk—a Mr. Jones he heard somebody call the fellow. Then when Mr. Jones's voice had droned to silence, he cleared his throat and heard his own voice saying steadily, never a quiver of fear sounding in it:

"With your permission, your honours, I want to ask Hunt a question."

It was Clutterbuck who answered, Clutterbuck who liked to talk to girls but who was afraid of his wife, Clutterbuck who, Ruthven said, had been sympathetic towards poor Anne. But he was not now sympathetic towards Anne's lover.

Brusquely he said: "I am sorry but you cannot be permitted at present to confront Hunt."

"I wish to ask him," said Thurtell quietly, "where he was on last Tuesday night."

"It doesn't matter what you may wish to ask him," said Clutterbuck. "At present you cannot be allowed to see the man."

Thurtell gave a faint bow. "Then," said he, "may I have leave, your honour, to write to Mr. Serjeant Vaughan for his professional assistance?"

"Most certainly, my good man," said Clutterbuck, "most certainly."

Half-relieved by the first refusal, Thurtell bowed. Already he was beginning to doubt the wisdom of asking such a question which had seemed forced through his lips; something within him rather than himself had spoken, in fury at Joe Hunt's betrayal. In his natural anger, he had been blinded to the peril in which he stood himself. The thought that he might be hanged by Hunt's treachery had so enraged him that he had not cared what happened to himself so long as Hunt was hanged beside him. That by turning king's evidence against his pal, the villain might escape the rope was a monstrous injustice, and Thurtell would have done or said anything to make the rogue suffer; for how could Hunt have satisfactorily explained his behaviour last Tuesday, that frantic day when he had driven back in terror from the Artichoke and afterwards had spent the night desperately trying to scatter Weare's belongings?

No, for his own sake it was perhaps best not to talk of that night, and he was almost grateful to Clutterbuck for having shut his mouth with a legal quibble. Ay, he was glad of it now! he decided while he stood and watched the irons being hammered about his ankles and running up, linked for easier movement between the knees, to his waist, as though he were professionally curious about the skill the smith showed in his handiwork.

CHAPTER TWENTY-SIX

SHUT FROM THE WORLD

They would not let him see the newspapers. That was one of the petty restrictions which infuriated Thurtell when, after the inquest, he had been charged with murder and lodged in Hertford Jail. This was not, of course, to say that he didn't see them. Although he was permitted no visitors, his legal advisers were in and out of the prison and they brought the newspapers and journals in their pockets that he might peep at them while assisting in his defence. Of all these papers, the *Times* infuriated him most. He would gibber at it until he lost all speech and, purple-cheeked, glared as though about to burst. Had he been free he'd have whipped the editor through the city. Mr. Chitty, his lawyer, strove to calm his choler; but that was difficult when every day this wretched paper found further mud to throw, already having dissected and hanged him in public; and there was nothing that Mr. Chitty could do to gag the anonymous enemy.

"I will bring it to the notice of the judge when the moment comes," he promised, "and I have no doubt he will reprove these—these pismires for such unjust, unsubstantiated allegations. However, I am pleased to say, we have lodged a criminal information against a certain Mr. Williams of the Surrey Theatre, and another against him for a high misdemeanour in attempting to pervert the course of justice."

"Excellent!" cried Thurtell, rubbing his cold hands. "Make em suffer, fine em, flog em, hang em, if you can."

"I am afraid," said Mr. Chitty with a wintry smile, "our powers do not extend so far as that; but I can assure you that this wretched play, the, ahem, *The Gamblers* it is called, will soon have to close its curtains."

"I'd like to have seen it first," mused Thurtell. "Wonder what the fellow was like who took the part of me?"

"I fear I cannot satisfy your natural curiosity," said Mr. Chitty, taking a dainty pinch of snuff from a silver box. "I never attend such places."

On the stage of the Surrey Theatre which often had Thurtell

visited when he had been free, the management had performed this drama based crudely on the events at Gill's Hill. Although unable personally to attend the performance, one of Mr. Chitty's clerks told Thurtell the plot, speaking of it with falsetto indignation while giving all the details he could remember.

"It's about a cove called Mordaunt," he explained, "which is intended as Mr. Probert and is as much like him as an apple's like a potato. This Mordaunt cove, he's the victim of the seduction of a couple of notorious gamesters and desperadoes called Woodville and Bradshaw."

"Which one of em's me?" asked Thurtell, already imagining himself in the part.

"I was under the illusion," murmured the clerk, "that the grossly libellous portrait of the ruffian Woodville was intended to typify yourself, sir.

"Well, this Woodville," continued the clerk, "and his confederate, Bradshaw——"

"This Bradshaw—he's Joe Hunt, I suppose?"

"Precisely," said the clerk. "The story runs this way. Woodville owes an old grudge for money against a certain Frankly which he'd lost to him at play, so he takes him down to clean out a flat, so he says, at a short distance from town, Bradshaw being placed in ambush for him at the entrance of a lane which is not unlike that one in which they say Mr. Weare was . . . well, you know. It's all a little confusing, but they're somehow traced from the ruins of a warehouse consumed by fire in Watling Street, when we see em getting into a gig, to the Bald-Faced Stag at Edgware, and subsequently to the lane at Gill's Hill. They weren't lying, either, when they had that on their bills. Almost thought I was in Gill's Hill, 'pon my honour, I did, when the curtain went up!"

"The villains!" cried Thurtell, grinding his teeth, "how can they tell such lies in public! . . . Well, hurry on. What happens next?"

"It went like this," said the clerk, after a moment's thought while he tried to sort out his impressions of the previous night. "Mordaunt has just tried his all at a common gaming-house and returned destitute to his Gill's Hill cottage when he is abruptly broken in upon by the . . . by, by Woodville and Bradshaw who in the scene before this we'd watched completing the murder, as we suppose it to be, and robbing of Frankly in the adjoining lane, when the explosion of a pistol is heard and Frankly falls out of the gig and is dragged by the accomplices through the hedge. The object of their unwelcome visit to Mordaunt is announced by Woodville informing him that he is come to relieve his necessities and that if he but assist him in one thing his difficulties shall be forever at an end. He presses money on him," cried the clerk, growing excited, gesturing as though offering money, then shrinking back as though appalled by the offer while his right hand reached forward towards the invisible booty. Even the sceptical Thurtell, snorting with indignation, was sufficiently impressed by this performance to gape at the clerk with admiration and a certain awe.

"Not only does he press money on him," cried the indignant clerk, "but he gives him also a bond of his for one thousand pounds which he tells him he has forced from the wretch, Frankly, who had been in part his ruin. Mordaunt sees blood-spots on the bond and forces them to leave the place, though he promises to conceal their guilt. Immediately after this, the officers of justice apprehend him; and whilst protesting his innocence, which is vouched for by his unhappy wife, who embraces him, Bradshaw and Woodville again make their appearance and are recognized by two men employed in mending the lane where the murder took place. To add terror to conviction, the bleeding body of the unhappy Frankly is borne in, supported by some countrymen, who call on the villains to look on their victim. He is discovered to be still alive, makes a formal recognition of their persons, and expires while the curtain falls."

"The things some coves'll think of!" cried Thurtell, trying to laugh although black in the face with rage. "It must be stopped!"

"It shall be stopped," said the clerk. "Leave it to Mr. Chitty, sir. It shall be stopped."

They were snapping at him from all sides, now that he was down. On the stage he was hissed and cat-called when he killed Weare nightly, in the newspapers every day he was hanged, and lies about his past were told as truth. When Weare was buried in Elstree churchyard, the *Times* gave five and a half columns to a description of the awesome scene; for it was at eleven o'clock, an hour before midnight, to the tolling of the bell, that Weare was carried to his grave, Thurtell read in the cuttings Mr. Chitty's clerk showed him.

Now that Hunt had blabbed, the evidence would be hard to fight; and although at the ensuing coroner's court Bill Probert had held out at first, denying any knowledge of Weare, eventually he, too, had begun to talk. Now was it a race between the pair of them to see who could spill the most. Thurtell's anger against Hunt, the clown of his entourage, remained high and steady, but when he heard of Probert's betrayal, he at first only shrugged. Had Hunt not talked first, and so soon, doubtless Probert would have held his tongue. Once he discovered that Hunt was trying to save his neck by blabbing, it was natural that the bastard should try to out-talk the other bastard. Both men were cowards, and Thurtell despised them; but Hunt, he swore, he loathed.

Not being allowed newspapers, Thurtell could rely only on what the turnkeys and his legal advisers told him, and he had little money left. Much of Weare's cash had melted on debts, on the gift to Hunt, on gifts to Tom's daughters and on a large sum which he was now pleased that he had forced into Tom's hand one night when he had been drunk. Ay, he was glad of that gesture. At least, Tom, although still in jail with the conspiracy charge hanging over him, need not starve and he had nobly surrendered back whatever was asked to pay for legal advice. Then there was Probert, who was penniless. As he had remained loyal for so long, Thurtell sent him what gold he could spare, and he furiously rejected the suggestion that he should help Hunt who was practically starving in jail.

"Not a farthing," he said with satisfaction when Hunt's lawyer asked his assistance. "Let him starve, the bastard. But for him, I'd not be here."

Inaction made Thurtell fretful, and the few walks he was permitted in the prison-yard were scarcely sufficient to stretch his strong muscles; besides, whenever he went there, strangers pressed to watch, and this irritated him. Even Ruthven had vanished. Alone save for the turnkeys, his visiting counsel, the magistrates who called to nag at him with questions on the excuse of seeing to his comfort, and the chaplain who called every day, he saw nobody; and he prayed that Anne might soon relent and in pity come to say that she forgave him. But he was allowed no visitors unless permitted by the magistrates, and the governor of the jail, Mr. Wilson, carefully read what few letters he received before passing them on to him.

That he was irritable and slightly feverish Thurtell tried to conceal, not wishing to be either pitied or consoled, and he maintained an air of unshakable firmness, while his health and his appetite remained good. Always polite, decorous in manner, he sat and smoked his pipe or took a pinch of snuff, and he slept soundly; and he began to find a certain pleasure in listening to the chaplain. Never having thought about religion, calling himself a Christian without troubling to consider what

Christianity might expect him to do and say, he was pleased to find a respectable clergyman interested in the state of his soul, although at times it was difficult for him to keep his temper before the fellow's impertinent probing into his conscience.

"Sir," said he one day, cocking up his chin, "this talk of yours would be all right if I were guilty, but I'm innocent."

Lifting his arms and rolling his eyes upwards, the chaplain groaned. "Before you speak so rashly," he cried, "I entreat you, sir, to weigh well the importance of every declaration which you make in your present awful condition."

Thurtell frowned and hung his head like a bad boy caught in a lie. After all, he decided, it were best to keep your mouth shut even when you were being talked at by a gentleman of God.

Determined to save the soul which Thurtell was satisfied stood in no spiritual danger, the chaplain left books and tracts and a volume called *Sherlock on Death* which Thurtell found both wise and solemn, but tedious.

More interesting to him were law-books, and these he obtained from wherever he could, hoping to find buried amongst them some key with which to unlock his prison. Day and evening, until light faded and his eyes grew tired, he read the tomes, making careful notes of any point that occurred to him as being a telling one. The chaplain's abrupt dismissal of his protest of innocence had annoyed him and he was not going to offer a second chance of being snubbed. When the subject was approached, he said quietly that in proper time he would establish his innocence; but once it was passed over, he joined in the mood of his visitor, being grave with the magistrates, respectful to the prison governor, devout with the chaplain, business-like with his lawyers and merry with the lawyers' clerks; and whenever possible, he drew the conversation to the sport he loved above all, boxing, and he demanded to be told the moment it should be known when the whole of the stakes were made good for Spring's bout with Langan.

Slowly time passed. November lagged through days and nights of cold, and the commission day of the special jail delivery was not until early in December. Greatly though he feared the outcome of that delivery when he would stand to fight for his life, Thurtell hated the waiting, the lonely nights, the few visitors, the little exercise, the silence about what was happening outside these stone walls and the mystery that remained about Anne and what she might be doing. Since his committal to Hertford, he had heard not a whisper of her

activities and to his knowledge she had made no attempt to visit him.
He had not believed that she who had seemed so loving could have
shown herself so cold and cruel.

Brooding thus one day in his cell, sucking at his pipe and watching
the blue smoke turn grey in the icy air as he slowly savoured a glass of
brandy and water, he looked up idly at the sound of the key in the
lock; then he sprang to his feet when Ruthven entered.

"Where the hell have you been all this time?" he roared.

"Cold in here," said Ruthven, drawing the capes of his box-coat
higher up the back of his neck. "What's this? Brandy? They treat you
well here, eh, Jocky? Bring another glass!" he shouted at the turnkey
and sat down on the bed.

"Why haven't you been to see me?" said Thurtell in an aggrieved
voice as though Ruthven were his closest pal.

"Not my fault, Jocky, not my fault," sighed Ruthven. "This here
case of yours . . . Ah! but it's started a rare yoicks, tantivy and soho
and away, I can tell you."

"What do you mean? what's it got to do with hunting?"

"Not hunting foxes, Jocky, something cunninger even than old
Reynard. When they heard you was nabbed, you should have seen the
rats start squeaking! Your pal Lemming—or is it Lemon?—seems to go
by both incogs, that cove—got away in time."

"He's no friend of mine," said Thurtell. "I hardly know the
fellow."

Ruthven winked, then with a contented grunt he took the glass
the turnkey had brought and poured himself a large portion of
brandy. "Here's to you," he chuckled, "and to your pal, Lemming."

"He's no pal of mine, I tell you . . ."

"Perhaps he ain't," agreed Ruthven. "No man ever likes the fellow
he works for and Lemming's a tight-fisted one, but I almost got my
grips on him. You probably ain't heard, but Sir Dicky Birnie, you
know, the chief magistrate, he started an investigation into what he
could find out about you. They all work together, these magistrates,
thick as thieves they are, and he kept me on my bunions, I can tell you.
I thought I had Lemming once; but, no! I got down to Margate but
the thick-headed constables there had let him slip; he'd paid em, no
doubt, and he's safe in France by now.

"Anyhow," he added, "the gang's smashed. That's one good
thing about having nabbed you, Jocky! They all thought you was
going to mace on em! fancy them thinking that!"

"I've got nothing to say," growled Thurtell. "I hardly know any of em!"

"Good for you, Jocky! I never did expect to hear you mace on any of em; it ain't your nature. But it just shows how they judge everybody by theirselves. By the way, they've let Miss Noyes go free."

"What!" cried Thurtell, dropping and breaking his pipe, "has she been in jail? You never told me!"

"Never had no chance, my lad; been too damned busy, but that's why I've rode all the way from London on a cold day like this, just to give you the office." Slowly, Ruthven drank that Thurtell might have the opportunity to appreciate the unselfishness of his act. "They held her on suspicion, her and her brother. Don't blame em for keeping Noyes. You never seen a fellow in such a funk. Fearfully agitated when he was first took up, he was, the sweat pouring off him. I seen him strike his two hands violently on his forehead and seem to choke in trying to say something. After that, anybody'd have kept a fellow like him in quod."

"But Anne? why Anne?"

"Don't ask me what I can't answer. They thought she knew more than she'd say, I suppose." Ruthven sighed. "They was right suspicious of her, kept on asking her questions, questions, and she saying she don't know nothing about you."

"Brave Anne!" he cried and joyously sat down again and drank.

"Ay, she's a real out-an-outer," agreed Ruthven. "Most she would say was she'd seen you with a gold watch but didn't think she could swear to it; saw you with it the night you did Weare—I mean, the night that Bill Weare wasn't seen no more. No offence, Jocky, no offence. She said she saw you with a knife once and heard you talking about being a Turpin. But nothing else agin you. Thought I'd tell you this so as you'd not misjudge the woman. Dreadful cut up she was over your situation."

"Ah," said Thurtell, smiling. The discovery that it had not been of her own will that Anne had stayed away gave him such delight that he could have danced, the coming trial forgotten. "So they've let her out, have they?" he cried. "And so they should! If ever there was a spotless angel, George, it was, it *is* Miss Anne Noyes. I drink to her."

"And I'll drink with you," said Ruthven, refilling his glass and tinkling it against Thurtell's. "Here's to the angelic Miss Anne Noyes," said he, "the one woman who knows when to keep her gob shut."

They drank and laughed, and laughed and drank; then Thurtell wanted to know all about Anne, how she looked, was she very unhappy, did she mention him. . . .

"I told you," said Ruthven, "she didn't do no talking, and she didn't mention you except to ask me on the quiet to tell you to keep in good heart and to know that she was praying for you night and day and just living for the time when you'd be out again."

"The dear woman," groaned Thurtell, and turned aside because there were tears in his eyes.

"You asked me how she looks," continued Ruthven, turning his back that Thurtell might not be embarrassed should he want to weep. "I'm no poet to go talking about how a young woman looks like," he muttered, "but she looked handsome enough to me with a black patch over her right peeper, only a little unwholesome in her complexion, perhaps, owing to jail atmosphere. Otherwise, she's what she was, only less so, if you understand me. You have a fine woman in her, Jocky."

"I know it," sobbed Thurtell. "I don't deserve such an angelic. I've been a bastard in my time."

"So have we all," said Ruthven; "wouldn't be a man now if you hadn't been a low hound when you was young. I like to see you show such sentiments. It's only the weak fellows what's afeared to confess that they've got a heart."

"Can—can I see her?" whispered Thurtell. "Could you bring her here, George, please? I'm not asking to see her alone, just to have a word with her, just to tell her something."

"If I could," cried Ruthven, "split me open, but I would, by glory, wouldn't I! but it ain't allowed, Jocky. It's old Clutterbuck. He won't do nothing for you, won't hear a word on your side. Did you ever know a cove called Graham, Jocky?"

"Graham?" repeated Thurtell, and shook his head. "No, I can't say that I did. Why?"

"This cove what is called Graham it seems is this Clutterbuck's nephew," said Ruthven in a hoarse whisper, "a flat what Lemming and some of your pals once hooked in St. James's and left him lighter of four thousand quid, or so it's said."

Softly, Thurtell whistled. "No," he sighed regretfully, "I wish I had met him. Four thousand, eh! No wonder Clutterbuck don't like me, but Weare was worse than me at that. Probably it was Weare that squeezed him, and he ought to be damned glad now that he's gone."

"Well, he ain't," said Ruthven; "he hates all sharps and gamesters and he swears to flog or hang any of em he can get his hands on. Damned bad luck, Jocky, that you should have chosen a place like this where there's a cove like him gasping to kick a sporting fellow in the backside."

"But what's this got to do with Anne?"

"Nothing," said Ruthven, "and everything. He's heard that you and Weare were gamesters and he's started Birnie at Bow Street getting busy to hunt em down. There's terror in St. James's now. No one dares open a door without a blunderbuss in his hands for fear it might be one of us coming to nab him. I don't like it, myself. I got nothing against gaming, but Clutterbuck's out for murder. That's why he won't let you have no visitors or newspapers or nothing, and he'd never let Miss Noyes get within sneezing distance of you."

"The bastard," said Thurtell, breathing heavily and clenching his fists, "the dirty bastard."

"Ay," nodded Ruthven, "it seems you done the wrong man, after all, Jocky. Weare wasn't a bad cove, if you don't mind snakes."

Because some petty magistrate's nephew had been fleeced by sharps, he had to be persecuted. They were determined to hang him: that was plain. Right or wrong, they were going to hang him because bloody Clutterbuck's fool of a nephew had fallen into the hands of one of Lemming's gang. Thurtell regretted that he had had no finger in that plucking: it would have been some satisfaction to have recalled an act that had stung this mercenary uncle to such illegal vengeance. Because it was illegal, he told Mr. Chitty.

"We are doing all we humanly can for you, Mr. Thurtell," sighed Mr. Chitty. "The high sheriff is very indignant at Mr. Clutterbuck's high-handed interference. Nor is Mr. Clutterbuck your only enemy. I regret to say that the sheriff's high chaplain, the Rev. Mr. Lloyd, a friend of Mr. Clutterbuck's, is equally as intolerant. As a preacher, he dislikes gaming and thinks this an opportunity to give him the text for enough sermons to last him till the end of his days. I have pointed this out to the high sheriff—Mr. Sutton of Ross Way who, unfortunately, lives about twenty-five miles from the town—and who until then was wholly unaware of what was being perpetrated in his name. That a man of God could be actuated by any improper and uncharitable motive I am not inclined to suppose——" Mr. Chitty gave a sudden smile that was more like a bite than a smile, "—but certainly his officious zeal in this instance partakes neither of the justice of the law nor of the merciful spirit of the gospel."

"If I could only get out of here," snorted Thurtell, trembling with anger. "Only for one day!"

Mr. Chitty raised his eyebrows and stroked his nose, regarding him rather as a bird might look on a worm, and he gave a rusty chuckle.

"In that event," he murmured, "I rather fear, sir, you might find yourself back again with a second capital charge hanging over you."

"No bloody fear," said Thurtell. "I'm too fly to let that happen again." He laughed at the look on Mr. Chitty's face showing horror at his client's honesty. "Only jesting, sir," he said. "My idea of a joke."

"A dangerous kind of a joke, Mr. Thurtell," said Mr. Chitty, "one which, if persisted in, would necessitate my withdrawal from the defence. My clients are always innocent."

"Of course, of course," said Thurtell hurriedly. "If they're all as innocent as me there'd be none of them ever hanged; but what can a man do, however innocent he is, when there're fellows like Clutter-buck set on hanging him?"

"Leave Mr. Clutterbuck to me," said Mr. Chitty. "I will deal with him. I am taking the matter to the court of king's bench to demand that cause be shown why a mandamus should not be issued commanding him to admit certain persons to consultation with you."

"Good," said Thurtell, "only I'd like to have old Clutterbuck here for half a minute."

Mr. Chitty was hard at work, and he was a capable man, but he did not know everything. Of that Thurtell was quite sure, and he remained puzzled and distressed by the extraordinary enmity he had aroused not only in Clutterbuck's breast but in the columns of the newspapers. Other men had done far more than he, torturing people and ravishing and cutting the throats of helpless females, but they never stirred up the hatred that his benevolent act of cutting the throat of a detestable scoundrel had apparently aroused throughout the country. It was all rather flattering, of course, but it was also bewildering. When he walked for exercise in the prison-yard the dislike of the other prisoners astonished him who could see nothing to frighten or anger strangers in a personal affair between himself and one of the most notorious sharps in England. One would have thought that Weare had been the darling of the nation, a noble warrior or sailor, a Nelson or some philanthropic saint, to see and hear the way the people carried on about his death.

What have I done? thought the astonished Thurtell, cut off from the world, not permitted friends or relatives to visit him, let alone the woman he loved. What have I done? could I have spifficated the wrong fellow, after all?

CHAPTER TWENTY-SEVEN

PIERCE EGAN MAKES A CALL

COLD the days and colder the nights; and during most of the day Thurtell sat by the fire in that enclosed area called the yard where the prisoners were allowed to exercise. Probert and Hunt apparently were being kept from him lest they conspire together or begin murderously quarrelling. It was a wise precaution, as Thurtell himself agreed. His feelings towards both men were rancorous, especially towards Hunt. From Probert, the lady's man, he had never expected much bottom; but although lacking bottom, Hunt had at least pretended loyalty and had behaved like a comrade. Thurtell was pleased he was saved the annoyance or disgust of being in their presence and he was able to concentrate on writing his speech, copying examples of miscarriages of justice from Percy's *Reliques* and other sources supplied by his solicitors, and wrapping all in bombast from the famous speeches for the defence by the Irish advocate, Charles Phillips, who specialized in criminal conversation, seduction and breach-of-promise cases. His extravagant style appealed to the actor in Thurtell, and he read aloud what he had copied, with additional flourishes from his own inspiration, to a fellow-prisoner, Randall, who had been deputed by the governor to act as a sort of companion and guard to attend to him.

"Mr. Thurtell," he said, mournfully shaking his head, "I do wish I was eddycated like you."

At the last moment, under strict orders from the high sheriff, Clutterbuck had permitted Thurtell to be given whatever morning and evening papers he should desire, and all morning he had been steadily reading through them, grunting and cursing to himself. The bloody lies they printed about him! nearly all of em lies! particularly the bloody *Times* and the *Morning Chronicle*. His hands trembled while he read. Already these cowardly assassins took him as dead and buried. There should be a law against such liars! How could a jury be found that wasn't already satisfied by the newspapers that he was guilty?

Fretting and fuming, spitting out tobacco-smoke, choking on his brandy and hot water, he sat by the fire when a turnkey strolled to him with a slip of pasteboard.

"Cove to see you, Jack," he said. "Mr. Wilson's with him in his office."

Carelessly, Thurtell took the card, then he caught his breath and his eyes sparkled.

"By gad, Randall!" he cried. "Bet you a pony you'd never know who wants to see me! Would you believe it, eh! That shows I'm somebody, don't it! for it's Mr. Pierce Egan himself!"

"Pierce Egan!" breathed Randall as though hearing the name of some visiting god. "Not him what writes for the papers!"

"It is," said Thurtell, crowing with delight. "It is! Mr. *Tom and Jerry* himself! Ain't I a real swell, now, old lad!"

Pierce Egan! They had met before, of course, often. No one in the sporting world could fail to know Pierce Egan, at least by sight. An agile man in his early fifties with quick eyes and a chuckling laugh, he was at every sporting event, racing, boxing, cocking, fencing, and his book, *Life in London, or Tom and Jerry*, had been read not only by followers of the fancy and the nobs in London, but by practically everybody in England who was able to read. Thurtell's own copy had long since fallen to pieces after constant reading; its language had become the language of the day, drawing-rooms had changed into chaffing cribs because of it, and rank and beauty had learned to patter flash like any Greek. And now for this man, the most famous man in England, to call on him!

Shaking with excitement though he was, Thurtell was not going to let the great man know how proud this visit had made him. Their acquaintanceship had been little more than a nodding one; they had scarcely spoken a dozen words together; but even of that slight intimacy had Thurtell often boasted. Now he had something indeed to boast about! Pierce Egan had condescended to visit him in a jail!

In the governor's office, beside the fire, Pierce Egan was standing, tapping his legs with his whip while talking to the governor, Mr. Wilson; and at Thurtell's entrance he turned, smiling sweetly, eyes twinkling, and held out his hand as though meeting again one of his dearest friends.

"What, Pierce Egan," said Thurtell, bowing a little and grasping that smallish hand in his great fingers, "how do you do?" Then he stood back, smiling. "This is kind," he said, "and I am very glad to see you."

He bowed again and shook Mr. Wilson's hand and, without asking permission, seated himself negligently in a chair beside the fire, crossing one clanking ankle over the other.

"You look well, Thurtell," said Egan gaily, eyeing him from top to toe, his quick glance missing little. "You look as if you'd been in training."

"Yes, thank God," said Thurtell, delighted, "I was never in better health and spirits. . . . And you are come down to Hertford to talk a few minutes about me, I suppose?" and he smiled as though it were all a foolish jest that he should be behind stone walls and iron bars and should have irons about his legs.

"Yes," said Egan, pushing up his coat-tails to warm his bottom at the fire, "to cast my eyes around, to report what's going on: you know my forte."

"Yes," said Thurtell, "I've read many of your sporting accounts with great pleasure; but I suppose you, like the rest of the press, have lashed me severely."

"No," said Egan, "no, upon my word, I have not written a single line at present about you."

"Well, I feel obliged to you for that," said Thurtell. "But what a piece of work this affair has made, ain't it?" He shrugged, feeling in his waistcoat-pockets for his snuff-box, and the movement made his fetters clink. Ruefully, he looked down at them, then smiled, wrinkling his brow as he glanced up at Egan. "What a parcel of lies the papers have asserted against me!" he said, laughing. "And in addition to that, they say I am sullen and dejected! Do I appear dejected?" Having found his snuff-box, he tapped open the lid, and laughed again, low and scornfully. "Those who know me well know that I have nothing to be dejected about," he crowed.

"You have seen the newspapers then?"

"Yes," said Thurtell, and his lips set as tight as the snuff-box lid when he clicked it shut, "I am now reading the whole of em. It's too bad; the paragraphs are all false. I never committed any serious crime in all my life. My friends know it full well. You may believe me, Mr. Wilson," he cried, turning earnestly to the governor and speaking slowly, emphasizing each word, "I never was before a magistrate on any charge in my life till the present. I do the crime for which I am charged, indeed!"

While he talked, recollection of old days, free days, gay days, curved his lips into a smile and the eyes, in their hollows, seemed to glow; and Egan, watching for any signs of fear, for any slip that might give him an inlet into the man's mind, marvelled at his courage and seeming indifference to his fate.

"I suppose you mean to read your defence?" he asked when Thurtell relaxed to silence.

"No, no!" cried Thurtell, hand raised in protest, and almost with anger he cried, defiantly: "I shall speak for myself . . . And I'll give some of the papers pepper for what they've said falsely against me. But I shan't be tried now, I want three witnesses to complete my defence, but so much prejudice has gone forth to the world, they're afraid to come. They must put it off without they mean to murder me. And I don't like Judge Park."

Agreeing with Thurtell's opinion of that dodderer of moral malignity, Mr. Justice Park, though he did, Egan thought it more discreet to change the subject. "I understand you wished to have Mr. Charles Pearson to conduct your defence?" he murmured.

"Yes, yes, indeed, I did. He's a clever fellow, but he's too much in difficulties to appear in court for me. When did you see him last?"

"About a month since," smiled Egan. "At Brighton."

Thurtell laughed and winked at him. "At Brighton? Ay, he wished me to appear some time since on the stage there as Richard III."

No sooner had he mentioned that than he regretted it and Egan pretended not to have understood its implications, while Mr. Wilson, seated at his desk by the window, looked down at his hands. A stupid thing to have said! Thurtell bit his tongue. With the newspapers howling at him as a bloodstained fiend who didn't deserve a trial, it had been careless of him, to say the least, to confess that a friend had considered him excellent for the part of Shakespeare's monster. Quickly, from his own abilities as an actor, he swung to rage at *The Gamblers*, the play of which Chitty's clerk had told him, and his indignation was unfeigned when he cried:

"Could anything be more cruel, unmanly, or diabolical than to publish in a play-bill at the Surrey Theatre that the chaise and horse should be exhibited in which it is said I committed the murder? It is a most infamous falsehood; and the press has dealt with me most unfairly."

Egan nodded agreement and raised his arms and shrugged to show that he was helpless in the matter; and Mr. Wilson took the opportunity of the pause to turn to Thurtell, saying: "Mr. Thurtell, I wish to call your attention to a letter I have received from Barber Beaumont.

He wishes me to read it to you, and wants to know whether you set your house on fire."

Appalled, Thurtell stared at him, tossing back his head, and he glanced at Egan with raised left brow.

"What do you think of such a fellow," he cried, "to send such a letter to me! to divert my attention at this period! An answer, indeed! To acknowledge setting fire to my house! Egad," he cried, shaking his clenched fist, "I'd like to break his head into a thousand pieces first!"

Wilson and Egan looked at that great fist, the knuckles showing white, the heavy brown hair on its back; but before either could speak, there sounded a rap on the door and a big dirty-faced ruffian with small eyes and a broken nose sidled in. At sight of Egan he ducked in a servile fashion, then he cringed towards Mr. Wilson and he eyed Thurtell with bright, malicious grey eyes.

"I am engaged," said Mr. Wilson, frowning; and the fawning ruffian went out backwards, bowing low.

"Who's that?" cried Thurtell with a dainty shrug.

Wilson turned away, sighing, and shuffled with his papers. "He brought your brother down today," he said softly. "That's Bishop, one of the turnkeys of Newgate."

"I should like to speak to Tom . . ."

"Personally," said Wilson, "I have no objection; but the magistrates assert that it would be improper, as your brother is to be called as a witness for the prosecution."

"Well, then, I suppose it must be so, but . . ." Thurtell sighed deeply, and Egan noticed how suddenly old he looked, ". . . I'd like to shake hands with him." Quickly, he recovered his indifferent air, turning again to Egan and speaking as though he talked to a friend in a chop-house or tavern.

"Can I do anything for you," asked Egan, and added hurriedly: "respecting your trial?"

"No," said Thurtell, then: "Yes. If you should see Mr. Chitty this morning, tell him I wish to consult him respecting my defence."

"I must take my leave," said Egan suddenly. "All luck go with you, Thurtell;" and he held out his hand.

Gladly, Thurtell seized and shook that hand. "Goodbye," he said, gazing earnestly into Egan's eyes. "I thank you kindly for this visit; but I'll see you again. My trial must be put off."

"One moment," said Wilson as Thurtell turned towards the door. "Mr. Thurtell, there is one thing I wish to impress on your mind and

U

I hope you will give me your promise, that on your meeting with Hunt you will behave decorously."

Thurtell wished he had not asked that request. The mention of Hunt brought hot anger to his sallow cheeks but, with Egan watching, he dared not show his enmities. Before this man whom he most admired in the world, he must remain insouciant, a gentleman who bore no rancour against an inferior such as Hunt.

"No, no," he said hurriedly, "I'll not hurt or abuse him. I will behave properly, you may rely on it."

Back to the yard he went under the watchful turnkeys, back to the fire and the adoring Randall, back to the inkpot, the writing-paper, the sand-box, the pens and the pile of creased newspapers.

The great speech seemed tame to him when he glanced through it again. This meeting with Egan, exciting and flattering though it was, had left behind it, like most pleasures, a certain disappointment now that it was over. He would have liked the conversation to have continued, to have talked of the noble art with this authority and perhaps have asked his opinion on the merits of Langan. No. Perhaps he had been wise not to have mentioned Langan. As an admirer of Tom Spring, he might have found himself in an argument he would not have liked, for he had heard that Egan and Langan were friendly and that Egan had talked of writing the Patlander's history some day. No, even amongst sportsmen, there were some subjects best left alone.

Soon, enthusiasm for rhetoric seized him again, the actor he had always longed to be, the second Kean, mastering the sportsman who feared that he might not have shone as he would have liked to have shone before the great Pierce Egan. Into the night, he wrote, rewriting, crossing out and writing again, repeating lines half to himself as though he munched them.

When he lay in bed, those lines kept revolving in his mind, exalting his spirit, until weariness dragged him to sleep; and it seemed he had only closed his eyes when he opened them again on the dawn and, with a shiver, remembered that this was December 4, the morning of the special commission for the trial of John Thurtell, Joseph Hunt and William Probert for the murder of William Weare on the night of October 24, 1823.

Such was his excitement as he leaped out of bed that he scarcely felt the cold which sprang at him with icy teeth, although counsel had warned him that they intended to ask for an adjournment. A tall glass of brandy reduced his pulse almost to normalcy and, with Randall's assistance, he carefully dressed himself in a blue coat with fawn-coloured trousers and a fawn waistcoat with gilt buttons and a black stock; and, to make movement easier, he tied up his irons with a silk handkerchief between his legs.

It was half-past seven and bitterly cold when he passed through the prison-gates to the carriage that awaited him in the free world outside. The street was packed, police beating back the people who roared like beasts at the sight of him, and some of them tried to spit towards him. Contemptuously, Thurtell looked at them, chin out-thrust and lips pressed out; then suddenly he grinned and, for a man with heavy irons on his legs, sprang with surprising agility up and into the carriage.

Inside its cold security, he sat with an officer on either side and pre-tended to ignore the riot in the street. As though he were alone in a study, he glanced carefully through the papers he carried, reading for the hundredth time snatches of the speech he had so carefully com-posed.

When Hunt appeared from the jail with his solicitor, Mr. Harmer, he looked so woebegone that Thurtell's promise to the governor had not been needed. Impossible for a man of his high stomach to hate such a miserable creature, although he was glad he was not placed beside him. Wisely, Wilson sent Hunt on to the box to sit beside an officer, and Thurtell remained undisturbed below.

Behind them, the javelin-men closed in and the driver whipped up his horse, starting off at a great pace, reckless of whom he might over-run; and the mobile howled as they hurtled by, howled and spat and shook fists and cried what they would like to do with the murderers.

Iron gates grated open at the rear of the court-house, then clashed behind him, shutting out the roaring multitude; and, feeling as though he were a French aristocrat about to appear before the tribunal of sansculotte justice, Thurtell stepped lightly to the ground.

Jailors and court-officials awaited him, and he pushed amongst them through the door while a constable conducted him to a smallish room which he knew must be the pound behind that dock in which he must later appear. The furnishings here were small, four chairs and a table, but he was glad to see a fire in the grate, and he stood before it, hands out.

Behind him, he heard the faltering steps of Hunt and turned to glare sternly at him; and Hunt could not meet his glance. Whimpering, he slumped on to a chair and looked away. Neither man spoke. Words were not needed. In the small eyes of Thurtell gleamed loathing such as a man might feel towards some noisome creature, a slug on his hand, and Hunt was too terrified to make any defence.

Thus they remained in silence, Thurtell before the fire, Hunt crouching on a chair, when Probert was ushered in. Again these three were together with their secret, held by the bond they detested and which chafed their spirits, apart yet indissolubly one, each fearing and hating the others. And still no one spoke while, slowly, Thurtell tapped open his snuff-box and took a pinch between thumb and forefinger, and despised them both in a look.

Into that uneasy silence with Probert twitching on one chair and Hunt slumped on another, the jailors not attempting to conceal their amusement and Thurtell watching like an offended schoolmaster about to swish a tawse, a waiter kicked open the door and entered with a tray upholding coffee and toast.

"Bear a hand!" cried Thurtell with the accent and the air of a lord or a judge. "Let me have some of that."

Instantly, humbled by that authoritative voice, the waiter hurried to him; and Thurtell took his time. He scanned the tray, then slowly poured himself a cup of coffee and chose two pieces of toast; and when the waiter would have moved away, he tapped him on the shoulder and, with a frown, commanded him to remain where he stood.

Not until he had drunk and eaten, then refilled his cup and taken two more slices of toast, did Thurtell permit the fellow to serve the others. Even in such small matters as this, these traitor dogs must be taught his supremacy.

When at last the door leading into the dock was opened, Thurtell did not move. The hero of the piece must always delay his entrance and let the supers supersede him. With rattling of chains, trying to stop himself shivering, trying to keep his chin erect, Hunt went first; and Probert followed, shaking his chains with trepidation, stumbling, head down. Lastly came Thurtell, walking easily, as though unconcerned and merely curious to learn what all this commotion could be about.

He had never expected an audience so large and so impressive as this, yet, like a well-bred gentleman, he concealed his surprise. Always the actor, when with gentleman, he became again the gentleman, careful in speech, courteous in behaviour, the true son of the re-elected mayor of Norwich.

And these were great people who had come to see him. Towards the bench he bowed and saw Mr. Justice Park sitting there, the same man who, annoyed with his enemy-advocate, had proved so good a friend in the insurance-action. Mr. Justice Park sat in his red robes, the great wig falling across his shoulders, and he did not answer Thurtell's bow. He glared at him, and shook the nosegay given judges that it might drive off the stench of prisoners.

Others did not disdain Thurtell's recognition. Egan bowed politely, as did certain sporting peers, and he was delighted to recognize them and to return their bows, particularly that of the Hon. William Lamb, foreman of the jury. His pleasure at finding himself in such exalted company and the centre of all eyes, dispelled whatever faint fears remained with him after last night's dark hours. Ignoring his companions in the dock, he chatted with Wilson, then called to Mr. Jay, his solicitor, and scribbled him a note, asking whether he thought the trial would be adjourned. Mr. Jay replied, writing that he hoped so, and Thurtell grinned as though very pleased, and deliberately he took little notice of the murmuring about him and he scarcely looked up from his papers when the crier began to bellow for silence and the clerk of arraigns gabbled through the long indictment phrased in legal lingo.

Then came the stupid question, yet a question which must be answered: How did he answer to the charge?

Quietly, he replied, as though replying to a commonplace everyday question: "Not guilty."

How tried?

"By God and my country," he said.

Hunt almost bellowed his replies just to prove how innocent he was; but Probert merely whispered.

What followed was of no interest to Hunt or Probert who did not even pretend to listen, but, carefully, Thurtell followed what the clerk read aloud, a long affidavit drawn up by his solicitors and complaining about the play at the Surrey Theatre and the scurrilous attacks in the press. This reading took some time, and when discussion followed, the judge was humane enough to order that chairs should be placed in the dock.

When at last it came for the judge to give his decision, Thurtell leaned forward, listening to every word. He frowned as the old fool made it clear that the defence had had time enough in which to prepare their case, and he cited the example of the murderer of Mr.

Perceval in the House of Commons in 1812 where the crime had been committed on Monday and the culprit hanged the following Monday. When he came to the question of the newspapers and other libellers, however, he was fierily on the prisoners' side, although he considered it scarcely wise of the defence to have read such papers aloud before the jury. He also considered these publications pernicious, not only because of their possible effect on the jury, but because they gave an undue advantage to the accused by showing them prematurely what might be brought against them during their trial. . . . Nevertheless he had decided to adjourn this commission until Tuesday, January 6, at eight o'clock in the morning.

The moment the judge announced this decision wellnigh everybody in court stood up and rushed for the doors, trying to push their way through that they might watch the prisoners being taken back to jail.

It was almost a battle to force a way out of the court-house, the police and the javelin-men beating and punching back the howling multitude which, kicked aside by frightened horses, closed in, roaring, behind the carriages and fought to spit inside or to throw stones or dead animals or filth.

Thurtell sat back, arms folded, amused by the uproar, confident now that he would never be hanged. First round to him. The judge had given him best, agreeing to a delay, and that was an excellent omen. No question now, he felt, that he would win in the end.

He could not see behind him the carriages bearing Hunt and Probert. He did not see Hunt on the edge of tears, biting his lip and trembling before the howling; he did not see Probert with his head sunk down as though his neck were broken.

But had he seen them he would have only laughed. Had he not said that they were a pair of cowards, both of them cowards; and what could you expect save cowardice from a coward?

CHAPTER TWENTY-EIGHT

TEARS FROM A CYNIC

THAT afternoon, smoking contentedly by the fire in the covered yard and again correcting and adding to his great speech, Thurtell looked up and was delighted to see Pierce Egan slowly approaching him. Immediately, he put down his pipe and strolled forward, smiling, while the other prisoners respectfully drew aside that the great men might talk together without an audience of eavesdroppers.

Offering his snuff-box, Thurtell gave a brief, friendly bow and said: "I am very glad to see you, Pierce Egan, but I was sure you would give me a call before you returned to London."

Egan bowed and took a pinch of the snuff, then followed Thurtell back to the table and his corner by the fire.

"Yes, I've kept my promise," he said, strolling beside him, "and I'm happy to say that now, in consequence of this adjournment, you will have plenty of time to prepare for your trial."

"Yes, I shall," grinned Thurtell, pouring out brandy for them both; "but I was sure they'd put it off; they couldn't do otherwise. I expected to have seen more persons, I assure you," he lied, being very proud at having found the court so fashionably attended. "I recognized lots of the *family* people."

He smiled, arching his thick brows, and Egan laughed. They had been there, all right, these "family people"; he had noticed them, too: anxious men who could not keep still, who looked furtively about them as though expecting a hand suddenly on their shoulders, Lemming's men terrified lest Thurtell say too much.

"How did you approve of the exertions made by your counsel?" asked Egan, after casting in his mind for something to say.

"Chitty was excellent," said Thurtell, "but Andrews was fine. His language was so good that he carried his point with the judge. Here is my defence . . ." Out of his pocket gently he drew the fat roll of his precious manuscript. ". . . I will read a few sentences to you, for your approval," he said almost bashfully.

"I should like to hear it," said Egan; pouring himself more brandy, and, settling into his chair, he stretched his legs to the fire.

Sitting back, chin up, waving his arms, Thurtell began to declaim, choosing passages from here and there, those he considered the most telling; and that Egan might not go to sleep, now and then he muttered in an awe-struck voice, "Beautiful" or "fine" or "very good," as though somebody else had written it. This skipping method failing to satisfy Thurtell's pride in his wonderful composition and Egan making no objections, he decided to begin at the beginning and to read it all aloud.

"I think I'd better read the whole of it to you," he said suddenly, eyeing Egan hopefully and dreading his refusal. "If you can assist me to improve it, I shall feel greatly obliged to you as I have more nerve than ability. Write to Mr. Fenton, Austin Friars. If you send any letters to me here, they'll be opened."

"Certainly," said Egan. "If anything occurs to me tending to your advantage, I will, without delay, communicate it to your solicitor."

Often had good nature and politeness forced Egan to listen to the screeds of amateur writers and he had acquired a certain self-protective deafness; and interested though he was in the progress of the Swell Yokel, he soon found himself, under Thurtell's histrionics, turning sleepy. Too much odomontade. Too much talk about nothing. Too many mythical or ancient examples out of dryasdust old books. And it was fatal to tire a jury who could take a too easy revenge on a bore. More fatal still was it to tire a judge, and Mr. Justice Park was not the kind of buffer who had much patience.

No one could deny his extensive knowledge of the law and his ability to sum up evidence concisely and, unless his prejudices were pricked, on the whole, fairly. But certainly, he was not the kind of judge before whom Egan would have chosen to appear should he ever be caught doing something of which modern society did not approve.

Even his long training in listening to amateur writers could scarcely keep his eyes open as the heat of the fire and the comfortable warmth of the brandy made him drowsy, while on and on and on went Thurtell. Undoubtedly, the fellow should have been an actor, although his methods were rather of the old school—a great halt or twitch in the gait, a very grave face on all occasions, and an inflexible regard when reciting for the interests of *ti-ti-tum*, *ti-tum*, *ti-tum*, *ti-tum-ti*. Having published a novel in the shape of a biography of an actor, Egan prided himself on his knowledge of the stage and, being a fellow with an appreciative eye for a lady's leg or any other portion of her person commonly and prudishly concealed, he haunted theatres and lounged in green rooms. Thurtell was an exaggerated example of a type he had often encountered there, the ambitious country fellow who for some extraordinary reason believed he was another Kemble or Kean and made a nuisance of himself wherever actors forgathered until somebody gave him a walking-on part, or he ended in a barn in the country. One saw them any night at Oxberry's Craven's Head, particularly on Friday night when there was always singing and fiddling there, actors, authors and poets drinking and smoking under the numerous framed prints of actors and actresses of past and present. That, far more than the refined if brutal hells of St. James's or the vicious surroundings of the Brown Bear in Bow Street, was Jack Thurtell's natural habitat.

When Thurtell spoke now of the piety of his mother and the universal good character of his father, his tongue faltered and he put up a hand to wipe his eyes; and Egan felt moved, although uncertain whether the tears were sincere. Not that that really mattered. A great actor must get into the skin of a part until he becomes that part, his own identity lost; and Thurtell unquestionably had in him the germs of a great actor.

At last the dramatic voice ended with the cry: "So help me God, I am innocent!" and Thurtell, eyes raised to heaven, pressed his hands over his heart. Egan almost applauded as though he were in the theatre. Instead, in a low voice he said: "You've not seen your father or mother for these two or three years past, I suppose?"

"O, yes," said Thurtell, sitting down again and heaving a heavy sigh, "it's not so long since I dined with them at Norwich."

"Since you've been at Hertford," continued Egan, probing deeper that he might test the sincerity of Thurtell's filial declarations, "your father's not been to see you, nor any of your relatives, have they?"

"No, no," said Thurtell energetically, "I couldn't see my father. My feelings wouldn't permit me; and if he was to come in at that gate over there I'd not see him. I couldn't; and I'd order the turnkey not to admit him. I saw my brother Tom yesterday; that was quite enough for my feelings to undergo. I wonder what he's been saying of? but he has no nerve, poor fellow! He has no strength of mind."

To display his own nerve and strength of mind, he smiled and stretched himself and took a few paces along the yard, nodding familiarly to the other prisoners. Walking beside him, Egan listened to the clink of metal at every step.

"Those irons are damned heavy," he said. "They must be troublesome to you."

"No, no," smiled Thurtell wearily, "they don't operate on my feelings. The only thing that's disagreeable to me is being locked up so early as five o'clock in the evening. But Wilson's a tender-hearted, worthy fellow. He does his duty like a man and no party can find fault with him."

"I'm so glad to hear you're so well-treated," murmured Egan, adding, "and I hope you'll be able to make it appear all right at your trial."

"I shall," said Thurtell confidently. "I want only a few witnesses to come forward and if they have any nerve at all, I shall get through it. After hearing that a murder had been committed in the neighbourhood, do you think I'd have been such a fool, if I'd been guilty of it, to have had a ball in my pocket and a pistol about me? I had been shooting some birds, and the blood about my waistcoat-pocket was from that circumstance alone."

There was sincerity, conviction in that voice, yet Egan knew that Thurtell was lying; and again he sighed to think of the actor which the stage would lose to the hangman. "I sincerely hope, Thurtell," he said, "you'll be able to substantiate in the proper place what you now assert to be fact."

"I would not attempt to impose on you in the slightest degree," Thurtell cried in a ringing voice and stopped and looked down at Egan. "I did not *commit* the murder. I declare solemnly to my God——" Grasping Egan's hand, with his free hand, he pointed towards the sky. "—I did not *commit* it. But ultimately, I suppose, I shall be convicted; and if so, it shall all come out! It is like my right and my left hand trying to hang me. . . ." So furiously indignant had he become that he could scarcely speak, the small shadowed eyes shining like pale fire. "Two such contemptible, cowardly rascals!" he cried, "wretches! Probert and Hunt! a disgrace to mankind. But during my trial . . ." The huge clenched fists rose as Thurtell put himself in a boxing posture, knees bent and far apart. ". . . I will hit that Probert to death. I will put such questions to him! Probert has been tried for sheep-stealing. I can prove it."

"I hope to God you'll be able to clear up your character."

"Probert is one of the worst men alive," cried Thurtell, his anger breaking all control when he thought how both of his companions sought to hang him that they might themselves escape. Hunt was a weakling, but Probert pretended to be strong. What Hunt might do from weakness, Probert would do from pure malignancy. Yes, he was the worst man he had ever met, when he considered it, although until now he had not fully realized how deep was his loathing. Putting it into words, trying to speak dispassionately to impress Egan, hatred broke its bonds and surprised him by its vehemence. Yes, he did hate Probert, hated him far more than he hated Hunt. "I lent him money to prevent him starving in jail," he cried; "and when I sent to him the other day to get a little from him in return, when I knew he had received five sovereigns, he sent me two shillings in a snuff-box, which I dashed upon the ground and sent back to him. He is such a bad man, so horrid a wretch, that I cannot keep my temper when I speak about him."

"Are you out of money, Thurtell?" asked Egan quickly. "Can I——?"

Thurtell smiled and caught his arm before the hand could reach the trouser-pocket, and putting his face close to Egan's, he whispered into his ear: "God bless you, No! But if I had, that wretch Probert would not have advanced any to have kept me from starving."

"Did you speak to either of them in court?" asked Egan, again the newspaper-man; "or on leaving it?"

"No! Speak to them, indeed!" cried Thurtell. ". . . I don't know who to trust!" Biting his lips, he glanced sideways at his companion walking beside him to the clinking of his irons, uncertain whether one could trust a writing-man. But Egan was not an ordinary reporter. He was also a gentleman. . . . Yet Thurtell found it difficult to ask a favour of anyone.

"Recollect, Thurtell," said Egan suddenly as though in answer to his thoughts, "as I must very soon take my leave of you, whether I can do anything for you in town or country."

This was his opportunity, no better one would be found, yet his accursed tongue spoke before he could use it for a different purpose. It said: "No, nothing at present," and inwardly he groaned. "But," he added furiously, "I must repeat to you that the conduct pursued by Barber Beaumont towards me has been cruel, nay, unmanly. I never had any intention upon his life. The most barbarous lies have been told about me bringing out an air-gun to kill him, but I have never had the most distant intention of using it against a human being."

"I am sincerely happy, Thurtell," said Egan, looking at his watch, "to hear you make this assertion. I must now bid you goodbye."

Thurtell could not let him go. He must not let him go like this.

"One moment," he stammered, "there, there is a lady I would, I would like you to speak to for me."

"Most certainly," said Egan. "Tell me her name and address and I'll give her any message that you like."

"She is Probert's sister-in-law," muttered Thurtell, "Miss Anne Noyes; and I don't know where she's staying."

Egan had expected the name and address of some high-flyer and the mention of Anne Noyes so startled him whom little could startle that he could merely gape at Thurtell. He had once met the woman and had seen her at the inquest. One-eyed. Rather mousey. Hadn't thought much about her. . . . He wished now that he had taken more notice. It just proved how little a man could tell about a woman from her outside! Who would have expected this handsome bull of a man to be fond of an insignificant little one-eyed female!

"She's staying with her sister," he told Thurtell, "at the Blue Boar. I know Major Wood slightly and he introduced me. Asked me to call and to have some shooting at his place."

"Then, please, do so; for my sake, do so," said Thurtell earnestly. "I am afraid Miss Noyes is offended with me. I failed . . . that is, I didn't keep an appointment I'd made with her, and I don't want her to think . . . Will you just tell her that I find it impossible to forgive myself for . . . O, she'll know why! Just say I can't forgive myself and that I pray she does not think too hardly of me."

"With pleasure," said Egan. "I will go at once."

"Thank you, thank you," cried Thurtell, pressing his hand in his. "Now I'll show you the way to get out of here," he laughed, "although I can't use it myself." Gathering up the chain between his legs, he rapped with its links against the lock. "Don't forget," he said, shaking Egan's hand again, "tell her and all the persons that I am in good health and spirits. And I have your word, you'll not mention Miss Noyes, will you, in anything you write?"

"I hope I am still something of a gentleman," said Egan with dignity, "even though I have to work with a quill for my living."

"I shouldn't have asked. Forgive me, like a good fellow. Come . . ." Thurtell slipped the snuff-box from his waistcoat-pocket, ". . . have a pinch of snuff before you go. . . . And don't be long before you call again."

Egan bowed and took the pinch of snuff while slowly the great door, studded with iron nails, began to open.

He did not like this mission to Anne Noyes. He was in a hurry as he had to return to London and write about this interview. His description of the opening of the trial he had already written and sent by a messenger to the *Weekly Dispatch*, yet he had little time left to spare. Already, as was his way, he was carefully repeating in his mind as much as he could recall of his interview with Thurtell; and taking some paper and a pencil from his pocket, he began to scrawl notes in his own peculiar shorthand.

Within a few minutes he had recorded the main details, then putting away pencil and paper he strolled to the lobby where he found Hunt's solicitor, Mr. Harmer, saying farewell to his client. Egan had known Hunt by sight for years and, whenever possible, had dodged being in his company. How a gentleman like his brother who had sung at Covent Garden and was now acting in Ireland could have had the same mother as this sinister scarecrow had often puzzled him. In his eyes, there was nothing likable about Hunt. What Thurtell could have seen in the fellow to have chosen him and the treacherous Probert as partners in murder puzzled Egan.

With Mr. Harmer he strolled into the open street, out of the sourish odour which all prisons have, and he took deep breaths of the damp free air looking about him at the noisy passers-by. Never had Hertford been so crowded with such merry, drunken multitudes. Being a mere twenty-one miles from London, it was a popular centre for sporting men and women, but usually it drowsed through the days while barges on the Lea carried its wealth in wool, meal and malt to the metropolis. Brewing seemed to be the town's main industry and there was a sharp and invigorating odour of hops hovering like an angel's hiccup about the streets and in its numerous inns and taverns. Every day since the arrest of the three and their committal to trial had become a kind of holiday, a seven-Saturday week, Saturday being market-day, a day of drunkenness and good cheer when farmers and their wives and labourers arrived in wagons, carts, buggies, curricles, chaises, gigs and tandems; and amongst the farmers now moved the country-gentry from their great estates with London swells and tulips, the furtive-eyed, quick-moving gamesters alert for a plucking and the young bucks attempting with dirty clothes and grimy hands to appear as much like a stage-coachman or a second-rate pugilist as they possibly could.

All was carnival; day and night, it was carnival. Everybody, from dandy to tramp, from lady to moll or twopenny-quean, had seemingly trudged or raced to Hertford to join the joyous dance of death. Not in a single face that passed, man's or woman's, could Egan detect a flicker of pity; all were eager for blood, like savages gathered for a cannibal-feast, excited by the ferocious diatribes in the *Times* and the *Morning Chronicle*, those leaders in the attack on a helpless man not yet tried let alone convicted. Himself a journalist, Egan had a fellow-workman's indulgence towards these unprincipled editors who forgot decency in their fight for larger circulations, yet it seemed to him that they were satisfying some personal fear or hatred by this noisy pretence of virtue which, as he knew by experience, few of them possessed. Their pens in acid, they scribbled insults at Thurtell, inventing tales to show his villainy when facts could not be twisted into a convincing lie, denouncing him as a cold-blooded monster, murderer, gambler and lecher and shuddering at mention of the debaucheries which they swore had taken place in the rural secrecy of Gill's Hill Cottage where, without a wisp of proof, they declared numbers of young girls had been brought by Thurtell, Hunt and other mutton-mongers.

This was nonsense, as Egan knew, having talked with residents at Elstree. Mr. Wardle, for example, the leaseholder of the cottage and a most respectable gentleman, had regretfully told him that he had never once seen a strange female at the house, and he would have known, he said, had there been any. As for the accusations that Thurtell was a notorious swindler and London sharp, Egan knew how wide were such insults from the truth. As a betting-man he had always been considered a complete novice amongst sporting people. As a gambler, he had never the talents to win unless his "luck" was ready-made. He had no true penchant for play. Neither rouge et noir nor hazard were his forte, but he had always been most passionately fond of boxing; and although many a boxing-match was on the cross, there were honest pugilists who disdained to throw a fight for money. Many, indeed, were the man's admirable qualities; and had he not become the friend of Probert, Egan felt, he might have lived to die in his bed.

"I can remember no trial," he remarked as they struggled towards the Six Compasses, "that caused such éclat as this."

"Nor I," panted Harmer; "can't understand it. Just another dirty murder. All ruffians together. Weare only got what he deserved."

"Scarcely the opinion one expected from counsel for the defence," smiled Egan.

"O, no," grinned Harmer, "my client's innocent. Wrongfully

accused. Thurtell and Probert are not my affair. They can hang tomorrow and I won't relish my dinner the less."

Like all the public houses in Hertford, the Six Compasses was packed and noisy, and it was with difficulty that Egan managed to interest a maid by pressing a coin in her hand and to cajole her into telling Miss Anne Noyes that he wished a word with her.

"Wait in the bar," he said to Harmer, "I'll not be long;" and he followed the servant up the stairs and down passages until with a rap on the panels, she flung open a door to announce that there was a gemmen to see the lady.

Anne was alone, Egan was relieved to find, her sister and husband —Caroline, he had learned, had recently married Major Wood— being out to see the sights, and although she greeted him with a faint smile, it was plain that the woman was distressed and had been recently weeping. Looked at closer to, he found her not so unfavourable as she had appeared when last he had seen her. Her skin was clear and delicately coloured, her hair a rich black in shining ringlets, and the left eye—the right concealed behind a black velvet patch—was of a glorious brown. Had she not been so unfortunate as to have lost that eye, she would have made a handsome woman; but you could not forget the disfigurement, no matter how you tried to dwell on the soft texture of skin, the plumpness of her hands and shoulders, and the shape of body exaggerated by the tight waist and the upward push of stays.

"Your servant, ma'am," he said. "My name is Pierce Egan and I have come with a commission from a mutual friend, Mr. Thurtell."

Hearing his name, she coloured and began to tremble. "I . . . I have nothing to say," she whispered, "nothing to interest the newspapers, nothing whatever."

"I have come, ma'am," said Egan, "in my private, not in my professional, capacity. I have but recently left Mr. Thurtell and he asked me to bear a message to you."

"How does he stand against it?" she asked. "O, they have been cruel, cruel. The vile things written about him, these terrible lies! How can men write such lies yet sleep at night!" She pressed her lacy handkerchief to her eyelid and brushed the tears from her cheeks, then daintily blew her nose. "Forgive me, Mr. Egan," she said, "I am not myself. These . . . these lies about Mr. Thurtell have unnerved me; and they have refused to allow me to visit him."

"That refusal," he said gently, "may appear inhumane but there is a sound reason for it. You are one of the witnesses for the prosecution and it would not do for you to see the prisoner and perhaps conspire with him."

"Conspire! what can I conspire with him! a helpless woman and he locked away, no doubt in irons. God forgive those who have done this to him. Conspire, indeed! I would mingle my tears with his, and that is all."

"Have you thought, ma'am, that such a meeting might help to unman him at a time when he needs all his strength, all his faculties sharpened to razor-edge?" said Egan. "The only thing that troubles him is fear lest you have not forgiven him."

"Not forgiven him!" she cried, amazed.

"Ay, ma'am," said Egan. "I know not the rights of it, but Mr. Thurtell wished me to tell you that he hoped you bore no ill will towards him. There was some appointment, something he had left undone—as a gentleman, he could not go into details nor could I question him. All he asks, so I understood him, is that you will realize how remorseful he is and how repentant of . . . well, of whatever it is."

"So he still thinks of me!" A slow smile edged the corners of her pale mouth as she sank into a chair; and she looked almost beautiful at that moment, her skin seeming to freshen, to glow, as though with sudden youth. "Even in this dreadful hour he thinks of me!" she sighed.

"I can assure you, ma'am," said Egan earnestly. "He thinks of little else. It is plainly the one thing that distresses him, for he seems most confident of escaping the charge against him."

"Thank you," she whispered, "thank you. O, if only I could go to him!"

"You could write, ma'am," said Egan. "I am certain a letter from you, just a few lines, assuring him that you still hold him in your affections would be a stronger fillip to him than even the sound of Not Guilty when he stands his trial."

"I—I do not deserve this!" she said. "O, that I could be worthy of such a gentleman! What he did, what you say he now laments, was the act of a gentleman. To be honest, I was angry and miserable at the time; but now I see the nobility behind what I had thought callousness or even cruelty. He would not take advantage of a woman's folly. Mr. Thurtell is a good man, Mr. Egan."

"I have never doubted it," said Egan. "At bottom he is a gentleman and his misfortune is that he fell amongst bad company. His reputation has always stood high in sporting circles and he is applauded for many acts of generosity."

"He has a noble heart," she said and sadly smiled.

"Ay, ma'am, a generous one," cried Egan, delighted to find that he had moved her away from fears and self-doubts to fondness again for her lover. "I recall him when taking leave of a friend who was at the point of death. Thurtell blubbered like a child until he was rallied by the afflicted person begging him to control himself."

"Yet they would kill this gentle person!" she cried, bursting into tears and springing to her feet as though unable to remain seated. "O, Mr. Egan, is there nothing we can do for him, nothing?"

"There is one thing that you can do," said Egan. "Write to him. Be discreet in your writing, tell him of your faith in his innocence and of how you condole with him. Only remember, all letters to him are read by the governor of the prison. Mr. Wilson is a good man, a kindly man, but he has a duty to perform. So pray be careful what you write."

"I have nothing to conceal, nothing of which I am ashamed!" cried Anne passionately. "I would be proud to proclaim my feelings towards him. If there was anything I could do, gladly would I do it and care not a fig for my reputation. What is this wretched thing, a woman's reputation, against the life of a good man? But why is he so hated, why are the newspapers so bestial towards him? He has done them no harm."

"He has done them a great deal of good, ma'am," said Egan. "Never have they been so busy. It is not for me to speak ill of those of my profession, but there are occasions when I am . . . well, not exactly proud of my calling. When society grows ashamed of itself, it seeks a victim. It is gambling, not John Thurtell, that society is intent on damning."

"Alas that a man should suffer for others' sins," she sighed.

"It was ever thus," said Egan. "There is cruelty in mankind, ma'am, and once it grows frightened, the most civilized of nations can show itself to be a realm of savages. Gambling has been deified too long, the world is weary of it, and certainly homes have been wrecked and families left destitute by this madness. But there are other evils; cheap drink, poverty which destroys ambition and robs a man of manliness, diseases which reduce strong men to idiocy, there is corruption in government which our rulers conceal by pretence of honesty and talk of benevolence, there are young women who have

X

been forced to barter chastity for a mouthful of bread and good work-men turned to thieving to keep wife and children from starvation. Ah, there is much wickedness in the world and the real sinners are often too exalted to be thrown down. They throw down instead some poor Jack Thurtell occasionally and hope thereby to make the world believe that they are the defenders of the home. God save me from the cant of politicians."

"Still, I don't see . . . why should he suffer for these others?"

"He has been found out, or at least, they think he has been found out." It was difficult to put into words the abstract ideas that made him indignant with civilization, and extremely difficult was it to explain to this distracted woman that her lover was being sacrificed to appease the nation's conscience. The murder of Weare had been a diabolical crime, cold-blooded and planned for gain and from revenge, but such murders were far from unknown and usually they were dismissed with little more than a shrug. But for some reason, difficult to understand, no murder had aroused such rage and horror as this; the inordinate excitement remained mysterious even to Egan.

"Well, ma'am," he said at last while she sat weeping, shaking and sobbing, in a chair, "it is time for me to leave you. I have a friend below whom I am driving back to town. If there is anything I can do, I am yours to command."

"Th-thank you, Mr. Egan," she said, lowering the handkerchief to reward him with an unhappy glance and a timid smile. "I am more than grateful to you. It is good to find that poor Jack has some true friends when all the world's against him. I will write to him as you suggest. It shall never be said that I was so cowardly as to abandon him in his hour of trial. You . . . you think there is hope?"

"There is always hope," said Egan. "Do not despair, and above all, ma'am, do not let Thurtell despair."

"I will write to him immediately. Thank you, sir," she said, rising and holding out her hand. "You have proved a true friend when he and I most need a friend. May God bless you, Mr. Egan. And should you visit Mr. Thurtell again tell him with all the fervency of which you are capable, tell him that I love him dearly and pray for his release. Yes, tell him that I love him with all my heart and that I have no fears for our future, knowing that truth must triumph in the end."

He shook her hand tenderly and slowly walked from the room, feeling more disturbed than he had believed possible. However wicked Thurtell might have been, the love and loyalty of this proud yet unhappy woman gave the man a dignity and fineness that submerged the murderer in the lover. Away from the evil Probert and Hunt, Thurtell, with such a wife as this, might well become a good and honourable man, like his father.

"A drink," he said to Harmer when he joined him amongst the shouting men about the bar downstairs, "a brandy, quickly. Never have I needed a drink as I need this." And when at last Harmer had fought his way to the bar and returned with the glasses, he took his glass and held it up. "A toast," he said, "to a nameless lady . . . Would to God we men deserved such creatures. A woman who loves a scoundrel and thinks him a saint. There aren't many of em, but when they come . . . damn it, they make a man ashamed to be man."

"I should have thought," smiled Harmer, "that it makes him proud to be a man."

"You have the right of it!" cried Egan, drinking the brandy to the dregs. "One should be proud to be loved by such a creature, however unworthy it might make one feel. . . . I'll think twice before I write against the sex in future. But we must hurry, I've yet to write the copy of that interview and printing-presses are as impatient as any hangman."

More impatient, indeed. The hangman had only to wait and he was fed his victims, but compositors, printers and editors lived with an eye to the clock and there was no reprieve for the pen of any working journalist. There were occasions when Egan was ashamed of his profession, and this was one of them. Damn it, in future he'd report no hangings. No, he would keep to sport whose record could scratch no tragic woman's heart; and he felt tears on his lashes as he hurried with Harmer to his gig in the yard, and he blinked and rubbed his eyes, pretending dust had blown into them, while Harmer turned aside and affected not to notice. Never before had he believed that newspaper-men had other than stones for a heart and the sight of Egan, prince of sporting-writers, knuckling his eyes and snuffling like a boy, turned even his lawyer's stone heart to amazement and incredulity like an atheist before a miracle in which he dares not believe.

CHAPTER TWENTY-NINE

THE FIGHT FOR A LIFE

As EARLY as four o'clock in the morning the streets close to the court-house were crowded with a noisy, laughing multitude, most of them drunk, whistling, singing, cursing and trying to keep their feet as they swayed back and forwards like a sea. In darkness, tightly packed together, the people stood, seeing only dimly the faces of those even beside and in front of them, while bottles were passed overhead from hand to hand. Gentlemen stood beside ragamuffins, harlots beside respectable women, all being united by a common urge to look on the face of a man who had killed, as though Thurtell were unique, the elect of God. Outside the court-house doors, watchmen had been stationed during the night to see that none entered who had no right to enter. Within a small space cleared by the constables, they walked up and down with lanterns and cudgels, strict orders having been given that no one should be admitted until seven o'clock.

Shortly before that cold hour, magistrates with their friends, and those influential enough to have been given tickets, began to push through the crowd which elbowed and tried to trip them, jeering into their faces. Only through one private door were they at last admitted; but such was the huge pressure of others trying to force their way in that the constables had to wield their cudgels and thrash them back. Around the other open door, the one admitting the gentlemen of the press and members of the jury, the more cunning interlopers sought with bribes and lies to edge inside, swearing by God that they were reporters or witnesses or magistrates, but unless they could produce tickets or could find an official to vouch for their credentials, they were driven back, kicking and bruising those behind. Some did manage to sneak inside, passing as barristers' clerks and carrying legal-looking bags borrowed from lawyer-friends.

At seven o'clock the doors opened, and in one wild rush the people surged forward, shouting and cursing and fighting as though all had become panic-stricken and sought to escape like refugees before an enemy. There were howls and screams and cries of anguish, yet, surprisingly, no one was killed and no one even injured beyond a few bruises. Within an instant, every seat in the court had been filled and the most experienced manager of a theatre could not have seated an audience more compactly.

The well of the court itself was also a confused medley of people while the places set apart for the magistrates and the friends of the high sheriff were filled until many men were practically sitting on others' laps. Some almost came to blows. Everybody seemed to be shouting and cursing, accusing this or that person of having no right to be there, while, frantically, ushers and constables tried to bring some order and quietness. Of all the many people present, only four were ladies, and two of these, the sheriff's wife and a friend, were close to the dock from where they could watch every movement and expression of the prisoners. The other two ladies were in the gallery, their laps heaped high with a stock of religious tracts which they had hoped to push into the hands of the prisoners. Even the great men, tardy in arrival, had difficulty to find accommodation. Lord Errol was there, Lord Verulam, Lord Essex and Captain Fitzclarence, Egan noted from the press-box, while two famous artists, Sir Thomas Lawrence and William Mulready, held pencils and sketch-books in readiness.

Depressed after a night's hard drinking, he looked about him through a liverish eye, and sneered. They had come to watch a man fight for his life as though it were a play; and when he thought of Anne Noyes, he felt that he wanted to kick his way outside and drink himself insensible while these others remained to enjoy this Roman holiday. He prayed that some new evidence had been found by the defence. . . .

Gradually, the light grew stronger, yet it was still very dim in the court-room when, at eight o'clock, plump Mr. Justice Park arrived, having spent a comfortable night as guest of Lord Verulam in the great rooms behind the Tuscan pillars of the portico of his manor at Gorhambury, and pushed and puffed his way indignantly through the press. Enraged at finding his court in such disorder, he refused to open the proceedings; and in that refusal, Egan considered him perfectly justified. The uproar was deafening and until those who had seats were seated and those who had no seats had been ejected, the judge sat back, growling and tossing his scarlet robes, his popping eyes as inhuman as granite.

After this irritating delay while the protesting interlopers were hustled out, there was still another long delay before the prisoners appeared. Watching the clock tick on, five minutes, six minutes, seven minutes, Egan even began wildly to hope that again the trial would be postponed, important evidence perhaps having arrived; but when at last the clerk of the arraigns, busy Mr. Knapp, asked what had caused such extraordinary unpunctuality, one of the under-sheriff's assistants explained to the judge that the prisoners were having their irons removed.

Fully ten minutes passed slowly while still there was uproar in the court as men were being pushed out and insisting furiously on their right to be present, and while two of Thurtell's counsel, Mr. Jay and Mr. Fenton, almost had their gowns torn from their backs in their struggle to enter. Even when the prisoners had advanced into the dock the uproar continued, and it was some time before there was sufficient silence and Mr. Wilson was heard shouting whether Probert was come to the bar.

"Yes," said Mr. Knapp, "Probert must be there."

So they had finally settled on Probert instead of Hunt to play the crown witness? That was understandable. With Probert in the dock, Mrs. Probert could not give evidence; now she would be able to back up whatever tale her husband might decide to spill, and he was not so obviously involved as Hunt in the actual murder.

While Hunt's counsel argued with the judge, pleading to have his client's trial postponed because of the alleged promises of favour held out to him by the magistrates if he would confess, Egan scribbled and studied the three men in the dock. Thurtell was dressed in a dark frock-coat, drab cloth waistcoat with gilt buttons, white corduroy breeches, and black stock. He looked, to Egan's surprise, a trifle embarrassed, and his countenance was very pale, almost waxy, perhaps from confinement and the restraint of his irons. There was still, however, a firmness and collectedness in his bearing which manifested a seeming indifference to his situation.

In a shabby suit of black, Hunt stood beside him, giving a more assured impression than he had the last time that he had stood there; while Probert, his hair now piebald with great white patches, seemed fully at ease and well in health, his respectable black suit being clean and new-looking. None of the prisoners spoke. As though they were strangers met by chance in some waiting-room on the way to eternity, they sat apart, while a desk was placed before Thurtell on which he rested a volume of the *Newgate Calendar*, an almanac and pens and paper.

Only now and then, during pauses in the talk, could Egan watch the scene, his pen being busy scribbling scribbling scribbling. Lawyers, however, were like politicians: they spoke slowly, with dramatic emphasis lingering over words. Therefore Egan, although a conscientious recorder, was able to survey the scene while setting it down in words to be read at thousands of breakfast-tables.

It was dull work, however, while on and on prosed Mr. Thesiger, pleading to have Hunt's trial postponed; and it was all unnecessary; the authorities had settled on Probert and were more than unlikely to let Hunt get away with it, too.

When at last Mr. Thesiger had droned to silence, there began again a struggle in the well of the court. Thurtell's solicitor could not reach his counsel, and although Mr. Justice Park, almost purple in the face, commanded that a way be made for him, it was many minutes before he could squeeze through the audience. Then, at long last, the prisoners were put to the bar and the jury was sworn; after that, Probert had to be discharged as not guilty, and Mr. Gurney was able to begin his case for the prosecution.

While Mr. Gurney talked, Thurtell listened attentively, occasionally making notes on the paper before him or whispering to his counsel; and, when the judge withdrew for a few minutes on some urgent but undivulged matter, he ate a slim sandwich passed him by Mr. Wilson. Despite his pallor, he seemed the most healthy and unconcerned man in that stuffy room, gazing about him and nodding to acquaintances as though this were some friendly gathering and they had not come together to explain why they were going to stretch his neck.

Scribble scribble scribble, again went Egan's pen when the witnesses entered the box. No new evidence. The old evidence. Damning evidence. First, the finding of the body, that treachery of Hunt's which had knotted the rope and which yet had failed to let him wriggle free. Serve the fellow right. He had knotted the rope for himself as well as for Thurtell. Then came puddle-faced Field of the Artichoke telling of the body being brought in a sack to his inn; Bow Street's Johnny Upson telling of the body being found in the pond; Rexworthy to swear to the identity of the corpse; Dick Weare to agree that he had seen his late brother soggy at the Artichoke; and the surgeon to describe the wounds he had probed. Then Ruthven . . . then a Watford constable . . . and, at last, Bill Probert.

While the constable was giving his evidence and taking up the red handkerchief, the broken knife, the gold watch-chain surrendered by

Mrs. Probert, the sack, a torn shirt and, particularly, the pistol, the judge kept bouncing on his chair clucking his tongue and crying "Be careful! be careful!" lest the blood and hair on the pistol be disturbed before the jury could examine them. When the pistol was finally put back on the table, he subsided with a satisfied grunt and took up his pen again while the constables escorted Probert through the dock to the witness-box.

Unashamed, quite at his ease, only the unhealthy pallor of his skin suggesting that he came from prison, Probert shouldered his way to the witness-stand and took the oath. Thurtell turned aside and would not look towards him while Hunt stood tiptoe, gaping at his old friend as though not recognizing him in this traitor, and for some time he did not sit down again. Gripping the rail of the dock, he stared, mouth open, and sometimes sadly he shook his head.

The others could hang, but Probert was careful about his own neck. With the royal pardon in his pocket, he nevertheless let nothing slip that might suggest he had been an accomplice in the actual murder. An innocent who had welcomed his friends to his cottage in the country and been rewarded by finding a corpse on his hands; and although the prisoners' counsel soon had him turned inside-out as a scoundrelly bankrupt and possibly a receiver of stolen goods, his evidence remained unshakable. Miss Anne Noyes would never embrace her bridegroom after that, sighed Egan: there could be no escape for Thurtell, nothing could save him unless Probert should be proved a liar. A liar he decidedly was, of course, but his description of the murder and the attempts to hide the body were broadly and undoubtedly true.

After the husband, the wife. Mrs. Probert, genteelly dressed in a blue pelisse, a Leghorn straw bonnet and a green veil, quivered her fat in the box, shuddered theatrically when she saw the prisoners sneering at her, and cringed towards the judge, bobbing and ducking when he politely suggested that she might be given a chair. Her voice was low, so low that, after his questions, Mr. Gurney had to repeat her answers that the court might hear them. Thurtell listened to her with more interest than he had listened to her husband, and he smiled wryly when he heard how she had spied and eavesdropped during the murder-night. Hunt opened his eyes wide and shook his head as though disgusted, and he looked appealingly towards the bench, shrugging and groaning, raising his hands, a good man helpless before a woman's lies.

After consultation with the judge on the propriety of such questions, Mr. Gurney led her to speak of what she had told her husband when he had come upstairs that night to bed. "Must I answer?" she squeaked, almost swooning in her agitation.

"I do not want you to tell us what was said," Mr. Gurney murmured soothingly; and the judge leaned down to say: "Pray, compose yourself, good woman. You need not be alarmed."

"Must I answer questions concerning my husband?" she sobbed, her voice so low and so hysterical that even Egan's sharp ears were uncertain of what she had said.

"No evidence you now give can prejudice your husband," said Mr. Gurney. "He has been this day put before a jury of his countrymen and acquitted of this murder."

"O, has he!" she screamed and fell backwards as though about to swoon; "has he!" she screamed again.

Slowly, ignoring the hysterics, Mr. Gurney repeated his question, and at last, holding her corsets where she presumed her heart to be, Mrs. Probert managed to gasp: "O, I'll answer anything! but has he been acquitted?" Her agitation was such that she waved aside every question counsel shot at her.

"Pray, compose yourself, pray, good woman," clucked the judge. "Don't be alarmed, we are not wanting you to say anything against your husband. Pray compose yourself. Pray do not be alarmed."

Hunt turned and grinned at the people about him, and raised his brows and softly whistled, as though inviting scepticism of this performance in the box; but Thurtell gave no sign of his feelings. He merely bent down a little and took snuff, drawing up his brows and closing his lips firmly, an expression which Egan knew to be more or less habitual with him.

Then out came Mrs. Probert's admissions. Once Mr. Gurney had uncorked her, out with a delighted rush came everything that she could say to damn her husband's friends and to exculpate her husband. Beyond hope now, sighed Egan, busily scribbling his hieroglyphs, were Thurtell and Hunt, particularly Thurtell. There was no hatred of Hunt in the court, he noticed. The little monster was dismissed by most people as a very minor actor in the tragedy; only on Thurtell was curiosity, admiration or hatred concentrated. Yet to Egan's thinking he was the most innocent of the three, the great bull led by a clown and a coward to the sacrifice.

At last, Mrs. Probert was led, loudly sobbing, from the court; then

Thomas Thurtell took her place. Tom did not want to say anything. His natural stutter grew exaggerated and he spluttered and spat, dragging at his cravat with one hand as though it were too tight, and he could not look towards his brother who remained calm, apparently unruffled as he took up his pen again to continue taking notes.

A most unwilling witness. Egan felt sorry for the poor devil trying to edge away from admissions, squirming in the box, spluttering and gasping, his face sweating in that close atmosphere. But the questions continued and could not all be shifted aside, squirm from them though he did, until the judge leaned down, swelling out his cheeks, and warned him to be careful.

At last, he was released and hurried from the court for Thomas Noyes to take his place; and after Noyes came his sister, Anne.

Trembling, she entered, scarcely daring to look at Thurtell. So agitated was she, so pale her cheeks, that the judge intimated that she might be seated and a chair was brought. With murmured thanks, she sank on to it and looked shyly about her while she swore the oath; and then at last she looked at Thurtell. This was the moment for which Egan had been watching and he saw a sad yet brave smile curve her lips, a smile of love and encouragement with no shame or reproof in it; and he saw how Thurtell straightened, faintly flushing, smiling in reply. For that moment, separated by the bobbing heads of counsel, court-officials and visitors, the lovers looked at each other; and Egan forgot the patch over the woman's right eye, forgot also that the man stood in defence of his neck, and pitied them and wished that Thurtell could go free to marry her. Whatever his guilt, it was less than the guilt of many who were respected in the world. He had killed, that was true, but the man he had killed had been worthless and the world was better for his going; and now the woman also was stained with his guilt, doomed by her love to a lifetime's misery and regrets. Yet, bravely, before that crowded court, before the four women quizzing her scornfully and the men noting with little interest her few attractions, Anne Noyes sat and in Egan's eyes she was a heroine ready to defy the world's censure for the man she loved. And the tragedy was that she could do nothing in his defence, nothing. Her sister and her sister's husband had knotted the noose too firmly for anything she might say to slacken it; and what could she say when she must only answer questions and not make any statement?

Yes, yes. She knew that her brother-in-law had a white hat which was kept in the hall. None of the three had worn a white hat that evening. They had a little brandy. .... Yes, yes. .... Pointless questions many of them seemed to her, an irritating buzz like an insect disturbing her, while she peeped and smiled shyly at Thurtell; and only once did she admit some damaging evidence, although it was not really important. When shown the bloodstained broken knife that had been found in the lane, she said, Yes, she had seen John Thurtell with a knife very like that.

Mr. Andrews, for Thurtell, then stood in place of the prosecutor, and he was careful not to tangle her in lies. Yes, she said, John Thurtell had been often at the cottage before. Yes, he slept there several times. He did not always sleep on the sofa. .... She sighed and looked down at her kid-gloved hands.

"I can swear he once slept nearly a week at the cottage," she said, then added: "He slept alone. ...."

Only two men in that court noted the sadness, the regret in her low voice when she said, "He slept alone." Egan was startled, not knowing whether she lied, and she had not seemed the kind of woman who would have lied from prudery; yet who could tell? There sounded sincerity, even sorrow, in that simple declaration. He glanced towards Thurtell and saw how he looked down at his papers, frowning and seeming angry with himself, as though there were a taunt concealed under her words. "He slept alone," she said and glanced at him, tears on her lashes.

With relief did Egan see her leave the court, glancing back at her lover as she went, and William Rexworthy took her place. His dislike of Thurtell, Rexworthy did not attempt to conceal. He glared at the man, and whenever possible stressed his evidence to make it tell against him, relating how Thurtell had visited his billiard-rooms in search of the deceased, how they had talked apart together and how later he had identified the body fished from the pond.

One after another, witnesses bobbed into the box, their evidence seeming scarcely necessary after what the Proberts had confessed. Yet come they must, to drive nails deeper into Thurtell's coffin. Weare's laundress, Mary Maloney, to tell of her master's leaving Lyon's Inn and to identify his watch and clothing. Thomas Carr, next, the hackney charioteer, told how Mary Maloney had called him from the Spotted Dog to drive to Lyon's Inn and how he had taken the deceased up Welbeck Street to the New Road and along to Cumberland Street where his fare had alighted, returning with a tall gentleman in a rough coat to pay him what he owed. A horse-patrol, Thomas

Wilson, had seen two men in a gig driving at a furious rate along the Edgware Road. The ostler at Cross's stables, James Shepherd, told of Hunt hiring a gig from his master. Another ostler, Stephen March, remembered Hunt hiring a horse and when it was returned it was a good deal distressed. "Yes," he said, "there was a little blood at the bottom of the gig."

The pawnbroker's assistant, Benjamin Coxwell, had sold a pair of pistols, a key and a mould to two strangers for one pound fifteen. The ostler at the Bald-Faced Stag, John Butler, recalled that on Friday night, October 24, between six and seven, Probert had called at his house in a horse and chaise. The landlord of the White Lion told of drinks and of suspicious talk by Hunt and Thurtell at his bar. David White, son of an Edgware corn-chandler, remembered Probert buying beans and oats on the evening of October 24, and, he replied in cross-examination by Mr. Thesiger, he had not seemed to have been in a hurry to get away. Stephen Probatt, landlord of the White Lion at Charing Cross, told of Hunt giving him a five-pound note out of which he had taken one pound five shillings for hire of a horse; and "a Mr. Reece," he added, "was in my coffee-room. He remarked that he was a smug sort of man and ought to get a knock on the head. Hunt afterwards pulled out a pistol and said: 'This is a good fellow to do business'. . . ."

Robert Field of the Artichoke told of visits to his inn; and Richard Bingham, ostler at the White Lion, told of visits to his inn; and Mary Maloney was recalled to agree that the last witness's description of a short man with large dark whiskers, a sallow complexion and high-cheekbones, fitted her master exactly. James Freeman, a labourer, had strolled on the night of October 28 out of his cottage—which was called the Folly, he explained to the judge—to meet his wife and had seen two gentlemen in a gig in Gill's Hill Lane. Philip Smith, a farmer, while driving his wife and child in a donkey-chaise had heard the report of a pistol or gun, followed by groaning, when he passed the corner of the lane leading to Gill's Hill. He had not investigated, he uneasily explained, because his wife had been alarmed.

Richard Addis, Probert's servant, had a great deal to tell. Everything that he said confirmed the Proberts' tale; and he was delighted to talk, and he would have talked all day had the gentlemen not wearied of asking him questions. After him, came his fellow-servant, Susannah Woodruff; but before she had taken the oath, the judge turned to the jury. It was not for him to consider his own convenience, he said, but that of the jury. By the law of England, he was not allowed to discharge juries in criminal cases nor could he let them return to their families before the verdict was given. If they should feel tired, however, he would dismiss them for the night and proper accommodation would be found. . . .

Everybody, including the prisoners, looked tired. Through the long day the procedure had continued with scarcely a pause and the court was ill-ventilated, the foul air bringing weariness. Only the audience in the gallery and pushing even into the well of the court remained at ease, prepared to sit or stand for weeks so long as they could enjoy the sight of two men being prepared for death. At the judge's suggestion of adjourning, they murmured angrily, while the jury whispered together. Egan prayed that they would agree to adjourn. His wrists and fingers ached after so much writing, the scribbled-on sheets of paper piling high beside him, and he longed for a glass of brandy and water.

Damn the jury. Confound the jury. They would be satisfied, said the foreman, with some refreshments taken in the box.

No brandy for an over-worked journalist. Groaning, Egan took up his pen again as Mr. Broderick, one of the three counsel for the crown, tucked up his gown behind him and started to question Miss Woodruff. She merely corroborated what her fellow-servant, Addis, had sworn, but she made one remark to set the court chuckling with that relief which even the silliest jest will bring in the tense drama of a murder-trial. Was the supper on the night of October 24 postponed? asked Mr. Broderick. "I don't know," she said. "It was pork;" and she gaped about her, bewildered, when they laughed.

John Harrington, labourer, followed her into the box to tell how he had seen the prisoners in Gill's Hill Lane on the Saturday morning after the murder and how they had told him that their gig had capsized the previous night and said that they were looking for a penknife and a handkerchief. After they had gone, he and his partner, Richard Hunt, had found a penknife dirty in the cart-ruts, and, later, a pistol amongst some brambles. He left the box for Richard Hunt to take his place; then Egan noticed that Thurtell was standing up, papers in hand, trying to attract the attention of the judge.

"My lord," he said when he could be heard, "I must pray you again to speak to the gentlemen of the jury on the subject which you have before mentioned, namely, the propriety of postponing further proceedings till tomorrow. I beg them to consider the peculiar situation in which I stand, having been up since six o'clock this morning. By the time the remaining witnesses, of whom I understand there are twenty still to be examined, have been gone through, I shall be too much exhausted to do justice to my defence."

"By the law of the land," said the judge, seeming to inflate within his robes as he leaned forward, "a case ought to go on until it is closed, and I am ready to go on with it. I am willing, however, to do what I can to accommodate either the gentlemen of the jury or yourself. It is with the jury, however, that the matter must rest."

"Yes, my lord," said Thurtell, "I am aware of that. I did not address myself to your lordship at this time."

"No, prisoner, so I understood," agreed the judge with an air of condescending impartiality. "But the law of the land supposes that we must go on to a conclusion, and in my experience I have sat sixteen and seventeen hours in a day."

"Gentlemen of the jury," said Thurtell, turning towards the box and giving a little bow, "I trust you will take what I have said into consideration."

Before the foreman could reply, the judge said: "The gentlemen who are counsel for the crown state to me that for the prosecution very little remains to be done."

Desperately, trying to conceal his indignation, Thurtell cried: "I beg to say that it will take two hours for Mr. Hunt and myself to go through our defence."

But the judge was giving him as little mercy as possible. "We had better go on at all events with the case for the prosecution," he said flatly, taking no heed of signals from the jury-box. "There are many reasons, I find, why we should do so. That case will now last only an hour or two; and after that, if we cannot conveniently go on, I will take an opportunity of again recommending your prayer to the jury."

There was no more to be said. Back into his chair sank Thurtell while Richard Hunt, the labourer, was being sworn; and Egan felt how impossible it was not to admire the man. Firmly, temperately, respectfully had he put his plea and he showed no gesture of resentment when it was dismissed. Yet the man must be dog-tired, his patience strung to breaking-point, despair gradually crippling all his hopes as witness after witness went into the box to swear his life away with little things done, little things said, little things seeming unimportant at the time but now being linked together in an unbreakable rope for his hanging. Yet he gave no hint of worry. As though perfectly at ease, a gentleman amongst gentlemen, he listened to the evidence while at his side Hunt seemed to sink lower into his clothes.

Richard Hunt confirmed what his fellow-labourer had said; another labourer, William Bulmer, on the morning after the murder had seen two men in Probert's garden walking towards the house. George Nicholls, who lived near Gill's Hill, said that on Monday a labourer had given him a knife and pistol which he had passed to Simmons, the officer. They were bloody. "On Monday evening," he added, "I observed what appeared like brains about the barrel of the pistol."

John Pidcock, a surgeon, deposed that he had examined the naked body of Weare at the Artichoke. John Fleet, who had been placed in charge of the Cock after Thurtell's flight, deposed that Hunt had called at the public house for some of Thurtell's property, including a red shawl. Caroline Williams, servant at the Cock, agreed that the red shawl had been Thurtell's. Another servant, Lucy Slater, also identified the shawl. John Marshall, gunsmith, identified the gun produced as having belonged to Weare. W. Blakesley, a lodger at No. 19, King Street, Golden Square, remembered Hunt arriving on October 27 in a single horse chaise with a carpet-bag, a gun in a dark case, a dressing-case and some coats which he had carried indoors.

The Bow Street officer, John Upson, was recalled to state that he had escorted the prisoners from London to Watford in two gigs, and the next morning he had told Thurtell about Hunt's confession. "I asked what he did with the watch," he said, "and he told me that he threw it away in a place among some trees where there were some palings." Thurtell had forgotten saying that, half in jest, that weary morning so long ago and he certainly had not expected this damned runner to recall his words so aptly. He should have remembered that it was dangerous even for an innocent man to admit anything to the police.

Here was another of the police, a constable from Rickmansworth, to repeat that Thurtell had called Hunt a rascal for so nosing him and had said that he would never have done the same to a friend, particularly after he had offered the watch for sale in Hunt's name and as his property.

Next Tom Thurtell was called again, but before he could answer, the foreman of jury was standing up and signing to the judge that he was weary and would like an adjournment. And not too soon either, thought Egan, gratefully putting down his pen for a moment. He was exhausted, the judge was weary, the jurymen nodding together, and even Thurtell looked a little tired.

But Egan could not rest for long. There was the judge's talk to the jury to record and the swearing of two constables to guard the jury during the night; after that, he could relax, jotting down a few notes about the scene until the judge, who had been chatting with some friends, noticed that Thurtell and Hunt were still in the dock.

"They must talk to them elsewhere," he cried when Mr. Wilson explained that they were conversing with their professional advisers. "You must remove them; you run a great risk by keeping them here."

Out of the dock amongst the jailors moved the two men, Thurtell looking almost gay, clutching his manuscript. Ay, gay! although plainly very tired; and was that, wondered Egan, because he would not now have to read his darling defence to an exhausted audience when he had not the strength remaining with which to expound it as he wanted to expound it, as though he were the hero expectant of applause in a drama on the stage?

CHAPTER THIRTY

HOW SAY YOU?

AGAIN at seven o'clock in the morning were the doors of the court opened, and again hundreds struggled to enter. Within a few minutes, every space inside was crammed almost to suffocation, the excitement being even more intense than it had been the day before, because of the interest in Thurtell's defence. It was for this that so many gamesters and rogues had travelled to Hertford, and horsemen were posted nearby to be despatched the moment the verdict was recorded that those interested should know whether Jack Thurtell had talked. In France, Lemming waited with trepidation, and in the St. James's hells men drank and conversed in hushed voices, unable to remain still and repeating again and again, to give themselves courage, that Jack had gumption and would never mace on his pals. Then when in the carriage, Thurtell was seen to hold that bulky manuscript and a heap of books and papers tied in a blue pocket-handkerchief, the watchers groaned in apprehension.

Egan was in his place amongst the other reporters when the prisoners entered the dock, bowing respectfully to the court, and again he marvelled at Thurtell's calm demeanour. As though he had slept soundly and had never a trouble on his mind, he looked about him and bowed to friends, while at his side, Hunt shook and simpered.

There were two witnesses for the crown to be examined before the defence could open, and once these two supernumeraries were out of the way, the audience settled for the dramatic hour when Thurtell would attempt to break down the web of evidence in which he was enclosed.

But the defence opened dully. The judge leaned forward, peering towards the prisoners, both hands on the bench, and said challengingly: "John Thurtell, this is the time that it becomes your duty to make your defence."

Again, Thurtell bowed, then he turned to Mr. Jay to ask whether his witnesses were ready.

"My lord," said Mr. Jay, turning to the bench, "my client wishes to call his witnesses first."

"I cannot in my capacity attend to wishes," grunted the judge. "I must abide strictly by the rules of the court. This, therefore, is the proper time for the prisoner making his defence."

Thurtell had hoped to keep his speech, like a general holding back his cavalry for a final sweep at a crippled enemy, until the last, but to Mr. Justice Park's ruling he had to bow. Then, half-turning towards the bench while facing the jury, he unfolded his manuscript, assumed a graceful attitude, and began in a firm voice.

"My lord, and you, gentlemen of the jury," he said. "Under the pressure of greater difficulties than, perhaps, it has before fallen to the lot of man to sustain, I now rise to vindicate my character and preserve my life. But appalling as are these difficulties, I have been supported under the impression that the hour would arrive when I should be enabled to defend myself in a land of liberty, before that tribunal which the free institutions of my country have awarded to the accused: namely, an enlightened court and a jury of twelve fellow-subjects uninfluenced by prejudice and unawed by power."

His voice was resonant, like an actor's, and seemed to grow more powerful, more confident, as he continued in that hushed court in which little was heard save his voice and the scratching of pens, while, from outside, the crowd still shouted and sang. Calmly, showing never a quiver of fear, he spoke, and it was difficult to believe that a man so unafraid could possibly have been a murderer.

"I have been represented by the public press," he cried, his tone rising in indignation, "as a man the most depraved, the most habitually profligate, the most gratuitously cruel, that has appeared in modern times. I have been represented as a murderer who had perpetrated his crime with greater atrocity, and under circumstances of more premeditated malice, than any that has hitherto been heard of in the sad catalogue of criminals. I have been stigmatized as a callous, cruel, heartless, remorseless, prayerless villain who had seduced his friend into a sequestered path in order the more securely to despatch him. I have been described as a viper who had nestled in the bosom of his victim with the preconcerted intention of striking a surer blow—as a monster who, having committed a deed of horror at which our common nature recoils and humanity stands aghast, endeavoured to extinguish the upbraidings of conscience in the tumults of debauchery. These have been the descriptions given of me, not only daily, but I may say hourly by the public journals, and communicated from one extremity to the other.

"You, gentlemen, have no doubt read them; I will not say that you have been influenced by them; but it would exact too much from the common virtue of human nature to suppose that you could entirely divest yourselves of impressions successively repeated, or that you could dispossess yourselves of those feelings—those creditable feelings I will say—which such statements, if justified, were calculated to excite. But I feel satisfied, gentlemen, that, as far as it is possible for men to enter into a grave investigation with minds unbiased and judgments unaffected by the atrocious slanders which have been published against me, you will decide as becomes the character of that sacred office with which you are invested. You shall hear from men of the most unblemished reputation, of the most unimpeachable veracity, that at least there was a period of my life when the bosom of him who now stands before you as an accused murderer flowed with the most gentle and kindly feelings of affection and sympathy, and that my faults were those of an improvident generosity and an unsuspecting confidence. Beware then, gentlemen, of preconceived opinions; O! beware of an anticipated verdict.

"Gentlemen, my entrance into life was under circumstances the most auspicious. I was reared by a kind, affectionate and religious mother who first taught my lips to utter their first accents in praise of that Being Who guides the conduct of your hearts, and of the learned judge upon the bench. My youthful steps were directed by a father whose kindness and charity extended to all who came within the sphere of its influence. . . ."

He wiped his eyes and his voice broke a little when he spoke of his parents who, as all those present knew, had made no attempt to visit him while he lay in jail; but soon his voice became steady again and he continued in the same deep, measured and unshaken tone as before, accompanying the words with gestures perhaps a trifle studied and theatrical. Nevertheless, thought Egan, busy with his pen, it sounded better now than when he had listened to it in jail.

On Thurtell talked, boasting of his services to his country as a marine in the recent war; and then he turned to the accusation of his having been a gambler. To this, he confessed, hand to his heart, he pleaded guilty, although, he insisted, for the last three years he had not entered a gaming-house, or attended a horse-race or any other sporting exhibition. And if this were an unpardonable vice, then half the nobility and most enlightened statesmen must stand as his apologists. From gambling, he spoke of his experiences in London, his bene-volence towards those in distress and his weakness in allowing sharps to beggar him. He had gone bankrupt, that was true, but he could not be blamed for it; nor could he be blamed for the fire that had burned down his and his brother's warehouse. As for Mr. Barber Beaumont who had dared accuse him of arson and who had persecuted him ever since, he was very hard on him, denouncing him for almost all crimes from suborning witnesses to rebellion against the king. Then his voice dropped, he looked about him, and said in a lower and yet not less indignant tone:

"You have been told, gentlemen, amongst its other unfounded calumnies, by the public press that a Mr. Wood has asserted that he was inveigled into a house in Manchester Buildings where he supposed it was intended to murder him and that he saw me standing in the passage. Happily, I am enabled, if such a charge were this day at issue, to prove from the unquestionable testimony of some most respectable individuals that I was, at the time I am thus described to be in Manchester Buildings, in my native city of Norwich. Of Mr. Wood I shall say no more at present: I abstain from doing so from feelings of delicacy towards an amiable and innocent female."

At mention of even "an amiable and innocent female," a rustle fluttered through the court, a sudden shifting of the listeners on their seats and a hissing indrawing of their breath.

From this tender reference to Caroline, Thurtell reverted to abuse of the press and then proclaimed his honourable service in the marines during the war.

"Towards me," he cried in a trembling voice, "the very order of nature has been reversed. The few days of my late misfortunes have thrown a livid shadow over the glories of days long past, and the pursuit of a profession hitherto held honourable among honourable men has been turned to the advantage of the accusations against me. The actions of my life have been misrepresented—every kind of connection and engagement which I might have formed has been ransacked to supply the magazine of slander."

For the moment he could not continue. Anger and indignation, roused by his own eloquence, began to choke him and he sobbed, leaning forward and pressing his knuckles on the rail of the dock. His recent defiance and cool courage had not had the effect as had this unexpected breaking of his will. Even the judge, who had been scribbling and listening without the faintest pretence of believing a word he was told, was sufficiently moved to grunt:

"Sit down for a moment; sit down."

Thurtell did not sit down. He remained leaning against the rail, shuddering and gasping, until he was able to breathe easily again. Then, once more erect, his great shoulders back, he seemed to gather up his frame. As before, he looked very steadily at the jury when he returned to his speech. For a while, he continued to denounce the tales of his cruelty in battle, then he softened his voice to thank those officials who had been kind and attentive to him in jail: the high sheriff, the magistrates, the Rev. Mr. Franklin, the prison chaplain, and, especially, Mr. Wilson whose fatherly conduct, he said, he could never forget.

Now came the moment which Egan had dreaded. Thurtell paused to drink a glass of water as he opened the paper containing the examples of past miscarriages of justice. Egan groaned to see him. Nothing, he knew, irritated judge and jury more than the thought that justice might ever have made a mistake. The bare suggestion infuriated them, seeming a slur on their own probity and acumen.

The paper was either ill-written or Thurtell, otherwise so splendid an orator, was so indifferent a reader that the effect, Egan noticed, was fatal to his previous flowery appeal. He stammered, blundered and seemed confused throughout, while people yawned and began to whisper and titter, almost ignoring him.

While in this state of irritable boredom, scribbling his notes, Egan chanced to look up and glance around the court and he was startled to see, standing by the door, a woman with a patch over her right eye. Beside her stood Ruthven, who apparently had conducted her inside. This woman alone of all those in that room gazed intently at Thurtell as though entranced by his halting eloquence. Rapt like a mystic listening to a saint, she stood, unmasked, unveiled, gazing at him with an almost holy adoration. Fortunately, Thurtell did not notice her or his confusion might well have become even worse than it was. On he stumbled amongst the words, speaking now hurriedly, now slowly, as though, realizing how he had lost control of the court's emotions, he was growing desperate.

It seemed that he would never end; and when at last he was about to falter, his fool of a lawyer whispered to him, and he spoke of yet another dryasdust case taken from the *Newgate Calendar* about someone called Coleman, in Kingston in 1748, who had been hanged for murdering a woman. Three years later, two men confessed to the murder. And that, thank God, was all.

With obvious relief, Thurtell put down the *Newgate Calendar* and took up his packet of notes to conclude his address. Again, he became the actor; again, there was silence before that powerful, confident voice as he stood erect and started to speak.

"And now, gentlemen," he said, "having brought these cases under your view, am I not justified in solemnly warning you against giving to circumstances a weight to which they are not entitled? Though circumstances may be considered and balanced, am I not justified in submitting to you that unless they are entirely irreconcilable with my innocence their weight ought to be small against me? Am I not justified in saying that, in justice to me and with a due regard to your own consciences that you may discharge your duty with satisfaction to yourselves, you are bound to consider whether all the circumstances which had been brought forward in evidence might not exist, and yet the individual who is now addressing you be innocent of the murder? Have I not a right then to call upon you, not only to confer upon me the benefit of a doubt or of that presumption of law which supposes every man to be innocent until he is proved to be guilty; but under the guidance of an unbiased and candid judgment to do an act of justice to yourselves, to the public and to myself by dismissing me from this bar by your verdict of acquittal? Remember, gentlemen, my existence hangs upon your breath, for if you bring in a verdict of guilty, the law afterwards allows no mercy. If you should not feel fully assured of my innocence, if you should even have a doubt of my guilt, the law gives me, and your own hearts will give me, the benefit of that doubt. Cut me not off—I implore it of your justice, of your humanity—in the very summer of my life. I implore it, not for myself, but for the sake of those whose memory is unsullied; for the sake of those whose name I bear and whose character accusation never stained; for the sake of their home, a happy home, which my death will render desolate. . . .

"Gentlemen of the jury, in your hands, I repeat it, are placed my honour and my existence—the hopes and fears of my family—all that is most dear to man. I stand before you as before my God, overwhelmed with misfortunes, but unconscious of crime, and while you decide on my future destiny, I earnestly entreat you to remember my last solemn declaration——

"I am innocent, so help me God!"

This last declaration he shouted, eyes raised towards the ceiling and his arms a little extended. Then slowly he drew back his arms and pressed his hands above his heart, and bowed. Ay, he bowed like an actor waiting for applause before he sat back, satisfied, in his seat!

Egan noticed that Anne Noyes was sobbing into her handkerchief and that most of the listeners let out their breath as though after some awesome moment; but Mr. Justice Park was not impressed. He smoothed his wig and turned with a curl of the lip to Hunt.

"Joseph Hunt," he said, his cold, flat voice like an icy wind through a stuffy room dispelling any emotion aroused by Thurtell's histrionics. "It is now your time," he said, "as your counsel cannot address the jury in your behalf, to say what you think proper in your defence; but before you begin, the purposes of justice require that the witnesses for the other prisoner should be heard first."

What possible witnesses could Thurtell produce? Tremulously, Anne lowered her hands and dared look out upon the world with hope again, while Egan chose a fresh pen. As he had expected, the witnesses were worthless. A Samuel Wadeson said that he knew Probert and that he would not believe him on his oath unless supported by other credible witnesses. Nobody doubted that. Nobody trusted Probert an inch. But there had been more than Probert's word to help twine the rope that would hang Thurtell. A Mr. Haydon said that he knew Thurtell and considered him humane and kind-hearted. A Captain M'Kinlay of the royal navy under whom Thurtell had served from 1812 to 1814 swore that he had always found him correct, humane and liberal. A Mr. W. Walmsley had known him for thirteen or fourteen years and considered him a humane, well-disposed man. And that was all. Nothing. Not even a bubble on which to rest a feather of hope. The man was doomed.

With the seating of Thurtell, much of the interest had vanished from the trial. Nobody cared a twopenny damn about the fate of Joseph Hunt and few even pretended to listen after he quavered: "My lord, I have a defence to make, but from the extreme anxiety of mind under which I labour I do not feel myself competent to read it."

"You had better hand it to the officer of the court and let him read it," said Mr. Justice Park, stifling a yawn as he began to glance through his notes.

While Hunt remained sunk on his chair, Thurtell beside him seeming indifferent to what was said and watching only the jury's faces, Mr. Knapp began to read from the papers Hunt passed him.

Hunt made no real defence. He did not even deny the crime. All that bothered him was the injustice of having been inveigled into giving a confession and afterwards not being admitted as king's evidence.

When Mr. Knapp had droned to a halt, Hunt seemed to have recovered something of his courage. Perhaps his horror at having heard his plea read so prosily as though it were the minutes of some aldermanic meeting or something equally as dull, inspired him to speak. He stuttered that he had another speech to make.

"I—I merely wish to add," he said, "that the greater part of Probert's evidence is false, and especially the part of it in which it is stated that I was acquainted with all the circumstances which occurred previous to the murder. In order to save his own life, Probert has found it necessary to sacrifice mine. One fact which Probert has stated, everybody must see must be false. Probert has said that I pointed out the place where I was to be set down on the road. Now it is in evidence that I had never before been in that part of the country. How then could I point out the spot?"

The judge did not bother to answer such an irrelevant question and Hunt flopped back, sweating, in his chair while the judge commanded that one of the Hertfordshire constables be placed in the witness-box.

A fat and unhappy-looking constable being sworn, he stood gaping about him while the judge asked if he knew where Gill's Hill Lane stood.

"No," said the constable, "I dunno."

Angrily, the judge dismissed him and the coroner stepped briskly into his place to swear emphatically that not only Gill's Hill Lane, but also the place where the body had been found, were both in the county of Hertford.

Then the judge, hitching up his robes and shuffling his notes, began his summing up, and those experienced in his ways had only to glance at him to know what emphasis he intended to give the evidence. Egan had expected nothing less, yet idiotically he had hoped for some last-minute miracle that might console Anne Noyes in her grief; and of course there had been none. Thurtell, and doubtless Hunt, would hang; and he noticed that Thurtell himself appeared to be of a similar opinion. Although still showing no hint of fear, there was a fatalism in his attitude, in the way in which he shrugged his shoulders, took snuff and talked to his counsel, which showed that he had abandoned hope. Yet carefully still he listened, even now and then interrupting the judge when he thought he had gone adrift; and he grinned sardonically when my lord baulked at the word "blunt."

No, it was impossible not to applaud Thurtell, murderer though he unquestionably was. While Hunt appeared ready to collapse whenever the judge made any observation against him, he showed only a manly fortitude which was plainly not forced or constrained, his mind keenly alert to seize and avail himself of any opportunity to help his doomed case.

While the judge meandered through the evidence, Egan noticed that Anne Noyes had drawn further back as though to shield herself behind Ruthven, no doubt fearful of breaking into tears before the court. Even she, he felt, for all her woman's faith in the power of her love, must have begun to despair. Yet Thurtell remained outwardly unconcerned as though he were seated at somebody else's trial.

Not until the jury had retired to consider their verdict did he relax and smile and chat with his advisers. Egan edged closer to hear what was being said and he was not surprised to find that, despite his air of confidence, Thurtell suffered no illusions about the verdict. He was asking Mr. Platt, one of his counsel, whether he thought the judge might postpone the execution until after Sunday. Mr. Platt shrugged and shook his head. It was most unlikely, he told him. Annoyed, Thurtell asked Mr. Harmer his opinion, and Mr. Harmer agreed with his *confrère*.

"What!" cried Thurtell, "has not the judge power to respite for a few days?"

"Ay," said Mr. Harmer, "he has the power, but I've never yet known it used in cases of murder, unless some doubt was entertained about the correctness of the conviction. However," he added in a hopeless voice, "there'd be no impropriety in your respectfully soliciting him to grant the indulgence."

It was impossible for Egan to edge close enough to speak to the prisoners himself, so great was the gathering about the dock. No popular actor, not Mr. Kean himself, had ever known such sycophantic adulation as buzzed about this nonchalant murderer. Gaily—or as gaily as was possible for so naturally grim a character—Thurtell talked, asking how the great fight had gone at Worcester; and nobody could tell him. But mostly he talked of his defence and of the great speech he had written and delivered. He jeered at Probert, damned him for a liar, tore his evidence to contemptible shreds; and everyone agreed with him, preferring far the murderer above the informer.

"To say that I said that Weare had nearly got the better of me!" he cried indignantly. "Weare was a very little man, and to think it possible that such a person could get the better of Me, that's all nonsense!"

"At all events," said one of the sycophants, "you can't be accused of betraying your companions."

"No," cried Thurtell emphatically, clenching his fists, "before anyone could have got the secret from me, he must have torn my heart out of my breast!"

"You mean, of course," said the other with a warning lift of eyebrows, "if you had been concerned?"

"Yes, of course," agreed Thurtell hurriedly, giving him a sudden smile.

"Well, no matter what they do to you, my boy," grinned a sporting gentleman cheerfully, "no one can dispute the firmness and talent you showed here today."

Thurtell smiled again, raising his chin. "I think," he said complacently, "I have taken a little sting out of the poisoned shafts levelled against me. I know that the lads of the village will be pleased at my conduct."

Not once did he turn towards Anne Noyes behind Ruthven at the door. For a moment, Egan considered speaking to her, and decided against it. Sympathy might unnerve the unhappy woman. It were best to leave her to stand the blow alone; and when the jury filed back into their places there was no need for the foreman to speak. Besides, they had been absent only half-an-hour and that was a very bad sign indeed. Not one of those twelve unhappy men looked towards Thurtell and Hunt, and some of them were weeping. When he tried to answer to his name, the foreman choked; and when it came to giving the verdict, for a moment he was unable to speak.

With horror, Hunt gaped at them; but, putting down the glass of ale he had been drinking, Thurtell drew himself to his full height, loosely clasping his hands together, and stared very intently at the jurors while they filed into their box.

With a great effort, at last the foreman managed to answer Mr. Knapp, the clerk of arraigns, whether John Thurtell were guilty or not guilty of the murder of which he stood arraigned.

"Guilty," he said in a low voice, tears running down his cheeks.

"How say you," asked Mr. Knapp, "is Joseph Hunt guilty or not guilty?"

"He is guilty also," gasped the foreman, "as an accessary before the fact."

"Then you say," persisted Mr. Knapp, "they are both guilty as they are indicted?"

"Yes," sobbed the foreman, hand covering his face.

In the hush that followed, all turned to stare at the prisoners who remained firm, impassive. While the square of black cloth called a coif was unfolded in readiness by the clerk, Thurtell pulled out his snuff-box, tapped it open and, with an air of profound pleasure, sniffed daintily at the pinch he had taken and held between thumb and forefinger.

Alone amongst all those present, Egan looked, not towards Thurtell, but in search of Anne Noyes.

Anne Noyes was no longer there.

CHAPTER THIRTY-ONE

THE DEAD GOD

ALL THROUGH that long night, his last night, Thurtell could hear men hammering while they raised his scaffold, driving in the last nails with steady blows. Work had begun on it the day before his trial, so certain had the authorities been that it would soon be needed; then they had rested until the expected verdict had been finally pronounced. Now, at the direction of the under-sheriff, Mr. Nicholson, carpenters had started to saw and hammer and whistle again. Doubtless, this work was of particular interest to them for, although the drop to quicken death by hanging had been introduced as long ago as 1783, Hertford-shire had remained old-fashioned and slow to catch up with such modern fashions. For the first time in the county the drop was to be tried on Thurtell and it was being built in such fashion that, after use, it could be taken down and put together again whenever it should be needed. A temporary platform had been erected, and this contained the falling leaf, the bolts being so arranged that they could be pulled in an instant. On this was Thurtell to stand while overhead stretched the stout crossbeam to which the halter would be attached. From the door of the prison, a short flight of steps led up to the platform; and below and around it, a railed enclosure was placed of about three yards' area in which would stand officials and gentlemen of the press without being trampled on by the audience.

Hearing the bustle outside, the steady tap of hammers, while lying on his bed and pretending to sleep, Thurtell smiled when he recalled how grimly he had jested with Mr. Wilson. "Why," he had said banteringly, "I understand that when you round people here, you put them in a tumbler and send them out of the world with a gee-up, gee-ho! and I suppose my ears'll be saluted with a smack of the whip? But that's rather an old-fashioned and ungentlemanly way of finishing a man."

Mr. Wilson must have reported these complaints to the magis-trates, for now, instead of his being hanged on a cart whipped up to leave him dancing on air, Thurtell was to be rounded off after the modern style. Not kicking to death from a moving tumbler but dropping through a trapdoor at the sudden release of the bolts. He supposed that this was progress, and he hoped that it might prove less liable to choke a fellow than the old method. The means, however, did not trouble him: it was thought of the hanging itself, of death, oblivion and the worm that dieth not that was like grit under his eye-lids, keeping him awake.

Hang he must, said the law. From that appalling thought there could be no escape. Therefore he struggled mightily not to think of it. He tried to think of other, happier things; but he could not escape for long, even on fancy's pinions, outside the thick stone walls of this living charnel-house.

Yesterday . . . yes, think of that! . . . the return from court after damned Park's long oration—that almost sermon miscalled judgment which had made poor Joe weep behind his handkerchief—came back to him with the stifling horror of suffocation. Glad was he now, and proud, that he had retained his dignity. Seeming emotionless, serious and profoundly attentive, he had stood beside the blubbering Hunt; and all the time his heart had been hammer-hammering and his blood had been like thunder in his ears.

This air of cool courage he had maintained during the drive back to jail through the twilight, and then he had calmly drunk his tea and eaten the slices of bread and butter while glancing through the Bible and the religious books Mr. Franklin, the chaplain, had left for his reading. His iron-like mask had not broken, and the jailors—two always to watch lest he seek to forestall the hangman—had marvelled at such indifference. Later, Mr. Franklin had entered the cell; and then, suddenly, no longer had Thurtell been able to hold back his tears. Like a boy to his father, he had wept. For the first time since childhood, he had wept and had found a certain satisfaction, almost a pleasure, in those tears, although he had struggled hard to restrain them. Sobbing, he had gasped out a few words in answer to the clergyman's gentle questions. Yes, yes, he was contrite, he had groaned: he was ready to make his peace with God. Already he felt, he had sobbed, that the world had closed in upon him and he realized that he had only a few hours remaining in which to live. . . . Only, he had cried, grasping Mr. Franklin's hand, only he could not contemplate that awful exit without recollecting those near and dear connections to whom his death would prove a source of affliction and shame!

That had been last night, after the pronouncement of his fate. Since that crumble-down he had mastered the woman in him and now no man could catch him weeping. What if, under the blanket he

raised to hide his face in pretended slumber, he twitched and stared
aghast at the thought of death tomorrow when he felt strong and
virile? The two watchers playing cards and Joe Hunt nodding by the
fire could not see his face. They thought that he slept. And sleep, surprisingly, he did at times, only suddenly to awake with suffocation up
his nostrils and fire in his chest.

He had asked Mr. Wilson if he might have Joe Hunt with him during this last night on earth; and trembling, the clown had cringed into
the cell. Plainly, the authorities did not intend to hang him. Otherwise they'd have been turned off together, and doubtless they'd trans-
port him to New South Wales. Yet in his uncertainty, hoping while
fearing to hope, the wretched creature showed himself no Turpin
lad, but a craven, shaking and blubbering.

As he had crept into the cell, Thurtell had smiled and gripped
Hunt's hand in forgiveness. "Joe," he had said, "the past's forgotten.
I stand on the brink of eternity and we meet now only as friends. It
may be your fate to lose your life as ignominiously as myself, but I
sincerely hope the royal pardon will be extended to you and that
you'll live to repent of your past errors and to make some atonement
for the injuries you may have done to me or others. Although you
have been my enemy, freely I forgive you."

Earlier that day, while they had sat side by side in the pew in the
chapel, he had sought to calm Hunt's distress, and it seemed that he
had not succeeded. . . .

"You brought it all on yourself," he had told him, mournfully
shaking his head. "If you'd not told where the body was there'd have
been no trial and we'd have been safe."

"It-it was to be-be-be so," Hunt had blubbered, tears running
down his nose and dangling on his newly grown whiskers. "It-it can't
be helped. If it hadn't been divulged, it-it-it'd have come out some
other time."

Still, Hunt had remained afraid, shuddering at any sound as they
had sat before the fire and in the light of the oil-lamp had drunk their
brandy and prayed and read devotional books until shortly after one
o'clock. Then Thurtell had yawned and said that it was time to sleep.
His last, no, almost his last, sleep. Fully dressed, he had flung himself
with the clash of irons on to his bed and had covered his face with the
blanket and lain still.

But not to sleep. Not yet to sleep. This last night he wished to grasp
at memories of living. Memories of laughter, of brightly lighted

gaming-houses, of noisy taverns and of women's shoulders dazzling above their gowns, of the clean patch of sunlight on which brave men fought inside the squared circle, of comradeship so rare and of love that had been rarer yet . . . Of sweet Anne Noyes.

No! not of Anne Noyes. Of his speech yesterday from the dock. He did not doubt that for many, many years to come it would be printed and reprinted as an exemplar of great and moving oratory.

He wondered what Anne Noyes was doing that moment. Could she conceivably be sleeping? he wondered; or did she lie awake, as he lay awake, remembering their brief yet precious intimacy? And he was glad that he had refrained from answering the impudent, madcap invitation the loving innocent had given him. Never could she say that Jack Thurtell had ruined her in her amorous folly. Nobly had he refrained, pitying her in her gallant simplicity.

Yet the damned world damned him for a villain! he who had spared a maiden's loveliest sacrifice! Never, by God, had he been a mutton-monger. Women's company had he liked, some women he had almost believed he had loved until he had encountered Anne and known in truth that she was the only her whom he desired. No other woman had seriously chafed his heart. Anne, she and no other, was his only sweetheart; and too late, too bloody late had he found the woman in her. . . .

Shifting angrily from that hot thought, he wondered how the great fight had gone. Langan could not possibly beat Spring. Yet Justice Park had beaten Jack Thurtell, flooring him clean with a dirty blow! After that calamity anything might be expected, the devil become God and even Langan beat Tom Spring.

The lads of the village would be watching to see him turned off. Lemming's legs and the sporting lads fresh from the battle between Spring and Langan, they would gallop to Hertford to watch how their pal behaved on the drop. And he'd not disappoint them, he swore. He'd show them how a man could die. And he hoped that Anne would be there to see him. He had sent to Egan, asking him if he would be kind enough to call on the lady after the execution to remind her of his love and to tell her that his last thoughts had been for her alone. Egan was a good fellow. He'd not forget to do it. You could always depend on Egan.

He did hope Tom Spring had won that fight.

A good life his had been. A full life. No regrets, no whining now, Jack my lad! a brave and merry life when the bums hadn't been too hot on his tail. Only he regretted having so few things to leave to his friends. His pistol, the pistol that had done for Weare, he had promised Ruthven; the air-gun he would give to Mr. Wilson, and there remained only his snuff-box, a plain, cheap box, alas, which he would leave to Mr. Wilson's kindly son; and inside it he would enclose a lock of his hair as a memento. There was nothing else he had to leave, except his eternal love to Anne.

Probert, damned Probert . . . He'd not have been damned Probert, he swore between his teeth, for twenty thousand pounds! Far better to die as he was going to die than to live degraded and spat on like Probert, always pointed at by the fingers of scorn and loathing. If only, by God, if only he could have had the bastard alone with him in that cell, if only for a few minutes. . . .

Yesterday the traitor had been released on the world, a free yet an accursed man, a worse than Cain. One of the turnkeys had told Thurtell about it. And, typical of the baseness of the beast, Probert had tried to crawl away without repaying that turnkey the two or three shillings he owed him, while a wretched fellow-prisoner from whom he had borrowed ninepence had been left to bewail his own silly, gullible nature and the baseness of the borrower.

"Parson Lloyd seen him at the White Hart," the turnkey had sniggered. "Him and her, the one what he calls his wife, that little fat un who won't never see forty again. There they was with a bottle of wine between em, drinking to liberty and laughing like pigs, for pig he is, the dirty pig. Parson Lloyd was shocked to the heart-bone, he says, and he told em what he thought of em. Seems the pig wanted to wait till the morning that he might see you turned off."

"I'd turn him off!" Thurtell had snarled.

"And I'd help you do it, that I would, sir, and with pleasure!" had the turnkey heartily agreed. "Parson Lloyd never used no such language to him, I don't think, although he has a rare roaring tongue with a cat's lick to it when he's hot against sinners. And he slang-whanged that Probert when he seen him, just as though he was in his pulpit, told him he ought to be ashamed of himself showing his ugly mug in Hertford when you was getting rounded in the morning, told him to get out of the place quick. 'You go and hire a post-chaise,' he tells him, 'and mizzle afore you gets yourself murdered,' he says. Bloody Probert, he ups and he says he ain't got no blunt, and Parson Lloyd—he always was a fool, that un, believing any lie he's told—he gives him two bloody quid, he does! They went then, the pair of em, for fear parson'd change his mind and want the blunt back; and, damme, when they left in the chariot, they never pulled down the blinds as though they wasn't ashamed to show their nosy dials to the world!"

His silence before his accusers, no whine from him to mace on his pals, and his almost insolent bravado in court had made of him a hero, Thurtell had learned. Those who before had execrated him, now applauded him. The gamesters, terrified lest he talk secrets, now swore that he was the bravest and most loyal cove who had ever rattled a dice-box; and harlots who had mocked him as a fool easily bubbled of his blunt with a sad tale of lost innocence, now wept at mention of his fate. Ay, and not only the harlots! Ladies, too, his jailors told him, piped their pretty lamps, and there was scarce a female in Hertford who would not have taken him instanter for lover or husband had he been quit of these fetters. Ballads were being sung about his bloody deed and his fortitude in court, and even the blasted newspapers— Judge Park having spoken bitingly in court against their viciousness— had calmed some of the froth on their mad-dog pens. He had become the nation's hero; and that was a warming thought.

He prayed he would not weaken when he stood on the scaffold and disappoint the people's expectations with a shivering fit. That was his main fear, lest in that final moment he should turn coward and reveal his terrors. For Thurtell was terrified. He did not want to die. With Anne Noyes waiting for him outside and her fortune soon to be unlocked from chancery, he had so much for which to live, not only for his own happiness and his exultation in being a man, strong, healthy, brave and alive, but there was also Anne to console, and his unhappy parents to be made proud of having bred a scamp who, before the end, would prove himself a generous, noble fellow and obedient son.

Into sleep he drifted and awoke suddenly, startled, not knowing where he was, feeling a hand on his shoulder. Wildly, he glared up to see the young Mr. Wilson leaning over him and Hunt nodding asleep by the fire.

"I am sorry, Thurtell," said Mr. Wilson, "but it grows late. I came half-an-hour ago and had not the heart to wake you. Seven o'clock has struck."

Seven o'clock! Thurtell shuddered, suddenly remembering everything, the murder, the excitement of the trial and the horror that lay ahead at noon. . . .

Z

"I hope you are well," said Mr. Wilson, not knowing what best to say.

Thurtell forced a smile. "Very well," he said. "I've had an excellent night and dreamt some odd things. But I've not dreamed anything about this business since I've been in Hertford."

"You are refreshed?" muttered the young man. "I mean—your inward comfort?"

"Yes, I am very well, very comfortable," said Thurtell and, yawning and stretching, he saw Hunt blink awake beside the dying fire.

The despair on that poor devil's yellow face brought Thurtell back his courage. He hoped to God he did not look as jaundiced as that when he had soon to face the people outside.

"May I have water?" he asked, stepping from under the blankets. "I had better wash and dress carefully. I'll not need much breakfast, sir. Tea will suffice for me, with a little bread and butter."

Carefully, indeed, he dressed as though preparing for a tryst with a pretty woman, and Mr. Wilson had the handcuffs and fetters removed that he might put on his clothing without trouble. A white cravat, not a black one. No, definitely white. He'd wear no mourning at his own funeral, dammit. White corduroy breeches, his best. Then drab gaiters and polished black shoes. Next, his dark brown great-coat with the black collar, and the black kid gloves. The wrists of his white shirt he pulled down that they might be seen below the coat-cuffs. Then again the damned handcuffs were locked on to his wrists and the heavy, jangling irons were put upon his legs. These irons he pulled up in the middle on a Belcher handkerchief and tied the ends about his waist.

Precious minutes now were running, each minute ticking him closer to death. Although he answered politely when jailor or chaplain spoke to him, he scarcely knew what he said or what he was doing while, pushing aside the bread and butter, he sipped a cup of hot tea.

The feeling that supported him and blinded him to the reality of what was going on was a peculiar yet not unpleasant feeling. He felt as though he were already dead. This body which they were set on destroying no longer mattered greatly. As though he stood outside himself, he watched with little more than detached interest the way everybody had become excessively polite and blinked away tears, and how Hunt sobbed loudly beside the fire. These men had become phantoms and all the world was ghostlike. A ghostly chaplain prayed beside him and Hunt, everyone on their knees, and his own ghost's voice read aloud a sermon on eternity from one of the books on the table. Other ghosts approached to speak to him, shifty-eyed ghosts who would not look at him straight and who talked either in flat voices or with a snuffle as though they had colds in the head.

His own calm and gracious demeanour he silently applauded. Not many men, egad, had died so bravely as this! And he condescended to speak to these unhappy phantoms from another world, and he went with them to the chapel and prayed again, Hunt being very noisy beside him in the pew. When the service ended, he turned pityingly on his companion, grasping his hand repeatedly and assuring him again and again of his perfect forgiveness of the past and saying that he was prepared to die in peace and charity with all the world.

Yes, in peace and charity. All he forgave, all, except Probert. That bastard alone remained outlawed from his love. But these others, these poor creatures who were the puppets of blind laws, could not be blamed for doing what they had been bidden to do. Freely, he forgave them and felt like a king dispensing largesse.

Then they were gone. They vanished in a blink, it seemed, while he had been complacently wondering what the newspapers would say about his courage on the scaffold. He looked up and found himself alone in the chapel with the elder Mr. Wilson who seemed troubled and ill at ease.

"Now, Thurtell," said Mr. Wilson suddenly, touching his arm, "as there is now no eye to witness what is passing between us but that of God, you must not be surprised if I ask you a question."

Slowly Thurtell turned and looked at him with astonishment that the man should ask him questions at an hour like this.

"If you intend to make any confession," continued Mr. Wilson hurriedly, "I think you cannot do it at a better period than the present." Still, Thurtell watched him, brows drawn down but that left brow raised like an amused, inquisitive circumflex; and desperately, beginning to stammer, Mr. Wilson concluded: "I ask you if you acknowledge the justice of your sentence?"

Quickly, earnestly, Thurtell seized both his hands and pressed them with fervour between his own.

"I am quite satisfied," he said, "I forgive the world; I die in peace and charity with all mankind. That is all I wish to go forth upon this occasion."

But Mr. Wilson was not satisfied. The part of his duty he detested most was this questioning the condemned so that the conscience of

z*

society might be appeased by the publication of a last confession. Falteringly he asked: "But, Thurtell, do you feel that the laws of my county have dealt justly and fairly to you?"

That poor Mr. Wilson might not remain uneasy, Thurtell smiled, saying: "I admit that justice has been done me. I am perfectly satisfied."

Then the ghosts returned, and Mr. Wilson who with his questions had for a time taken on flesh drifted back to vagueness; all were vague, were phantoms gesturing and whispering and weeping, and Thurtell let them remain as phantoms. All his strength was needed to concentrate on himself, on making certain that he played his part without faltering before the critical multitude and, particularly, before those reporters who had written of him with barbaric insults.

Even through the thick stone walls the noise of the expectant audience could be heard. The crowd had waited with more or less patience and its talk and laughter entered the prison only as a subdued murmur like the ebb and flow of a great sea outside. This noise was heartening to Thurtell, as the sudden, sitting-erect movement of a theatrical audience is heartening to the actor when he steps on to the stage. Soon, very soon, would come the great, the last moment of his life. Beside that gigantic moment, everything else appeared shadowy, as Mr. Franklin, the chaplain, was shadowy when in a trembling voice he asked whether there were anything he could do to ease Thurtell's mind with respect to his family and friends.

"Why, yes," said Thurtell with a grateful smile, "I would be indeed indebted to you, sir, if you would write to my father and inform him of the extreme contrition, resignation and penitence with which I meet my end."

"It shall be done. On my word, Thurtell," sobbed the chaplain, "it shall be done."

"Then pray for them," said Thurtell, "as I am praying that the minds of all my family might be strengthened under the deep affliction they must feel and of which I, alas, was the unhappy author."

He lowered his head and moved his lips as though in prayer, but he was not praying. He was thinking how well he performed his part of penitent, and how these men, in their grief, must be admiring his stoical imperturbability.

Then suddenly he remembered and looked up, astonished that even his imminent hanging could have driven such an important matter from his mind.

"I have one more favour to ask of you if you can oblige me," he said to Mr. Wilson.

Eagerly, hoping that this might mean the beginning of a confession, Mr. Wilson swung round. "What is it?" he asked.

"It is," said Thurtell with a shy smile, "to tell me how the great fight terminated."

"Fight? Great fight?" Mr. Wilson blinked, not understanding what he meant for a moment; then he realized and felt faintly shocked that a man, loaded with sin and a bloody conscience, soon to stand face to face with the recording angel, could at such a time be interested in whether some pugilist had knocked another one down.

"I—I don't know," he said a trifly primly. "I will inquire."

Only a few minutes was he out of the room, and then he hurried back.

"It was a hard-fought battle, I'm told," said Mr. Wilson; "it lasted two hours and five minutes and Spring was a great deal punished, but he won."

"I am glad of it!" cried Thurtell, lifting his manacled arms, fists clasped. "God bless him! He is an old friend of mine."

Spring had won. Thurtell had known that he would win! Pierce Egan would be hangdog this morning, his pal hammered in the ring, and his other pal . . . his other pal soon to be nubbed. . . .

Suddenly sounded a tapping on the door, and Thurtell shuddered. From toe to crown, he shuddered, strive though he did to control the tremor. Under his wrinkling skin, the cowardly spirit seemed to struggle to break free, terrified before this summons to a sudden death, for that was Mr. Nicholson tapping with his wand as a signal that the hour of execution had at last arrived.

Mr. Franklin also flinched and shuddered, as though the summons were for him; and in that dim chapel all remained very still, white-faced, until in a strong voice, Thurtell said: "I am ready." Again, he seized the chaplain's hands and again thanked him for all the pains he had taken to redeem his soul; he thanked him for the many personal kindnesses he had done for him in the goodness of his heart, and he thanked him also for the contrite and Christian spirit his teaching had bestowed on one about to die so that he was now ready cheerfully to leave this world.

The chapel-door was thrown open and Thurtell, chin up, walked steadily, his hand on the chaplain's arm, along the paved passage that crossed the yard and led to the tread-mill. Mournfully, the church-bell tolled and the clock began to strike the first note of midday.

Behind Thurtell and the chaplain walked the few officials led by Mr. Wilson; slowly, at funeral pace they went, their shoes shuffling over the stone and Thurtell's chains clinking at each move. Thurtell alone seemed indifferent to his fate. Around and behind him, the others wept, until at the door they paused and he again, for the last time, shook hands with these men who would live after he lay dead.

"God bless you, sir," he said, wringing the chaplain's hand, "God bless you." Young Mr. Wilson was noisily weeping and Thurtell placed his handcuffed hands on his shoulder, saying cheeringly: "Come, come, don't cry, don't grieve . . . We shall meet again, we shall meet in heaven." Then to the under-sheriff, quickly he said: "Pray, Mr. Nicholson, I beg of you to see that there is as little delay as possible. I want no long waiting on the scaffold."

Mr. Nicholson bowed; and the moment of death could no longer be delayed. The bell still tolling, the clock finishing on the stroke of twelve with a resonance that echoed hollowly along the stone passage, the door was flung open and Thurtell walked into the damp sunlight. He walked out to be temporarily blinded by the glare and deafened by the shouting. Above him reared the scaffold and before him and around him stood uncountable men and women laughing, talking, whistling, singing; but when they knew that he stood there, silence was immediate, and the men took off their hats.

Up the steps, steadily walked Thurtell, the fetters jingling, and no longer was he in his world of phantoms. That illusion which had sustained him through the morning fled, and he knew with a reality that appalled him that he was about to die. Pretence now was finished. He and not these men about him was to become the phantom. They would continue living, able to touch things with their fingers and to taste spiced foods and strong drink on their palates; but he would not be with them. No, he would be lying motionless under the surgeon's cold knives, the secrets of his being laid bare to science; and his soul . . . he did not know where his soul would be. . . . Only he knew that he did not want to die.

They were watching him. Thousands of people watching him. A muddle of faces, men without their hats and women hiding their cheeks in their bonnets. Anne? was Anne there? He could not see her. He could not see anyone he recognized; yet in such a multitude there must have been dozens of his friends riotous after Spring's flooring of the Irisher. A nearby clock, the laggard, began to strike midday, striking as the hangman shifted Thurtell to make him stand immediately over the drop. Kindly clock that would postpone time to give him a few more breaths of life.

The drop was like any other trapdoor. Impossible to believe that it was to open on to sudden death with a jerk on his neck. For a few moments, he stared down at it, seeing each knot and splinter of the boards; then he looked up again, trying to appear nonchalant while he sought for friends. There was one fellow he knew down there amongst that anonymous horde. What was his name? Of course! Johnny Dale, the old Horncastle jockey and horse-dealer, waving at him, tears running down his cheeks, a little man splashed high with mud. He must have driven far and hard to have got himself into such a state. What was he saying? Thurtell strained to hear and caught only a whisper on the wind. "God Almighty bless you, Jack." Was that what the old horse-thief was trying to tell him? Thurtell smiled and nodded, and Johnny Dale burst into tears, his face wrinkling like a monkey's.

Not wishing to embarrass the poor man further, Thurtell looked away; he looked down into the railed enclosure surrounding the scaffold, and there he saw Pierce Egan stand bare-headed, a pencil and paper inside the grey topper he held in front of him, while he looked up at him quizzingly. He bowed, and Thurtell bowed, like two old friends gravely exchanging greetings in company.

From around the throat, the executioner cut collar and cravat, and Thurtell craned his neck to help him in his work. Instead of a collar then was coiled the noose, itching his skin; and slowly a white cotton nightcap was drawn down over his face. The cloth was thin. It did not hide the world from Thurtell although it hid his countenance from the world so that the grimaces of the dying might not be seen. And for that he was grateful. Behind this frail mask he could let the muscles relax and could blink, if he wished, in terror; but he was too anxious about the way of being killed to allow terror of death to worry him. Executioners could be bunglers, and as this was to be the first use of the drop in Hertfordshire, they might easily make some wretched mistake. He had asked to have two half-hundred-weights attached to his legs to make certain that he would fall with a thump, but Mr. Wilson had said that such questions must be left to the hangman to decide. Thurtell had seen hangmen at work, the coarse, drunken savages, and he had little faith in their skill. This damned drop looked too short, decided

Thurtell, watching the assistant hangman tie the rope to the cross-beam overhead.

"Don't forget," he cried, "let me have fall enough."

The hangman, Tom Cheshire, brought all the way from Newgate for the occasion, frowned at criticism. He was, however, only the second-hangman, Jemmy Foxen being temporarily indisposed, and he did not like to be rude to his clients, particularly to one like Thurtell whose hanging was so great an honour.

"It's quite sufficient, I can assure you, sir," he growled.

Still, Thurtell did not believe him and he felt angry that Foxen should have failed to answer the call.

"Do you think, Mr. Wilson," he asked, "I have got enough fall?"

"I think you have, sir," said Mr. Wilson, measuring the slack rope with his eye. "Yes, quite enough," he said, and held out his hand. "Goodbye, Mr. Thurtell," he muttered huskily, "may God Almighty bless you."

Thurtell grasped his hand and shook it warmly. "God bless *you*, Mr. Wilson," he said, "God bless *you*."

Choking back sobs, Mr. Wilson moved away to the farthest part of the scaffold and gripped the rail to steady his hands. All became silent. The great multitude held its breath, afraid even to blink lest it blink during the fall to death, and stared at the man with the white featureless face. Like a statue, Thurtell stood, his hands perfectly steady under the handcuffs, waiting, listening to the step of the hangman, for the squeak of the bolt.

He was so intent on listening that he had no time for thought. Even love, even Anne Noyes, was forgotten during that moment of tension; then he heard a faint movement and leaned to listen better, and found himself flung suddenly in a flurry of terror and a clatter of irons into darkness. The breaking of his neck sounded like a pistol-shot; yet, to make certain, Old Cheese, as friends and enemies called Tom Cheshire, climbed down to grip the legs and pull and tug on them, like a monkey clinging to the body slowly going round and round with its head to one side.

That crack of the neck sent the people helter-skelter into panic. They ran, they kicked and pushed against one another, in a fever to escape they knew not what. Screaming, they smashed down a fence and trampled to shreds a cow-house. Some fainted, many wept, and all, even the most callous, showed with twitching lip or blinking eye emotion they sought to conceal. Never had Egan seen such behaviour amongst a hanging-crowd. Usually they remained riotously merry and concluded the amusement in debauch. Yet now they ran squealing and pushing and tumbling over one another in a frantic desire to get far away from the jail.

Egan shrugged. At least, it cleared the road and he could walk without great difficulty back to the Six Compasses; and he was half sorry for that, not liking his coming interview with Anne Noyes. Of all distressing things, few could be worse than a woman hysterical with grief when it was impossible to console her. But he had promised Thurtell to see the woman, and a promise to the dead was a sacred one.

But Anne Noyes was not hysterical. He found her in her room, white-faced, but calm and even smiling. Before her stood her sister and her sister's husband, and when he entered Egan had the unpleasant feeling that he was intruding on a family quarrel. That was the last thing he wanted to do. As it was, his nerves were over-wrought, after the horror of Thurtell's brave end and the memory of his body twirling while Old Cheese held it in both arms and tugged; that he should now have walked into some private argument was more than he could bear. He decided to leave as quickly as he politely could.

"I have come, Miss Noyes," he said, "at the bidding of a late mutual friend. He asked me to tell you that he would die with your name on his lips."

"Thank you," she said with the gracious air of a queen. "But you have addressed me wrongly, Mr. Egan. I prefer to be known as Mrs. John Thurtell!"

"This is madness!" cried Caroline, fists clenched as though she would belabour her sister. "Take no heed of what she says, Mr. Egan, I pray you; it is only to vex me and my husband."

"It is true," said Anne quietly; "we were married in secret. I would have thought you would have preferred that, Carrie. After all, you'd like my baby to have its father's name, wouldn't you?"

"I don't believe it," howled Caroline. "You're lying, you cat; even you couldn't have done such a wicked thing!"

"In eight months you will have your answer," said Anne, smiling. "Mr. Egan, I would like you to announce it in your newspaper. Say that Mr. Thurtell leaves a widow, Anne, née Noyes, who expects to be delivered of his child."

"But . . . but, ma'am . . ." Egan did not know what to say. It might be true, it might not be true. Desperately he looked at the angry-red cheeks and glittering eyes of Caroline Wood, and then at the stiff little major who was her husband.

"She's not herself," cried Caroline. "Please, Mr. Egan, if you are a gentleman, take no heed of her ravings. She scarcely knew Jack Thurtell. It couldn't be."

"It is," said Anne, "and you know it. O, yes, pretty sister, you know it's true; and you're jealous. All the gentlemen were in love with you; it was always like that, wasn't it? Well, Mr. Thurtell was one gentleman who preferred your sister, even though she might have only one eye; and I'm proud, proud, to be carrying his child!"

She faced her sister, her chin up and a tight smile on her lips; and Egan then understood how Thurtell could have loved this woman. She lacked Caroline's bold beauty, she had only one eye, but there was fire in her, and spirit; ay, a spirit to match Jack Thurtell's! Caroline seemed a pale flame before her, quivering back from the fury of her passion. If only Thurtell had lived, this was certainly the wife for such a man.

"Mr. Egan," she said imperiously, "pray don't forget. I want my marriage announced and my condition known to the world."

"No! No, no, no!" screamed Caroline, falling, sobbing, to her knees.

"I—I will do what I can," said Egan, bowing; and turning quickly, he hurried from the room.

Outside, on the stairs, he halted to regain his breath and to clear his thoughts. That noble woman remained too strong a memory to be dismissed. Like Thurtell, calm and heroic on the scaffold, his beloved had stood with angry dignity before that blubbering bitch of a girl; and he wished, he prayed, that she had not lied and that she was indeed Thurtell's widow.

Behind him he heard quick steps and turned to see Major Wood hurrying down the stairs.

"Mr. Egan," hissed the major, "you'll not publish all those farradiddles, please? Miss Noyes didn't know what she was saying. A good woman, but . . . you know, women when they lack a husband have strange fantasies at times. You'll not suffer for it, I promise you. I am not a rich man, Mr. Egan, but if a hundred or two——"

"I am a poor man," said Egan furiously, "and I may be only a damned journalist, a poor devil who has to live by his pen, but even if I may not be a gentleman, sir, I am determined to be considered as one. If I could be certain that Mrs. Thurtell was sure of her facts, of course I would publish her announcement."

He turned his back and strode down the stairs, not turning to see the major wringing his hands in despair. Had he remained he might have hit the rogue and he did not want to find himself challenged to a duel. A better revenge by far was it to leave him in the agonies of doubt, waiting in terror each day for the newspapers that might break a scandal in his little world and proclaim him the brother-in-law of the notorious Jack Thurtell.

Much as he would have liked to publish the story, Egan knew that he would not write it. Anne might have invented it that she could whip the complacency of her sister and brother-in-law and be recognized as a woman capable of attracting lovers. And if it were true, it were best concealed. For the moment, wild with grief, she might wish to proclaim her womanly triumph to show that, no matter how shameful his death, she remained proud of her bully lover; but later, when excitement ebbed, when she would have to sink back into the everyday world of unexciting things, she might well prefer that the child should be reared without knowledge of its notorious parent.

Ay, true or false, the tale were best forgotten, for whether true or false, it proved Anne Noyes—or Anne Thurtell—to be a woman above most women, the worthy half of such a man. There were tears in Egan's eyes as he stepped into the crowded street and saw the noisy pack of drunken men and women rioting in the winter's light with an abandon rarely seen in daylight. All classes were there, from the dandy and dandyzette to the thief and his moll, from the country gentleman to the cow hand, with farmers, butchers, bakers, meal-men, legs, swells and tulips, and women of respectable appearance beside raggletaggle drabs in semi-nudity.

This was the world of Jack Thurtell crowded into Hertford to pay him homage with ribald ballad and the ballum-rankum of carnival. Ay, here was saturnalia on a cold rainy day, a sacred if most profane dance before some heathen god of violence and debauchery. And they had been promised an especial treat. In the morning, in St. Bartholomew's Hospital, London, the anatomized corpse of Thurtell was to be displayed for their inspection. Until then, when they could gloat with love and pity on their dead god of violence, they celebrated his apotheosis in true ruffianly fashion, not even waiting for the screen of nightfall for acts which should be performed only in the strictest privacy.

Under the surgeon's busy knives, the dead god lay with his head to one side and his strong neck grooved by the bite of the rope; and the chosen bride of that god sat smiling defiantly, spitefully at her sister who wept and wailed, seeming almost insane with terror before thought of the scandal that would break in the morning should Egan prove himself no gentleman. After that, she, the wife of Major Wood, the daintiest, most prudish lady in all Hertfordshire, would never be able to lift her pretty head again.

Anne Noyes sat back in her chair, too contented in her malice to mourn her lover's passing. Her sole regret was that her tale, alas, was not true, although she could not blame herself for that.

Grief, she realized, would come later, when she awoke to see the empty, endless future open in barrenness before her; but she would not think of that; only she felt faint annoyance that she had neglected to buy herself a wedding-ring. First thing in the morning that must be rectified. Until then she would remain sitting like this, silent and tightly smiling, while pretty Caroline wept as though to bleach the colour from her eyes, with her fool of a husband standing beside her first on one leg, then on the other, uncertain what was best to be done. Dear Jack, she felt certain, would have been delighted to see suffer the two he hated; and she looked up as though for his approval, feeling him at her side. But he was not at her side. He was not there. Only emptiness enclosed her. All her life she would walk through this emptiness, this vacuum, this dried heart of love.

Swiftly she tossed that horror aside, shaking her dark ringlets, and slid back into the warm security of dreams, into the arms of a man whom no woman could possibly steal from her. And that was something of which few wives, and certainly not Caroline, could boast. Jack Thurtell was hers, forever hers in her heart; and in the morning, in widow's weeds, she would drive to St. Bartholomew's. She prayed that they had not cut that splendid body too cruelly and she wondered whether she would be permitted a farewell-kiss. Surely, as his only widow, she might be granted that small privilege, so few were the memories she had to support her through the long, long years ahead until dreaming ended in an embrace of souls in some rapturous heaven where there would be no hangman to part poor lovers. Yes, that meeting was worth waiting, worth living for; and meanwhile, there was the ring and a sable gown to be bought.

Life at last had found a meaning for Anne; and Caroline was maddened, outraged, to see her sister smile upon some secret bliss which she would never share.

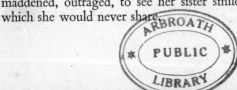